S0-AAZ-157

Praise for Anne Schulman

"An intriguing novel."
Family Circle

"A blockbuster novel by Ireland's answer
to Jilly Cooper.
Image

"*Intrigue* is a wonderful page-turner."
It Magazine

"A gripping read."
Woman

" . . Is great fun."
The Bookseller

"*Intrigue* is a compulsive blockbuster."
Sunday Press

"A sizzling read."
Farmer's Monthly

Chapter & Hearse

Also by Anne Schulman

Intrigue

Encounters

Published by Poolbeg

Chapter & Hearse

Anne Schulman

POOLBEG

Published 1997 by
Poolbeg Press Ltd,
123 Baldoyle Industrial Estate,
Dublin 13, Ireland

© Anne Schulman 1997

The moral right of the author has been asserted.

The Publishers gratefully acknowledge the support of The Arts Council.

A catalogue record for this book is available from the British Library.

ISBN 1 85371 780 0

All rights reserved. No part of this publication may be reproduced or transmitted in any form or by any means, electronic or mechanical, including photography, recording, or any information storage or retrieval system, without permission in writing from the publisher. The book is sold subject to the condition that it shall not, by way of trade or otherwise, be lent, resold or otherwise circulated without the publisher's prior consent in any form of binding or cover other than that in which it is published and with out a similar condition, including this condition, being imposed on the subsequent purchaser.

Cover photography by Michael Edwards
Florist: Marcella Thorne
Cover design by Poolbeg Group Services Ltd
Set by Poolbeg Group Services Ltd in Garamond 10/12.5
Printed and bound in Great Britain by
Cox & Wyman Ltd, Reading, Berks.

A note on the Author

Anne Schulman lives in Dublin with her husband and has two children. With several puzzle books and a biography to her credit, she prefers to write fiction. *Chapter & Hearse* is her third novel with Poolbeg having previously published *Intrigue* and *Encounters*.

Acknowledgements

Hand on heart, *all* the incidents and events in this book are fictitious, so too are the characters.

Kate Cruise O'Brien, my friend and editor whose unflagging enthusiasm and encouragement made the writing so enjoyable. (Even when you trod on my angels, Kate.)

Nicole Hodson, who went to great trouble to explain the vagaries of publishing. (We've been thrown out of better places than that, Nicole.)

Kieran Devlin, the voice of reason, only a phone call away.

Paula Campbell, whose ideas and inspirations are infectious.

Sarah Farrelly, who not only created the wonderful cover but led me through the process step by step.

Nicole Jussek, who gave me a glimpse into the complexities of children's book publishing.

Margaret Daly who showed such kindness and gave me a real rose.

Lucy whose cheerfulness never fails to brighten the day. Karen and Simon, unsung heroes, and Conor, the only man to whom I will never wish, *many happy returns!*

Every flock has its shepherd and in Poolbeg that is Philip MacDermott. A Man of Dreams.

Thank you is such an inadequate way of expressing my gratitude for all the unstinting help and advice but is sincere nevertheless.

To DR for sharing her painful secrets.

To Richard Buchalter for his legal help.

Dr Gerry Tolkin, aka Dr Gerry Oscar, who helps me kill off my characters by e-mail. Ireland's loss, Canada's gain.

Christine and Ian Hadley for a magical night in Paris.

Patricia Scanlan for keeping me on my culinary toes. The sandwich maker is always at the ready.

The computer find and rescue team, Noirin Scully and my son-in-law, Pat. (Wouldn't you think I'd have learnt by now?)

When I emerge from the cocoon of words and chapters, my patient family and friends are always there for me, ready to pick up where we left off.

My daughter Lynda, my sounding board. My son Paul, who takes it all in his stride.

Lastly, but most of all, my husband David who supports me every step of the way and doesn't in any shape or form resemble Derek Grant. Thank you for your fortitude and caring.

For my darling husband, David
who makes everything possible

Prologue

She was lovely – slim, blonde and dead.

The office swarmed with forensic people, each with their own task; to them just a matter of routine. As yet this woman was unknown to him, a stranger whose life would undoubtedly touch his own.

"What details do you have for me?" Michael Moore asked the young constable, the folds of her new uniform still visible.

She read her notes with shaking fingers, her skin a paler shade of green than the dead woman's eyes.

"First time?" He recognised the signs.

"Yes . . . sir?" She fumbled for his title.

"Detective Inspector Michael Moore. Don't worry, it'll get easier. You'll get used it," he assured her sympathetically. Maybe she would, but in all his years in the police force he had never managed to accept death and violence without stomach-churning revulsion.

He stepped around the body and made his way to the window. From there he could get a clearer picture of the office. Half-sitting, half-leaning, he scanned the room.

Anne Schulman

The office was pleasantly feminine, nothing over the top; pastel shades, pale woods, softly-coloured upholstery on the chairs. An overturned vase of yellow tulips, deprived of their life-supporting liquid, were already beginning to wilt. The raw-fibred rug under the pale-oak desk was rucked and bunched; he resisted the urge to straighten it and its tangled fringe. He photographed the room slowly with his eyes and stopped every now and again to make a memory-jogging note. Satisfied that he had done all he could for the moment, he heaved his bulky frame away from the glass. When he retired he would definitely go on a diet.

"She's a cracker, isn't she?" Bill Brown, the police photographer, trod carefully around the body.

"She was," Michael Moore corrected and found it difficult to look away.

There was something clenched in the curled fingers, a tiny scrap of beige paper, barely visible.

"What's that, there, in her hand?" he asked.

Bill Brown bent over and peered closely. "Some sort of paper?" He frowned. "Reminds me of my kids' school note-books, a cover perhaps? Don't worry, the boys will get it."

"It's OK, we've seen it," the white-overalled crime examiner assured them with a smile as he moved cautiously in their direction. Michael Moore didn't miss much.

Michael relaxed. He tried hard not to do other people's jobs, but old habits . . . "Thanks, Kenny, what else have you got for me?"

Kenny Brandt gave him a brief résumé of what they had found so far.

"Anything else?" Michael asked.

Kenny stooped and from his case, an untidy jumble of tweezers, brushes, assorted containers and powders, he produced a small plastic bag which he held between plastic-gloved fingers. At first glance the transparent bag appeared to be empty. "A blonde hair." He pointed to the side of the bag with a glove-wrinkled finger. "We lifted it from the edge of the desk, it was embedded in a splinter. She must have given her head one hell of a bang."

Michael nodded his thanks, that would account for the dark red, spreading stain under the softly-waved, blonde head.

He made his way downstairs to the front door and examined it for himself. Kenny Brandt was right, there was no damage, no sign of a forced entry. He added that information to his notes then returned the book to his pocket. He spoke to the leader of the contract cleaning firm who had discovered the body. She was white-faced and shaken but answered his questions without hesitation.

" . . . and now I suppose I'll be handcuffed and taken to the station," she finished with an attempt at nervous humour.

"Relax, you're not a suspect," he assured her. "You get off home now, we know where to contact you." Michael patted her arm. He had seen it all before.

He returned to the preserved scene and took a last look round. "I'm off," he called to anyone who was listening. Could it have been an accident? he wondered. He doubted it.

3

"We must keep an open mind," Kenny Brandt teased him laughingly as he approached the door to dust it for prints.

Michael smiled. For all their good-natured mockery and their smart mouths, they would miss him when he retired.

Michael Moore put the key into his front door with a sigh of pleasure.

"It's good to be home," he told his wife.

Book One

Spring

Chapter One

Holly Grant put her key into the front door and took a deep breath. "It's good to be home," she lied to her husband.

"You're late," he accused from the living-room.

"I'm sorry, we were really busy today." She put her heavy holdall on the floor and hung her coat in the hall cupboard with the buttons facing left, the way Derek insisted. She slotted her bag in between the wall and the cupboard and made sure that the strap did not poke out and trip someone – like Derek. He always warned her about that.

"You should object to these long hours. Either that or get paid overtime," he groused when she entered the immaculate living-room. "I left my office at five."

Holly plumped up a cushion on the big easy chair but didn't reply.

"What have you planned for dinner?" Derek asked.

"I thought we might phone and order Chinese." She held her breath.

"Junk food. *Again?*"

7

"We haven't had a Chinese takeaway for at least five or six weeks. Besides, it's quite healthy food," she objected mildly. "Lots of vegetables, very little fat, low in cholesterol."

"I don't wish to pump myself full of monosodium glutamate, thank you. I hope you won't suggest it again."

"Please, Derek, just this once."

"I said, no, Holly, and I *mean*, no."

"Then we'll have to make do with an omelette."

"I don't consider that a meal. I've been working all day."

And what do you think I've been doing, sky diving? she shrieked silently. "There's some salad left from last night, some nice brown bread. And there's a piece of that pie that you like . . . I could make some custard. Didn't you have a proper lunch today?" Only Derek thought that two full meals a day were a necessity, everyone else made do with one.

"If you call that slop they serve in the canteen, lunch, then yes, I had lunch."

Holly's head began to throb. *Not long now, not long,* she consoled herself as she went into the kitchen. Derek followed her. The hairs on the back of her neck bristled. He made her so nervous.

"That knife is dirty," he accused and pointed to a knife on the gleaming stainless steel draining board. "You must *watch* what you're doing when you wash up, doing everything twice is a total waste of time and energy."

She cut viciously into the loaf. "Bread or toast?" she asked.

"Bread, but *thinly* sliced, please."

"Would you like to do it yourself?" she said sweetly, but could hear her own sarcasm.

His eyes narrowed.

"I mean you're so much better at it than I am," she added hurriedly.

Derek took the knife from her trembling hand. "It's not difficult, just watch carefully."

Holly thanked her invisible star there were mushrooms in the fridge, a bit curled and wrinkled, but they'd be well hidden inside the folded eggy-pancake. Ten minutes later they sat down to eat.

"We'll go for a ramble tomorrow, the forecast's good." Derek cut his bread into even smaller pieces.

"I can't. Remember? I need a new suit for work." She was glad of the excuse, she loathed those outings. Derek fancied he knew everything about the countryside and, whether he did or he didn't, the walks bored her rigid. She would love to have spent the day alone, wander round the shops, have lunch. Heaven. "Why don't you go? I'm quite happy to shop on my own."

"No. I'll go with you. Last time you went out alone you bought that disgusting red jacket."

Holly clamped her lips firmly together while her stomach did a one hundred and eighty degree roll. *Not long now,* she told herself. She would burst if she didn't say something in her own defence.

"It was a perfectly respectable jacket," she reasoned, quietly. "People do wear red. It is not a tarty colour, it's a warm colour."

"Please, don't argue, Holly," Derek snapped, his

voice rising. "I don't *want* you to dress in lurid colours, they make you look like a slut. Brown and green are the colours for you, beige if you must."

The fight seeped out of her. He was probably right. Who cared anyway? As Derek often said, no one was the least bit interested in her or the way she dressed. But sometimes she longed to be trendy, particularly at book launches and those publishing lunches when everyone wore nice clothes, bright colours. On those occasions she always felt dull and dowdy.

Derek placed his knife and fork neatly on his plate and rose from the table. "There's a documentary on television that I want to watch. Don't take too long with the washing-up," he instructed.

"I won't. But I've brought work home with me."

His temper erupted on cue. "More work," he stormed. "It's not enough that you put in all those hours during the day, now they're making you work at night also. I'm going to phone your boss and tell her it must stop. If I've told you once, Holly, I've told you a thousand times, we can manage. *You do not need to work.*" His voice thundered to a crescendo.

"Please, Derek, don't shout. I've got a headache. I enjoy my work, really I do. We're just a bit rushed at the moment. It will all be over soon." *It will all be over soon,* she repeated the comforting words to herself.

"It bloody well better be or I'll go and see that slave-driver myself, tell her to find herself another mug." He slammed the kitchen door so hard that a chip of plaster fluttered to the floor.

Holly relaxed for the first time since she had come home. Once Derek settled in front of the television, he wouldn't move again until bedtime. She ran some water and clattered the dishes into the bowl. If he was so concerned about her, why not help with the washing-up?

She washed each plate, every spoon, knife and fork, meticulously. Derek was fanatical about cleanliness, fanatical about tidiness, her appearance, her work, her money, her friends, even her sister.

At first she was flattered that he took such a close interest in everything she did. She'd been quite happy to hand him her pay cheque each month, let him take care of her finances. Derek liked things to be exact. She didn't object when he advised her about her hair and her clothes. As he pointed out, she had very little sense of style. But she had been bitterly disappointed that he disliked her friends. Perhaps they *were* a little silly but so was she until Derek taught her how to behave in a more dignified manner. Her friends didn't care much for him either and they soon drifted away. What distressed her most of all was that he thought her attachment to her sister childish. Liz was childish. Stupid and immature. Holly was deeply hurt by the nasty things he said about her sister and her husband. In Holly's opinion, Robert was a wonderful husband and Liz adored him.

Not long after they were married, Holly began to realise that Derek found fault with everything she did. She worked too hard in the office, not hard enough at home. The flat was never tidy enough.

"Towels ought to be folded neatly. Your wardrobe should be colour graded, drawers turned out thoroughly, once a month . . . " His litany was endless.

No matter what time of the day or night Liz phoned, he grumbled, found it inconvenient. Liz soon sensed Holly's lack of spontaneity, her nervousness, whenever they spoke, so, in spite of the higher cost of daytime calls, she began to phone Holly at the office instead. Derek unnerved her too.

The first time her workmates invited Holly to join them for a celebratory drink after work, Derek had objected so vehemently that she automatically refused any further invitations. She longed to be part of the crowd but the row that was certain to follow would not be worth it. She was lucky to have someone who cared so much about her, Derek told her frequently. Lucky to have someone with good taste, a husband to look out for her. After all, there were so *many* girls, far *prettier* girls, on their own.

"Those single girls at Pagett must envy you like mad," he often said. But that wasn't the impression that she got when Derek showed up uninvited at the evening launches, anxious to drag her home.

Their sex-life became loveless, on demand. It never occurred to Holly to refuse, she didn't want to be labelled cold.

"I'd like a glass of beer, that omelette was salty," Derek shouted from the sitting-room.

"Just coming," she answered. Lazy sod, couldn't he get his own drink?

"Haven't you finished in there yet?" He took the glass from her hand without looking away from the television.

"I was just washing around the tiles." Why should she admit she'd been day-dreaming?

"They could do with it too, they looked grubby."

Dear God, we can't have grubby tiles, can we? Holly asked herself. An indictable offence, surely? I wonder which is worse, being in jail or living with you? There can't be much in it.

She switched on her laptop computer and waited for the file to load. Mentally she thanked Norma Downs – her passport to escape.

Proof-reader and editor required, she'd read in the local rag. Just up her street, a way to earn some extra cash. Nervously, Holly had hidden the paper under the settee in case Derek noticed that it wasn't in the re-cycling bundle. He would go berserk if he discovered that she'd taken on extra work. She was so frightened of his reaction that it didn't occur to her just to jot down the number. It took her three days before she plucked up enough courage to reply to the advertisement. After a quick glance at Norma's manuscript, Holly could see that Norma Downs was an author who needed help.

"I'm very patient when it comes to my stories and my characters," Norma explained. "But I become impossibly bored when I have to sit down and correct the nitty-gritty. I like to move forward not backwards."

Quite reasonably, she asked for proof of Holly's capability. Holly promised to put Norma in touch with her boss, but Holly needed to speak to her first, put her in the picture. It had taken a lunch-time of soul-baring with Simone Pearse, her immediate boss, and the job was hers.

"Do you have to make that noise?" Derek grumbled as Holly's fingers sped over the keyboard.

"Sorry, I'll type more softly."

After the ten o'clock news ended, Derek announced that it was bedtime.

"I'll only be a few more minutes," she said. With a bit of luck he wouldn't want to make love tonight, or *have sex,* as she privately called it. He had forbidden her to use that expression.

"Makes it sound so cold, so clinical," he objected.

Spot on, she muttered to herself.

"Be sure it *is* only a few minutes, you'll ruin your eyesight staring at that computer. Come to think of it, you'd better wash your hair tonight, we don't want to waste time in the morning. If we finish shopping early, we could still get our walk in. Goodnight, Holly."

"Mmm," Holly answered as she fought with one of Norma's awkwardly-worded sentences. With a bit of luck, Derek would be asleep as soon as his head touched the pillow.

Her nail jammed between two keys as his fist crashed on the table.

"I said, *goodnight, Holly.* Don't you even have the manners to answer me when I speak to you."

"Goodnight," she mumbled as tears of fright stung her eyes.

"Goodnight, *Derek*." He clutched a clump of her hair tightly between his fingers and twisted hard.

"Goodnight, Derek," she repeated obediently as the tears spread to her cheeks. *Not much longer, not much longer*. The words had become her mantra, her safety valve.

· · ·

"This egg needs at least another half-minute." Derek threw down his spoon in disgust. He was always bad-tempered on Mondays.

"I cooked it exactly as you like it, three and a half minutes," Holly objected as she wiped the splattered yolk from her new brown suit. Maybe she should leave it there, at least it gave the miserable suit a bit of colour.

"It's disgusting, runny. Your time would be better spent at cookery classes instead of hammering away at that computer."

"Oh, Derek. *Shut up*." The words escaped involuntarily.

"*What* did you say? *What did you say?*" His voice bellowed in her ears. His eyes glinted maniacally. And then for the first time, he hit her. A hard well-aimed blow on her cheek with his clenched fist. In shock, she sat in stunned silence.

Without as much as another glance in her direction, he left the table, left the kitchen and slammed out of the flat.

Chapter Two

"Holly Grant on line two, Simone," the receptionist said.

"Holly? Where are you?" Simone had been quite concerned, Holly was never late and it was almost ten-thirty.

"At home."

"I can barely hear you, are you OK?"

"No. No, I'm not."

Simone could hear the distress in her voice. "What's wrong? You sound awful."

"I think my jaw's broken."

"Did you fall? What happened?"

"Derek hit me."

"Holly, that's terrible." Simone was not surprised. She had met Holly's husband and thought that he was loathsome, had one of the cruellest faces she'd ever seen. "Are you at home? Do you want me to come round? I can be there in ten or fifteen minutes."

"Would you? If you don't mind . . . I'd be so glad . . . "

Simone grabbed her coat and bag and practically

ran out of her office. "I don't know when I'll be back. Cancel my lunch appointment," she called over her shoulder to the startled receptionist.

She dashed outside and flagged down a taxi – easier and quicker than using her car. She gave the driver Holly's address and told him to drive as fast as he could.

The offices and houses were a blur as they passed. She had been shaken rigid when Holly first told her about her husband that day at lunch. Imagine anyone putting up with a man like Derek Grant, in her opinion he had all the charisma of a cornflake. In Holly's own words, he was a domineering bully.

"But how do you stand it? Why do you put up with that kind of . . . torture?" she had asked, uncomprehendingly. "Has he ever hit you?"

"No. He's pulled my hair, pushed me out of his way, but no, he's never hit me. But, Simone, I've had all I can take. I want to leave him. That's why I need to earn this extra money," Holly explained – unnecessarily by that stage.

"Of course. I mean, go ahead, take the work," Simone encouraged. Although she and Mark were no longer together, Holly's marriage made her own seem positively idyllic by comparison. "Maybe *I* could find something extra for you. As you know, authors are often glad to have someone to edit their manuscripts before they turn them in to us. Forgive me, Holly, I still don't understand, why did you put up with this kind of treatment for so long?"

A ghost of a smile touched Holly's lips. "I don't

understand either. Stupid, isn't it? I suppose I believed him when he told me that no one would be bothered with me, no one would care. I thought of myself as worthless," she admitted. "It took a bad cold and a television programme to make me finally sit up and take notice."

"I'm not with you."

"It was when I was stuck at home with that rotten dose of flu. I was so bored that I switched on the television and watched one of those daytime talk shows – people discussing their problems – you know the kind of thing?"

Simone nodded.

"A woman, obviously suffering badly from depression, began to talk about her life, her control-freak of a husband. It could have been me, *my* life she was discussing. Before I knew it, I found myself kneeling by the set, crying with her. I recognised all the things she'd suffered. I was way ahead of her. Then the audience joined in. They weren't shy about airing their views. *Get rid of him, dump the bum. Don't let this man control your life. You are worth something.* It was as if they were advising me, reaching out to me . . . I suppose now you really think I'm crazy? But I'd lost all my confidence, my self-esteem. I was certain I couldn't manage alone, exist without Derek."

Simone was beginning to get the picture. "So what are you going to do about it, Holly?" she asked gently.

"That's simple. When I've saved some money I'll

just pack up and disappear from his life. He would never agree to a divorce, I'm positive of that."

"What does your sister think of all this?" Simone knew Holly and her sister were close. Holly always talked about Liz.

"She doesn't know. She *mustn't* know. Liz would want to tear him apart."

"Just what he needs," Simone remarked, acidly.

"You won't tell her. Please Simone, promise me . . ."

"Relax, of course I won't."

Holly's face was taut with misery and tension. Her outpourings explained much more than she realised. Simone had often wondered why such a pretty girl would go to such lengths to hide her assets. All those dull clothes, that unattractive hair style. She never joined the rest of the staff for a drink after work. And yet, Simone reflected, when Holly attended launches and warmed to the subject of publishing, she sparkled. The authors who had met her, liked her. Everyone at Pagett liked her.

The taxi swerved round the corner with a squeal of tyres. The driver was taking Simone at her word. She pulled herself upright, huddled into a corner and clung tightly to the safety handle. Poor Holly. Of course she would help her if she could, but how? Holly wasn't the decaff-coffee-and-sympathy type. And she herself wasn't exactly the perfect example of a marriage guidance counsellor. Her own marriage had ground to a halt, killed by a lethal dose of apathy and ambition.

Thoughts tumbled round Simone's head. Did she

have the right to interfere in Holly's affairs? Where would Holly go? Her sister lived in Oxford, quite a way from the town, too far for Holly to travel each day. The last thing I want to do is lose her, Simone acknowledged selfishly, she's the most reliable editorial assistant that I've ever had.

Simone leant forward and knocked on the glass panel. The driver slid back the partition.

"When we get to my friend's house, would you mind waiting for a few minutes?" she asked.

"My time is yours," he agreed amicably, his eyes fixed lovingly on the clicking meter.

* * *

Holly's face was swollen, but not so badly as Simone had imagined.

"You poor duck," she sympathised.

Holly promptly burst into tears. "I promised myself that I wasn't going to cry again," she sobbed.

"You're entitled to," said Simone soothingly. She doubted that Holly's jaw was fractured, she was able to speak quite clearly.

Simone put her arm round Holly. "First things first, do you still think your jaw is broken?"

"I can move it now, look." Holly chomped her jaw up and down. "It's sore, but not that bad."

"I don't have any vast medical knowledge but I'm sure if it was fractured you'd be in absolute agony."

"I think so too. I panicked," Holly apologised.

"I don't blame you. I'd have gone barking mad."

Simone refrained from stating the obvious – she wouldn't have put up with Derek for one night, let alone two years. "Let me pay off the taxi, then we'll decide what to do."

"Do you want to stay with him?" Simone asked as she went into the spotless kitchen to put on the kettle.

"Absolutely not. But where will I go? I could stay with Liz and Robert but they live outside Oxford, too far away to commute. I don't have much money. Most of my savings are in a deposit account and Derek looks after that."

"Don't worry about where to stay, you're welcome to use my spare room for as long as you need. As for money, at least you have *some* savings. Do you have your own account or a joint one?"

"It's joint."

"And the deposit book? Is it here in the flat?"

"Yes, I think so. It should be." Holly rose painfully from the settee and crossed to the little inlaid desk in the corner. She searched through some envelopes until she found the one she wanted. "Here it is, it's here."

"Good. Do you know how much of the money is yours?"

"About half of it, I think."

"And your passport?"

"I've never used it but I think it's in the desk, why?"

"You should have your own passport. You'll need a record of mortgage payments, bank statements. You should also have your birth certificate, your marriage licence and anything else you can think of. If you're serious about leaving Derek, you must have copies of everything. At least that's what I was told when I went through my divorce."

"I *do* want to leave him. More than you'll ever know. I can't take one more minute of his bullying, another second of treading on eggshells. The papers, everything you mentioned, they should all be here in the desk."

"Is there anywhere nearby that does photo-copying?"

"There's an office suppliers round the corner, they've done work for me before."

"Right, then here's what we do . . . "

Holly averted her face from the curious stare of the girl behind the counter.

"We want two copies of each, please," said Simone firmly. Then for the benefit of the girl, she added, "Don't take any notice, Holly. Only ignorant people stare."

The girl blushed furiously. "That will be one pound, seventy-five pence," she said in a cowed voice a few minutes later.

"What next?" Holly asked.

"We go to the bank. I think you should withdraw your money right away." Simone removed her scarf and draped it round Holly's neck and chin. Even in her sorry state the scarf gave Holly a real colour-lift. She should wear those pastel colours.

The bank teller was more subtle but Holly could

feel his eyes fixed on her jaw as the scarf slipped. "Thank you," she mumbled as he handed her back the deposit book. Simone was relieved that Derek's signature wasn't necessary for the withdrawal.

"Why do I feel like a thief?" she asked Simone.

"You've become conditioned to handing over your money?" she suggested.

"It *is* mine."

"I know it is. Don't feel guilty, Holly," Simone said a trifle impatiently. "Plenty of women would have wiped out the whole account. By the way, what time does Derek get home from work?"

"About five-thirtyish, a few minutes either way."

"That gives us plenty of time. After lunch you must pack, do you have suitcases? Something to put your bits and pieces into?"

"I have one case and a grip, they'll hold my clothes. I don't want anything else. I don't want any trouble, Simone. All I need are my clothes."

"No personal mementoes? Wedding presents?"

Holly paused. "I never thought of that. There are a couple of pieces of furniture that are mine. But Derek will be even more angry if I take them."

"Sod Derek. You don't have to care *what* Derek thinks any more. From now on it's what *you* think, what *you* want."

"It is, isn't it?" The smile made her wince with pain, but it was worth it.

While Holly busied herself in the kitchen, Simone phoned the firm of couriers that their publishing firm, Pagett, always used. They could send a van the following day. She spoke softly, urgently, into the phone.

"They'll be here by four-thirty." She smiled, she had practically blackmailed the poor dispatcher. "When I've eaten this sandwich, I'll pop back to the off-licence on the corner and scrounge some boxes. Pack everything you need or want and take it with you now. I think this will be your one chance to avoid mega-aggro with Derek."

"You won't find my flat as tidy as this," Simone warned as she sat on the bed and watched Holly pack her clothes.

"Good! I wasn't allowed to leave here in the morning until everything was vacuumed and dusted. I don't intend using a duster ever again!" She managed a lopsided grin. "I'd love to chuck all these clothes in the bin." Holly held up a shapeless, sick-green sweater. "I will throw *this* out, it's revolting isn't it? And these." A pair of baggy jeans followed the sweater into the empty drawer. *Tight jeans were unladylike,* according to Derek. "I'll get rid of everything else just as soon as I can afford to. I'll never wear green or brown again."

"I felt the same way when I got rid of my school uniform, it was a ghastly shade of muddy-brown," Simone remembered.

"All done." Holly zipped up the grip and snapped the lock on her suitcase.

The couriers arrived a few minutes later than they had promised. It took the two men less than ten minutes to load her possessions into the van.

Simone gave them her address and tipped them handsomely. Suddenly she was anxious to leave.

"That corner looks bare without Granny's desk," Holly said guiltily as she picked up her handbag and holdall. She preferred to keep the bag containing her laptop and manuscripts in her own custody.

"You'll find a new corner for your desk. It would be heartbreaking to part with such a treasure. I'd die if I had to give up that little Pembroke table, it's gorgeous. And, as for that Susie Cooper breakfast set, it's the prettiest china I've ever seen."

"They're family heirlooms, I suppose. My grandmother adored those cups and saucers. She never used them, just washed and dried them with loving care then put them back in her glass cabinet. I'm afraid I did the same thing. I must tidy up those papers on the floor, Derek will go nuts when he sees that . . . " Holly's eyes lit up with mischief, this time she remembered not to laugh.

"Come on, Holly, we should get out of here." Simone appreciated the humour but felt uneasy. The quicker they left this pristine prison of Holly's the better. "I'll phone for a taxi."

"Wait a minute, Simone. There's something I must do before I go."

"OK, but make it quick." Simone felt the tension between her shoulder blades spread upwards to the back of her neck.

"Follow me," Holly ordered as she strode purposefully into the kitchen. She opened a cupboard above the sink. "Stand back," she warned. Two at a time the cups crashed to the floor. Saucers and plates followed at quite a rate and the sugar bowl broke neatly in half at her feet. She opened a drawer and pulled it free of its rollers. The cutlery clattered and bounced noisily, then lay glinting amongst the broken fragments of crockery. "Just one more thing." Sugar crunched under her feet as Holly opened another cupboard. She grasped a plastic ketchup bottle firmly in both hands then squeezed it as hard as she could. The effect of the red sauce on the white cupboards and counters was really quite artistic.

"*Now* I'm ready," she said triumphantly as she stood back to admire her handiwork.

"*What the hell do you think you're doing?*" Derek's voice boomed.

The two women were immobilised with fright.

"I . . . I . . . Why are you . . . back so early?" Holly stuttered, then was silent. Her body shook uncontrollably.

He ignored her and turned on Simone. "What are *you* doing here?" he snarled. "*Well?* I'm waiting for an answer."

"Don't try your scare tactics on me." Simone met his furious eyes steadily.

"Simone is waiting for me. I'm leaving you." Holly's voice was faint but firm.

"Rubbish! You're not going *anywhere*," he threatened.

"I don't think you understand, Derek. It's over, I've had enough. You're nothing more than a bully, a control-freak," she heard herself say. It was astonishing, suddenly she felt liberated, no longer

afraid of him. For a split second she even felt sorry
for him.

"How *dare* you speak to me like that?"

"I dare because it's the truth. You've made my
life a living hell." Now that she'd found the courage
to stand up to him, she was determined to have her
say. "Find yourself someone else to torture, Derek.
Better still, find yourself a doctor. You're *sick*. All
this time I felt so sorry for myself, now I feel sorry
for you. Goodbye, Derek. Ready, Simone?"

Derek grabbed Holly's arm, his face contorted
with rage.

"Let go of her," Simone screamed, her anger
overcoming her fear. She looked around wildly then
grabbed a coffee jar. She raised it in the air and
brought it down as hard as she could on his wrist.

"You bitch!" he yelled as he nursed his hand. *"I'll
sue you."*

While he was off balance, Simone pushed him
as hard as she could. He stumbled backwards
against the cupboards. *"Go, Holly. Go,"* Simone
yelled.

The sudden attack winded him. "Stay where you
are," he gasped.

Holly balled her hand into a fist, if he made any
attempt to stop them she would punch him.
Nevertheless, her legs trembled as she passed him.

"You'll be back," he bawled. "You'll come
crawling home. How far do you think you'll get
without any money? That bitch won't help you for
long. You'll be back . . . "

"Don't answer him," Simone warned her as she

grabbed Holly's bag and pushed her through the open doorway.

They stopped just long enough to scoop up the holdall and her laptop.

They ran along the street, the bags banging painfully against their legs. Simone looked over her shoulder. There was no sign of Derek, just a couple of women shoppers, wheeling identical plaid shopping-carts, identical looks of astonishment on their faces.

"Did you get hold of Liz?" Simone looked up from the trade magazine she was reading.

"Yes." Holly nodded her head in disbelief. "I'm amazed. She wasn't the least bit shocked or surprised. And I thought I'd done such a good job of hiding my feelings. Then Robert came on the line and actually congratulated me!" Holly held her hand to her mouth. Her jaw was now badly swollen, her bruise a kaleidoscope of blues, blacks and yellows. "Liz is coming to see me tomorrow – if that's all right with you?"

"Of course it is. I've told you, for as long as you're here, you must treat this as your own home."

"Without the dusting privileges, I hope?" Holly attempted a smile.

Chapter Three

It took Holly a moment to remember where she was. Then the events of the previous day slotted back into place. What a relief – no more rows, no bullying and, best of all, no Derek. Her jaw ached and her head throbbed. She squinted at her watch, it was almost ten o'clock. She edged cautiously out of bed, a shower would wake her up.

She rubbed her hair with a towel, then remembered there was no longer any need to force it into its root-tearing pleat, she could wear it loose now.

A cup of tea worked wonders, and she began to feel almost human. As she sipped, she read Simone's note again. She would be home around five o'clock and Holly should rest as much as she could. She smiled gratefully without moving her mouth too much. It was wonderful of Simone to take care of her like this. Although they worked together, had lunch every five or six weeks, they were not really close friends. Friendship was something that Derek did not understand, regarded as a sign of weakness. *Never rely on people,* was his warped dictum.

Holly luxuriated in a daydream as she dressed.

Surrounded by laughing faces, the clink of ice in glasses, she held them spellbound with her witty stories, her clever management of agents and authors. She was embarrassed to admit it, but she was almost bored to tears by those endless compliments – her clothes, so *now*. Her hair, could that possibly be its true colour? She was asked about her make-up so often that she considered compiling a computer printout of the products she used. Yes, her flat was a real find. The furniture? Purchased from one of the zillion antique shops she visited regularly. She agreed, modestly, it had been worth all the time and effort. She supposed it did look rather wonderful. And all of this achieved without Derek's guidance. Derek! For a few glorious moments she had forgotten all about him.

A frisson of alarm dimmed her bravado. What if she had to see Derek again, if she weakened? Impossible. It was his cruelty that had finally liberated her, he wasn't going to lure her back into that whirlpool of despair. There must be no meeting with Derek. She would find a solicitor, let him handle the divorce. Simone had used one for her divorce, she would know who to contact.

"Hello, Liz." Holly put a brave smile on her swollen face. Her curling hair hid most of the multicoloured damage.

"I didn't know what to expect," Liz said truthfully as she hugged her sister.

"I'm OK," Holly assured her. "Simone has been incredibly kind."

"She certainly has," Liz agreed but felt guilty. The one time that Holly needed her, she'd been miles away.

"Let me make you some coffee, then we can talk. I'm sure you must be parched."

"I'd love some." Liz stretched her back and her arms. "That old wreck of ours isn't the most comfortable car in existence."

"Stay put, rest yourself, I won't be a minute."

Liz flopped gratefully into a chair and looked about the room. Although she was perfectly content with her own chintzy, well-worn furniture, she couldn't help admiring this state-of-the-art room. She liked Simone's deep comfortable chairs, the carefully placed paintings, thriving green plants. She envied the swathe of pristine, beige carpet. The carpets in their cottage were positively threadbare in parts. She leaned forward on her chair and from there she could see into the open-plan dining-room. It too was attractive, a pale oak table surrounded by six comfortably upholstered chairs. More pictures, water-colours this time, and more plants, none of which straggled the way hers did.

"It's a lovely flat, isn't it?" Holly asked. "When Simone and Mark broke up, she decided to keep it on. I can't see myself affording a bachelor-pad like this, can you?"

"So you've definitely decided to leave Derek?" Liz asked cautiously.

"Definitely and absolutely. I'll never go back."

Liz exhaled. "I can't tell you how glad I am, Holly, how pleased we both are. How relieved. I don't know how I managed to keep quiet for so long. What a bastard Derek was. I was always so afraid of what he might do to you, mentally, I mean. Robert begged me not to try and influence you. It was your marriage, your life, he insisted. You changed so much, Holly, you were like a dog that had been beaten. It was cruel."

"He never actually struck me before, just pulled my hair," Holly said quickly.

"Oh brilliant! Let's hear it for Derek. Why are you defending him?"

"Was I? To prevent myself from seeming like a total idiot, I suppose. But you have to admit, when he did become physical, I had the good sense to get out."

Liz held her tongue, Holly had suffered enough. "There are worse forms of cruelty," was all she said.

"You don't know the half of it. It took me a long time to realise how much he controlled my life. Completely controlled it."

"We guessed that. That's what upset us so much. I don't think we've heard you laugh for years."

"There wasn't a lot to laugh about," Holly replied sardonically. "Anyway, it's over now. I'm a free agent again, a liberated woman." And as if to prove it, she flicked her hair in triumph.

Liz caught her breath. "My God, look at that bruise . . . "

"It's OK, it will fade in a few days," Holly said dismissively.

"You should have it photographed, have some proof of what he did to you." Liz was horrified.

Holly's hair had hidden much of the damage. Come to think of it, this was the first time in ages that she'd seen Holly wear her hair loose like this, long and wavy like her own. It looked good.

Liz stirred her coffee thoughtfully. When they were young they had done everything alike, they looked remarkably alike; brown-haired and blue-eyed. Liz faithfully copied everything her sister did. She thought of Holly as her much older sister even though there was only an eleven-month difference in their ages. Their father had died just after Liz was born. Liz could never quite decide whether it was the narrow gap in their ages that made them so close or if it was because of their mother. There were many things for which she would not forgive their mother. Holly could remember the day she left, quite clearly, but her own memory was not as vivid.

"I'm going to work as a housekeeper," she'd told her daughters.

What she didn't bother to tell them, or their grandmother, was that the job was in America. After a few months she married the man she worked for and, although she sent regular cheques for the girls' upkeep, she never returned. She remembered their birthdays but they never saw her again. When Holly turned sixteen, the cheques stopped. They knew neither her married name nor her address.

The sisters clung to each other, closed ranks and made their grandmother's task a difficult one. In time, their mother's memory faded. Their hostility towards their grandmother also faded. As they grew into bright intelligent teenagers, their affection for their surrogate mother grew, too. She ceased to think of them as a burden, and *her girls* became the entire focus of her life. They cherished the memory of her proud face as she watched each of them in turn graduate from university. They worried as she became tired, less able to cope. Then one day she slipped from their lives.

"You must come and live with us, of course," Liz insisted as she shrugged off her memories.

"I'd adore to, Liz, but you live too far away. I have my work, I couldn't bear to give that up. I'm happy at Pagett. In a few days I'll find a place of my own to rent. I'll manage beautifully. I could come and visit you at the weekends, that would be wonderful."

"But you'll be all alone. I'm sure you could find another job, nearer to us."

"I probably could, but I won't mind being on my own, honestly. Imagine. I'll be able to do my own thing, come and go as I please. If I want to work late at night I can, and not feel guilty. There'll be no one to tell me what to wear, how my hair should look, who I should speak to. We'll be able to chatter on the phone – until the bills get out of hand. If I feel like having a meal after work, I won't need anyone's permission. Oh Liz, there are so many things that I'll be able to do."

"I suppose so," said Liz doubtfully, then lapsed into silence.

"How did you stand him?" she burst out angrily after a minute.

Holly shrugged. "Stupidity, addiction, lack of confidence? Who knows?" She didn't want to talk about Derek any more.

It was an absolute treat for Holly to spend the day with her sister. No rushing to get back to Derek, no nasty comments about wasting time.

They talked non-stop until it was time for Liz to go, she wanted to avoid the heavy traffic.

"We'll see you on Friday," Liz confirmed as she got ready to leave. "Then we can continue where we left off."

"Poor Robert! I'm looking forward to it so much." Holly smiled.

"Me too. Don't forget, have that bruise photographed and contact a solicitor as soon as possible," Liz said in a serious voice.

"Give me a day or two. Then I will, I promise." Holly clung to her sister for a moment. "Don't worry about me, I'll survive."

Chapter Four

Simone dumped a brown paper bag unceremoniously on the coffee table, and said, "Your husband is evil."

Holly's face paled. "What's he done?" she asked.

"He stormed into Pagett, yelling that he wanted to see his wife. When the security people tried to eject him, he began to rant and rage and said that I'd kidnapped you. And that's not all. When I went to get my car from the car park, all four tyres were flat," Simone fumed. "That's why I'm so late."

"I'm sorry, Simone," Holly said weakly. What else could she say? "I really am, how can I make it up to you?"

Simone instantly regretted her outburst. Holly's stricken face made her bruise even more livid and pronounced.

"Take no notice of me, I'll calm down in a minute. Let me get out of this suit, have a drink, then we'll eat, there's Chinese in the bag, pop it into the oven to keep warm."

"Does he know that I'm staying with you?" Holly asked fearfully.

"I'm sure he does. But don't worry, he doesn't know my address," Simone began reassuringly, then stopped. "He doesn't, does he? You never mentioned where I live, did you?" she questioned.

"No. There was never any reason to."

Simone was relieved. Another meeting with Derek Grant was more than she could take.

The fracas in the reception area had brought Pagett's managing director, Arthur Lord, scuttling from his office. He issued strict instructions that, if Holly's husband made any further attempt to enter the building, security should call the police immediately. Arthur liked Holly, she was a gentle girl, and he was genuinely sympathetic that she had been subjected to such trauma. But Pagett was a publishers, not a bull-ring.

The wine soothed and calmed them both. The foil dishes and cartons soon emptied.

"That was divine," Holly said appreciatively as she broke open a fortune cookie. "Derek would rarely agree to a take-away."

Simone shrugged. "It saves cooking."

"Listen to this," Holly said as she read the motto. "Woman who wishes to equal man shows little ambition."

"Especially if that man is Derek," Simone replied sardonically.

"What else happened at Pagett today, apart from the obvious?" Holly asked.

"Not a whole lot. We finalised plans for Della Armstrong's book launch, it's on the eighteenth.

Martin Crowe phoned and kicked up hell because his local book shop had no copies of his book and Esme Wright wants to do a feature about me – with photographs – for the *Sunday Globe* magazine."

Holly whistled. "The *Globe*, I *am* impressed." One look at Simone's glum face prompted her to ask, "Aren't you pleased?"

"It *is* flattering, I suppose." Simone frowned. "It will certainly be good publicity for Pagett, but I don't particularly enjoy discussing my private life. It makes me feel uncomfortable."

"She can only print what you want her to."

"You must be joking. Where did you get that idea? Esme is a hard hitter. The less you tell her, the more she writes."

"When's the interview?"

"Tomorrow."

"Tomorrow? That doesn't give you much time."

"I'm lucky it wasn't today. Which reminds me, I must go and fish out something suitable to wear."

"You look good in whatever you wear." Holly's praise was sincere. Simone knew exactly what suited her. Her tall slim figure made her a perfect clothes-horse. She never wore her skirts too long or too short, and had a flair for colour, a casual elegance which appeared effortless. Holly had lost count of the number of times she would have given her all for a touch of Simone's glamour.

The bedroom was the essence of tranquillity, just like the rest of the flat. Simone liked those neutral shades and had introduced subtle touches of colour which added to the charm of the room.

"What do you think of this?" Simone held a blue silk blouse against a pale-beige suit. It was still too early in the year to wear her cream one.

"Perfect," Holly said enviously. When she wore beige it looked drab.

Simone scrabbled around the bottom of her wardrobe for the shoes that she needed, then stretched to the shelf above the hangers to find a matching bag. "With all the fuss and bother today, I completely forgot, Arthur has called a meeting for Wednesday. All very mysterious. No one has a clue why."

"Not even Lois?" Holly laughed.

"Not even Lois!" Pagett's receptionist, Lois, was the eyes and ears of the firm. No one on the staff could quite fathom how she managed to glean all her information, so they'd given up trying. They'd christened her *radar-lugs* but were careful to keep on the right side of her.

"I wish I didn't look such a mess," Holly said morosely. "I want to get back to work."

"Another couple of days' peace and quiet will do you no harm."

"I suppose everyone is gossiping about . . . my problem."

"Nobody except Arthur knows what happened," Simone reassured her.

"But surely they couldn't have missed Derek's . . . performance?"

"Well . . . Don't let people get to you. Everyone

is . . . or would be . . . on your side . . . " Simone floundered. Not even the office cat could have failed to hear the ruckus that Derek had created earlier. "I have an idea. Why don't I bring home some manuscripts for you to read? I'll never get through them all. You can jettison any that you don't like. Just to keep me in touch, scribble a short report. You know exactly what's right for us, what we need."

"I'd be delighted. Bring home as many as you can carry. Tomorrow I'll work on Norma's book, it's almost finished."

"How's the book going?"

"Very well. It's a pity we can't publish her, she'd be ideal for us."

"Has she ever suggested changing?"

"No. But she does have a little grumble every now and again. I think the book I'm doing now is her best so far. Great plot," Holly said admiringly.

"Maybe some day she'll change to Pagett. I'm sure you help her enormously." Simone yawned. "I'm going to bed. I need all the beauty sleep I can get tonight. I take a lousy photograph at the best of times."

"Oh, that reminds me, talking of photographs, Liz drove me spare today – she insisted I must have my bruise photographed. Do you have a camera? I'd be too embarrassed to go to a professional." Holly pulled a rueful face.

"She's right. I do have a Polaroid somewhere. Let me try and find it now while you're still technicoloured."

Simone stood on a chair and searched the top of her wardrobe. "Here we are, I hope there's some film in it, it's ages since we . . . I . . . used it." Sometimes she forgot that Mark was no longer there.

They examined the camera. "We're in luck, there are still about six shots left," Simone said. "Sit here on the chair and I'll see what I can do. Patrick Lichfield I'm not."

The first photograph was blurry and faded.

"I wonder if the film is past its best?" Simone wrinkled her nose. "Let's try again."

The second, third and fourth exposures were more clearly defined and the close-ups of the two remaining photos quite horrifyingly detailed.

"Put them away until you need them," Simone advised as she watched Holly's face crumple.

Holly brushed her hair gently so as not to hurt herself. Even though she had seen the bruises in her mirror, the photographs had upset her. The past two days had been hazy, a series of mind-stabbing events linked only by moments of reality.

"What have I done? How will I cope alone?" she asked herself. She was seized with panic. It was two years since she'd had to think for herself, two years of total dependence, of cruel controlling guidance. The brush rested idly in her hands. How was Derek feeling now? Remorseful? Lonely? Could he change? Holly pushed back her hair and stared at her reflection. She continued to stare at the bruise. And then she saw it. Really saw it. Was she losing her mind, how could she even *think* about going back to that ogre?

How long was it since she had been her own person, in control of her life? At university? A wisp of a smile twitched her lips. She'd been independent then, fiercely independent. Nothing fazed her. They were wonderful times; the shared house, the beer-impregnated furniture, the tipsy intellectual discussions which lasted into the small hours, none of which they could remember the following morning as they scrambled to lectures. And people, there were always people, students, friendship and warmth. She was popular then, not like now – alone, isolated, practically invisible.

Tears of self-pity oozed from her eyes. Derek had destroyed her life, dominated her, separated her from her friends. The only one left was Liz – and Robert of course. She had never allowed Derek to come between her and Liz. *Not allowed him to part her from Liz.* Holly stirred. She blamed Derek for her weakness but she had been strong where Liz was concerned. Liz – the most important person in her life. The tears stopped. She *could* build a life for herself, make friends again. She was quite capable of earning a living. The time for blame and recrimination was over.

Chapter Five

Derek Grant looked at the empty corner disdainfully, he'd never liked that fussy little desk of Holly's. And the way she'd scattered those papers all over the living-room floor was disgusting. It would take him most of the night to clear up the mess she'd made in the kitchen.

He sat on the carpet and put the documents back in their envelopes. At least the damn desk had served a purpose, now he'd have to find a new place to store the papers until she came back. A white fury seized him as the reduced balance in their deposit book registered. How dare she do that without his permission? When had she withdrawn the money? Another of Simone's contributions to their otherwise happy marriage? It had to be her fault, Holly would never steal money from their account. Simone was fast becoming the controlling factor in their marriage. She had to be stopped before Holly fell totally under her spell. He would deal with her in his own way, but only after Holly came home.

Derek waited quietly in the doorway opposite until

Simone left the flat. He didn't need that cold bitch's interference again, he wanted to talk to Holly alone. He was furious that he'd spoiled his perfect record by taking time off this morning, but that was what Holly had driven him to.

He ran his finger down the list of names and rang the bell marked Pearse.

"Yes?" Holly answered.

"Holly?" he questioned.

"What do you want? How did you know where to find me?"

"Let me in, I need to talk to you," he said.

"I have nothing to say to you, go away."

"We *must* talk," he insisted.

"No. If you want to talk to me you can contact me through my solicitor. You'll hear from him in a few days."

"Don't be ridiculous. Just open the door and stop behaving so childishly."

Holly could hear that edge in his voice, the menace that had always terrified her.

You're free of him now, she told herself sternly, he can't frighten you anymore.

"Let's get this straight," she said firmly. "I don't have to talk to you. Not now, not tomorrow, not ever. *I know my rights and, if you don't leave immediately, I will seek a restraining order. I will also advise your firm of my status . . . your abused wife.*" Holly's confident warning was a quote from the text of Norma Down's last book.

"Holly! You don't mean that." His laugh had a hollow ring to it but it infuriated her nevertheless.

"Go to hell," she shouted and slammed the intercom phone back on its cradle. It buzzed again almost immediately. This time she removed the receiver and stuffed it into the drawer of the telephone table beneath it.

"Now ring," she challenged the closed drawer.

Derek stood motionless in front of the solid street door. He was puzzled by Holly's new-found determination – Simone's tutoring no doubt. Holly had always been such a reasonable person, looked up to him, never argued. Simone's influence had obviously warped her thinking. He pressed the bell again, but Holly didn't answer. Totally frustrated, he hammered the door with his fist, but she still didn't respond.

Derek wrapped his aching fist in his hand. If this was the way Holly wanted to act, let her. She'd be the loser, not him. She'd miss him, see sense in a day or two, then he might, or might not, take her back. Imagine Holly trying to live alone, look after herself, she was such a helpless creature. It was just as well that he'd taken a note of the names and addresses in her diary. The phone numbers could prove useful too. He'd even jotted down Simone's car number as she swept away from one of those launches, though at the time he hadn't known why. He would phone Holly tomorrow, enough of the morning had been wasted knocking on her door like a beggar.

Chapter Six

Holly tossed aside the manuscript she was reading and tried to focus her thoughts. The news that Pagett were adding children's books to their list fired her imagination. Simone appeared completely uninterested in the new venture. It was all right for her, she was at the top of the heap.

Holly was anxious for every bit of information that Simone could give her.

"It's not my province, let them get on with it," she answered vaguely. "I really can't tell you any more than I already have. I was in a rush today and had to leave before the end of the meeting." An edge of impatience crept into Simone's voice.

Holly rolled and unrolled the cover of the manuscript. This would be the perfect opportunity for me to get ahead, she fretted. "Simone, I'm sorry to go on about this children's thing, but won't they need an editor?" she persevered.

"I'm sure they will."

"I've been thinking, would I be able to handle it? I'm well used to dealing with adult books," Holly added quickly.

"I really don't know. I imagine there must be great skill in handling children's work. You'd need experience, possibly even a list of established authors. It's not for me to say, you'd have to talk to Arthur about that."

"Do you think you could put in a word for me, recommend me?" Holly asked with a frown.

Simone listened to Holly's request with a sinking heart. Her eyes darted to the pile of manuscripts which she'd brought home for Holly to read. She'd already made short work of two of them and had written a short report spelling out why they were unsuitable for Pagett. There was no need for Simone to read the discarded texts, Holly's judgement was good enough for her. She makes my life so much easier. Perhaps I should promise to do as she asks. Arthur would certainly listen to what I have to say, but it's up to me how I ask. Now was the time to nip Holly's editing aspirations in the bud.

"I can't guarantee anything but I'll have a chat with Arthur, find out what he has in mind," Simone promised reluctantly.

"That would be wonder . . . " Three long trills on the doorbell stopped Holly short. Not Derek again. She hadn't told Simone about his earlier visit and she was still trying to work out how he'd managed to get hold of her address.

"Yes?" Simone said sharply into the intercom. More interruptions. At this rate she'd never get to grips with all she had to do.

"Pizza? I didn't order pizza. You must have the

wrong address." There was silence as she listened to the disembodied voice. "You have the right name, but I'm telling you, I did not order pizza." Again she listened then frowned. "Twelve large pepperoni pizzas? I'm sorry but . . ."

"Oh God, Derek!" Holly groaned as she stood beside Simone.

"Come up, second floor," Simone said as she pressed the entry phone buzzer. "It seems to be a genuine mistake. Besides, Derek doesn't know where I live."

"I'm afraid he does," Holly admitted. "He showed up this morning but I refused to talk to him."

Simone's eyes darkened with anger. "I thought you said he *didn't* know my address?" she accused.

"He must have read it in my diary . . . I'm so sorry." She always seemed to be apologising for Derek.

"Not as sorry as he'll be," Simone said as she opened the door.

"Do you know who ordered these?" she demanded angrily.

"No, Miss. My boss took the order," the young delivery man said.

"Right. Step inside for a moment. Put the boxes there on the floor and ring your boss."

His finger shook slightly as he punched in the number, his boss would flip. "Ron? It's Tommy. That order for twelve peps, there's been a mistake." He held the phone away from his ear as an abusive stream of invective bleeped from the instrument.

48

"I don't know. It's not my fault," he whined. "Here, speak to the woman yourself."

Tommy stuck the phone into Simone's hand and shrank back.

"There appears to be a mistake here," Simone informed Tommy's boss. "We didn't order *one* pizza, let alone twelve. Who gave the order?"

"Are you Simone Pearse?" The irate man enquired.

"I am," she replied icily.

"Then twelve pizzas it is."

"Don't be ridiculous. I'm not responsible for your mess-ups."

"The man said he wanted twelve pepperonis delivered, and twelve you've got."

"Listen, there *isn't* any man here. You've been had, chum."

It was Simone's turn to hold the phone clear of her ear. She dropped it back into place without uttering another word.

"Hang on a minute," she told Tommy. She put a couple of pound coins into his hand. "Sorry you've had this hassle. I think he said to take them back."

Simone kicked the door shut with her foot. "Right, why didn't you tell me that Derek was here today?" she demanded.

"I was upset that he'd found out where you live – I didn't want to worry you."

"I'd be a lot more worried if he just showed up one day, wouldn't I?"

Holly could feel tears welling in her eyes. She

swallowed hard. "Obviously he must have read my diary."

"And written down my address," Simone pointed out acidly. "I suggest you mention this to the solicitor tomorrow. I don't want your husband anywhere near my flat again."

Holly picked up her manuscript and the tears which had been threatening fell unchecked. Simone was livid, quite rightly. But what could she do to stop Derek? Perhaps the solicitor would advise her. It wasn't fair to Simone, to either of them. She must start looking for her own flat tomorrow, the last thing she wanted was trouble with Simone. If only Liz and Robert lived nearer.

Simone chose to ignore the waterfall which cascaded down Holly's cheeks. Now that Holly's demented husband had shown up, she no longer felt safe in her own home.

"You positively *must* tell the solicitor about this," Simone warned, emphatically. "I don't want him here again, don't want to get involved with courts and solicitors again. I've been through all that once." Her own divorce had been no picnic but at least there had been no acrimony. "In fact, I suggest that you make a list of all your grievances. Try and remember everything bad that happened during your marriage, every little incident, then everything that's happened since you left." Simone picked up her pen.

Holly switched on her laptop with a feeling of desolation. Perhaps she should offer to move to a hotel.

"Would you like me to leave tomorrow?" Holly asked forlornly.

Simone drew a deep breath. *Yes please,* she thought. "Don't be silly, it'll all work out," she answered unconvincingly. "Just prepare your statement for the solicitor. Besides, if you have everything ready, it will save you time and money."

Holly typed long into the night. Page after page scrolled on to the screen, Derek's injustice, his bullying, her frustration and fear. She dredged her mind for incidents of his cruelty, some long forgotten, others unrecognised at the time. Finally tiredness forced her to stop. If she thought of anything else she could add it in the morning before she printed out the sum total of two years of misery.

The one thing she couldn't remember was why she had married him in the first place.

Chapter Seven

Holly sat primly on the leather chair and waited as the solicitor examined the papers she had given him. As he read, Vincent Harper ran his finger backwards and forwards across the front of his thinning, mousy-coloured hair. Holly had never been to a solicitor's office before and expected to find bookcases crammed full of law books, a dusty leather desk piled high with ribbon-tied briefs and everyone talking in hushed tones. This glass and chrome room with its expensively potted trees, state-of-the-art machines and comfortably upholstered chairs wasn't what she'd imagined.

The solicitor set the papers aside, then eased his glasses upwards from the bridge of his nose with a nervous gesture.

"You certainly have been thorough." Vincent Harper nodded approvingly. "The photographs will be most useful, but I don't see any medical report, I must have missed it," he commented as he searched again through the pile of documents.

"No, you haven't, I don't have one. When I found that I could move my jaw without too much difficulty . . . I . . . I didn't visit a doctor," Holly finished lamely.

"It's important that you have a medical report. But don't worry, it's not too late." His eyes focused impersonally on her bruised face. "There's still plenty of evidence – unfortunately."

"Could *you* recommend someone?" Holly asked. She didn't like the doctor who had looked after her when she had flu – Derek's doctor – he was unsympathetic and cold, just like Derek.

Vincent was well aware that some women were reluctant to attend their own GP in these circumstances. He scribbled a name and address on a piece of paper and handed it to her.

"Doctor Philips is very understanding, you'll like her. She's attached to a clinic that deals with this sort of . . . problem." He did not care to use the word abuse.

Holly folded the paper and slipped it into her bag. "What happens next?" she asked.

Vincent Harper explained the procedure in detail. " . . . and so it's up to him whether or not he agrees to a divorce. I hope for your sake that he does. Now, what about finances?"

"I withdrew my savings from our joint account," Holly said proudly.

"That was sensible. I'm sure you were entitled to do that," Vincent replied tactfully.

"Do you mean, was I entitled to take it? Yes, I was. I only took what was mine. I don't want his money, or anything else from him come to that – except my divorce."

"Actually, I meant what about financial support? For instance, what about the money you contributed to the mortgage, are you going to walk away from that?"

"Yes. I don't care, he can have it."

"And costs? Are you prepared to pay your own costs? A divorce can be expensive."

Holly frowned. "I can't afford an expensive divorce." Simone had said his charges were reasonable and fair.

"I understand. But I think that your husband should bear a certain amount of responsibility. At least let's try and get back some of the money you contributed." It sickened him that women could be scared like this, frightened to even discuss their rights. This pretty woman with her stabbing, blue eyes was a perfect example. And then there were the others determined to grab anything and everything they could. "I think we should explore that avenue. Agreed?" he enquired.

"OK, I agree, but only so long as I don't have to see Derek or speak to him again. There's something else . . . " Holly was hesitant to mention it. "How do I stop him from harassing Simone Pearse and myself?"

"Simone told me about the incident at the office when she phoned. It may just be a reaction, shock, on his part. First day denial, that kind of thing. I suggest that you let the dust settle for a couple of days then, if you have any further trouble, let me know immediately and we'll apply to the court for a restraining order."

"Will that stop him?" Holly asked innocently. Maybe he was right. She could tell him about Derek's visit and the pizzas another time.

"If it doesn't, he'll be arrested."

"Oh," was all Holly could find to say. She wouldn't like to be responsible for sending Derek to jail.

"We seem to have covered everything for now. Unless you have any other questions or suggestions?"

"I don't think so. It's all a bit strange, difficult to grasp. As I said before, I can't imagine Derek agreeing to a divorce. One thing that *might* be of help is that . . . he would hate anyone at work to find out how badly he's treated me. He likes to think he's perfect, you see. I think if anybody saw those photos, he'd have a blue fit . . . I don't know if that's any use?"

"It could give us some leverage. But perhaps that won't be necessary, we'll just have to wait for his reaction. I'll keep you informed of our progress. In the meantime, go and have your medical examination. The sooner the better. There's no need to make an appointment, just go along. I'll ask my secretary to phone Dr Philips and explain what we need."

Holly shook his outstretched hand. She felt strangely comforted when he covered her small hand with his own. "I know you're feeling frightened and upset now, Holly, but don't be, sooner or later we'll sort everything out. If you think of anything else, or are worried, feel free to phone me, that's what I'm here for. I'll do my very best for you."

There was a lightness in her step as she strolled along the street towards the newsagent. She had made the first move towards her independence, now she must find somewhere to live.

Vincent Harper was right, Dr Philips was a compassionate woman. As Holly suspected, the X-ray proved that her jawbone wasn't fractured. Dr Philips gave her a thorough check-up. She prescribed a mild tranquilliser should Holly need it, then made out a full report, in duplicate. She even offered to include Vincent Harper's copy in their post bag later that day.

Her kindness brought the hint of a smile to Holly's lips.

Chapter Eight

Holly circled all the advertisements for flats which might be suitable. She was stunned that rents were so high. Perhaps if she went to an estate agent instead . . . The telephone interrupted her thoughts.

"I'm phoning about the massage," a man's voice said.

"Excuse me?" Holly answered, puzzled.

"The massage – Swedish massage," the voice leered.

I'm sorry, you must have the wrong number," she said politely.

"Sorry to have troubled you," he said.

A couple of minutes later the phone rang again.

"So you're offering massage, darling? How much?" A male voice drawled.

"I told you, you have the wrong number," Holly snapped.

"You didn't tell me anything darling, is that . . . " the caller repeated Simone's number. "That right?" he asked.

"You've made a mistake." Quickly she replaced the receiver in its cradle.

She returned to her chair under the lamp and tried to concentrate on her paper. The phone rang again.

"What's your address?" a husky voice enquired.

"I beg your pardon?" Holly replied, coldly.

"Your address, where do you live? The massage?"

Her throat constricted. Someone was playing nasty games and it didn't take a genius to work out who it might be. She slammed down the phone.

Before she could return to the flats-to-let column, the doorbell rang.

"Yes?" Holly answered the door-phone nervously.

"Taxis for . . . Ms . . . Simone Pearse."

"I . . . er . . . there must be some mistake. We didn't order a taxi." This was turning into a nightmare. For a second she wished Simone was here and then was glad she wasn't.

"Three taxis," he corrected. "You sure you didn't ring us?"

"I'm really sorry, but we don't need any taxis."

"Stupid cow, says it's not her."

Holly could hear the sound of car doors slamming, engines revving.

Derek, again. She had to stop him, right now. She fumbled in her bag and pulled Vincent Harper's card from her wallet.

" . . . yes . . . I see, mmm," he drawled infuriatingly. "The problem is that you don't have any proof that it's Derek, do you?"

"Who else *can* it be?"

"But you don't actually *know* it's him?"

"I thought you said you'd help me," Holly accused.

"I did, and I will. But if you tell the police what you've just told me, they'll also need proof," Vincent explained patiently. "I have a suggestion. If anyone else phones, ask them where they found your number – Simone's number. Tell them that someone is playing a sick game on you and you need to stop the calls. At least that way you may have a chance to find out where the ads were placed and, perhaps, discover who was responsible. Will you do that?"

"OK," Holly agreed reluctantly.

"Of course, we could hire a private detective if you like."

"No, I won't do that." Holly was adamant. The idea of involving a private detective frightened her even more. If she hadn't left Derek, none of this would have happened.

"I'll leave it up to you then. Keep in touch," Vincent instructed and she was left holding the purring phone.

She sank disconsolately onto her chair. Simone would be furious when she found out. I'm not going to tell her about the taxis, Holly decided.

The phone rang again. Twice. But neither caller would give her the information she needed.

"Hello, hello," she shouted in frustration at the next caller. But the line was dead, the man probably half-way down the street.

Simone closed the door and dumped her heavily laden bag on the floor.

"Thank heavens that's today over with," she called.

59

Holly's mouth went dry and she prayed that the phone would remain silent until she had time to explain.

"My word, there are a lot of messages," Simone said as she pressed the button on her answer phone. "What the hell . . . ? What's going on?"

Holly joined her in the tiny, square hallway. She hadn't realised that the answerphone was on the blink and had recorded the phone calls. At least the taxi driver wasn't on the tape.

"There have been some odd calls," she admitted. "Wrong numbers, obviously."

"Wrong number my foot, it's that warped husband of yours."

"Oh, he wouldn't do that," Holly said ingenuously.

"Get real, Holly. Who else would pull a stunt like this?"

Holly remained silent.

"I'm going to phone Vincent Harper, get his advice."

"No point, I already have." Holly fixed her eyes on Simone's shoulder, afraid to meet her blazing anger.

Holly's admission seemed to infuriate Simone even more. "And what did he say?" she asked coldly.

"That we need proof. He told me to ask the . . . men . . . where they'd found the number."

"And then what?" Simone demanded.

"I don't know. Phone him, I suppose." I'm not going to tell her that Vincent suggested hiring a detective either, she'd probably insist on it.

Simone peeled off her coat and threw it on the little padded stool beside the phone. What had possessed her to get embroiled in Holly's mess? she asked herself for the umpteenth time. She went into the kitchen, opened the fridge and took out a bottle of wine. She took one glass from the cupboard and poured herself a drink. Holly watched silently as Simone gulped it down then poured another. The golden liquid slopped over the side of the glass. Simone was shaking with temper, obviously blamed her. Why hadn't she listened to Liz? If she'd moved in with her and Robert, none of this would have happened.

"Please, don't start crying again, Holly, I can't take it," Simone begged as Holly's face finally crumpled. "I've had a hard day. Give me a few minutes to unwind, then we'll decide what to do."

Simone wished that her motive for helping Holly was altruistic, but it wasn't. Holly could easily find another job, but could she find another Holly?

By nine-thirty they'd discovered that the suggestive advertisement had been placed in at least two shops and one public phone box. They left the phone off the hook for the rest of the evening. Holly wasn't due to return to Pagett until after the weekend so she promised to track down the shops the following day. The last of their callers was sympathetic when Simone explained the situation, he promised to remove the card from the phone box himself. The following morning, after another call, Holly discovered that a third shop was involved. There was no point in telling that to Simone.

Chapter Nine

"I've never been so embarrassed in all my life." Holly felt her face flame with indignation.

"But you don't think it was Derek?" her brother-in-law asked as he refilled their glasses.

"To be honest, I don't. Two of the shopkeepers said that a middle-aged woman had placed the advert, a woman with a lisp."

"And the third?" Liz prompted.

"He couldn't remember but was almost sure it was a woman, he didn't take much notice."

"Do you think Derek could have paid someone to do it for him?" Robert puzzled aloud.

"I suppose he could have done but, much as I hate Derek, I don't think he'd allow himself to do anything so sleazy. But then there were the pizzas . . . and the taxis, Simone doesn't know about the taxis."

"And her tyres?" Liz reminded her.

"Those too. I wish I knew who was responsible." Holly sighed.

"I think you should wipe the whole thing from your mind, at least for the weekend," Robert advised, perhaps their questions were just making matters worse. "There's nothing you can do about it now. You've been through so much this past week, try and relax. Enjoy your couple of days. I'm sure you two will find *something* to talk about," he teased.

"I'm sure we will," Holly answered with a half-smile. "I'll do my best. But I'd like to phone Simone. She was at a booksellers' lunch today so I didn't have a chance to speak to her. I left a message on her machine and it's playing up a bit."

"Go ahead." Liz smiled encouragingly at her sister.

Holly shivered slightly as she sat at the bottom of the narrow spiral staircase that led to the attic. She dialled Simone's number. It had been gloriously sunny when she arrived at the cottage but, as the sun began to set behind the budding trees, warmth had deserted the lovely old cottage garden and the grey stone building was plunged back into the grip of a wintry chill. The cottage, a listed building, was the fulfilment of Liz and Robert's dreams. They had fallen in love with it the moment they laid eyes on it. Decrepit electric wiring and out of date plumbing had eaten up every penny they had. Robert's Oxford degree had earned him a prestigious post in medical research, but without the prestigious salary to go with it. Liz considered herself fortunate to have found work in the local prep school even if it was only part-time. Two and a half days each week. But they were content to invest their earnings in their home, wouldn't have it any other way. Central heating was their next target. In spite of its stone walls and floors the atmosphere in the cottage was shabbily cosy, filled with plump cushions, early spring blossom and, Holly recognised with a stab of envy, love. Robert had even lit a fire in her bedroom.

Simone answered her phone after the first ring. "I got your message, tell me about the woman," she urged breathlessly.

"Yes, of course. As I said, she was middle-aged, had a lisp. She paid for the . . . cards in cash. One week in each shop." It was pointless telling Simone that she'd found the third shop.

"Anything else?"

"No, not really. One girl thought that she spoke very quickly, as if she was nervous."

"I doubt that," Simone said quietly.

"Why do you say that? Do you know who it is?"

"It doesn't matter, forget all about it. Have a good weekend, I'll see you on Sunday night."

Holly stood frowning at the phone. Simone had been so steamed up last night, now she wanted the whole incident forgotten. Weird.

* * *

Simone watched for her exit then left the motorway traffic roaring behind her. Five minutes later she pulled up in front of Maggie Tweed's house.

"Thimone!" Maggie said as she cautiously opened the door.

Simone pushed it wide and swept unceremoniously past the dumpy woman.

"Thith ith a . . . thurprithe." Maggie Tweed lisped uncertainly.

"I'll bet it is. What are you playing at, Maggie?" Simone snapped.

"What do you mean?" Maggie smoothed her untidy hair then pulled quickly at her rumpled cardigan. Simone's immaculate appearance had always irritated her.

"Come off it, you know *exactly* why I'm here. What possessed you?"

"Thimone, what are you on about? I haven't the faintetht idea what you mean," Maggie claimed again.

"Swedish massage, my phone number? Cut the pretence, Maggie. Middle-aged woman with a *lithp*," Simone mocked unkindly. "Why, Maggie? Because I turned your book down? And don't bother to deny it was you, I have three witnesses who are willing to testify that it was."

Maggie eyed her furious friend. Ex-friend, as she now thought of Simone. Arrogant bitch. What gave her the right to trash her wonderful book, dismiss it with nothing more than a standard refusal slip? A stranger would expect better. But Simone's hostility frightened her, there was no point in feigning innocence. How had Simone found out it was her? And so quickly?

"I'm waiting for an explanation before I go to the police."

"Don't do that, pleathe. It wath jutht . . . a joke."

"A joke? You call that a joke?" Simone spat. "For God's sake, Maggie, the phone almost rang off its hook last night. God knows how many perverts have my phone number. Some joke."

Maggie toed a bare patch on the carpet with her slippered foot. "Do you want a drink?" she asked.

"No I don't want a drink, I want an answer."

"I did it becauth . . . you didn't give the book a chanth. Jutht turned it down, didn't even have the curtethy to phone me."

"I begged you to send it to someone else, Maggie. I didn't want to chance causing a rift in our friendship, but you just kept on and on. Insisted I read it. I warned you that I'd have to give you an honest evaluation. And to be fair to you, I gave it to my assistant to read also. She vetoed it too." Simone saw the hurt in Maggie's eyes, but she wasn't in the mood to pull her punches. She'd known Maggie all her life, liked her and her quirky wit. But Maggie's talent didn't lie in words.

"You didn't even read it yourthelf?" Maggie accused.

"I said, we *both* read it. And what about the pizzas you had delivered? Twelve pepperoni pizzas, another touch of spite on your part? And my car tyres, what about those?"

"What peet-thath? Car tyreth? I don't know what you mean, honetht, Thimone," Maggie insisted as she watched Simone's eyes narrow.

"The pizzas, ordering those was plain stupid. You might as well admit it now, Maggie, I know you were responsible for those too. Also you know my car, know where I park it. I suppose you didn't let the air out of my tyres either?"

"I admit I acted like a fool putting the cardth in the windowth but I don't know anything about peet-thath, or your car, I *thwear* I don't."

Simone stared hard at her. She believed her and wished that she didn't.

It would have been so neat and convenient if Maggie had been responsible for everything. Less worrying. She could handle Maggie but Derek . . . he was an unknown quantity, an angry man.

"You realise that I'll have to report this to the police?" Simone said.

"Don't, pleathe don't. I wath hurt, dithappointed, I admit it. I know that it wath wrong of me. But I didn't do the other thingth, don't involve the polithe. It will cotht me my job if you do."

Simone appeared to consider Maggie's plea. She had no intention of contacting the police.

"Thimone? You won't, will you?" Maggie begged.

"All right, I'll let it go this time but, if you ever pull a stunt like that again – I won't hesitate. And I mean that, Maggie."

"I know you do. I won't ever do anything like that again."

Simone's glare softened. Maggie seemed to have shrunk a couple of inches in the few minutes she had been there. "I'm sorry about your book, Maggie, but it was no use lying to you."

"Now that you're here, can you tell me what *wath* wrong with it?'

"I really don't want to upset you any more than I already have."

"You won't. Tell me," Maggie pleaded.

"OK. I felt it had no direction, no plot. The writing was stilted and overly-sentimental. The characters were . . . wooden, unreal. People don't speak to each other like that, Maggie, not even in books. That's the way I saw it, but I could be wrong. You could always try another publisher, get *their* opinion."

Maggie accepted the criticism without comment and hated Simone even more.

"I'm sorry, Maggie, but you *did* ask me." Simone had done everything in her power to persuade Maggie to send the book elsewhere but Maggie's entreaties had worn her down. She had read it with a sinking heart. The book wasn't suitable for publication and it had spoilt their friendship. Apart from one terse, accusatory phone call, she had not heard a word from Maggie for months. Under the circumstances perhaps a more personal note or a phone call would have been much kinder. It was cowardly of her, she knew, but at the time she was furious that Maggie had forced her into that position.

Win some, lose some, she sighed to herself as she walked towards the door. "Goodbye, Maggie," she said simply as she let herself out into the night. She doubted she would hear from Maggie Tweed again.

* * *

Relief, then concern, crossed Holly's face. The

soothing effect of the weekend began ᴛᴏ
rapidly.

"Do you really believe that Maggie Tweed wasn't
responsible for letting the air out of your tyres, or
sending the pizzas?" She almost added, or the taxis
and their angry drivers.

"I wish I could give you the answer you want to
hear, we both want to hear, but I know she was
telling the truth, she was too scared not to."

"What a spiteful thing to do. Imagine anyone . . . "
Then she had a vision of her parting gift to Derek;
the kitchen cupboards smeared with ketchup, the
smashed crockery.

"Imagine anyone . . . what?" Simone asked.

"Nothing." What a sordid mess it had all turned
out to be.

Chapter Ten

Holly caused quite a stir as she walked down the corridor, her head held high. It was not her bruises, well disguised under a layer of make-up, that commanded attention but her shining hair, loose and waving, her figure, trim in a short-skirted red suit. The high-heeled red shoes pinched her toes and the narrow strap bit into her heels but she felt so glamorous, so trendy that she barely noticed the discomfort. She giggled when the receptionist challenged her.

"It's *me*, Lois, Holly." They saw each other every working day.

Arthur Lord glanced at the pretty woman and wondered idly who she was.

Holly hesitated, then turned and ran back a couple of steps to catch up with him. "Arthur, could I have a word when you have a minute?"

"Holly! I didn't recognise you! My dear, forgive me. You look . . . different."

"That's OK," she assured him with a satisfied smile.

"I'm sorry to hear about your . . . problem," he said awkwardly.

"Thank you. It's over with now, well, almost."

"I'm glad. I'll be free in about ten minutes, come to my office then." Arthur Lord continued on his way to the art department. He hoped that Holly was not going to tell him that she was leaving Pagett. She looked so different with her hair long, that fetching red suit. He'd never suspected that she could be such a beauty. The break-up must have done her good. But now he must concentrate on Ellen Dawson's book, she was due in this afternoon and he wanted to check the artwork for her cover.

Holly came straight to the point. "Simone said that you were branching into children's books and I wondered if I could apply for the post of editor?"

Liz and Robert had urged her to talk to Arthur Lord as soon as she could.

Arthur was taken aback by her direct approach. This was not what he expected-tears, yes, explanations, perhaps, a tale of woe but the job of children's editor? Simone should have warned him.

"I . . . er . . . This is very difficult," he admitted honestly. "It's not that we don't appreciate your talent, we do, but . . . you see, it's a very specialised job. There's so much involved." He shifted his pen from one side of his desk to the other while he played for time. "For instance, you have to know what's right for toddlers, good for youngsters, for teenagers, also whether a first novel is suitable, that the story is right. And then there's the supervision and laying out of illustrations, designing the artwork is always hugely important in children's books . . . "

Arthur hated to disappoint the eager young woman. Why didn't he just tell her he had someone in mind? "You do understand?" he asked with a frown.

"Yes . . . but surely with my experience that shouldn't be too difficult to pick up?"

"I'm sure that's true, but we need someone . . . who's already qualified, someone with a list of established authors."

"So you're saying I'm not right for the job?"

"You could be, given time, but we want someone who can start right away." He wouldn't meet her gaze.

"Thank you for listening."

Liz and Robert obviously had more faith in her than Arthur did.

"Holly, I'm glad to see you back with us again," Arthur said, relieved to change the subject. "I'm sure it has been a most difficult time for you."

Holly did her best to hide her disappointment. "It wasn't pleasant. Simone has been fantastic."

He gathered from what Simone had told him that she bitterly regretted her offer of help. And who could blame her with that crazy husband of Holly's in the background? Derek Grant's visit the other day had upset him. He'd been jumpy ever since, they all had.

"Have you made any plans?" he probed gently.

"My sister and her husband want me to go and live with them in Oxford."

"Are you going to?" he asked sharply. He was well aware that Simone relied heavily on Holly and hoped that she wasn't going to take her family up on their offer.

"I don't know, I'm tempted." Holly astonished herself with the lie, especially as she had an appointment to see two flats later that evening. She sensed Arthur's disquiet, maybe her uncertainty would help him change his mind about the editorship.

"I hope you don't," he said. "I wanted to discuss something with you, but it can wait."

Derek's intrusion, no doubt, Holly thought morosely. "Can't we talk about it now?"

"I'm not sure that it applies now. Because of your . . . predicament, I was going to suggest that we increase your salary. Say, a thousand a year? That should help with living accommodation or any extra expenses that you may have."

"That's very generous. It would certainly help." In a flash, Holly realised that she'd been bribed. Was this a spur of the moment decision on Arthur's part or pre-planned? It wasn't a question she could ask.

"Also," he continued, "I thought you should have your own office, the one at the end of the corridor, next to accounts."

"You mean the room we use for storage – stationery, the manuscripts?"

"Yes. Of course we'll have it decorated," he added quickly. "It has plenty of light for reading, it's nice and quiet. It will be ideal for you."

She had been neatly shunted sideways. To make room for the children's editor, no doubt. She enjoyed sharing an office with Emma, Pagett's copy editor. I bet she'll be moved too, Holly guessed.

Where will they would put *her*? she pondered. In the broom cupboard?

"Think about it. Let me know what you decide." Arthur fidgeted then stood up. He had never learnt how to end an informal meeting without feeling rude or abrupt.

The female staff at Pagett made no comment about her absence, nor did they mention Derek's visit. Instead they complimented her on her suit, loved her hair, admired her make-up. This time she wasn't daydreaming, this time it was real. Even Simone had stared disbelievingly when she'd walked into the living-room earlier that morning.

Holly's mind kept wandering. Had Derek received Vincent Harper's letter yet? How had he spent the weekend? Would he dare show his face at Pagett again? She fervently prayed not. The two days she'd spent with Liz and Robert had been healing. A couple of times she had been close to tears but they soon chivvied her out of her uncertain moods.

Liz refused to take no for an answer and had dragged her sister into town, "to buy something red."

She and Robert enveloped her in their warmth without crowding her, bolstered her ego. By the time she arrived back at Simone's flat, a little of her lost confidence had been restored.

The *Sunday Globe* magazine, with its full page article about Simone, had been circulating around the office all day. It was, for the most part, quite flattering. There were one or two fictional additions but her photograph was excellent. Even Simone admitted it was better than she'd expected.

Holly forced her mind back to the screen and its winking cursor; she was getting nowhere, fast.

She looked around the small flat with dismay. It was tatty and miserable. Holly accepted that she couldn't expect to find a flat as spacious or well-equipped as the one she and Derek had shared, but she couldn't live here.

"May I think about it and phone you later?" she asked the poker-faced man who paced impatiently up and down.

"Up to you. But I'm warning you, we've had a lot of enquiries. It'll probably be snapped up tonight."

The first four advertisements she phoned had already been let. Holly shrugged. "Then that'll be my bad luck."

The second flat was a little better, but not much. The landlord offered to give it a lick of paint.

"I can change the colour of the walls if you don't like them," he said shrewdly as he noticed Holly's grimace of distaste.

This was the second time today she'd been bribed. The flat was only a twenty-minute walk from Pagett's Chelsea offices. Unless it was raining she would enjoy the walk and it would be a great saving on bus fares. She couldn't hope to live in Chelsea, the rents were far too high.

"Would you change the curtains?" she asked.

"They're very nice," he objected. "They don't need changing."

"Give me a minute to think about this."

"OK. I'll be downstairs. I have another appointment in ten minutes so you'd better look sharp."

It doesn't have to be forever, Holly consoled herself as she looked around again. The living/dining-room was tiny and the over-stuffed couch and chair made it look smaller still. The dining-table would seat two at a pinch, no more. There would be no space for her desk or her little table, not even enough room in the kitchen to store her precious china. She was sure Liz would look after her few possessions for her until she could afford something bigger. Poky though this flat was, it was well within her budget.

"I'd better take it," she muttered to herself as she closed the door. She determined to save every penny that she could. She wouldn't feel happy or secure until she could afford a flat of her own.

"I'll take it, providing you change the curtains," Holly said stubbornly.

"Done," he said without hesitation.

And she felt she had been.

Chapter Eleven

As a result of the feature article in the *Sunday Globe* magazine, manuscripts arrived by the sackful. They were stacked knee-high along one wall of Simone's office.

"We'll *never* get through this lot," she complained to Holly. "I think you should get rid of the hand-written ones for a start."

"What will I do with them? Don't forget *I'm* moving into the dump-room," Holly pointed out sarcastically.

Simone looked at her sharply. "I would have thought you'd enjoy having an office of your own."

"An office, yes. There'll be no space to swing a cat once the desk and chair are put in that . . . office."

Enough is enough, I must stop complaining, Holly chided herself. It wasn't Simone's decision to have her moved.

Simone hadn't seen much of Holly during the past week. It had been a week of launches, trade dinners, prize awards, meetings with agents and authors. They had taken up most of Simone's nights, and the days were a rush too. That suited them both. Holly was either in bed, or ready for bed, by the time she got home. Just another couple of days, then Holly would be moving to her own flat. Simone sensed Holly's resentment and wondered if Holly blamed her for the loss of the editorship, for not speaking to Arthur sooner.

Simone struggled back to the present. Learn a lesson from this, my girl, she lectured herself silently, next time someone's in trouble keep your lip buttoned and stay out of it.

"Do you have time to make a start on these manuscripts now?" she asked briskly.

"I can tackle a couple of them. I won't have much time this week between moving house and the office. What do you want me to do with the hand-writtens?" Holly bent down and began sorting out the bound and typewritten texts.

"I don't know, don't care. Get rid of them, send them back. We'll have a difficult enough job to do, just reading the typed ones."

In spite of Simone's kindness, Holly was relieved that tonight would be her last night at the flat. A tension had grown between them and their relationship had deteriorated. It would have been nice to have had Simone as a friend; they were both on their own, free to come and go as they pleased. But like everything else in her life, Derek had ruined her chance of that happening. When she was settled in her own flat, she would take Simone out for a really good meal. Find a special gift for her but, for now, the bouquet of flowers sitting in a bucket in Pagett's sink would have to suffice.

* * *

"That's the lot," Simone said as she closed the boot of her car.

"Thank you for everything, Simone," Holly replied and gave her a tentative peck on the cheek. "Are you sure that you won't change your mind and come up?"

"Another time. Remember? That mountain of work waiting for me at home?"

"See you on Monday. Thanks again, Simone."

Simone brushed off her thanks with an embarrassed wave of her hand, slid into her car and in seconds had merged into the traffic.

Holly unpacked her clothes, then made up her bed. She vacuumed every inch of the flat, then searched in the plastic carrier bags for a duster.

The knock at her door made her jump. Derek? What nonsense, she was becoming paranoid. Was she going to leap in the air every time a doorbell rang?

"Who's there?" she called.

"Your neighbour," a male voice answered.

She opened the door and found herself staring at a jar of coffee held by a man whose head was as bald as an egg. His body was egg-shaped too.

"I'm Terence Warren. I know I don't exactly look like the man in the Nescafé advert, but I'm the best available at the moment."

Holly was lost for words. She stared at the man, then at the jar of coffee, and began to laugh. His brown eyes twinkled as he laughed too, a hearty chuckle that shook his rotund frame.

"I'm Holly," she volunteered.

"How d'you do, Holly? I thought you might be in dire need of some caffeine."

Holly glanced at the watch on her wrist, it was almost three o'clock. "I didn't notice the time, I could certainly do with a drink. Come in, excuse the mess."

Terence stepped round the empty cases and plastic bags and handed her the jar.

"Oh, no!" she groaned. "I haven't got a kettle. I completely forgot to buy one. I even forgot to go to the supermarket."

"Don't worry, that's the beauty of neighbours, I'll just pop back next door and make us a cup. Milk, sugar?"

"Neither. Thank you."

In a couple of minutes Terence was back with two mugs of coffee, a packet of biscuits and the jar of coffee which he popped on to the counter in the kitchen. "Keep it." He waved away her protest. "It's not the most exotic flat-warming present, but it'll be useful."

As they sat at the cramped little table, Holly's nervous energy drained away.

"You've been lucky, I can smell fresh paint," Terence said.

"The landlord offered to decorate the flat. I had to bargain for the curtains."

"Well done! I've been nagging him to change my carpets and curtains for ages. If I wasn't so lazy I'd move. I'm kept pretty busy – I'm a quantity surveyor – and I suppose I've settled for the easy option."

She liked his open manner and his candour. He asked no questions, made no attempt to pry.

"I'd better leave you to it," he said suddenly. "I've taken up too much of your time already. Local knowledge – there's a small supermarket just round the corner if you're stuck. If you need a frying pan or anything, just ask."

"I will, thank you. I would like to borrow a saucepan until I can get to the shops on Monday. Something I could use to boil water? Food isn't a problem, I'll eat out this weekend."

"You can borrow my spare kettle, I'll be back in a minute. In the meantime, it's been nice meeting you."

"You, too," Holly said.

There was a knock at her door a few minutes later.

"Come in," she called. "it's open."

"Isn't it dangerous leaving a door unlocked in this day and age?" Derek's face was partially hidden by a large bunch of flowers.

"What are *you* doing here?" she gasped. "How did you find me?"

"That's not important," he said calmly. "May I come in?"

"No, you may not. And if you don't go away immediately, I'll phone the police."

"Such nonsense. I *am* your husband, don't

forget. We need to sit down and talk, find out what went wrong."

"It would be easier to find out what went *right*. And the answer to that is *nothing*, absolutely *nothing*."

"I must insist that you explain things to me yourself, Holly. No solicitors' letters, no interfering busybodies like that bitch you work for . . . "

Holly backed away from the door. Derek's voice was rising and her fear with it.

"Everything all right, Holly?" Terence Warren asked as he appeared in the doorway trailing a kettle flex behind him.

Holly's knees almost buckled with gratitude.

"This man is just leaving," she said.

"No, he is *not*," Derek insisted.

"Please phone the police, Terence, ask them to come right away."

Derek turned and eyed her neighbour coldly. "There's no need for that."

Terence's eyebrows met in a frown.

"Then get out, now," Holly ordered. "If you ever come back here again, you *will* have the police to deal with."

Derek glowered at them both, dropped the bunch of flowers where he stood and pounded down the stairs. Calmly, Holly picked up the flowers, walked a couple of steps and dropped them over the banisters to the ground floor. She watched Derek kick them aside viciously as he left the building.

It was the first time he had ever bought her flowers.

Terence followed her back into her flat. It didn't take much intelligence to work out the situation.

"I'm sorry you had to get involved in that, but so glad you were here. Thank you," she said simply.

"Here's the kettle I promised you." If she wanted to talk, fine, if not, that was all right too. Everyone was entitled to their privacy.

"Thank you, again."

"Look . . . I . . . I was thinking, if you fancy joining me for a spaghetti dinner, homemade . . . you may not be in the mood to go out . . . you'd be very welcome. As you can see, I don't exactly starve." Terence's eyes twinkled as he patted his rounded stomach. "You might be able to use some company."

Holly hesitated for a moment. "You don't have to feel sorry for me. God, that sounds awful, I didn't mean . . . I mean . . . Derek always has that effect on me."

"I understand. But, if you change your mind . . . "

"If it isn't any trouble, I'd like that very much."

"Seven o'clock suit you?"

"Perfect. Terence . . . do you think that we could lock the street door?"

"It usually *is* locked. Don't worry about it, I think your friend must have put the latch on when she helped you in with your things. I'll go and lock it now."

She heard Terence puffing down the stairs. Maybe the flat wasn't up to much, but she was lucky to have found such a good neighbour.

"Why do you say that?" Terence asked as he emptied the last of the wine into their glasses.

"Because I don't have the imagination that it takes to be a writer, never have had, not even in college," Holly explained. "But I do recognise a good book when I see one. I can take a manuscript, reword it, clarify sentences, my punctuation is pretty good too, but that's it. I could never write a novel, not in a million years."

"Maybe you've just persuaded yourself that you couldn't."

"Thanks for the vote of confidence, but I don't think so."

"Well, it's all foreign to me," Terence admitted. "I never realised how much work goes into producing a book. I just walk into a shop, pick what I fancy, and off I go. From now on, I'll examine the cover, look at the print size and think of someone like you checking every word," he promised with a smile.

"Will you have to read all those manuscripts that you have in your flat? I couldn't help noticing the boxes piled up."

"Heaven knows what my boss has given me," she said ruefully.

"How long will it take you to get through them? I'm a three or four book-a-year-man myself."

"It depends. If a manuscript isn't any good I'll give it about ten pages – skipping as I go – but if it's good, I read every word."

"That must take a lot of time."

"I have plenty of it. Terence, I feel I owe you an explanation." Holly held up her hand as he was about to object. "I know I don't *need* to explain, but I'd *like* to. Derek, the man who was here earlier,

and I broke up a couple of weeks ago because . . .
well, he controlled my whole life . . . "

Terence let her speak without interruption. He
could just about detect the faded yellow bruise
under her cheekbone.

" . . . so you see, in the end I *had* to leave him."

"It must have taken a great deal of courage to do
what you did."

"But it's making *him* realise that it's over, that's
the problem," Holly admitted.

"Surely you can get a court order? Then he'd
have to leave you alone." How a man could raise
his hands to a lovely woman like Holly, or any
woman come to that, was beyond him.

"I'll have to phone my solicitor first thing on
Monday, ask his advice. I can't understand how
Derek knew where to find me. Only a couple of
people have my new address and there's no way
they would have given it to him, of all people."

"Could he have followed you here?"

Holly considered the possibility. "Surely I would
have noticed him?"

"Not necessarily. We're not always aware of what's
happening around us. But I think notifying your
solicitor is a wise move. He'll know what to do. For
what it's worth, my recollection of bullies is that they
crumble if they're bullied in return. Derek backed off
quickly enough when you threatened to send for the
police, didn't he? Anyway, if you ever need me, just
holler. The walls are thin here as you'll probably
discover. By the way, if my telly's too loud, just bang
on the wall with a brush. I'll get the message."

Chapter Twelve

Holly rubbed her eyes and stood up. Her head ached. It's that office, it's airless, she decided. "This is the second headache I've had this week," she grumbled to herself as she went to find some aspirin.

Through the thin walls she could hear the faint sound of laughter, Terence must be watching television. Restlessly, she overturned a box of manuscripts and rooted through its contents. She cast aside a dog-eared, hand-written text that should have been returned with the others. A flicker of annoyance crossed her face, someone must have dumped them all in the box without checking. She searched for the covering letter that would normally be clipped to the title page of a manuscript. But there wasn't a title page, no clue as to the author, just a pencilled note of the date it was received. Ages ago, she noticed with a frown.

"You must have been kicking around for years," Holly said to the thick, silent wad of paper.

She sat back on her heels and glanced at the first page. Honoria was such a fanciful name, and

Wilberforce? That's a bit off-putting. Just one more page then I'll pack it in, she promised herself. I must also pack in this habit of talking to myself.

She sat back on her heels, straightened her legs and leant back against her chair. Finally she moved to the settee and stretched herself out, her long legs dangling over one of the arms. She forgot about the names and ignored the grammatical shortcuts. It was the most moving story she had ever read. She was fascinated by the struggles of the deserted mother left to cope with five young children, ageing parents and a batty aunt. The tribulations of the abandoned family were sensitively balanced by a good deal of humour which prevented the story from becoming morbid. She chuckled at the antics of the children. She could visualise them. See their home, feel their sorrows and their joys.

"Brilliant!" Holly said and forgot she wasn't going to talk aloud to herself any more.

She separated each chapter, straightened its pages, then stapled them together. Why on earth hadn't the author included her name and address, or given the book a title? Holly assumed the writer was a woman. It was told from a female's point of view. Wilberforce! The male character needed a more simple name, Tom. John, perhaps. Honoria was definitely miles off target, she needed a softer name, like Amy. Yes, Amy.

As Holly tidied the room she continued mentally to edit the manuscript. This was one book she would have enjoyed licking into shape. But what was the point? She didn't even know who had written it. She'd mention it to Simone tomorrow but doubted that she would have any idea where it had sprung from either.

"If you take my advice you'll keep out of Simone's way for the moment," Lois warned her.

"What's up? Holly asked.

"She's incognito for the next half-hour."

"Incommunicado," Holly corrected automatically. "Why?"

"Search me," Lois replied but her eyes spoke volumes.

"Come in," Simone called irritably in answer to Holly's tentative knock. "Holly! I was just going to send for you."

"Something wrong?" Holly asked.

"It bloody well is. Look at this." Simone threw an envelope across her desk. "Read it," she commanded.

Holly withdrew the single sheet of paper and read it. It advised Simone that her ex-husband, Mark, had contacted AIDS and that she should make an appointment at her local clinic to be tested as soon as possible.

"That's ghastly, I'm so sorry, Simone." Holly's jaw dropped.

"Don't be," Simone cut across her. "It's that husband of yours, again. More of his sick humour."

Holly's heart stapled itself to her ribs. "What does Derek have to do with *this*?"

"He sent it."

"What!"

"Don't worry," Simone relented. "I thought it was genuine at first – until I spoke to Mark. He just laughed. According to him you can buy these disgusting hoaxes in most joke shops – see – there's no address, no phone number on the letter."

"I'm delighted it's a joke, I mean I'm delighted it's not true. Are you sure it was Derek?" The question was pointless.

"No, I'm not sure, but who else could it be?"

"Maggie?"

"No way. I phoned her, she practically threatened to sue me."

Since Vincent Harper had written to Derek and warned him that they would seek a restraining order if he as much as *thought* of speaking to Holly, he had vanished from the scene. Neither she nor Simone had been bothered by him again.

"Are you going to report this to the police?"

"That was my immediate reaction," Simone admitted. "But I think there maybe a better way of stopping him. Actually, it was something that you said which gave me the idea."

"Remind me." Holly frowned. Simone had calmed down considerably.

"You said that Derek would go bananas if his firm found out how he'd behaved towards you. Well, now they're about to find out just what that vicious little creep has been up to . . . "

"You mean you're going to go to his office?"

"No. I'm going to send him a fax."

"But everyone will be able to read it, he doesn't have his own . . . Oh!"

"Exactly. That's what I'm counting on." Simone smiled triumphantly. "Here, read this."

Holly read the cleverly worded fax. Simone didn't accuse Derek of anything, merely sought his help – as a friend – to find a solution to her problems. Had he noticed anyone lurking around the car-park the other day when he visited the office, someone who might have let the air out of her tyres? Did he think that the same person could have had unwanted pizzas delivered? How should she deal with a hoax letter which said that her husband had AIDS? How should she go about finding the culprit? She would be deeply grateful for his help.

"There's something else you can add to this." Holly replaced the sheet of paper on the desk and told her about the three taxis.

Simone clamped her lips together in a thin line. "Is there anything else I should know? Any specific reason that you kept that from me?" Simone asked sarcastically.

"You were upset enough . . . I didn't want to make things worse . . . " Holly faltered.

Serves me right, she thought. I should have kept quiet.

"Give me Derek's fax number, the sooner he gets this the better. That's all I need for now." Simone dismissed her abruptly.

Chapter Thirteen

Holly reread Vincent Harper's letter. Derek had refused point blank to consider a divorce. Even though this was the reaction she'd expected, she was disappointed. Unless Derek had a sudden change of heart she could resign herself to a long wait for her freedom. But so what, she wasn't going anywhere and no one was banging down her door with proposals of marriage.

Living alone was nowhere near as exciting as Holly had imagined. She'd taken Simone out for dinner as she'd planned to do, but Simone hadn't asked her to visit the flat again – not that she blamed her.

She looked forward to her weekly evening with Terence. They took it in turns to cook. He was wonderfully cheerful and entertaining but he had his serious moments too. She spent every second weekend with Liz and Robert. They wanted her to make it every weekend but she couldn't impose on them like that.

The thought of her sister brought a smile to Holly's lips. It was her turn to phone Liz tomorrow but she longed to talk to her now.

"Holly! I wasn't expecting to hear from you," said Liz.

"I felt like a chat," Holly explained. "Everything OK with you? You sound a bit down?"

"I can't hide much from you, can I?"

"Hide what from me?" Holly asked.

"That the school doesn't need me next term. The other part-time teacher has been taken on full-time. They notified me today."

"Oh Liz, that's a bitch. I'm sorry."

"Me too, but Doreen's been there longer than I have."

"Is there no other school nearby?"

"Not that I know of. I've had my name on the register for ages. I'll keep trying, of course. And as if that wasn't enough for one day, the old rust-bucket started acting up. Luckily a neighbour saw me and stopped to see if he could help. He gave me a lift home. Robert says it can be fixed, but the poor old car hasn't much life left in it. Other than that – everything's peachy. Right, that's my tale of woe, what's news with you?"

"I had a letter from the solicitor today. *Surprise, surprise,* Derek doesn't want a divorce."

"Now it's *my* turn to be sorry."

"We've both had better days. But if he leaves me alone, I'll settle for that – and the wait."

They chatted for almost an hour.

"See you at the usual time on Friday," Liz said finally.

Silence descended on the room again. Holly wished she could afford to buy Liz a new car. She could see it now – a huge blue ribbon tied round a gleaming black car, Liz and Robert's delighted faces as they discovered the gift-tied automobile in the weed-strewn drive outside the cottage. That was the first thing she'd buy if she won the pools. The fact that she never did the pools didn't detract from her fantasy. But dreaming like this wouldn't finish her work for her. Holly reckoned that another hour should see the end of Toni Johnson's book.

She closed her laptop with a satisfied click. The book was a long one and had needed a lot of painstaking editing. She was pleased with the result. There were times when Holly felt that *her* name should be the one on the cover, she should be the one receiving the accolades. She envied authors sometimes, glowing with pride as congratulations were heaped upon them at their launches. It must be a marvellous sensation but one she would never experience.

Her mind drifted lazily to the untitled manuscript in her bedroom drawer. Somehow she'd never got round to mentioning it to Simone. She was so cranky these days that Holly avoided her. I must take another look at it, she thought idly as she tidied away her papers.

She settled into bed, the manuscript on her knee and a bar of chocolate on the bedside table. It was four o'clock before she turned her light out. She *must* discuss this manuscript with Simone tomorrow.

"Do you have a minute?" Holly stuck her head round Simone's office door.

Simone waved her in with her free hand and signalled to the chair facing her desk. She covered the receiver. "Won't be a sec," she mouthed.

Holly looked round the familiar room. Like most of the Pagett offices it was bright but not overly spacious. Simone disliked clutter and, apart from the necessities – a desk, her swivel chair and two semi-comfortable upright seats – the room bore Simone's minimalist stamp. There was always a fresh flower in the narrow tall-stemmed vase on her desk. That too took up very little space.

"Sorry about that," Simone apologised as she ended her call.

"That's OK. Toni Johnson's manuscript is finished."

"Well done! You really walloped through that."

"Mmm, not really, I've been at it for a while. But it's a good book. She seems to have changed her style this time; shorter sentences, not so much narrative. Although it needed a fair bit of work, it wasn't as difficult as usual."

"When are we launching it?" Simone asked as she reached for her schedule.

"March – for the Easter market. We don't have a lot of time to mess about."

"Right. By the way, I found a hand-written manuscript in one of the boxes that you gave me. It didn't have a pink slip, no author's name or address, no . . . It's a . . . "

"Don't tell me, just dump it. I don't care if it's another *War and Peace*, dump it. We're publishers not clairvoyants," Simone said as her phone rang again.

Holly picked up the diskette and Toni Johnson's manuscript and made her way to Emma's office.

She hated the thought of destroying that marvellous story she'd read again last night. What a waste – and all because of one missing page. Not even a page, just a few lines; a name and an address.

Chapter Fourteen

"Hang on to your seat belt, Robert has been invited to give a lecture in America and I've been invited too." Liz's voice bubbled with excitement.

"That's wonderful! I'm thrilled for you both," Holly said with genuine delight.

"When do you go?"

"August. We leave on the Friday before the bank holiday. The only fly in the ointment is that you'll be stuck on your own in London."

"Liz, for heaven's sake. Don't give it another thought. What a super opportunity for Robert and for you. Tell him I'm proud of him."

Holly hid her disappointment well. She had planned to take her annual holiday in August and had been sure that Liz and Robert wouldn't mind if she spent most of it with them.

"We will only be away for a week," Liz fretted.

"Perfect. I was planning to take my holidays in September."

The August sun burned with a vengeance. The flat was more claustrophobic than ever. From her window Holly could see the pavement shimmering in the relentless heat. She longed for the fresh perfume of Liz's garden, the dappled shade of the trees, the cottage with its cool stone floors. She returned to her laptop and scrolled down a page. She centred it, then in large, bold print she typed

Tomorrow's Joy
by
Emily Howard

Impatiently she waited for the printer to spew out the sparsely worded page. With delicate fingers she added it to the neatly stacked block of typed sheets. She took a step backwards then stood stock still. She stared at the bundle of pages as though she expected them to vanish into thin air. The book was complete. As near perfect as any she had edited. But this time it was her book, her baby, her adopted baby. Abandoned, forgotten, by its natural author.

Holly had read often enough about *running the gamut of emotions* and here she was in a tail-spin, experiencing most of them: pride, joy, guilt, fear, guilt, terror, depression, elation but above all, guilt. The full horror of what she was about to do gripped her, she found it difficult to breathe. She could never even tell Liz the truth about the book, never share her secret with anyone.

For weeks she'd practised how she was going to introduce the book and its author to the Pagett board. An agoraphobic author who not only couldn't leave her home but was unwilling to talk to people. A publicity tour was out of the question, even telephone interviews were taboo. She herself could only communicate by letter.

If Pagett wouldn't publish the book then she'd contact an agent. Goodness knows, she knew enough of them.

"You know the rules, Holly. If an author doesn't agree to publicity, we don't publish the book," Arthur Lord reminded her mildly.

"I understand that, but it's an *excellent* story." Holly lowered her head to hide the blush that spread to her cheeks. "When you read the manuscript it's easy to see how Emily Howard's agoraphobia arose – and why. That could generate its own publicity. She accepts that, doesn't care what anyone writes about her as long as she doesn't have to talk to them. I think that type of publicity could be very interesting." The silence that followed seemed endless.

"I've never heard you so fired up. What's the book about?" Simone asked.

"Yes, tell us about it," Arthur Lord urged with an indulgent smile. He had never seen Holly so animated.

Holly related her carefully adapted version of the hand-written manuscript.

Simone watched the glow of excitement light up Holly's face as she spoke. She had faith in Holly's judgement and, if her assistant editor was so enthusiastic, then she was willing to accept her assessment.

"I think we should go for it, make an exception in this case," Arthur Lord said.

Holly could have kissed him on the spot.

"All agreed?" Arthur Lord was anxious to get on with the meeting. There was a general buzz of approval.

"Another bonanza for Kleenex?" Roland Green, Pagett's literary editor, sneered as he examined his cuticles. Women and their true-to-life fiction.

"You should be so lucky," Simone snapped.

Arthur Lord hoped that Simone and Roland weren't going to argue. They were at loggerheads far too often for his liking. "What's next on the agenda?" he asked.

They got on with the meeting. Holly heard little of what followed, her head was spinning with delight. After a decent interval she would produce the finished manuscript, make it appear that she'd just finished the editing. This would give her an opportunity to check her writing, make any further changes. Surely she must have missed *something*? When that was done she'd hand it over to Jane. After it was type-set and proof-read, she'd give it one final check before it was sent to the printers. Then it would be out of her hands.

She could liaise with the art department about the cover, keep an eye on the review copies despatched to the journalists and booksellers. The publicity department was always eager for any input . . .

"Holly! *Holly!*"

Holly jumped as Simone's voice registered. Everyone at the table was laughing. Embarrassed, she joined in. "Sorry," she apologised.

"What dastardly deed are you planning in that little mind of yours," Roland drawled.

"You'd be surprised, Roland. You'd be surprised." Holly's cheeks flared a glorious sun-set red.

"I'll strangle that man one day," Simone said as she and Holly sat eating their sandwiches in Pagett's kitchen.

"Don't take any notice of him."

"He drives me nuts, he's so patronising. Anyway congratulations on your victory, you were very impressive. You couldn't have fought harder if you'd written the book yourself."

Book Two

April a year later

Detective Inspector Michael Moore asked not to be disturbed. He closed the blinds which separated the squad room from his office and made sure that there were no cracks of light. Calmly, he emptied his pockets, then glanced up at his suspect board. He had his own system of working even if his method was a constant source of amusement to his fellow detectives. But in all his years as a detective only one of his murder victims remained unavenged and, to this day, he was never a hundred per cent convinced that her death was not suicide.

He placed the surveillance video into his machine and settled down to watch it, but not before he took the first of his guilty stash and began to unwrap it. If only he hadn't gone public with his diet, there would be no need for all this secrecy. He was sure his wife had the other detectives on chocolate-watch. They had taken to popping into his office unannounced lately and for no good reason.

He fast-forwarded the tape and found what he was looking for, made a note on his pad, then re-wound the tape. The second tape was as he expected. He scratched his head in frustration. He had already eliminated three of the four names on his board, and now the tapes had provided a perfect alibi for the fourth. One of them was lying, yet all four of

*them had cast-iron alibis. He would have to question
each of them again, see if they changed their stories,
tripped themselves up.*

*He broke off a finger of KitKat and chewed it
contemplatively.*

Chapter Fifteen

"I can't believe my ears," Simone exploded. "We've spent the last hour and a half trying to find a way to recoup some of our losses and you have the neck to suggest that we give Patrick Worrall a whopping great advance for his next book."

"*Clouds* is a marvellous book. A magnificent book . . . " Roland Green thundered, his face purple with indignation.

"I'm not disputing that," Simone conceded. "But it doesn't change the fact that this *magnificent* coffee-table book has lost us a packet. For God's sake, Roland, don't the sales figures mean anything to you? *Clouds* sold seventy-eight copies. And now, a month after publication, it's remaindered from one end of the country to the other, forty-nine pounds ninety-nine, on offer at a fiver. Your answer to this is that we give him an enormous advance and fund him and an assistant to swan around Japan with his camera for three months. Why don't we just save time and heartache, and file for bankruptcy now?"

"Simone, Roland, *please*! This bickering won't get us anywhere." Arthur Lord rapped the table sharply with his pen. Even he was astonished at his friend Roland's stupidity. They had discussed the folly of publishing any more of those aesthetically pleasing but financially crippling books several times. He fully understood and shared Roland's enthusiasm for Patrick Worrall's brilliant work, took pride in the critics' acclaim. Patrick was undoubtedly their most prestigious author, a world class photographer but, genius though he was, Pagett could not afford Patrick Worrall. Their bank couldn't afford him either.

Only the click of the digital clock broke the charged silence of the room. Arthur was aware that they were waiting for him to censure Roland, and he would do so, but in his own time, in his own way. He would not reprimand him in front of the others. After all, he and Roland went back a long way. Twenty years of successful publishing and friendship. Roland was as much a part of Pagett Publications as he was himself. No, it wouldn't be right. Simone's outburst surprised him; she wasn't usually so confrontational, neither had she chosen the most tactful way of expressing herself. Reluctantly, he accepted that everything she had said was true. Patrick Worrall – another commercial flop – suicide. This time he would *have* to put his foot down, Roland must be stopped. But later, privately.

"If there's nothing else, I've got a plane to catch." Simone closed her folder with a slap. Arthur Lord had ducked the issue again.

"Going to Dublin to edit the king of blood and gore, are we?" Roland sneered.

"I'm going to edit John Barrett's book, yes, also to discuss the third reprint of his last one." Simone glared at Roland. "His books are extremely profitable. But then you've probably forgotten what that's like," she added spitefully.

Arthur Lord tapped the table again. "Meeting adjourned," he announced sharply. He couldn't face another altercation between these two.

With gloomy faces they gathered up their reports and financial statements and stuffed them into their folders. They threw the empty polystyrene coffee cups into the waste bin and straggled out of the boardroom in depressed silence.

"Have a good trip, Simone, give my regards to John," Arthur said wearily.

"I will," she promised.

Simone glanced up at the clock then rushed along the corridor to catch up with Tim Brown, their financial controller. "Bloody awful meeting," she said.

"The worst," he agreed.

"Are things really as black as they seem? I'm not too bright where balance sheets are concerned, not good with numbers."

"You mean am I being my usual, overcautious, pessimistic self?" he asked.

Simone flushed slightly, then smiled. "Something like that," she admitted.

"OK. I'll explain in words then. Just two words, plus and minus. Plus means profit, minus means loss. The buzz word for today is minus. *Minus, minus, minus.*"

"That bad?"

"That bad."

"What's going to happen?" she asked but didn't really expect an easy solution.

Tim paused at his office door and shrugged his shoulders. "I wish I knew. But one thing I *am* certain of, we're not going to find our answer by sending Worrall to Japan!"

"*That's* for sure," Simone agreed.

Chapter Sixteen

"It's difficult to take your worries on holiday," her mother used to say.

Let's hope you're right, Mum, Simone reflected as she stored her travel-grip in the plane's overhead locker. The aisle seat was occupied by a large woman who had already fastened her seat belt. Simone squeezed past her and, after some awkward manoeuvring, settled into her seat. She opened John Barrett's manuscript, she wanted to check the final chapter.

"Would you like something to drink?" the stewardess asked as she reached their seats.

Simone hesitated, they would be landing in twenty minutes. "A mineral water, please." No doubt John Barrett would pull several corks before the day was over. John Barrett, one of her favourite authors. Was it really only four years since he had marched into her office and slapped his manuscript, *Murder and Co Ltd*, on her desk?

"You'll *love* it," he insisted.

"Do you have an appointment?" Simone was startled by his sudden appearance.

"Er . . . no. There was no one at the reception desk . . . " His warm smile belied the apology in his voice.

Before she had a chance to tell him. *We don't accept unsolicited manuscripts,* he was helping her on with her coat and they were on their way to lunch at the Savoy.

"I don't usually have lunch with strangers," Simone protested as the waiter flicked open a gleaming white napkin and spread it across her knees. If her authors had presented her with a situation like this in their books, she would have put her red pen through it.

"If you think that all this will sway me, it won't." Simone made a broad sweep of the room with her hand. "Your manuscript goes on the pile with all the others and we're stacked to the ceiling."

"I'm sure you are. But you'll read mine tonight, won't you?" John Barrett placed his fingers and palms together in supplication. "Let's order, then you can tell me all about yourself."

And much to her surprise, she did.

As Simone sipped the sparkling mineral water she smiled at the memory of that first meeting. John Barrett could charm the birds from the trees or, more correctly, an editor from her desk. It was almost four o'clock before they'd left the elegant restaurant overlooking the river. She never discussed her private life with her authors, or anyone else come to that, but somehow in those few short hours, with a little sympathetic coaxing from John, she had broken her own rule.

When she left her office later that evening, Simone found herself slipping his manuscript into her work-worn leather bag. She felt quite light-hearted as she changed from her business suit into a comfortable robe, John Barrett had brightened her day. He was a nice man, if a bit zany. She heated some soup, grabbed a packet of cream crackers, then lay in her usual position deep in the comfortable, soft-cushioned couch. She opened John's large brown envelope and frowned. The manuscript was everything that she would normally reject; hand-written on both sides of the paper with barely a space between the lines, impossibly narrow margins. In her experience hand-written manuscripts invariably spelt trouble, texts which started off neatly almost always degenerated into an illegible scrawl. Narrow margins were an editor's nightmare and, using both sides of the paper utterly taboo.

Simone quickly fanned the pages but John Barrett's even, neat writing didn't falter. Perhaps she'd just have a quick look at the first chapter before she began editing the text she'd been working on the previous night.

She lowered the last page and rubbed her eyes. John Barrett was right, she loved it.

"I knew you wouldn't let me down," John said excitedly when he heard her voice on the phone.

"I'm sorry, John, but I must return your manuscript." Simone managed to keep her tone sombre.

"I see. Well it's very kind of you to let me know so quickly, Simone. Perhaps I had inflated ideas . . . got carried away. Anyway, I enjoyed our lunch, enjoyed meeting you."

Even in his disappointment John Barrett was charming. It was time to stop winding him up.

"Don't you want to know why I'm returning it?" she asked.

"Because I thought it was good and you didn't?" he suggested.

"Not exactly. It shouldn't be hand-written . . . "

John listened without interruption until she finished.

"I really did make a mess of things . . . "

"One other thing, John," Simone cut across him. "I *loved* it! I think it has the makings of a terrific book." She sat back and enjoyed the stunned silence at the other end of the line.

Within half-an-hour of their phone call, John swept into her office, his eyes shining like beacons. "I'll have the manuscript typed and back to you in a couple of days," he promised. "We have to celebrate tonight. Will you have dinner with me?"

"I'm sorry, I have to work."

"I'm sorry too. I hate eating alone, especially today," he said wistfully.

Simone was wary of invitations like that.

"In that case I'll have to wait until I get home tomorrow to break open the bubbly. My wife was so excited when I rang her, she's planning a special dinner for tomorrow. She's been my inspiration, deserves as much credit as I do, more perhaps. But

I mustn't hold you up. If you change your mind I'd be absolutely delighted to see you."

John's visit left her feeling depressed. Eve and John Barrett appeared to be a devoted couple. She and Mark rarely had a meal together nowadays, let alone a special dinner. His job in communications meant that he had to spend a considerable amount of travelling. When he was at home, her nights were taken up with book launches, entertaining out-of-town authors, and her editing. They never seemed to have time to spend together. Quietly, imperceptibly, their marriage was falling apart and they were both too busy, too involved, to do anything about it. Why not make *him* a special dinner, make a special effort, pay Mark some attention, make a fuss of him?

She dialled his office number. "Hello, Maria," she said pleasantly. "Is Mark back from Brussels yet?"

"May I ask who's calling, please?"

"His wife, *Simone*, Maria." Cheeky little cow. Maria knew exactly who she was.

"I'm sorry, *Simone*, I'm afraid Mark hasn't contacted me yet. Would you like me to ask him to get in touch when I hear from him?"

"Do that," Simone said sharply. She could imagine Maria's smug grin as the line went dead.

The hours dragged by but Mark didn't phone. Had Maria given him her message? She could try again but didn't fancy another tangle with Maria. She didn't know why Maria disliked her so much, they'd never even met.

It was almost five o'clock, too late now anyhow.

She might as well pack up for the day and go home. She tidied her desk and closed her diary, half-rose from her chair, then changed her mind.

John Barrett answered on the second ring. "Simone! Are you going to take pity on an old, lonely man in a strange town after all?" he teased.

"What time would you like to meet and where?" she asked stiffly.

He suggested a restaurant.

They arranged to meet at eight o'clock. That evening cemented the beginning of her friendship with John Barrett and, eventually, with his wife, Eve.

Simone looked eagerly through the small window as the plane taxied to a halt. She couldn't imagine anything more appealing than spending the weekend with Eve and John.

She could well understand why Holly looked forward so much to those visits with her sister and brother-in-law – and they didn't live by the sea.

Chapter Seventeen

John Barrett released Simone from his bear-hug and
eyed her critically.

"You look washed out," he announced.

"I love you too," she laughed.

He took her travel grip from her and steered her
through the airport to his car.

"How's Eve?" she asked as they drove through
the airport grounds.

"She's terrific, dying to see you."

"I'm looking forward to seeing her, and longing
for some of that wonderful Howth sea air."

Eve was waiting at the door of the bungalow.
She enveloped Simone in her strong arms and they
hugged affectionately. If Eve thought she didn't look
her best she was too polite to say so.

"I'm sure you want to go and change, you know
where your room is," she said.

Simone zipped up her jeans and pulled a light
cotton sweater over her head. From her bedroom
window she could see the well planted garden and
the gently rolling waves. She loved the peace of this
Irish seaside town. She picked up the books she

had brought for Eve and John and went to join them.

"Fresh prawns. Fantastic!" Simone's eyes lit up.

"I thought we'd eat right away, then you and John can take a leisurely walk," Eve said as she passed Simone a bowl of homemade garlic mayonnaise.

"We really should get down to work!" Simone replied unconvincingly.

"And we will. Tomorrow. Today is for relaxing," John insisted.

They strolled along the sea front and made their way towards the West Pier. They paused briefly to watch a television crew setting up a shoot.

"Maybe someday they'll film one of my books," John said jokingly.

"Maybe," Simone answered, vaguely. She didn't want to raise John's hopes at this stage but their foreign rights agent was fairly confident that she was close to completing a contract with an American publisher. If his books sold as well in the States as they had in Britain and Ireland, who knew where it might lead?

"I'll only be a moment," John said as they reached the pier. "I must collect Eve's order from the fish shop."

Simone strolled along to the edge of the jetty while John went into the fishmongers. She watched the fishing boats tugging at their moorings. Foamy waves slapped noisily against the concrete walls. They matched her mood exactly; grey, turbulent and angry.

She hardly noticed John when he rejoined her. She was totally lost in thought, her forehead creased in a deep frown.

"Eve will be delighted with the beautiful black sole," he said, swinging the parcel in his hand.

"Mmm," she answered absently.

"Do you want to start walking back to the bungalow?"

"Hmm?"

"Would you like to walk a bit further or make tracks for home?" he asked.

"I don't mind. You decide."

"We'll head for home and on the way you can tell me what's bugging you."

Simone tilted her head and looked at his wind-tanned face. "What makes you think there's something bugging me?" she asked.

"The fact that I'm talking to myself and people are staring at me," he replied with a sheepish grin.

His good humour brought a smile to her lips. "Intuitive as always," she said. "We had a ghastly meeting this morning and I ended up in a slanging match with Roland Green. The man is a financial moron."

John waited for her to continue. "Things have a habit of solving themselves, perhaps by the time you get back . . ." he suggested.

"No way. Not this time. If he's allowed to continue the way he has been doing, you'll be looking for another publisher, my friend."

"Want to talk about it?" he asked.

Simone hesitated. Discussing Pagett's problems

was disloyal, but as long as she had known him, John had never betrayed her confidence.

"Remember the book of photographs that I told you about last time we met, Patrick Worrall's *Clouds*?"

John nodded his head.

"It cost Pagett the earth to produce and we lost a packet on it. Now Roland Green wants to commission another one, about life in Japan. The cost of sending Patrick Worrall and an assistant to Japan for a few months, plus the cost of producing the book, would be astronomical. Pagett can't afford another disaster like that. It would ruin us. But these cold hard facts don't seem to have filtered through Roland's thick head."

John's business mind ticked over. "Surely one disaster, as you call it, couldn't ruin Pagett? They'd have to be in a fairly sticky financial situation for that to happen."

"I didn't tell you the full story. They are in trouble. *Clouds* was the third book of Roland's to bomb this year. He wafts around in a haze of impossibility, without the slightest thought as to how damaging his failures are. In my opinion, Arthur Lord is even more stupid because he allows him to produce them."

"Strange, Lord always struck me as an astute man, very much on the ball."

"Off the wall, you mean," Simone said bitterly. "He protects Roland, they've been friends for years. Their families are friendly. But at the end of the day, Roland is a loose cannon, a danger to Pagett."

"Why are his books so unsuccessful?"

"Because he celebrity-hunts. Also he's a born snob, anyone with a double-barrelled name is a shoo-in. If they can't write their own book, he'll provide them with a ghost-writer."

"Lots of people use them, don't they?"

"Yes, of course. But how does a book about the *Political Wranglings of the Peloponnesian Wars* grab you?"

"Not a lot," John admitted.

"What about *Touring Albania on a Tandem,* or *Cattle Grid Technology* with full colour-plate illustrations? And aren't you just itching to learn all about Melanie Beckworth's career move from *Film Star to Falling Star* – all you need to know about astronomy?"

John's lips twitched. "That's quite a selection!"

"And that doesn't include his literary fiction. I don't even want to get into that. If I produced that load of *scrape-bys,* I'd be out on the street, red editing-pen and all." Simone's face was pink with fury. She refrained from repeating Roland's opinion of John's thrillers. "He wouldn't know a best-seller list if he fell over it, not these days."

John matched her quickened pace. Simone needed to simmer down. He had met Roland Green, briefly. He struck John as an effete man, a man with no time for anyone outside his own orbit. Few people patronised John and although Roland had tried, his attempt had failed.

"Didn't Arthur have *anything* to say about all this?"

"Basically, no. He tapped his pen on the table, glared at me, then adjourned the meeting."

"Who else was involved?"

"Kathy, the children's editor, Tim Brown, Arthur, Roland and myself."

"Didn't any of the others have anything to say?"

"Not really. Kathy didn't get involved. Tim read his financial report in a gloomy voice. Roland puffed up with temper and Arthur, as I said, chickened out. Holly wasn't there unfortunately, she took today off – she's going to Paris on Monday – she might have supported me."

"If Roland has such poor judgement how come he's lasted so long in publishing? Wasn't he originally Pagett's sole editor?"

"Yes, he was. And from what I've heard, a damn good one too. But over the years he's become more and more fanciful, egotistical. In our business, tongues wag, you hear a lot of gossip and that's what I've heard on the grapevine about Roland. At this moment I'd like to grab him by his affected bow tie and swing him out to sea."

"He really has got to you, hasn't he?"

"Do you blame me? My job could be on the line thanks to him. I work bloody hard. I've had a good success rate and I don't want to see it go down the drain because of that creep. My job, as you know, cost me my marriage."

They walked up the hill towards the bungalow, Simone had given him plenty to think about. What she needed now was a good stiff drink, he was upset to see her so agitated. He had never understood why she'd allowed her work to override her marriage. True, she worked long hours, was totally dedicated, but so were lots of other people and their marriages survived. But that was Simone's affair.

As they reached the gate of the bungalow, the door opened and a blue-jeaned figure hurtled down the crazy-paving drive into John's arms.

"Lucy! You'll knock me over," John protested as he steadied himself.

Lucy disentangled herself from her father and kissed Simone on the cheek.

"Hello, venerable editor! Mum said you were here."

Simone smiled fondly at the boisterous girl. "This is a bonus, I didn't expect to see you this trip."

"If the hot water hadn't packed up, you wouldn't have." Lucy shared a flat with two other students and adored living in filth and squalor. "I don't mind mess but I do mind washing in freezing cold water."

"Well, for whatever reason, I'm pleased to see you," John told her.

"And I'm pleased to see you, aged-father."

"Not so much of the aged, if you don't mind," he said as he ruffled his daughter's curly head. "Eve, we're back," he called.

"I'll get rid of this revolting parcel," Lucy offered, crinkling her nose. "I *hate* fish. I'm sure Mum has some decent food in the freezer."

Simone threw her jacket on the back of a chair and warmed her hands at the fire. "This is glorious. A real fire," she said appreciatively.

"That's my job, looking after the fire. I must admit I love a coal fire too, especially after a brisk walk. Now what are you going to have to drink?"

Eve refused help in the kitchen. Lucy and Simone sat by the fire while John went to his study to answer some mail.

"How's college?" Simone asked.

"Hard slog, but I enjoy it."

"Are you keeping your diary up to date?"

"Yeah, more or less. I leave it sometimes, get bored. But then I think, what the hell, and catch up again."

Lucy's throw-away attitude didn't fool Simone for a second. She knew that Lucy desperately wanted to get into journalism and eventually become a novelist. John had shown her some of Lucy's short stories and they were very good for someone so young; bubbly, upbeat and infinitely readable. It was Simone who had persuaded Lucy to keep a diary.

"Time plays tricks on the mind. Even with the best memory in the world, you can forget things," she warned.

Lucy hadn't been enchanted by Simone's idea. "I'll certainly take your suggestion on board," she'd promised. It was then that Lucy had christened her *venerable editor*.

Simone stared into the dancing flames. The Barretts were a talented family. Eve was modest, almost coy, where her art was concerned. She utterly refused to exhibit her pictures, claiming, "I'm an amateur dabbler and that's how I intend to remain."

Simone had pleaded with her to show her paintings to a gallery, but she stubbornly clung to her resolve that her art was a hobby, nothing more.

"Why are you smiling?" Lucy demanded.

"I was thinking about your Dad's last book, *Blood Sails*."

Lucy giggled. "I thought Mum would go ballistic when she saw the cover."

"I'll never forget the look on her face," Simone admitted. "I was scared she'd sue us."

A painting of Eve's was the inspiration for John's second book. Everyone except Eve agreed that her picture would make the perfect cover for his book. But Eve had laughed, declared it nonsense, out of the question. John knew she wouldn't change her mind so when the time came to make a decision abut the cover, he sneaked the canvas out of her studio and took it to London, to Simone.

At the launch they'd watched Eve's reaction with bated breath. Surprise, annoyance, doubt and finally, delight.

During dinner Lucy entertained them with stories about her flatmates and their tenement-like existence. Exaggerated or not, her tales were hilarious.

"Write all this down," Simone begged when the girl finally ran out of steam.

"Pass me your glass, Simone." John was pleased to see her laugh.

"Not another drop, thank you. I can hardly keep my eyes open as it is. The meal was delicious, Eve."

"Lucy and I will make coffee," John announced.

"Slave driver," Lucy objected but bounced from her chair. She paused to gather a stack of plates and glasses. Simone held her breath and waited for the crash, but Lucy and her precariously balanced burden made it safely to the kitchen.

Simone curled up in the deep armchair and her eyelids began to droop. This was wonderful, nothing existed outside this cosy, mellow room.

The Barretts drank their coffee, talked in soft voices, cleared the table and left Simone to sleep.

Chapter Eighteen

"But I *like* that bit," John objected as they came to the heavily underlined passage of text.

"I do too," Simone said quickly. "But it detracts from the tension. You've worked hard to build it up, you mustn't diffuse it."

"I suppose you're right."

They rarely argued about changes that needed to be made but, if they really disagreed, Simone would wield her strongest weapon. "It's your book, and if you really feel so strongly about it, that's fine. But if you want my advice . . . "

Inevitably John came round to Simone's way of thinking.

"Now, this bit here, *he stood in the dark shadow* . . . " Simone frowned.

"*Under a brightly lit lamppost!*" John laughed. "What an idiot I am, how did I miss that?"

"You probably moved him or changed something," Simone suggested.

They were almost halfway through the manuscript when Lucy tapped lightly on the door. "Am I disturbing you?" she whispered.

"No," Simone whispered back.

"I've come to say goodbye before I go back to my squat."

"Lovely to see you, Lucy." Simone was happy to take a break.

"You too. Where's Mum?" she asked.

"In the garden. See you, sweetheart." John gave his daughter a peck on the forehead and slipped something into the pocket of her anorak.

"Thanks, Dad," Lucy said without looking to see what it was. She could always depend on him to top up her allowance.

She bounded away to find her mother. Lucy always moved at speed, she reminded Simone of a greyhound springing from its trap.

"I think we've earned ourselves a cup of coffee," John said as the door settled back into its frame. "Besides, I want to talk to you about something."

They moved from the desk to the window seat in John's study, very much a man's room. There were papers everywhere, stacked in neat confusion. He had clung to his battered old leather office chair and his huge desk which was in a permanent state of clutter. A mass of photographs, his word processor, a printer, innumerable pens, paper clips and pencils added to the jumble. Bookcases lined three walls and, apart from one visitor's chair and a small table which held cups and saucers and a coffee flask, the room was free for pacing. Which John liked to do when he wrote. From the padded window seat with its biro marks and coffee stains, they could see the sea and the garden. Eve had long abandoned any hope of establishing order in the room, so they had come to an arrangement. He didn't make any comment about her paint-strewn studio, and she didn't reorganise his study.

"This may be premature, Simone, but Eve and I discussed your problem last night. There's no doubt in my mind that, if you *are* forced to leave Pagett Publications, I'd follow you wherever you go – if you're agreeable. But there's something else. How would you feel about starting afresh, going it alone?"

"You mean, start my own publishing house? Oh, John! I don't mean to be rude, but you haven't got a *clue* what that would take." Simone smiled sympathetically at his naïveté.

"No I don't, but I'm sure I could hazard a rough guess." There was an edge to his voice that she hadn't heard before. "I'm not exactly a novice when it comes to business matters, Simone."

Simone felt the colour rise to her cheeks. She hadn't intended to patronise him, but really, the cost of establishing and running a publishers could be astronomical.

"I'm sure you're not, forgive me. Although I make a fair living, there's no way in the world I could afford to even think along those lines."

"I understand that, but I could. Even though I've retired from active work, I still have an interest in the business world, am always on the lookout for a good investment. I don't think the financial end of it should be a problem. I would hold the controlling interest. Sean could combine the accounting side of

127

it with Barrett Engineering. You would be responsible for the day-to-day administration – plus your editing, of course."

Simone lowered her eyes. She knew that John had taken early retirement – accepted a generous offer for his Irish company. Now he was doing what he loved best; writing, sailing his small boat and spending time with Eve. Simone knew nothing of his financial situation but she was aware that he still had a lively interest in Barrett Engineering UK which his son managed. It was that and his editing sessions which brought him to London.

"I'm flabbergasted," she admitted. "I suppose I've become ostrich-like, don't want to even consider the possibility that I could soon be back in the market place, back to square one."

"I doubt that, Simone. My guess is that you're well established in the book world, have earned yourself a fine reputation. If I'm any judge, you'd be snapped up in no time. But to get back to my point, it's an option you might like to consider. Obviously there's no need for any immediate decision. After all, things may work out at Pagett. It might be just a temporary glitch, a situation that could be reversed with some prudent management."

Simone twirled a button on her blouse. John's words had jolted her from her safe world. She adored her work and the thought of starting all over again made her stomach turn cartwheels. But it was comforting to know that there was an alternative. Life without Roland Green.

"I really appreciate your confidence in me and

perhaps you're right, the situation might resolve itself." But how? she asked herself.

They drank the rest of their coffee in silence. John didn't bring the subject up again until he said goodbye at the airport.

"Don't forget my offer," he said as he kissed her cheek.

Chapter Nineteen

Simone tutted with irritation as she manoeuvred her way in and out of the London traffic. She must keep her cool, otherwise she would destroy the benefit of those few days – more therapeutic than a health farm – that she'd spent with the Barretts. She smiled. If they could bottle that brand of warmth and well-being, they'd make a fortune.

The smile stayed on her lips as she pushed open the glass door and dashed up the marble steps which led to Pagett's first-floor offices.

"Hi, Lois," she called cheerfully as she swished past the reception desk.

"Hi, Simone. Simone, Arthur wants to see you at nine-thirty if you're free. Good luck."

Simone stopped in her tracks. Lois was in one of her I-know-something-that-you-don't moods.

"Why do I need luck?" Simone asked.

"Big row on Friday after you left." Lois looked cautiously towards Arthur Lord's closed door then lowered her voice. "Roland and Arthur. Locked in mortal . . . er . . . "

"Combat? And?" Simone itched to hear the

outcome but Lois always enjoyed aiming for maximum impact.

"There was a lot of shouting and yelling."

"About what?"

"About Pagett."

Simone raged inwardly. She didn't think they'd been arguing about the price of knickers in Marks and Spencers. "What about Pagett?" Outwardly patient, she played Lois's game.

"Money. Roland's books."

"And then what happened?"

"The phone rang."

"So you don't know how it ended up?"

"Oh, yes, I do. The call only took a minute."

It would only take a minute to strangle Lois. "Give me the bottom line," Simone urged.

"Bottom line?"

"The end of the story."

"Oh, right. Well, Arthur's door opened with a crash – I think it hit the table behind it, then Roland came out."

"Did he look pleased?" Simone's nails bit into the palm of her hand.

Lois shook her well-coiffed head.

"Happy?" Simone suggested.

"No."

Simone's patience gave out. "For God's sake, Lois, I've got work to do, tell me!"

"He looked furious. Purple."

"Did he say anything?"

"Something about hell freezing over." Funny, Simone's face was beginning to take on the same colour that Roland's had. "That's really all I know, except . . . "

"Except what?"

Simone was not in good form, Lois thought. "Except he had an appointment yesterday with one of his authors and he phoned just an hour beforehand and told me to cancel it."

"And that's it?"

"That's it. We haven't heard from him since."

Simone hung her trench coat on its hanger and digested Lois's news. Had Roland Green left Pagett? Did wishing make things come true, or was she just awake and dreaming?

"Come in," Arthur Lord called in answer to her knock.

"You wanted to see me?"

"How was your weekend, John and his wife well?"

"Fine, they send their regards."

"Sit down, Simone," he suggested.

Arthur made no move towards the more informal couches which they often used for their discussions. She perched on the edge of a chair and faced him across his desk.

"I didn't appreciate your outburst on Friday," he began.

"I didn't mean to be offensive, but it needed to be said, Arthur."

"It caused considerable upset."

"To whom, to Roland?"

"To everybody."

"You mean Roland."

"And to me."

"I didn't mean to upset *you*. It would have been much easier if you'd tackled him. But you didn't, so . . . "

"Is that an implied criticism?" Arthur bridled.

"Just a simple statement of fact," Simone retorted. "Is that all you wanted to say? I've got a stack of work to do."

"I haven't finished. Roland is furious. He is threatening to leave Pagett and . . . perhaps join Harbour Books."

"Now that *is* good news," she interrupted.

"Let me finish. He says he can no longer work in this atmosphere. In his words, Simone, 'It's me or her.' That's the problem I'm faced with."

"Then you have no choice, do you?"

"What's that supposed to mean?"

"He is the cause of your problems, he's the one-man-bankrupt-them expert. Your worries would be over, Arthur, let him go and scuttle Harbour Books."

"Just like that? Twenty years down the drain on your say-so?"

Simone felt butterflies begin to stir in her stomach. Why was Arthur still defending Roland? No matter how friendly they were, surely he couldn't be that much of a fool.

"So in effect what you're saying is, I should be the one to go." There, she'd said it.

"I didn't say that. Stop putting words in my mouth."

"Then what *are* you saying, Arthur? Stop

pussyfooting about. If it's not him, and that doesn't look likely, then it must be me."

"What I'm saying is, I'd like you to apologise to him. Show him some understanding, some faith in his ability, his talent . . . "

"Like hell I will! How dare he issue an ultimatum like that?"

"It's not like that. It's embarrassing for him to be harangued in public by someone fifteen years his junior, he is the managing editor."

Fifteen years and the rest, Simone thought bitchily. "He wasn't *harangued* in public, it was a private board meeting and I don't see where age comes into it." The butterflies changed mood to *ring-a-ring-a-rosies*. "If his own inadequacies embarrass him, tough."

"You never used to be so hard, Simone."

"I never used to be treated so unfairly. We both know that my books, which he trashes at every available opportunity, are keeping Pagett alive. Three best-sellers in five months, that's not a bad record. Even you would have to agree with that." There was no mistaking the bitterness in her tone.

"Please, Simone, try and see it from my point of view. I'm well aware of your unerring good judgement and all your hard work. And I agree that Roland has made a few . . . shall we say, less fortunate choices. I've had a long talk with him . . . "

"So I've heard."

"If you'd just apologise we could all get back to being a team."

"Arthur, I'd like to continue working at Pagett, I

really would, but if it means that I must apologise to Roland, then I offer my resignation now." Simone walked towards the door, then turned. "Perhaps you'd like a day or so to think about it, decide what you want to do." *Atishoo, atishoo, we all fall down.* The fluttering creatures ceased their dance. They lay in the pit of her stomach like a lead weight.

Simone slammed her office door with a resounding crash. She stood in the centre of the room, not knowing what to do next. Never had she been so incensed, a piston hammering where her heart ought to be. She could see the shadow of her shaking body in the sunlight on the carpet. Her resignation had tripped from her tongue with frightening speed, the last thing in the world that she wanted. But apologise to Roland Green? *Never.*

* * *

Arthur Lord sat motionless at his desk and waited for the pain to subside.

How was he to find the solution which would end this war between his editors? It had blown up into a full-scale war. They were both pig-headed, stubborn and clung to their arguments.

Arthur reached for the silver water jug and poured a slug into the beaker-top which served as a glass. Be honest, he told himself as he sipped the reviving liquid, who do *you* think is right? The pain reared again. He took a deep breath and waited. Let the dust settle, he advised himself, why kill yourself worrying? It was barely ten o'clock and he was exhausted.

Chapter Twenty

Holly was almost weak with excitement. It was her first trip abroad and in a couple of minutes she would be in Paris. Paris! She tried not to skip as she followed the other passengers through passport control into the clear, plastic-tubed travelators which led to the baggage carousels. Charles de Gaulle airport was enormous. She watched anxiously for her new suitcase, proud of its retractable handle and solid little wheels. Even though she hadn't allowed the matching grip out of her sight for a moment, she hoisted it from her shoulder on to the trolley and felt for the manuscript. It was still there. So too was her laptop and its adapter.

She waited patiently in the queue for a taxi. People jostled impatiently and she almost missed her turn as a group of musicians elbowed her out of their way. The taxi driver refused to take the five of them in his cab and Holly couldn't resist a smirk as she sank into her seat. The taxi hurtled along the busy road and after a while she began to recognise some of the sights: the Eiffel Tower, far taller and more imposing than she'd imagined, and the tree-lined Champs Elysées that appeared to stretch forever. Her eyes darted from one building, one street, to the next, then suddenly they were passing the Louvre museum. She knew it was the Louvre because of the steel and glass Pyramid, cradled snugly in the protection of the old, honey-stoned walls. Ancient and modern. Astonishing juxtaposition. Before she had time to give it any further thought, they arrived at the hotel.

Holly smiled with delight as she watched the activity in the square beneath her window. A mime artist clad in an enormous white sheet, his face and hair white-chalked, draped himself on a white plinth and assumed the pose of Rodin's *Thinker*. A crowd gathered from nowhere. A crocodile of little children and their teachers crossed the square and stopped to gaze at him. Without warning, he flapped his arms and gave a roar which sent the children screaming and scuttling around the blue-jeaned legs of their laughing teachers. Holly shifted her gaze to a small group of teenage skate-boarders as they threaded their way along a diagonal line of miniature traffic cones with incredible speed and agility. Her smile widened as one of them interrupted his suicidal display to shake hands politely with a new arrival. The mime artist picked up his white hat from the ground, laden with coins. He removed the sheet. Dressed in tight black trousers and a black polo neck, he resembled a stick insect. He mounted a bicycle no more than ten inches high. A new crowd gathered as he began to ride the tiny machine in wide circles. She could have stayed at the window all day but she was in Paris to work, to edit a book.

A biting wind whistled through the canvas awning of the brasserie but Holly was determined to eat outside. April in Paris, and no sign of Spring. She chose a seat near one of the tall, outdoor gas heaters and strained to read the menu on the board above her head.

"Croque Monsieur and coffee, please," she ordered.

The waiter scratched his head. "Café, Madame?"

"Oui," Holly ventured.

He reeled off a list. "Café grand? Espresso, cappuccino, décaféiné . . . ?"

"Cappuccino, s'il vous plait," she said shyly as the strange words tripped off her tongue.

She translated the francs into pounds and was horrified as she checked the bill. Bloody hell! Four pounds for a cup of coffee, and only half a one at that, ten pounds for the open toasted sandwich. What would a meal cost? But there was no time to delay, Lucinda Rockingham was due at the hotel at two o'clock and, although the café was only next door, she didn't want to keep her waiting.

Lucinda's unfortunate fall was the reason for Holly's trip to Paris. She couldn't possibly travel to London in her condition and utterly refused to be edited by post. Rather than contend with any more of Lucinda's phone calls, Arthur had reluctantly agreed that Holly should edit the book in Paris. Holly had stifled her whoop of joy until she was well out of Arthur's earshot, then she grabbed for the phone and called Liz.

She sat in the quiet lounge off the foyer, the manuscript on the table, her pen at the ready. There was a flurry of footsteps. Lucinda Rockingham, a great drift of a woman, was preceded by her bosom and followed by a phalanx of porters, hotel managers and her driver. She paused at the step which led down to the lounge then carefully placed one crutch in front of the other. Holly rushed to help but Lucinda waved her away and staggered bravely on to firm carpet.

"I have arrived," she announced imperiously.

Lucinda directed the placing of her cushion, a footstool, her handbag and a tiny jewelled glass bottle.

"Smelling salts," she informed Holly.

When she was comfortably settled, her plastered leg on its tapestried rest, she dismissed her flunkies then waved a crutch at the barman. "Whisky," she demanded. "And I think you should switch off that music. Oh! Holly, what will you have?"

Nothing like being an afterthought. "Nothing for me, thank you." A drink in the middle of the day always made her sleepy.

"Nonsense! Your first trip to Paris – you must have something."

Holly needed to keep her sweet. "In that case I'll have mineral water – sparkling."

"Such depravity," Lucinda tutted.

Lucinda downed her drink in one swallow. With her half-specs perched on the end of her nose, she graced Holly with her full attention.

"So, what have you done to my book? I suppose the margins are full of red-inked changes."

Holly cleared her throat. "Very few."

"*Your* ideas of very few and mine differ, I'm sure." Lucinda liked to attack first, she could always retreat later.

"Take a look for yourself," Holly invited as she pushed the manuscript across the table.

When they first met, Lucinda had taken a shine to Holly. Simone had been delighted to get the difficult woman out of her hair. Holly's compliant temperament suited Lucinda although, in a weak moment, she confessed to Arthur Lord that Holly was not quite the push-over she'd first thought her to be. Holly could be stubborn too.

"Huh! Very few, indeed!" Lucinda snorted. She was actually quite pleased to see so many virgin pages, but what fun was life without a grumble?

Holly moved to her side and they began their editing.

"I want that kept in," Lucinda insisted as they came to a deleted passage.

Holly was prepared for this. "I did too, at first, but then I thought, no, it weakens your point. You worded that previous sentence so beautifully, there's no need for any further emphasis."

Holly waited. Living with Derek had taught her

to hold her tongue; she supposed she could thank him for that if nothing else. Besides, Lucinda was a sucker for flattery.

"Well . . . maybe you have a point."

Round one to me. Holly hid her grin. In spite of Lucinda's intimidating bluster, she had grown quite fond of her.

As they turned to the start of Chapter Six, Lucinda asked for help. She needed to move her leg. Pain was deeply etched on her pale face.

"Perhaps if I move the footstool, or would you prefer to stop?" It must be dreadful for her, Holly thought compassionately.

"No. Let's keep going, you didn't drag all the way to Paris to watch me having an attack of the vapours. But another drop of whisky might do no harm."

Holly noticed that the jewelled bottle remained tightly closed. She signalled to the bored barman. Apart from themselves, the room was empty.

"Keep going," Lucinda instructed as she sipped her Scotch.

"No, relax for a few minutes, there's no rush." Holly leant back in her chair.

Lucinda was furious with herself. She was fed up being stuck in the apartment but her determination to meet Holly at the hotel had backfired. Her leg was throbbing and she was finding it difficult to concentrate. But she'd wait, the booze would probably hit the spot.

"I hear that you've disposed of your other half," Lucinda said as casually as if she was discussing the weather. "Good on you. Keep it that way. Next time, take a lover, one with his own washing machine and an iron," she advised.

Holly was speechless. Was nothing sacred?

"Don't look so shocked, that's what I did after I left *my* husband. It was terrific. All moonlight and candles, flowers and sex. Wonderful!"

"But . . . but I thought you were married, *are* married."

"I am. That putty-hearted idol of mine persuaded me that, if I married him, I would never have to wash socks or boxer shorts again. So I did, and I haven't." Lucinda grinned. "I have my charms you know, I'm good in bed," she said.

Holly smiled, she couldn't see Lucinda in that light.

"You should see the look on your face, Holly. How do you think I'm able to write all those sexy bits in my books? Practice, my girl, practice. And here's another shock for you, there *is* sex after thirty, you know. I probably won't give it up until I'm a hundred."

Holly's laughter rang in the quiet room. Lucinda was incorrigible.

"By the way, I've told my devoted slave that he's to take you to dinner tonight. He's entertaining a couple from London and you can act as hostess in my place. But remember, keep your hands off Dominic, he's mine."

"I will. I mean, I can't . . . go to dinner."

Lucinda laughed at Holly's confusion. In spite of the pain she was enjoying herself enormously.

"Thank you for the thought, Lucinda, but I don't even know your husband. I'll manage beautifully on my own."

"Nonsense! I won't hear of a lovely girl like you wandering around this wicked city on your own. Now, if I was able to get about, that would be a whole different scene, we could trawl the town together." Lucinda's eyes sparkled with mischief.

I hope I have her spirit when I'm her age, Holly said to herself. Lucinda must be the wrong side of fifty.

"My pain is getting worse, so don't argue. Dominic will pick you up at eight o'clock. Trust me, you'll have a fabulous time."

"Lucinda!"

"Holly!"

It was useless arguing, Holly could see that. She didn't fancy getting stuck with Lucinda's husband, never mind another couple.

"Not another word or I'll take to my bed, then you'll be here for a week."

"I could live with that." Holly grinned. "But I don't think Arthur would be overjoyed." How true that is, Holly thought with a stab of concern.

Ugly rumours had been going the rounds at Pagett for some weeks now. The firm's finances were in a bad way, according to Lois. Her own book, *Tomorrow's Joy,* was due for publication in about four or five months and she prayed nothing would go wrong.

Lucinda managed to last for another half-hour, then admitted, "I've had enough for today. I think that you should come to the flat tomorrow, then, if I'm uncomfortable, I can stretch out on my death bed. We'll continue no matter how ill I feel."

"You sure you're up to it?" Holly felt she should ask.

"'Course. We'll work like mad. Finish in record time, then the following day you'll have a bit of time to explore, to shop. You can't come to Paris and not see the sights. You're here until Wednesday evening? I'll expect you in the morning, nine o'clock sharp? You have my address."

"I have it here in my diary." Holly patted her bag. "About your launch date, Lucinda. How do you feel about going ahead with it in July as we planned? Or under the circumstances, would you rather postpone it?"

"I'd prefer to stick to the plan. My ankle is badly fractured and the doctors say it'll be six or seven months before I'm mobile. I imagine it would be at least a year before I could even think of doing a publicity tour. So sure, go ahead. I've had so much time on my hands since my fall that I've already started a new book. It's based in Paris so it'll be fun to drive around and find locations."

The barman and a porter helped Lucinda from her chair and the earlier procession reversed itself. Her driver appeared as if by magic and the head porter led the way to the car.

Holly waited until Lucinda was out of sight. The urge to grab her coat and walk through the Tuilerie Gardens to the Place de la Concorde was overwhelming, but she had to make those changes while they were still fresh in her mind.

Chapter Twenty-One

Holly liked what she saw in the mirror. Never plump at the best of times, the walk to and from her office each day had trimmed her slender figure even more. Her legs, in their sheer black tights, were shapely and she loved the new, short, black skirt with its box pleats. The red jacket gave her skin a wonderful glow and the lacy black body, which she just couldn't resist, brought the outfit together. "Tarty, indeed," she snorted as she clipped Liz's silver earrings in place. "Eat your heart out, Derek Grant. It's *you* who has no taste."

She still thought of Derek – a lot. But he no longer dominated her every waking moment. Nowadays it was more a see-how-I-can-manage-without-you scenario. How different Terence was. Like a roly-poly bolster, always encouraging, endlessly patient, never judgemental. How lucky she was to have him as a friend.

Holly waited by the front door of the hotel and suppressed a giggle as Lucinda's sex-god emerged from his car. She recognised Lucinda's driver from that afternoon. Lucinda had to be double his weight and at least five or six inches taller.

"Holly?"

"Yes. Dominic?"

He grasped her outstretched hand. "No wonder Luci told me to behave myself tonight." The warmth of his smile eclipsed his sombre look.

Holly couldn't imagine that formidable woman being called *Luci*.

"I got the same warning!" she confided. What on earth had possessed her to say that?

"Then we'll have to take heed and do what *she who must be obeyed* suggests. That's what Lucinda calls herself, by the way."

Holly was pleased to hear it – nasty husbands were not her scene.

As they sat in the back of the car, Dominic pointed out places of interest. "Lucinda tells me she plans to work you to death tomorrow. She wants you to have a chance to see even a little of Paris before you leave. Pierre will be at your disposal for the day on Wednesday and then he will take you to the airport. Won't you, Pierre?"

"Oui, Monsieur." The chauffeur nodded.

"That would be fantastic." And even better that he understood English. "I'd *love* to go to the top of the Eiffel Tower," she mused.

"Your wish is my instant command. Look."

The car drew to a stop and Dominic directed her gaze to her right. The Tower towered. It was awesome. An enormous mass of intricate metal which glinted eerily in the night light, and reminded Holly of a giant Meccano sculpture.

"That's where we are going to eat." Dominic pointed upwards to a metal platform. "The restaurant is on the second *étage,* not quite at the top, but I guarantee you'll be thrilled by the view."

They walked between the stanchions and across the open square towards the Tower.

"We're lucky tonight," Dominic said as he looked at the sky. "It's a perfect night. Last night was cloudy."

A small group of people stood by one leg of the structure. A faint light glowed and, as they reached the waiting couples, a metal door opened. Dominic gently elbowed Holly inside and she found herself in a glass lift. As it glided upwards towards the skies, her stomach fluttered and she looked straight ahead, not down. This wasn't the time to disgrace herself by being nervous. When the lift came to a stop and they stepped into the dimly lit foyer, her misgivings vanished.

They made their way to the bar.

"The couple that we're meeting, the Nelsons, are also in France for the first time. They're here to see if they'd like to live in Paris. I'm considering taking him on . . . "

But Holly wasn't listening, the view from the dimly lighted bar was stunning. Paris lay at her feet like a glistening jewel.

"Come and sit by the window," Dominic smiled. He remembered his delight the first time he'd eaten at the Jules Verne restaurant.

"I've never seen anything so beautiful in all my life," Holly gasped as she swivelled her chair to drink in the view. The brightly lit avenues stretched as far as the eye could see. Cars moved in a twinkling flow.

The Nelsons arrived a few minutes later and they too could barely keep their eyes from the windows as Dominic introduced them. The couple, whom Holly instantly labelled thirty-something-city-types, were polite, personable, and distant.

Their window table in the dining-room had an equally breathtaking view. When they were seated Holly appreciated the ingenuity of the decor. The tables in the pale-grey and black room were illuminated by low, black down-lights no taller than the drinking glasses, obviously designed to prevent any reflection which would spoil the panoramic view.

Only Dominic gave the menu full attention.

"I think I'll have the soup," he decided.

"Me too." Ryan Nelson wasn't particularly interested in food. "I must confess I eat to live, don't live to eat."

How ungracious. Holly felt her flesh creep.

"I'm going to try the carpaccio, I presume it's all right to eat the beef here?" Sue Nelson asked.

"I should think so," Dominic said. "If you're unhappy with the idea, why not order something else."

Holly peeked at Dominic, did she detect an edge of sarcasm in his reply? She had no idea what beef carpaccio was and wasn't going to show her ignorance by asking. Sue wasn't exactly the chummy type. There was something about her which had immediately put Holly on the defensive.

Dominic noticed her discomfort. "Have you ever tried carpaccio, Holly, or is raw marinated beef not your thing?" No wonder Lucinda loved him so much.

The wine waiter brought the wine list.

"Red or white?" Dominic asked each of them in turn.

Sue Nelson frowned and began to question Dominic about the wines. Ryan Nelson squirmed in his black swivel chair. The table rocked ever so slightly as he kicked his wife underneath the crisp folds of the cloth.

"How is your starter?" Dominic asked Holly as she speared a little frill of truffle on to her fork.

"Absolutely delicious," Holly said, and it was. *Fresh asparagus and truffle on a delicate bed of salad leaves.* She must remember the description exactly. Liz had warned her that she'd want to hear every minute detail.

"And how was the carpaccio?" Dominic asked.

"Mmm. Not bad at all."

Good or bad, Holly noticed the transparent slices of beef had vanished in a trice.

When her *carré* of lamb arrived, Holly forced her eyes from the window and joined in the conversation. She adored those little cloves of roasted garlic.

"So you're in Paris to edit Mrs Rockingham's book?" Ryan gave her a rare smile.

"I should write a book," Sue interrupted before

Holly had a chance to reply. "I have so many wonderful stories, it's just finding the time to sit down and put them on paper."

"It *is* time consuming." Holly wished she had a pound for every time she'd heard that.

"I'm sure it's not that easy though, is it, Holly?" Ryan frowned.

"Rubbish!" Sue snorted dismissively. "Anyone who puts their mind to it could do it. Providing they have the right story, of course." Her cheeks were flushed from the wine and her husband cringed deeper into his chair.

"Well, Holly? What do *you* have to say?"

Ryan's put-down was not lost on Holly. Or on Dominic. Only Sue tossed a disdainful head as she drank her wine. Normally Holly would have been quite happy to explain the ins and outs of writing, but why bother? Sue Nelson was a lost cause.

"I'm sure Sue's right," she said amicably.

"There you are, told you. Straight from the horse's mouth." Sue gave a triumphant smile that was more like a smirk.

They finished their main course in stilted silence.

"I must go and find the little girl's room," Sue said.

"Good idea, I'll walk with you." Ryan put his napkin on the table and followed his wife.

"What do you make of them?" Dominic asked after they'd gone.

"They're very . . . worldly."

"Worldly?" Dominic questioned.

"I . . . not my type." She wished Dominic wouldn't put her on the spot like that.

"You mean rude? Pushy?"

Holly shrugged. "If you like."

"I don't like. I bet you that at this moment he's giving her a right earful. His job would entail a fair amount of entertaining and would also involve his wife," he said, more to himself than to Holly.

Holly had no idea what the job was nor what Dominic did for a living. Lucinda had mentioned something about *the business* and Holly knew that they expected to live in Paris for a year or so, but other than that she was in the dark.

If Ryan Nelson had given his wife a good tongue-lashing, it didn't show. She returned to the table unchastened and swivelled her chair towards the window.

Holly exclaimed with delight when her chocolate pudding was put in front of her. The white chocolate mousse was covered with a delicate cage of finely spun caramel. Exotic fruits spilled from a crunchy cornucopia of almond and ginger and the base of the plate was covered with smooth chocolate sauce, which lay in a rich dark pool.

"This is so beautiful I can't bear to cut it," Holly said.

Dominic smiled. Ryan thought how nice it was to find someone who wasn't blasé and Sue who, up to now appeared to be lost in her own world, suddenly leaned across the table and brought her spoon down on Holly's plate with a thwack. The cage shattered into dozens of tiny splinters and stuck to the flattened mousse. Fruit and sauce flew in all directions.

"There!" Sue slurred. "Your problem solved."

"Sue! Just look what you've done." Ryan jumped up from his chair. "I'm sorry, Holly. Did you get sauce on your jacket?"

"I don't think so. It's all right, I think I escaped."

"I'm sure Sue is sorry, aren't you?" Ryan glared at his wife.

"Just trying to help," Sue shrugged. And that was the nearest thing to an apology that they were going to get.

As people began to leave the dining-room, Holly realised she hadn't even noticed any of the other diners. Several people came to the window tables to take a last look at the shimmering city below. Holly enjoyed studying people, wondering who they were or what they did. She had drunk far more than usual tonight and the wine was beginning to play tricks on her eyes. If she didn't know better she would have sworn that the couple at the table at the far end of the room was the double of Derek and herself. She shook her head.

The Derek-lookalike busied himself paying the bill. Fascinated and sleepy from the wine, Holly continued to stare. The couple stood up and made their way towards the window beside their table.

It *was* Derek. It was. She wasn't seeing things. His companion was almost a mirror image of herself – as she used to be. The woman's hair was shorter than her own, but scraped back into a flat pleat; she wore a little more make-up, perhaps, but not much.

And, if there was still any doubt, there it was, the inevitable brown suit.

Holly grasped her glass of mineral water and almost threw it down her throat. The iced water revived her, but Derek was still in recovery. Their eyes locked. He had barely recognised his glamorous wife.

Holly gulped air. "Hello, Derek," she heard someone say in her voice.

"Holly." He nodded his head curtly.

"Aren't you going to introduce me?" she asked. Where she'd found the nerve she would never know.

Derek just continued to stare.

"I'm Bunny," the woman answered for her silent companion.

"Bunny . . . Bunny what?" Holly prompted.

"Buh . . . eye" she mumbled.

"Sorry, I didn't catch that."

"Bh . . . Bly."

Derek stood motionless at her side.

"Oh, Bly! . . . Bly?" Holly frowned, the name was familiar. "Isn't that your boss's name, Derek?"

The woman's mouth flew open and then snapped shut.

Derek was galvanised into clumsy speech. "We're in a dreadful rush. Come on Bunny, we must hurry. Goodbye Bunny . . . I mean, Holly." Derek grabbed Bunny's arm firmly and steered her ahead of him into the darkness of the room. Holly could almost feel his cruel grip.

"Well, what was that all about?" Sue demanded.

An interesting little *contretemps,* anything to break the boredom of the evening.

"Just someone I used to know." Holly's reply was almost inaudible.

Dominic regarded her shrewdly. "Would you like another glass of water?" he asked. She was trembling like an aspen.

Chapter Twenty-Two

Holly dangled the little brown and gold gift bag by its chubby strings. A smile of pleasure crossed Terence's face when he saw her at his door. "Welcome home. Come in, come in," he urged.

Holly handed him the bag of chocolates and flopped into her usual chair. "I came to see if you fancied going out for a bite – if you haven't eaten already. The flight from Paris has made me lazy." Holly shook her head as he offered her one of the rich chocolates.

He popped a rum truffle into his mouth and chewed it with noisy relish.

"I haven't been home long, either. I wouldn't mind going out," he agreed. "I can't wait to hear all about your trip."

Terence heaped his plate with fried rice. "I suppose after the fleshpots of Europe this is poor fare?"

"I love Chinese food, you know I do," she said.

"Just teasing!" Holly was touchy.

"Sorry, I'm a bit uptight. I'll tell you all about

Paris in a minute but I've something else to tell you first, something very odd."

Terence barely missed a chew as he listened to Holly's account of her meeting with Derek and his *friend*.

"Fancy Derek of all people, having a bit of nooky with the boss's wife. That's a bit of luck. Just what you need."

"Lucinda Rockingham said the same thing. What a character she is! She practically had me in court waving a divorce petition. *Shop him to his boss. Screw him for every penny he has,* was her actual advice."

"She sounds like a real bitch – I like that in a woman." Terence gave her one of his broad grins. "But there are two ways to boil an egg, hard or soft. I think you should go for the hard option."

Holly pulled a wry face. "It was a row about an egg that got me where I am today," she reminded him.

He became serious. "I think that if you use your information cleverly, you could cease to be Mrs Derek Grant."

"How do I do that?"

"Simple. Blackmail the bastard."

"Idiot!"

"I don't suggest that you send him a ransom note or an anonymous letter, nothing so crass. Your solicitor will know how to tackle him, how to use the information. That's all supposing he's guilty, of course."

Doubt crossed Holly's face. "What if she was the boss's daughter, not his wife?"

"Don't fret. If the relationship was innocent, why was Derek's lady-friend so reluctant to give her second name?"

Holly munched a crispy won ton while Terence turned the lid of the teapot upside down. He eyed the remains of her chow mein and she pushed it across the table. He emptied the contents of the metal dish on to his plate. How could she prove that Derek and Bunny were having a fling? What explanation did she herself have for being in the restaurant with a married man? How could she prove *her* innocence? But then she had Lucinda Rockingham on her side. No one would get the better of Lucinda.

"I want to hear more about Paris, what you did today?" Terence demanded.

He could always distract her from her worries.

• • •

Robert stood in the shadow of the tree. His wife and her sister were chattering like magpies, a rake and hoe abandoned on the grass beside them as they lolled on the bench in the watery sunshine.

"If you two put as much energy into the garden as you do into talking, we'd be open to the public tomorrow," he laughed.

"There's a lot to talk about," said Liz.

Their non-stop flow of conversation was a constant source of amusement to him. Holly was almost unrecognisable as the woman she'd been a year ago. Although still a little reserved, she'd regained some of her vitality. She had blossomed.

"Tell Robert what happened at the Eiffel Tower," Liz prompted as she put the bowls of soup on the table.

Holly repeated the story of her meeting with Derek.

"It sounds as though you've got him nailed, material for adultery."

"I think so too. At first I wasn't sure if *Bunny Bly* was his boss's wife or his daughter. And then this morning I suddenly remembered Derek bitching like mad, Alan Bly had had a huge party for his 35th birthday and hadn't invited Derek."

Once Holly had worked out that the woman wasn't Alan Bly's daughter she invented a new worry.

"Of course, she could have been his sister," she fretted.

Robert crumbled some of his roll into his soup. Holly had obviously given the situation plenty of thought. On the face of it, it sounded more likely that Bunny Bly was a wife, playing away, not Bly's sister.

"I presume you contacted your solicitor and told him about meeting Derek?"

"First thing yesterday morning."

"And what did he have to say?"

"He was away on holiday. Will be for another ten days. His assistant said that if it was urgent I could speak to his partner. But it wasn't, so I didn't." Strange how relaxed she'd become about it all now.

Liz was impatient. "Forget about Dracula, let's hear about the rest of your trip. We were up to Wednesday. Holly had the day to herself," she explained to her husband.

"I was dressed and on my way by seven! Dominic arranged to give me the use of his car and driver for the day but I wanted to walk in the Tuilerie Gardens, take a look at the Pyramid at the Louvre."

"Were the gardens fabulous?" Liz asked, her expressive eyes full of longing.

"Unfortunately, no. It was all paths and bare branches. They're redesigning the gardens. I must admit I was very disappointed." If I make any money with my book, I'll arrange a weekend break for them in Paris, Holly promised herself. *My book,* she thought with a stab of conscience.

"Then what?" Liz sat forward eagerly.

"By then the traffic was tearing around the Place de la Concorde at a frightening rate so I used the underpass and walked back by the river."

"Then?" Liz urged.

"Pierre arrived about ten and, on Lucinda's instructions, drove me to the Faubourg St. Honoré. You should have seen it, Liz. Every fashion name you've ever heard of, they all had shops there. And the prices! They were mind-boggling," Holly rolled her eyes at the memory. "And there was this wonderful arcade, full of crystal and china, Lalique had three shops there . . . " Holly's face was alight and her eyes shone. She stopped now and then to take a mouthful of food.

Liz and Robert glanced at each other. It was good to see Holly so alive, so vibrant. At that moment Liz knew that her sister would be all right. In time the effects of her awful marriage would fade. Having that neighbour of hers, Terence, for a friend was no harm either.

Chapter Twenty-Three

The Jordan Award had fast become one of the most sought-after literary prizes. The ten thousand pound prize was awarded for a best first novel. Pagett were not in contention this year but they always attended the dinner, looked forward to it. It was one of the highlights of the year, a grand social occasion.

Simone cast aside the red chiffon dress, she wasn't in a frivolous mood tonight. Her unexpected trip to the Brussels book fair last week hadn't helped. Louise Marcham, their foreign rights' agent, had been rushing downstairs when she tripped, fell, and broke her wrist. Simone was just about to leave for the office when the phone call came – she would have to take Louise's place. By noon, she was on the plane to Brussels. Apart from that hurried call, she hadn't spoken to Arthur Lord since the day she had offered her resignation. The wait for his decision was almost unbearable. Perhaps he'd say something tonight; the Jordan Award always put him in a happy frame of mind.

The enormous ballroom was practically empty, most people crowded around the bar. Simone took a deep breath, pasted a smile on her face, then joined the thronging mass of publishers, agents, PR people and authors.

"White wine, please," she said to the barman. She waved to Annabelle Strong, one of their sales representatives. Annabelle waved back then nudged her companion, who turned to look at Simone. Simone moved into the crowd. Wherever she stopped to say hello, conversation ceased. She sensed an atmosphere. People glanced at her briefly then turned away. Was her bra strap showing? Had she forgotten her make-up? Had she remembered to put on her dress?

She was relieved when dinner was announced and the slow shuffle towards the ballroom began. Could that be Holly in the gorgeous blue two-piece?

"Hello, Simone," Holly greeted her gaily.

Simone did a rapid scan of Holly's outfit. It shrieked designer, expensive.

"Pretty suit." Simone cocked her head on one side.

"Thank you." There was no mistaking the question in Simone's voice. There was also no reason why she should tell Simone that she had picked up the gorgeous blue silk and chiffon two-piece at a second-hand bazaar in Oxford. Liz warned her, on pain of death, not to tell *anyone* where she had found the beautiful jacket and skirt, just accept the compliments that were sure to come her way. And they had. Lots of them. It had taken her and Liz half of Saturday and all of Sunday to cut away the muddy hem, the only give-away sign of wear. It was Holly's good fortune that the suit's previous owner must have been of Amazonian height, but as slim as Holly herself.

Simone stopped at the bar for a top-up, then seated herself at the Pagett table. Jeremy Hide, their marketing manager, stood and pulled out the chair beside him for Holly. Last year he had done the same thing for her. There wasn't any sign of that dowdy girl of a year ago, Simone thought resentfully. Holly laughed gaily at something Jeremy said and Simone scowled at the pair of them. Roland Green came to the table with Emma. She smiled at Emma and ignored Roland.

"What a ridiculous tie," Simone snorted to herself. Only Roland could come up with the affected idea of a red and white spotted tie with a formal dinner suit when everyone else wore black. Stupid git.

She watched the door, but Alfred Lord's chair remained empty. No one seemed to know why. He hadn't been seen all week, according to Lois.

Simone pushed the food around her plate but ate very little. Instead she nodded to the hovering waitress who refilled her wine glass.

The recipient of the Jordan Award made a breathless speech. The young writer, probably no more than twenty-two or three, was terribly nervous and in awe of her surroundings. With flaming cheeks and the magical cheque clutched firmly to her flat chest, she almost ran back to her table and her delighted publishers.

Holly could imagine herself on the podium this

time next year, collecting the prize for *Tomorrow's Joy*.

Simone stared moodily into her glass. She wanted no part of the goodnatured banter which flew backwards and forwards across the table and couldn't wait to escape. But she stayed.

"Something bothering you, Annabelle?" she snapped at the pleasant young rep. She had felt Annabelle's eyes on her all night.

"No! no," Annabelle answered quickly, "I was thinking how quiet you are. Are you all right?"

"Just rearranging my prejudices," Simone retorted sharply.

Roland Green's smug smile was more than she could stomach. She picked up her bag and headed for the ladies' cloakroom.

"Hello there."

Trudy Friel. Of all the people she would rather not talk to. "Hello, Trudy. Haven't seen you for ages," Simone managed in a friendly tone as she rooted through her make-up bag for her lipstick brush.

"I hear little whispers, Simone. Dare I ask if they're true?" Trudy's tabloid column was fodder for millions every weekday. It was rumoured that after the Friday edition went to press, she climbed back into her coffin and remained there for the weekend.

"I haven't heard any whispers." Simone waited for the follow-up.

"Big changes at Pagett?"

"None that I've heard of and *I* would know,"

Simone said decisively as she blotted her lipstick with an unsteady hand. What whispers? What changes? Simone knew better than to question Trudy. Anything she said or asked about would be quoted.

"If you say so." Trudy lit a cigarette, smiled and raised her hand in farewell.

Simone paused for a moment before going into the ballroom. If she left now, would she be missed? She swayed slightly on her feet. A hand at her elbow steadied her. She looked up into a pair of mellow, chocolate brown eyes, set in a handsome, sun-tanned face.

"I'm sorry, I must have knocked into you," the blurred Adonis apologised.

"Not at all. It's these heels, they're higher than usual," Simone lied with aplomb. It was a long time since a man had set her heart racing.

"I'm Ian Trent."

"Simone Pearse. I'm with Pagett."

"I'm delighted to meet you, Simone Pearse. And grateful to your high heels."

As they stood in the doorway she felt as though the whole room was staring at them. And well they might, Ian Trent was easy on the eye.

"May I buy you a drink?" he asked. This was turning out better than he'd hoped.

"Sure. But . . . if you're not involved, come to our table, let Pagett buy you one instead." She could do with a lift, a shot in the arm. Ian Trent was just the serum she needed.

Heads turned their way as they reached the

table. All night heads had been turning in her direction.

"Let me introduce you." Simone smiled possessively. "Annabelle Strong, one of our sales representatives, Jeremy Hide, . . . "

Ian walked round the table and shook hands with each of them in turn.

"Where did she find him? He's drop-dead gorgeous," Annabelle whispered loudly to Marianna Berry from the art department.

Lois, whose intention it was to look like Ivana Trump, stared at him openly. Emma rolled her eyes at Holly who gave a slight giggle. Tonight was the stuff that her dreams were made of.

Simone signalled to the waitress and ordered a bottle of champagne. To hell with the expense, to hell with Pagett, she deserved something that would brighten up her night.

By midnight, she and Ian were the only two left at the table. His face became mistier, more handsome with every sparkling sip she took. She supposed it had been rude of her not to offer the champagne to the others, but blow them, they'd done nothing to make her evening a pleasant one. Quite the opposite in fact, she'd spent most of it wondering what *she'd* done wrong.

"I suppose we'd better go too, before we're thrown out," Simone said. She groped under her chair for her bag, then rose unsteadily to her feet.

"Do you have a car or can I give you a lift home?" Ian asked solicitously.

"I didn't bring my car tonight, I'd be glad of a lift."

"Would you like to come in for a night-cap?" Simone asked recklessly as the taxi drew up outside her flat. I must be nuts, the man's a total stranger, she warned herself as she handed him her key.

"That would be nice, coffee perhaps?"

Simone gathered up the skirt of her black dress, swayed slightly, then plunged up the stairs.

Ian examined the watercolours while Simone busied herself with cups and saucers.

There had to be a catch. This man was polite, handsome, charming and caring. All too good to be true. She stared dreamily into the column of steam that spiralled upwards towards the ceiling, then realised the kettle had boiled.

Ian heard the clatter of china. Simone Pearse was a tiny bit the worse for wear. She looked stunning. The ornate gold necklet with its sunburst drops softened the severity of her simple black dress.

Simone carried the tray into the room. Her green eyes glittered and her lips were soft and dewy. Ian walked smoothly towards her. God, she was beautiful. He held out his arms. She bent down, placed the tray carefully on the table, and passed out.

Chapter Twenty-Four

Why was there a jack-hammer drilling away in her bedroom, in her head? Simone struggled back to consciousness. She wasn't in her bedroom, she was in the living-room.

"Oh shit," she groaned as memories of the evening came tumbling back. "How *could* I? What day is it?"

She shook her head – which was foolish. The big question was whether Ian Trent was as handsome or as kind as she remembered or whether she had made a total fool of herself in his chocolate brown eyes. Chocolate. A wave of nausea gripped her. This was her worst and definitely her last hangover. Simone shrugged off the duvet. How had that got there? Ian! She pushed the cover away quickly; apart from her shoes she was still fully dressed. With her hands holding her head on to her body, she staggered into the kitchen. Soda water might help. She sloshed some water – mostly into a glass – swallowed a couple of aspirins, then staggered back and fell shivering on the sofa. She pulled the duvet around her.

The soda water was helping, the aspirins were kicking in too. The hammering had eased slightly. Who was Ian Trent? That was probably academic now, last night would have seen to that, she thought. Pity.

By the time she reached Pagett, Simone was in reasonably good shape. The strange feeling in the pit of her stomach was due to nerves. She'd had no time to think about herself in Brussels. It was the first time she had been alone at one of these book fairs and all her energy had been spent in talking to foreign publishers and arranging possible sales.

Now she must face reality, did she have a job, or were her days at Pagett at an end?

Everyone was gathered around Lois's desk, intent on something that she was reading aloud from a newspaper. Emma saw Simone first. The paper practically flew into the air. Lois grabbed it and pushed it out of sight.

"Morning, Simone," she said.

There were more hellos and good mornings then, one after the other, they beetled back to their own rooms.

"What's going on?" Simone demanded.

"Nothing, Nothing at all." Lois's voice rose an octave and came out with a squeak.

"Come on, Lois, I'm not an idiot, what were you reading and why did you hide the paper?"

"It's just a silly article."

"Let me see it."

"It's nonsense, Simone."

"Show me." Simone held out her hand and kept it there until Lois reached under her desk and produced the crumpled paper.

"Which page?"

"Trudy Friel's column."

The builders were back at work in her head, the hammer doing overtime.

"May I borrow this for a few minutes?" she asked.

"Sure, I've finished with it. But take no notice of her, you know what she's like."

With as much dignity as she could muster, Simone walked slowly along the corridor to her office. Bloody Trudy Friel. She had forgotten all about their meeting in the cloakroom.

She smoothed out the paper. The item was in bold print, impossible to miss.

A little bird tweeted last night – things are
all a flutter at Pagett Publications.
The greater red and white spotted buzzard
is soon to become
Pagett's sole adult editor.
A disappointment for the golden-haired eagle
high on her perch?

Simone read it twice then crushed the paper between her taut fingers. Pagett always made good copy. Blind anger bubbled to the surface. So that was what last night was all about; the sly glances, the whispering huddles which dispersed as she came within earshot. Roland Green, the preening monster, he had fed Trudy this information. She could kill him, strangle him with her bare hands. How *dare* he make statements like that? How dare he tell such blatant lies? Arthur Lord must be told . . . But was it true? Had Arthur already informed Roland of his decision? No, not even Arthur was cowardly enough to use a gossip column to inform her that he'd accepted her resignation.

Her phone rang.

"Simone, can you go to the boardroom – right away?" Lois asked.

Before she had a chance to reply, Lois cut her off.

"As a matter of courtesy, I have come to tell you that, as from today, Pagett is on the market."

Simone stood at the foot of the table, rigid with shock. What more could the day throw at her?

Amanda Lord sat alone at the big table. Simone had met the grey-haired, almost fragile, woman a couple of times before. But fragility was not a word that sprang to mind now.

"The day after your argument, Arthur had a mild coronary. I have little to thank you for, Simone. You or Roland," she said in clipped tones.

"Oh! I'm so sorry to hear that Arthur is ill." There had been no hint, no whispers. Then the full force of the accusation hit her. Why should she be held responsible? She had fought her corner, nothing more.

"I think that's extremely unfair, Mrs Lord. Unjust. I've done nothing wrong, Roland was the one who . . . "

Amanda Lord held up a hand to silence her.

"You're doing it again, Simone. Whatever you think or say no longer concerns me – us. My husband has suffered as a result of your . . . power battle, and therefore so have I. *He* is my only concern now. The doctors have advised him that he must not have any stress and the only way to avoid that is for him to sell Pagett. On your way out would you tell Lois to phone accounts and send for Tim Brown, I'm ready to see him now."

"But what about our jobs? Do we keep . . . "

"Please ask Lois to send for Tim Brown," Amanda Lord said, icily.

Simone reeled in to the corridor and leant against the wall beside the closed door. Waves of nausea made her stomach heave. If she didn't get to the ladies' cloakroom right away she'd be sick where she stood.

She felt no better. The image that stared back at her from the mirror said it all. Her mascara obviously didn't realise it was supposed to be waterproof, her all-day lipstick was nowhere to be seen.

But for once her vanity took second place. She could accept that ill health would force Arthur to take things easy, perhaps even to close Pagett, but Amanda's bald accusation seared through her like a branding iron. It had all happened so fast; no room for discussion, just a statement and close-the-door-on-your-way-out.

Simone wanted to kick and scream, tear the basin from the wall. *"It's not fair,"* she yelled at her reflection. *"That's slanderous. How could she say such a thing?"*

She soaked a paper towel and did the best she could with her streaked face. The pounding returned with a vengeance. She escaped to her office and sat with her head in her hands.

"There's a call for you on line one," Lois said.

"Who is it?" she asked irritably. Would that girl never learn to say who was calling?

"Your ex."

It was unusual for Mark to phone. "Put him through."

"Hello, Simone. How are you?" Mark's deep voice set up a fresh attack of head-banging.

"I've had better days."

Mark Pearse hesitated. "Is this an awkward time for you? Should I phone you later, this afternoon, perhaps?"

"What was it you wanted to talk about?" she asked sharply. She hadn't meant to snap at him, this calamity wasn't his fault.

"I . . . there's something I wanted to discuss with you."

"Sorry, I didn't mean to be grouchy. It's been a bitch of a morning, go ahead."

"Could we meet for a drink later? Say about six o'clock?"

Even the thought of a drink made her stomach churn again. "I don't think I can manage that. Can't you tell me what it's about?"

"I would have preferred to tell you in person, but . . . actually, Simone . . . I'm getting married again."

Mark squirmed uncomfortably in the silence. "Simone, are you still there?"

Simone wiped her sweaty palm on her skirt. "Yes," she mumbled.

"I'm sorry to spring it on you like this."

"Oh, Mark." She couldn't trust herself to speak.

"I really didn't want to tell you . . . " Then he stopped. "Simone, *please* don't cry like that. I know this is sudden, but I didn't think it would affect you so much." His tone was gentle. He would always be cursed with a soft spot for this woman he had married.

"It's not just that, it's everything." Simone made no effort to hide her anguish. "Everything's fallen apart today, gone from bad to worse."

"What can I do? Can I help?"

"No one can help. It's all so dreadful."

"Listen, how about if I come round and take you to lunch, then you can tell me what's wrong?"

"I can't go anywhere. I look terrible, my eyes are swollen . . . "

This was more like Simone. "If things are as bad as that, then surely what you look like doesn't matter, does it?"

"I s'pose not."

"I'll be there at one o'clock."

Simone wiped her eyes on the back of her hand. Why had she let him go? Why hadn't she tried harder to make a go of their marriage? Mark needn't have taken the trouble to phone her, he could just have remarried and told her later. But he'd always been a softie, never wanted to hurt anybody. A fresh spurt of tears made their way down her cheeks and on to her blouse. What a fool she'd been. What did she have to show for all her years: a blemished career, a broken marriage and precious few friends?

Chapter Twenty-Five

Simone made no effort to work. She just sat at her desk and waited for the knock on her door. Mark's sympathetic smile rekindled her self-pity.

"Come on, no more tears. Let's get you out of here," he said firmly as he produced a pair of sunglasses from his pocket. "They'll probably be too big, but they'll do the job."

Simone took the glasses from him with a pale imitation of a smile. "I'll just tidy my hair," she said and dashed from the office.

Mark paced up and down. Simone looked like hell. What on earth could have upset her so much? She'd never been a cry-baby. His eyes wandered to the crumpled newspaper on her desk. He glanced at the door, then picked up the scrunched pages, and smoothed them out.

"So that's it!" Quickly he crushed the pages again and put them back. What a rotten way to find out that you'd been sacked. *Nothing* meant as much to Simone as her career. But Simone would always succeed. For a second he thought of Susie and her unconditional love for him. Susie's wants in life were simple; a slew of babies, a home of her own, and him.

They sat in the dimly-lit bar.

"Drink this all in one go," Mark said as the barman put a small glass containing some dark liquid in front of Simone.

It was revolting. She gagged as the cure stuck in her throat.

"Drink it, Simone." He leaned forward and gently tipped the glass to her mouth.

"You'll feel a lot better in a few minutes, I promise."

He waited quietly until she was ready to talk. Silences between them had never been awkward, just unrewarding.

"I'm really sorry to inflict my misery on you," she apologised. "You chose the wrong moment to phone."

"Or the right one?"

"Either way, I'm really glad you rang when you did. I can't pretend to be over the moon about your news, but you deserve to be happy, Mark. I'm being very selfish. What's . . . she like?"

Mark chose his words carefully.

"Susie sounds very nice and I'm sure you'll be right for each other."

Damn the little paragon of virtue, she thought uncharitably.

"I hope so. But we're not here to talk about Susie. I want to know what upset you so much?"

Mark sat back and let her speak, but he soon

leaned forward again as she told him about her meeting with Amanda Lord.

"That's a dreadful thing to lay on anyone," he protested. "She had no right to blame you – or Roland Green, come to that. They can't hold you responsible, Simone. Unless Arthur Lord has changed radically in the last couple of years, I'd lay the blame fairly and squarely on his own cowardice. He was always weak – but you don't need me to tell you that. Blaming you is cruel."

Simone had tried all morning to tell herself that but hearing it from Mark helped. Suddenly she felt lighter. It didn't change anything, but it definitely helped. And the revolting hangover cure seemed to be working too.

"I want to believe you, Mark, I really do." She told him about the article in the morning tabloid. "Do you think Roland Green was telling the truth? Has Arthur decided to let me go?"

"Would he have had time to make that kind of decision? Didn't Amanda say that he took ill after your meeting last week? But either way, Simone, forget that rag. Concentrate on the future. Have you given *that* any thought?"

"All I've been able to think about is Amanda Lord."

"I can understand that but I'm positive you'll have no problem finding an equally good job, maybe an even better one."

Why did I not love you enough? Simone asked herself bitterly.

"Thanks, Mark. I suppose I'd better get my act

together and decide what to do. I can't afford to be out of work."

In fairness to Simone she'd never asked him for a penny. "Look, if you have any problem with the mortgage . . . I can tide you over."

"I hope it won't come to that."

"I'm *sure* you'll cope, but I want you to know that I'm here if you need me."

He had never known Simone so vulnerable. In spite of her red eyes, she was still beautiful, almost tragically so. Susie's image faded. If only Simone had needed him more. They had been happier than a lot of couples he knew. But the others had stayed together, tackling their problems somehow. If only he'd been firmer . . .

"Where did we go wrong, Simone?" he asked with a sigh.

"I'm here if you need me." Mark's words triggered her memory. That was what John Barrett had said. She must phone John, tell him what had happened.

"Simone?"

"Sorry. Did you say something?"

"Nothing important."

"I've just remembered something. One of my authors was interested in starting up a publishers. He wanted me to run it. I must phone him as soon as I get back to Pagett, tell him what's happened . . . " Simone glanced at the time. "I must go. The sooner I get hold of John the better."

This was the Simone he remembered, every sign of vulnerability banished, only raw ambition glittering in those lovely eyes.

"I'd better give you back your glasses now, Mark. I don't suppose we'll see each other too often in the future. I hope you and . . . Susie will really make a go of it. By the way, I don't know if you were going to invite me to the wedding, but I'd rather you didn't. I would find it difficult. Thank you for caring, Mark. I feel a lot better now."

"I'm pleased. I hope things work out for you. Let me know how you get on."

Inadvertently, Simone had helped him too. Susie would never be Simone, but Susie loved him unconditionally and suddenly that meant a great deal.

Simone had a brief word with Eve Barrett, then asked to speak to John.

"Nice to hear from you, Simone, how are things going?"

Just listening to his voice made her feel more positive. The short walk from the pub to Pagett had given Simone a chance to get her mind in gear. It would have been foolish to speak to John before she was in full command of herself. She would not go to him cap in hand.

"Not so good, I thought I'd better put you in the picture. Arthur Lord is ill and has decided to sell Pagett. I was worried about your book, John, and felt I owed it to you to tell you right away. If Pagett is sold, I'm not sure that your contract will be valid."

"I see." Simone's phone call was not entirely unexpected. John had read Trudy Friel's sniping article but obviously that wasn't what she wanted to discuss now.

"I appreciate your concern. But don't worry, it's probably far too soon for any decisions yet. These things take time. Is Arthur very ill?"

"He had a mild coronary, I gather he's not in any danger." She had no intention of divulging any details of that stinging meeting with Amanda Lord.

"I'm pleased to hear it," he said. Simone sounded very calm and collected. "I suppose all we can do now is hang on and see what happens."

"My feeling exactly," she lied tersely. "I'll keep you posted." Where was John's offer of *if you need me*? Should she try and draw him or play a waiting game?

"I'll be in London early next week so if you need me, you know where to find me."

Simone slammed down the phone with a crash. *Of course I need you,* you idiot, she railed inwardly.

John frowned and rubbed his ear. Simone must be in quite a tizzy. Either that or she'd dropped her receiver by accident. He peered at the pre-set numbers on his phone and pressed the button he wanted.

Chapter Twenty-Six

Holly was on a high. She whizzed round the flat in record time and sang loudly under her unpredictable shower. What a night it had been. They were all there; new authors and famous ones, renowned agents, the big publishers. She'd never had so many compliments and Jeremy Hide had invited her to dinner. Although she was flattered, she had shied away. That was how life should be, exciting and rewarding.

"Loved the recital," Terence said as they met outside their respective doors.

"Sorry! I forgot about those walls." They rarely disturbed each other.

"Don't apologise, I enjoyed it." He stood aside and Holly sped down the stairs. "How was the award night?" he panted as he caught up with her.

"Brilliant! Absolutely brilliant."

Terence smiled. Holly was positively sparking with high spirits.

"Are we still on for tonight?"

"You bet. I have *oodles* to tell you."

"See you at seven-thirty." Terence watched Holly

as she bounced down the road, her hair springing in time to her movements. Of all the fools in the world, Derek Grant had to qualify as the biggest.

Holly's plan of action was set. Today she would hand over her book. In the end she had done her own copy-editing and the manuscript, in Pagett's house style, was ready for typesetting. Holly quickened her step. She could hardly wait to give it to Jane Scott who had promised to read it before she began to typeset. They had similar tastes in reading and she trusted Jane to give her an honest opinion. Jane would be the first person to read the finished book and Holly could barely wait for her reaction.

Every doubt known to writers swept through her mind. What if her judgement was wrong, what if the book was no good? What if no one liked it? What if it bombed as Roland Green's books had done? What-ifs frolicked round her head like mischievous goblins. But the biggest what-if of all she refused to think about. It lay buried deep in her mind. *What if the author recognised the book?* She pushed the thought away.

"Hello, Holly." Lois was at her desk early.

"Hi, Lois. Did you enjoy yourself last night?"

"I had a ball. The *Jowardan* is always terrific."

"That's a good name for it," Holly laughed. It would take very little to make her laugh today.

"You looked fab last night, your gear was really cool."

"Thank you. You looked great too, especially that hair-do – Ivana Trump better watch out."

Lois grinned, wrinkled her nose à la Trump, and turned back to her newspaper.

"Jane in yet?" Holly asked.

"Uh uh, not yet."

"Marianna?"

"Nope."

"Anyone?"

"Nope, just you and . . . Oh, my God – listen to this."

"What is it?"

"Listen . . . " Lois insisted and read the article, not once, but three or four times as the crowd around her desk grew. They dispersed quickly when Simone arrived.

Holly followed Jane to the typesetting department.

"So what do you think of them little apples?" Jane demanded as she closed the door.

"I'm stunned," Holly admitted. "But I'm sure it's not true, it can't be. Arthur wouldn't fire Simone. We'd have heard, wouldn't we?"

"Who knows? Of course there was that bust-up between her and Roland. And Lois said that Simone had had some sort of disagreement with Arthur last week, before she went to Brussels."

"Yes, but . . . " Holly began.

"But what?"

Holly shrugged, she was impatient to discuss *Tomorrow's Joy,* not debate Simone's future. "We'll hear soon enough if it is true. Here's the diskette and the manuscript of my . . . eh, Emily Howard's book." She must stop referring to it as *my* book, or *my* MS. "Could you run me off another copy?"

"No problem," Jane agreed willingly.

"You will read it, won't you?"

"I'm looking forward to it." Jane slapped the manuscript on top of the pile on her desk.

Holly itched to tell her to treat it with special care but she mustn't draw any extra attention to the book. "Thanks, Jane," she said instead.

"Is Toni Johnson's MS nearly finished?"

"It's with the proof-reader now. It should be back in another couple of days then I'll give it a last check and let you have it."

"Good. Now scoot, I've loads to do."

Holly took one last lingering look at the manuscript and left.

The art department was busy but seemingly not too busy to discuss Trudy Friel's column. Holly didn't want to get involved in any more supposition. "I'll pop back later," she told Marianna. They really needed to make a start on the cover, time was running out. Only four months to publication, Holly thought with a shivery thrill. She sympathised with the author who had suddenly stopped writing, but had been delighted to grab the vacant slot. *Tomorrow's Joy* had been scheduled for Spring of the following year, but Simone had voiced no objection, and left Holly to make all the arrangements.

Holly smiled as she passed a small, tense, grey-haired woman, but the stranger regarded her stonily. Probably a nervous author, poor thing, but there was something familiar about her.

Holly found it impossible to concentrate. She swung her chair away from the computer screen and stared unseeingly at the plain wall. She usually did that when she needed to rest her eyes or to think. Was it possible that Simone's reign at Pagett *had* come to an end? Roland Green – *their sole editor?* Surely not. He disliked most – all – of the fiction they produced and never hesitated to voice his caustic opinion.

Holly let her thoughts stray, ideas take root. Could she replace Simone?

Her reverie was interrupted by Tim Brown. Unless she was editing, Holly liked to leave her door open.

"Holly, when you have a minute, Emily Howard hasn't signed her contract yet. When you're finished there, pop in to me, we need to discuss her advance."

Holly nodded silently. Contracts, advances – she'd only dealt with them occasionally. She'd have to sign Emily Howard's name – a false name. A fraudulent signature. Holly's toes curled in fear. Suddenly the ramifications were terrifying. What would happen when she received the advance, the royalties, how could she cash cheques made out to a fictitious person? Tim Brown would need Emily Howard's address, what address could she give him?

A dreadful sense of isolation gripped her, she had forgotten that sensation of loneliness, the alarm and dismay that had been so much a part of her life with Derek.

O, what a tangled web we weave, When first we practise to deceive! – the words mocked echoingly, and every nerve in her body screeched, *confess.*

185

Holly blessed the temporary break in thought as she waited for Liz's call to be put through.

"I couldn't wait to hear about last night, how did the suit look? How was your hair? Did everyone say you looked wonderful? And what's that article in this morning's paper all about?" said Liz, without pausing for breath.

Holly felt mean, but she wasn't in the mood to cope with Liz's rapid-fire questions. If only she could confide in her sister.

"Can I get back to you later?" Holly asked. "I'm up to my neck this morning."

"Of course. Bye."

Holly was awash with misery. Why hadn't she foreseen what would happen? Lies and more lies lay ahead. And to Liz of all people. How could she explain to Liz what she'd done when she didn't understand it herself? The advance, royalties – how could she account for the money?

"Stop!" Holly shook her head violently from side to side. "I've got to get out of here."

She left Pagett and walked blindly past offices and shops. She must think things through carefully while there was still time to back out.

Chapter Twenty-Seven

After lunch, rumours ran round Pagett faster than maple syrup down a clean shirt front. Lois's desk was surrounded but even she had no answers today.

"Roland Green came and went – like a whirlpool." Lois felt the onus on herself to give them some snippet of information.

"Whirlwind," Emma said.

"That too." Lois grinned, unfazed.

"Didn't Mrs Lord say *anything* to you?" Jane Scott asked.

"Yes. *Send for Simone Pearse. Ask Tim Brown to come to the boardroom.*" She gave a fair imitation of Amanda Lord's clipped tones.

"So you don't know why Tim has called this meeting?"

"No. Maybe to tell us that Simone has got her marching orders?" Lois suggested, helpfully. Simone had been acting so strangely all morning it wouldn't surprise her in the least. "She left at lunchtime with her hunky ex, she was wearing dark glasses." It wasn't much, but it was a bit of gossip.

"I bet he wasn't as handsome as the guy she picked up last night," Emma remarked sardonically.

"Did anyone find out who Ian Trent is?" Jane asked.

"Doesn't anyone have any work to do round here?" They leapt at Simone's voice.

"Do you know why we've been summoned to the boardroom, Simone?" Emma's brow was creased with concern, she needed her job. All morning she'd experienced a feeling of disquiet, nothing she could put her finger on, just a sixth sense that something was wrong.

Simone glanced at their anxious faces. "There are going be changes at Pagett, Tim will explain at the meeting." Why should she admit that she was as much in the dark as they were? She was on her way to the boardroom now in the hope that she would catch Tim Brown before the meeting started.

Simone sat at the head of the table. She still couldn't come to terms with John Barrett's about-face. One minute he was offering her her own publishing house, and now that the situation they'd discussed had become reality, he was practically ignoring her. Serve him right if his book suffered. The longer she lived the less she understood people.

"You're early, Simone," Tim Brown said as he swept into the room carrying a slim folder.

"Sit here," she said. She left Arthur Lord's chair and moved to the one next to it. Even at this late hour, it was important to her to establish rank.

"Right mess, isn't it?" Tim muttered as he searched through his folder.

"Mrs Lord was in quite a flutter this morning," Simone suggested casually.

Tim threw her a sharp look. "Don't let her fool you, she's the iron hand in the steel glove. Tough old bird. Here's the statement she wants me to read at the meeting, you might as well have a look at it now."

Simone didn't actually grab it, more wafted it out of his hand.

Due to ill health, Arthur Lord has made the decision to sell Pagett. Business will continue as usual until such time as a buyer is found.

During this period no new work will be accepted. No further contracts are to be issued.

Tim Brown is authorised to act on our behalf and will keep you informed of any developments.

Signed on behalf of Pagett Publications, Amanda Lord.

Simone read the brief communication with a stony face. "In other words thanks, and goodbye. No, not *even* a thank you. Does she expect everyone just to hang around and await her pleasure?"

"I suppose she's so wrapped up with Arthur . . . isn't thinking clearly," Tim said.

"I'd hate to meet her when she isn't muddle-headed, Lucretia Borgia would have been no match for her."

"We're all in the same boat, Simone, and some of

us have to row harder than others." He gave a half-grin at his pun but his tone was bitter. "Be thankful you only have yourself to think about. I have a wife and two kids to clothe and feed. And what about the others? They have commitments too."

Tim's mood had changed pretty rapidly, Simone thought, as she mumbled a vague agreement.

Tim glanced at the clock on the wall. "It's time," he said. He wasn't looking forward to this. He wished he had some answers for them, for himself.

A gasp, then shocked silence, greeted the short statement. Then everybody began to speak at once. Tim held up his hand for silence.

"I know as much or as little as you do. The way I see it, we can either hang in there and hope Pagett will be sold quickly or start looking for another job right away. I don't want to depress you, it's not going to be easy. You all know that with the breakdown of the Nett Book Agreement, publishing has been hard hit – there's a lot more firing than hiring going on at the moment. Obviously the decision is yours. I can't advise you. I'm sure that Mrs Lord will be in touch as soon as she can. In the meantime, I think we should put some money in the kitty and send Arthur some fruit and a get well card. That's about all for now, folks. Oh! – Simone, Kathy, Holly, could you come to my office in, say, half an hour? Bring your book schedules, would you?"

Holly nodded, then edged her way towards Danielle Peters, Tim's assistant. "Emily Howard hasn't signed her contract yet," she whispered.

Danielle nudged her. "Consider it done," she said in a low voice.

In spite of Tim's professed lack of knowledge, they all crowded around him looking for any vestige of hope that he could give them. Simone sat at the table. The same table she'd sat at more times than she could count. This was the first time she had seen all the staff gathered together in the boardroom – a room that meant more to her than her own living-room. But not everyone was there. Roland Green was missing. As the room emptied she asked Tim Brown, "Why isn't Roland at the meeting?"

"Haven't a clue."

"No doubt you saw the article in this morning's paper?" she asked. Was it really only this morning?

"Yes, I did. I presume it was Roland who fed her that rubbish. Come to think of it, he hasn't put in an appearance all week – except for last night at the awards and a couple of minutes this morning. According to our beloved Mata Hari at the front desk, he spent about two minutes with Amanda Lord and was not in the best of form when he left. Anyway it hardly matters now, does it?"

"It does to me, I'd like to find out once and for all who told Trudy those lies."

"Simone, you're not going to try and talk to Trudy Friel, are you?" There was a strange crusading look in her eyes. "Don't be a fool. Trudy will never divulge her source and, if you phone her, she won't hesitate to hang you out to dry."

Simone didn't reply. There were ways to get to

Trudy and she had just come up with one of them.

Trudy Friel smirked with satisfaction and pulled her notepad towards her.

Her article must have got up Simone Pearse's nose.

"Hello, Simone, what can I do for you?" She'd never liked the self-assured bitch.

"You could tell me who gave you that information," Simone asked lightly.

Trudy laughed. "Nice one. You know I'm not going to tell you that."

"Pity. Never mind. Your loss." Simone waited for the question that was sure to follow.

"Why, *my* loss?"

"I was prepared to do a trade."

"Trade?"

"Swap information."

"What kind of info?"

"You can't expect me to divulge that. Anyway you're not interested."

"Stop playing games. I might be interested, but it's difficult to judge if I don't know what you're offering."

"Stop press, inside information."

"Such as?"

Simone smiled, Trudy was biting. "Such as, if you don't want it, I'll give it to any other paper you care to think of."

"What information?" Trudy persisted.

"Up to the minute news about Pagett."

"*Have* you been fired?"

"Sorry to disappoint you, Trudy, no I haven't."

"Then Roland Green has?"

"No comment." Let her take what she will from that, two could play Roland's game.

"Well, what is it then?"

"Do we have a trade? And by the way, you don't quote me."

"I don't like this . . . all right, I'll trade, but I'm warning you, if you're making an ass out of me . . . beware."

"Would I do that?"

"Don't push it, Simone. *What's going on?*"

"You won't quote me?"

"I won't quote you." The woman was exasperating.

"You first."

"OK. I overheard Roland Green talking to the MD of Harbour Books last night. He said that you were for the chop and he'd be responsible for all the adult publications at Pagett. Sole editor."

"But I thought he actually *told* you that he'd been appointed."

"You didn't read the item properly. I merely repeated what I heard him say."

Simone caught her breath. It was obvious now. Roland had been doing a bit of self-promotion, pushing up his worth with Harbour. Suddenly she felt a lift.

"Your turn – now that I've sold my birthright."

"Arthur Lord is selling Pagett." Simone heard Trudy's whistle of surprise. "When did all this happen?"

"About ten minutes ago."

"Why?"

"Why, what?" Simone employed Lois's technique.

"Why is he selling Pagett?" Was Pearse really as thick as she appeared to be?

"Doctor's orders."

"Is he sick?"

"He's fine now. He had a . . . mild warning. He just wants to retire."

"Thanks, Simone. Not a bad swap, I suppose. But don't even think of talking to Roland Green about this. I'll deny everything and crucify you at the first opportunity. By the way, I've taped this conversation."

"So have I, Trudy. So we're both safe."

So she wasn't as daft as she liked to make out. "Not many flies on you, are there?" Trudy said grudgingly as she put down her phone.

Chapter Twenty-Eight

"Are you serious, Dad?" Sean Barrett asked.

"Absolutely. I've been thinking about getting into publishing for a while. According to Simone, things are tight financially at Pagett. That, plus the fact that Arthur Lord is anxious to get out, could make it a very attractive proposition for us," John Barrett explained.

"But we don't know anything about the publishing game. I mean, I know you're a writer, and a damn good one, but . . . "

"Don't worry, son, I didn't know much about the engineering business either when I started, but I managed. I learnt on the job."

"What does Simone have to say about all this?"

"Simone knows nothing about it. And I think it's better that way. Don't contact her, I'm not going to discuss this with her until, or unless, there's something concrete to tell her."

"How come?"

"I don't want to raise her hopes. Besides, it may all fizzle out to nothing. At this stage the fewer people who know of our interest, the better. Just let's get a team of auditors into Pagett and see what happens."

"OK. I presume you know what you're doing."

"I hope so."

"I must admit, I'm astonished that you want to go back into business. You're enjoying your freedom so much."

"That's true. But I'm not going back into business. I'll keep a watching brief but basically this is for you and Lucy. Don't worry, you won't be turfed in at the deep end, you'll grow into it. That is, if we're successful. They may be asking a ridiculous price, someone could outbid us. Pagett may be strapped for cash. They're not as big as some publishers, but pro rata, they do command a healthy share of the market. I think the quicker we move, the sooner we'll find out whether it's a viable proposition."

"I'll get on to it right away. By the way, did you see that article in this morning's paper?"

"The one about Pagett?" John asked.

"Yeh. I presume it's about Simone and Roland Green?"

"I'm sure it is. She didn't mention it when I spoke to her, so I didn't bring it up. And that's another reason why I'm hesitant to mention this to Simone. I'd like to find out if there is any truth in the rumour, and if so, why?"

"But from what you told me, Simone practically carries Pagett, single-handed," Sean said.

"Correction, that's what she implied," John explained. "I don't want to appear cynical but that's

just one of the many things that we need to find out
– officially."

"I'll contact Fowles and Rayburn, they're tough
negotiators and I can trust them to do a thorough
job. Madeline Rayburn is a wily operator."

"Do I know her?" John asked.

"You've met her – she hums to herself all the
time, has a face like a landfill."

John laughed. "I remember her now, she did
some work for us on the Preston contract?"

"That's her."

"God help Pagett and poor Tim Brown!"

"Will you be in London next week?" Sean said.

"I'll be there from Tuesday to Thursday."

"Good. There's someone I want you to meet,
Dad."

"Business or social?"

"Social."

"Male or female?" John persisted.

"Female. And don't tell Mum! She'll have me
married with two children by Friday!"

"I won't. Neither will I say that, at your age, I
was married with two children."

"Thank you, Dad. I *really* appreciate your not
saying that!"

"My pleasure. Any problems at Barretts, any news?"

"No. Everything's running smoothly – today!
How's the squatter?"

"Lucy's fine, she tells us she's working like a dog
for her exams."

"Send her my love if you speak to her. I'd better
get off the line now and try to collar Madeline."

"OK. I don't suppose it'll happen but if you could organise it so that we had some idea of what's happening by the time I get to London next week, we could make an appointment with whoever is acting for Pagett."

"I'll do my best," Sean assured him. 'Bye, Dad."

"Bye, Sean. Keep me in touch."

Chapter Twenty-Nine

Simone slid into the perfumed bathwater and closed her eyes. Not even the most fervent optimist could claim that the day had been a good one. The only positive aspect she could think of was that she hadn't been fired. Other than that, it had been downhill all the way. Mark's impending marriage had thrown her, she couldn't bear to think of him with someone else. The way he'd talked about Susie – she sounded as though she'd be the perfect little wife. Perfect but boring.

She reached the phone in time to hear Ian Trent leaving a message on the answer machine. Simone had placed him in her minus column, hadn't expected to hear from again.

"How are you feeling?" he asked.

"Fine, thank you." She supposed she should thank him for looking after her but she was in a cussed mood and, in her book, that meant never apologise, never explain.

"I know it's terribly short notice, but are you free tonight? Would you have dinner with me? I didn't expect to be in London or I would have phoned earlier."

"I don't think so, Ian, thank you. It's been a long day."

"And not a very nice one for you."

"Why do you say that?" she asked sharply.

"I read Trudy's column."

Was there anyone who hadn't read it? "It's utter nonsense, a Trudy fabrication."

"I'm not surprised. Roland Green isn't . . . " Ian stopped short.

"Is not what?"

"Sorry, I'm overstepping the mark. Forget it. Won't you change your mind? We could eat locally, there's a lovely little bistro just near you, Trudy's. Oh! I'm such a dipstick! Simone, that was so insensitive of me."

"It's OK." She laughed at his discomfort.

"I could pick you up in half an hour."

Maybe it would do her good to forget her troubles for a while and, if she remembered rightly, Ian was very easy on the eye. "Make it eight-thirty."

She sneaked a look over the top of her menu. Drink or no drink, he was certainly as handsome as she remembered, thoughtful too. They had by-passed Trudy's in favour of a comfortable grill-room which specialised in up-market fish and chips.

Simone looked about the room. The restaurant was attractively appointed in brushed-steel and pink, with enough space between the tables to allow privacy.

"This is nice. Have you eaten here before?" she asked.

"No, it only opened last week – in fact I've never known such a fast about-turn. It was intended as a steak house but the owners panicked when beef became such a no-no, and within a few days they were advertising it as the greatest fish and chip experience since Harry Ramsden's."

Simone ordered a grilled Dover sole and a salad while Ian settled for *filet du carrelet, avec pommes frites et petits pois*. They laughed at the pretentious translation of plaice, chips and peas. With a little persuasion, Simone agreed to a glass of white wine.

"I don't think you told me which publishers you're with?" she pumped as she took a tentative sip.

"Partingtons – we specialise in medical books," he explained as he saw her frown.

"What brought you to the Jordan Award?"

"The sales manager of Hedges is a friend of mine, they had a space at the table so I went along for the hell of it."

The sole was delicious and Simone realised she hadn't eaten all day. Her lunch-time sandwich had remained untouched and Mark knew better than to force her. Mark. Her heart gave a slight jolt. Soon he would be someone else's husband.

"How are things in the world of fiction?" Ian asked as he poked idly at a chip.

Had he heard about Pagett's demise? He couldn't have. Should she tell him or not? She was having difficulty making up her mind about anything tonight.

"Would you mind if we didn't discuss publishing?" she asked.

"Of course not. Tell me about yourself, instead."

"That's even more taboo at the moment." What a scintillating companion she was. If he skipped dessert and asked for the bill, she wouldn't blame him. "I'm sorry, Ian, perhaps I should have stayed at home tonight."

"I'm glad you didn't, solitude magnifies troubles."

Was he fishing for information or just being kind? What the hell, Pagett's sale would be public knowledge tomorrow anyway. Besides, if she appeared vulnerable, it might score some brownie points with him.

"Arthur Lord has decided to sell Pagett Publications and my ex-husband is getting remarried." Nothing like the short, sharp shock for attention grabbing. "I heard about Mark's . . . wife-to-be . . . last night, just before I left for the Awards." A bit of face-saving as to why she was drunk was no harm. It wasn't lying so much as altering the time scale a little. Ian looked upset.

"But that's *dreadful*, what will you do?" he asked.

His concern was touching. "I'll get over it. I suppose it was on the cards that he'd marry again."

"No, I mean where will you go if Pagett close down? Will you find another editing job?" All this work to get to her and now it was probably a total waste of time. "Will you stay in the same field?"

Simone frowned. Why was he so anxious that she should be employed?

"I really don't know what I'll do yet," she replied tersely. "We only heard about this today."

Ian reacted swiftly to her bristling tone. "I hope I haven't offended you, it's just that I know your reputation as an editor. You're highly respected. It would be such a loss to the profession . . . " he said smoothly.

He is concerned and I'm being paranoid, Simone told herself. "Don't worry, I have no intention of leaving publishing. But it's unsettling, that's all."

Ian's face cleared. "To say the least," he soothed. "Let's forget about Pagett. Do you want to hear about my trip to Liverpool today?"

Within a few minutes Simone was laughing heartily. He was a natural raconteur and obviously made the most of life.

" . . . and then I snapped open my brief case with a flourish, the sale was in the bag, but the presentation pack wasn't!" Ian slapped his hand to his head. "What an idiot, all that spiel and then no info. Now you know why my tour was cut short."

"I can imagine how you must have felt."

"A prize fool is how I felt," Ian admitted. Simone had warmed up considerably. He doubted if anyone could be that testy all the time, especially someone in her position. It would take time to get to know her, but that was all right.

When they arrived back at her flat, Ian asked the taxi-driver to wait. He had an early start next day. Simone wasn't sure if she was sorry or glad. It avoided the temptation of inviting him in for a night-cap.

"I'll phone you next week, if I may?" Ian said.

"Do." She smiled.

He bent forward and kissed her lightly on the forehead. "Thank you for a lovely evening."

Before she had a chance to reply he took the couple of strides to the kerb and hopped back into the taxi.

"The Barbican," he said and sat back with a satisfied smile. Brigette would be waiting.

Chapter Thirty

Holly escaped from the meeting as soon as she could. The walk at lunch-time had cleared her mind and the thought of *Tomorrow's Joy* lying discarded in a waste bin, or forced through the cruel blades of a shredder, was too much to bear. She must see the book in print.

Holly had been as stunned as everyone else to learn that Pagett Publications was on the market. Amanda Lord's statement had certainly sorted out her priorities – she must get the contract for *Tomorrow's Joy* into her hands as quickly as possible.

She pushed her way through the chattering staff and made her way along the corridor to her office. Danielle Peters was ready with a large brown envelope. "If anyone asks, you collected this earlier today," she warned.

"You're a love, I'm really grateful," Holly said as she hugged the envelope tightly.

"That book means a lot to you, doesn't it?"

"Emily Howard is a good writer." She always shrank a little when Emily Howard's name was mentioned.

"What do *you* think will happen to Pagett? To us?"

"I don't know. I suppose we'll be bought by another publisher – I hope."

Danielle stared hard at Holly. "Is that unlikely? Do you know something that we don't?"

"No, no. I was just wondering whether contracts that have already been signed will be honoured or if Pagett's new owners would be entitled to scrap them and start from scratch?"

"Who can tell? Maybe Tim would know. Why does he want to see you and Simone and Kathy?"

"He wants to go over the lists of forthcoming books. Perhaps that's a good sign."

"If you hear anything – *anything* – will you tell me?"

"It's a promise. And thanks again, Danielle."

Holly locked the contracts in her desk drawer. They would have to be signed with one of her carefully practised *Emily Howard* signatures, something she couldn't do now, it needed a steady hand.

The full impact of Amanda Lord's statement began to sink in. The day had started out so well but now she felt like a swatted fly. If Pagett was swallowed up by another publisher, what guarantee did she have that *Tomorrow's Joy* would ever be published? Less than two hours ago she'd been terrified of what would happen when the book was in print, now she was upset that it might never see the light of day.

"Grab a chair, Holly," Tim said as she joined Simone and Kathy.

"We need to sort out exactly which books are contracted and which we must put on hold."

"Can I go first?" Kathy asked. "I have an author due in about twenty minutes."

"Sure, fire ahead."

Holly listened to them discussing the children's list. Kathy, in her own unflustered way, had collected a fine stable of writers.

" . . . is almost finished, the illustrator should be ready by Friday and it's due to go to the printers on Wednesday week."

"What about *Lucky the Laptop Leprechaun*?" Tim asked.

"I'm just waiting for one amended illustration and it's complete."

"And *Basher's Last Bean*?"

"That was despatched yesterday."

"You seem to have everything under control. Any other problems?"

"Just the same one as everybody else." Kathy always kept her cool.

"Thanks, Kathy, that's all I need for now."

"Cheers." She smiled and left them to it.

"I might as well do your list next, Holly, it's shorter than Simone's," said Tim.

"OK. Toni Johnson's book is almost ready and Maria Stoppard's thriller is with Emma now. *Tomorrow's Joy* is ready for typesetting . . . "

"Hang on a minute, Emily Howard hasn't had her contract yet. That's one we can pull."

Holly's breathing stopped for a moment. "She *has*. You left them for me, told me to collect them this morning, remember?"

"Yes, I do, they must still be in the post bag . . . "

"No they aren't, I posted them myself at lunch-time." Holly was positive that he must have noticed her heightened colour and was grateful that Simone was preoccupied with her own thoughts.

"I haven't signed them, we could still cancel them."

"Don't do that to her, Tim. She has so little in life, let her have something to look forward to."

"Everything's such a mess at the moment I suppose one more cock-up won't make any difference. Get those contracts back here as fast as you can, I'll sign them. Amanda Lord would freak if she found out that we're still issuing them."

"I'll get on to that right away."

"It's open," Terence called, but his welcoming smile faded as he saw Holly's grim face.

"Something wrong?" he asked, his stirring spoon in mid-air.

"Loads wrong."

"Have a drink first?"

Holly groaned. "I forgot to buy wine."

"Not to worry, I have some. Would you like to open it while I stir, I'm afraid this will spoil."

Holly sniffed the contents of the pan. "That smells good, what is it?"

"Wait and see. Get the glasses and then tell me what ghastly happening removed the sunshine from your smile."

"I'm probably out of a job."

"How come?" No wonder she looked so down.

Chapter & Hearse

"Pagett Publications are selling out. Arthur Lord had a mild heart attack and wants to retire. His wife came in this morning, drafted a brief statement, and we were informed about his retirement this afternoon."

"That's awful," he sympathised.

"Yep. But maybe it'll turn out OK, they're looking for a buyer."

Terence moved about the tiny kitchen as Holly told him the full story. While she talked, Terence switched off the hob and removed a griddle pan from the small oven. The fillets of monkfish were attractively seared and Holly watched as he divided them between two plates and carefully spooned a pungent sauce round them. From another pan he produced tiny new potatoes and buttered and herbed carrots.

"That looks so professional," she admired as he put the plate on the table. It wouldn't be fair to tell him that she wasn't hungry. "Smells wonderful too."

"And you feel it's going to stick in your throat," Terence said as he put the wine on the table. "Pick what you want of it."

Holly smiled at him gratefully. She had never met anyone with such understanding. "You are wonderful, Terence Warren," she said.

Terence flushed. Praise from Holly was always a delight.

At first Holly struggled but the meal was so delicious, she soon cleared her plate.

"That was brilliant, chef. I'd have taken a bet that *nothing* could have tempted me tonight."

"Then make sure you leave a good tip!" he teased.

Terence tripped the switch on the kettle and busied himself preparing coffee. Holly watched his calm movements. Although he went to great lengths to hide his feelings, she guessed that she had come to mean a good deal to him. His long-term relationship with a nurse had broken up after four years and, as far as Holly could tell, he'd made no effort to pursue anyone else. She knew he was popular by the number of times his phone rang each evening, but he didn't appear to encourage people. Right from the start of their friendship she had followed his example; never question, never pry. She longed to confide in him and felt instinctively that if Terence knew about the book, he would conceal his disgust. He would discuss it with her rationally, support her in any way he could and advise her to come clean, confess all. But much as she yearned to share her secret it would be unfair to involve him in such duplicity.

Chapter Thirty-One

John Barrett believed in moving quickly and was pleased that Sean had arranged for him to phone Amanda Lord.

He introduced himself and told her briefly what he had in mind.

She heard him out.

"If I understand you correctly," she said, "you're proposing to offer us half the amount we're asking and, in return, we get to keep forty-nine per cent of the shares? Arthur would be a sleeping partner, take no active part in the running of Pagett?"

"That's correct. Basically Pagett would be run by its working directors. All you and Arthur would have to do is pick up the dividends."

"Tell me, Mr Barrett, what makes you think that you could turn Pagett into a worthwhile investment? How do you propose to increase the profits, make it a viable proposition? After all, my husband is an experienced publisher and the last couple of years have been extremely difficult." John's auditing team had scrutinised the books very carefully. He was aware of Pagett's sorry financial state.

"I appreciate that. I have several ideas, but there's no point in discussing them on the phone. But take your time, think about it, talk to Arthur. In short, you would receive a lump sum and still retain almost half the business. This would only apply to the UK company, of course."

"Do you plan to expand elsewhere?" Amanda asked.

"Ireland, possibly, but that's way down the line. Perhaps you would ring me and let me know what you decide? If Arthur is interested I'll explain my plans in detail."

"You understand that Arthur cannot take part in any complex talks, don't you? His doctors insist on a stress-free life and I intend to do everything in my power to see it remains that way."

"I take your point, but I'm perfectly willing to negotiate with Arthur through you."

"I'll talk to him and contact you later today."

* * *

The immaculate putting green was almost lost in a corner of the huge garden. John cast an appreciative eye over the house. Starched-apron white and red-roofed, it was almost dwarfed by its surroundings. He could hear the sound of unhurried footsteps crossing a wooden floor.

"Mr Barrett?"

John held out his hand to the woman whom he presumed was Amanda Lord. She returned his handshake with a firm grip.

212

"Come in," she invited and led the way through a wooden-floored, sunny hall to an even brighter garden room at the back of the house. "Arthur will be here in a moment, can I offer you some coffee or tea?"

"Coffee, thank you."

"Excuse me a moment, I'm sure the kettle's boiled by now."

John was delighted to be left on his own. From the corner of his eye he had glimpsed the sheen of water. He crossed to the window to have a proper look at the garden. It was enormous. Beyond the plant-strewn terrace that led down to a perfectly striped lawn, a blue-tiled swimming pool glittered in the sun. Magnificent herbaceous borders were already full of colour and, as John craned his neck to the right, he could just see a mesh-enclosed all-weather tennis court. How Eve would adore all this. As soon as he got home he'd get out the mower and give their grass a good scalping.

"Please help yourself to coffee," Amanda said as she set the tray on a table. "I'll go and see what's keeping Arthur."

John sat on one of the cushioned bamboo chairs and poured himself a cup of fragrant coffee. What a great place to sit and read a paper, he thought.

"He's on the way," Amanda said as she sized John up shrewdly. Their brief telephone conversation had impressed her. "As you've probably gathered, Arthur is rather in favour of your idea. But I really must inisist you keep your discussions . . . "

John leaned forward and gently touched her tiny

hand. "Please don't worry, Mrs Lord, I won't cause Arthur any distress."

She stared at him for a moment. "Call me Amanda."

"I'm bowled over by the garden, Amanda."

"Thank you." A smile unfroze her serious little face. "It's my abiding passion. I'd spend twenty-four hours a day there if I could."

"It looks as though you do. My wife is quite a keen gardener, I'm the odd job man, ours is tiny by comparison . . . " John jumped to his feet as Arthur appeared. Whatever his physical state there was nothing fragile about his appearance.

"John, good to see you again," he said cheerfully. He gripped John's hand firmly. "Please sit down."

Amanda fussed with the cups and saucers while Arthur settled himself on a bamboo lounger. "Your idea intrigued me," he began without preamble. "I gather you must have some magic up your sleeve, otherwise you wouldn't have proposed this half-share situation."

"I don't know about magic, but I do have plans."

"I'd like to hear them."

"I'd start by moving Pagett out of its existing building and utilising Barrett Engineering's offices – that would save a packet in rent. In the beginning I'd concentrate mainly on paperback fiction, then, when we were showing a healthy profit, I'd have a look at the hard-cover market again."

"Do you still intend to publish paperbacks in A and B format?" Arthur asked.

"Absolutely. The shorter, literary books are perfect for the larger B format, but the mass market books – like mine for instance – are much better suited to the smaller A."

"That sounds like a sensible way to tackle things. But I don't see how I fit into all of this," Arthur admitted.

He was pleased that John recognised the literary value of some of their authors; writers who would never grace a bestseller list but who wrote beautiful, flowing prose, poets who gave enormous pleasure to the all too few who bought their books. But, in the light of today's competitive market, and Pagett's losses, he was the first to admit that popular fiction was the way ahead.

"Obviously if you remain on as a major shareholder, it would mean a smaller capital outlay for me," John explained. "That money could be used to extend the fiction lists, allow me to spend more on marketing and publicity. From your point of view it would be a risk, I admit. But I don't intend getting involved in a loss maker. You would, of course, be free to do as little or as much as you felt like. I'd like to be able to call on your expertise and know that I'd benefit greatly from your experience. A sleeping partner in effect, that way your retirement would still hold good. Also I'm sure it would be handy to have the extra income – especially with all that to look after," John said craftily as he waved a hand in the general direction of the garden.

Arthur smiled. "That's true, now that I'm not

allowed to do any of the heavy work we'll need some extra help."

"You'd also have the satisfaction of remaining in the company you founded. I'm probably a sentimental old fool, but that would mean a lot to me," John said.

"You're hardly what I would describe as old or a fool, but I know what you mean. The offer is tempting, John, I must admit."

"Tell us more about your plans for Pagett," Amanda demanded. She had been so quiet John had almost forgotten she was there.

They listened intently to his every word.

In spite of Simone's character assassination, John had always respected Arthur and, since his arrival, Amanda had thawed conspicuously. He was careful now to address them both equally. Amanda would have as much say in the decision as Arthur, he was sure. More perhaps.

"You've certainly done your homework," Arthur approved as John showed his considerable knowledge of Pagett's financial shortcomings.

"One area where you would be of enormous help is in the choice of personnel – who to keep, who to let go." John frowned. Nothing concrete had been said but, if Arthur's questions were anything to go by, the deal appeared to be on.

A wide smile lit Arthur's face. "That would be a pleasure. I sat on the fence for so long I had stripes on my rear end. Do you plan to keep on all the staff?"

"Only those that you recommend. This would be a good time to dead-head."

Amanda snorted indignantly. "If you want to hang on to your health, take my advice, get rid of Simone Pearse and Roland Green. It's thanks to them that Arthur took ill." Her eyes hardened.

"That's not fair, Amanda," Arthur said quickly. "Simone has always done a good job, Roland too – until recently. We go back a long way, Roland and I," he explained. "But in publishing, as I imagine in all businesses, times change, tastes change and, unfortunately for Pagett, Roland didn't change with them. I found it very difficult to censure an old friend and colleague and I know I was criticised behind my back for not reprimanding him. I'm afraid he doesn't have much time for what he calls *Kleenex fiction*. That led to arguments between himself and Simone. He even had a go at poor Holly one day."

This more or less bore out what Simone had told him, also it explained the innuendo in Trudy Friel's column. Simone's job hadn't been in jeopardy.

"What do you think of Simone?" John asked.

Arthur stroked his chin. "Simone's all right – better than all right, she's totally dedicated. She's feisty, I admit, speaks her mind, but then you probably know that already."

John sat quietly for a moment. "In view of what you've said, I think that Roland Green would be happier elsewhere."

Arthur smiled again. Amanda saw that he was hugely enjoying himself and left them alone. She would have taken great pleasure in firing both editors.

"That's your prerogative," Arthur said. "Much as it grieves me to say so, I had reached the same decision. I was dreading having to tell him, but then I took sick and Amanda wouldn't allow me to even think about Pagett."

"What about Holly?"

"In my mind, a rising star. Confidentially, I think Simone is anxious to keep her where she is, which would be a shame. She's a very bright young woman, the best editorial assistant we've ever had – and quite capable of becoming an editor. Since she dumped that husband of hers she's a different person – pretty too!"

John hoped that all this talk wouldn't make Arthur's heart race.

By the time Amanda reappeared with a tray of sandwiches and some fresh coffee, John had a pretty fair idea of who was who at Pagett.

Amanda looked searchingly at her husband, then relaxed. John Barrett's visit had obviously done him no harm.

"What are you two up to?" she asked.

"Well, I don't know about John, but I'm having a marvellous time filling him in on everyone's strengths and shortcomings."

"And they say women are bitchy," said Amanda archly.

"They are! But we have our moments too." John helped himself from the tray.

He and Arthur arranged to put the matter into the hands of their solicitors. Barring any hitches, they hoped to conclude their transaction within a few days.

* * *

Jane Scott was the first of Pagett's staff to hand in her notice. Tim Brown couldn't blame her, although it would mean their production department would be severely hampered. The last few weeks had been a nightmare for Tim; endless queries from his anxious workmates, entreaties for any snippet of news, and wall-to-wall auditors. He'd given up trying to remember which publishers were represented by which eagle-eyed number crunchers. There were days when he felt as though he personally was on trial. Amanda Lord stolidly refused to give him any hint of what was happening. He warned her that the staff was becoming disheartened, but she didn't seem to care. *We must wait and see what happens* was all she would say.

Tim's patience was running short. "What is it now, Simone?" he snapped as she appeared in his office for the third time that day.

"It'll keep." She turned to leave, her excuses for visiting the accounts department *had* worn a bit thin.

"Hang on, I'm sorry, I'm feeling the strain a bit – a lot. If one more person comes in here and asks if there's any update, I'll throw the heaviest thing I can lift at them."

"I won't need to duck then, that's not why I'm here," Simone lied glibly.

"Thank goodness for that, so what can I do for you?"

"I heard about Jane Scott and wondered whether we could hire a replacement? Mandy won't be able to manage on her own and there are still quite a lot of books in the typesetting queue."

Tim sat back in his chair and linked his fingers behind his head. He noticed that Simone had expressed no personal regret about losing Jane. "I asked Amanda Lord the same question this morning and her answer was . . . "

"We must wait and see what happens," they chorused together.

"She's a bloody frustrating woman," Tim growled as his phone rang. "Yes, Lois? Who? OK, put her through."

Simone sat on the edge of Tim's desk and watched him. His face was creased in concentration, perhaps this was the long-awaited announcement.

"That was Amanda Lord," he explained as he replaced his receiver. "I've to go and see Arthur tomorrow. Keep that under your bonnet, Simone, it may be nothing. I don't want anybody to think that there are developments if there aren't."

"I won't say a word. If you get a chance, ask Arthur what we do about replacing Jane." Even now Simone wasn't prepared to let things slide.

Chapter Thirty-Two

Tim followed more or less the same route that John Barrett had taken the previous day. Paranoia best described the mood at Pagett during the last few weeks. He had made up his mind, today he would ask for answers. Amanda Lord had made it quite clear that Arthur mustn't be upset in any way. Why should Arthur expect to be upset? Only bad news caused upsets. He wound down the window and switched on the car radio. The rap made his nerves jangle so he switched it off. He was prepared to wait just one more week, then he'd start contacting employment agencies. He'd had always been content at Pagett and, although his position was demanding, he enjoyed the bustle. They were a good bunch to work with. Except perhaps for that shit, Roland Green. Roland didn't single out anyone specifically, he was obnoxious to everybody but Simone Pearse was the person least likely to get his last Rolo, Tim thought with a smile. They hated each other, those two.

He was pleased by Amanda Lord's welcome. Up

until now she had been extremely abrupt with him. But in fairness to her, she'd probably been very frightened by Arthur's attack.

"He mustn't have any stress," she warned in a whisper, then her voice returned to normal. "Arthur's in the garden room."

Tim nodded. He was pleasantly surprised to see Arthur looking so well. The strain of years seemed to have dropped from his face.

"Tim! It's good of you to come. Take a seat."

Tim looked around him.

"I call it my tropical rain forest," Arthur said as he noticed Tim's interest. "If Amanda's been watering the overhead plants you can get a sudden sluice of water down the back of your neck."

Tim smiled warmly at his boss. "It's marvellous to see you looking so well. We were all really sorry that you had . . . " He fumbled for the right words.

"*Had* is the operative word, Tim. I'm fighting fit again and intend to stay that way. That's why I asked you to come today. I think we have a buyer for Pagett, one that will please you."

Amanda carried in the tray.

"I can't imagine *anyone* new pleasing me," Tim said as he rose to help her. He liked Arthur enormously, he was a gentleman in every sense of the word. That was his trouble.

"It's kind of you to say that, but I'll still be around on a consultancy basis."

The scones were warm from the oven and the raspberry jam reminded Tim of his childhood. "I haven't tasted jam like this for years," he told Amanda.

"Amanda grows the raspberries herself," Arthur said proudly.

Her face softened. She could see that Tim's visit wasn't going to present any problems. "I'm going to do some work in the garden, call me if you need me," she smiled.

"We will," said Arthur and turned his attention back to Tim. "Before I tell you who Pagett's new owner is to be, I must ask you to keep it confidential – until the contract is signed."

"Of course."

"It's John Barrett."

Tim's eyebrows knitted in a frown. "You mean . . . our John Barrett? John Barrett the author?"

"The same." Arthur smiled as he watched Tim's bewilderment.

"But he's a writer, not a publisher."

Arthur laughed out loud. "You look shocked, Tim."

"Stunned! John Barrett, I can't believe it. I thought it would probably be that American firm, Pages Inc, their auditors came back three times."

"John's offer was similar and, quite frankly, I like the man. Even more confidentially . . . " Arthur hesitated until Tim nodded his assurance. "If John takes over, I will retain an interest in Pagett. To be honest, I would find it difficult to sever my ties with Pagett."

"I'm sure you would," Tim said.

"So when John came up with his offer, I was

223

delighted. I'll be able to bumble around giving unasked-for advice, but without any of the headaches."

Arthur could see his bombshell had really shaken Tim. "More coffee?" he asked.

Tim nodded. This could be disastrous for Pagett or an excellent move. He couldn't make up his mind which.

"First reactions?" Arthur asked after a short silence.

"Either he'll revolutionise Pagett or we'll go to the wall."

"He's confident. I've listened to his ideas and I think you'll be pleasantly surprised. Also he'd be able to give Pagett the financial injection it needs."

"What about the staff? What does he propose to do about them?" Tim asked.

"That's up to John."

Tim looked worried.

"Strictly between ourselves, Tim, there's no reason for you to be distressed," Arthur assured him. "But I must let John speak for himself."

A weight fell from Tim's shoulders. He hated to adopt an I'm-all-right attitude but that's exactly how he felt.

"How are you managing?" Arthur asked, lazily munching a scone.

"Everything's running smoothly . . . no major problems."

"And minor ones?" Arthur guessed shrewdly.

"The only . . . " Suddenly Tim remembered Amanda's warning. "Nothing I can't handle."

"Amanda's warned you off, hasn't she? She tends

to be a bit over-protective at the moment. But I'm still your boss, so out with it, Tim."

"Jane Scott has found herself a new job. That leaves Mandy to do the typesetting on her own. She's quite competent at that but she really doesn't know how to cope with type faces, paper selection, print size, deadlines, the printers – all the things that Jane usually deals with."

"So what are you saying?"

"I'd like your permission to hire someone else, someone with experience. A temp might do. We'll all miss Jane terribly, she's so much part of the team."

Arthur ran his thumb up and down his neck. "Leave that to me," he instructed.

"Thank you. I hate to burden you," Tim said guiltily but only Arthur could make the decision.

"I'm just as anxious as you are that things run smoothly, I always will be," Arthur said as he stifled a yawn.

Tim looked at his watch. "Time for me to head back." He could see that Arthur had begun to droop. "I hope everything works out the way you want it to. It goes without saying that I'll respect your confidence, have no worries on that score."

"I know you will. The moment I have the all-clear from my solicitors, I'll let you know. And don't worry about Jane, I'll look after that."

On the way back the radio didn't bother Tim, on the contrary, he sang along to the music and looked forward to his future.

• • •

He guessed it would be Simone at his door. She probably had Lois on lookout duty.

"Well?" She nervously twisted her fingers.

"No news yet but there are several possibilities," Tim said. A promise was a promise.

"So why did he want to see you?" she asked suspiciously. "He could have told you that on the phone."

"He needed to check some financial details, find out how we stood with the bank."

"Did he say who those possibilities were?"

"He said he'd let me know as soon as he had a buyer." At least that part was true. He hated lying to her but it shouldn't be long before they had their answer.

"Did you ask him about replacing Jane?"

"Yes, I did. He said he'd look into it and let me know."

"*Everything* is bloody well on hold," she grumbled.

"It'll be sorted eventually. In the meantime let's get the priority books on the move – while Jane's still around. We can worry about the rest later."

"I think I'll put John Barrett's book to the back of the queue." Simone was still furious with him.

Tim bit his tongue.

"Why John's book?" he asked nonchalantly.

"Because I feel like it," she said spitefully.

"Come on, don't be silly. John hasn't done you any harm, has he?"

"He hasn't done me any good either," she snapped. If Tim knew about John's retracted offer maybe he'd share her view.

"His books have always been good sellers," Tim argued. "Don't lose heart, I'm sure we'll hear something very soon."

She shrugged and flounced from the room. He wished he could tell her the truth but, if he did, Arthur would never trust him again.

Holly wasn't in her office and he found her sitting on Jane's desk.

"I needed to check Lucinda Rockingham's publication date with you," he said. "Also find out how Emily Howard's book is progressing."

"It's coming along just fine," Jane answered for her. "And it's a *terrific* story." Jane had promised Holly that she would see the book finished no matter what.

"Lucinda is early July – the eleventh I think," Holly said, pleased by Jane's enthusiastic interjection.

"OK. Jane, I think we should put Lucinda at the end of the list for the moment, there's only so much we can do."

Jane flushed. "I feel so dreadful leaving you like this, but I *have* to have a job."

Tim squeezed her shoulder lightly. "It's not a rebuke, Jane. But we must make sure that the books are typeset in order of publication, otherwise we'll end up in a mess."

Tears stung her eyes. "I'd give anything to stay."

Tim gave her a sympathetic smile. Maybe Arthur would come up with an answer.

Arthur did, just as Tim was leaving for home. "Offer Jane a rise and promote her to production manager."

"Arthur, that's terrific! She's in bits about leaving. But how do I tell her without giving the game away?"

"You don't. Tell her that I was upset to hear that she was leaving and most anxious that she should stay with Pagett. Knowing Jane as I do, you can trust her not to tell anyone of her promotion until the time is right. All she needs to say is that she changed her mind."

"I'll tell her right away. The mood is so black here it'll be nice to be able to put a smile on someone's face."

Tim raced along the corridor to the production department. "Jane," he called as he pushed open the door. She was slumped across her desk crying like a tap.

"Dry those tears, I've got some good news for you," he said.

She shot up into a sitting position. "We've got new owners?" she asked.

"Not quite. But I've just spoken to Arthur Lord and he's offered you the position of production manager and an increase of a thousand pounds a year to go with the job."

Jane stared at him dully. "But I don't understand, what difference does it make? We mightn't be here next month, never mind next year."

"I think you can trust Arthur."

Something in Tim's voice silenced her. Was he trying to tell her something?

"Come on, what do you say?" he urged.

"I say it's a wonderful offer."

"Keep it to yourself until you hear otherwise," Tim warned.

"No problem, I swear it on the bestseller list!"

Tim laughed. "If anyone asks, you changed your mind, couldn't bear to leave Pagett."

"OK." She winked at him conspiratorially.

Chapter Thirty-Three

Holly recoiled as she recognised the neat, tight writing on the envelope. Derek! Just when she'd begun to push him to the back of her mind. She picked up the letter and turned it over. The back of the envelope was blank, no sender's name or address, no clue as to its contents. Derek had ruined far too many days of her life already, he wasn't going to wreck this one. The letter could wait. She flung it unopened on to a chair.

Holly was unaware of the smiles of passers-by as she breezed along the road, her eyes shining, hips swinging. Within the hour the typeset book would be in her hands. Never again would she be blasé about an author's excited response to that first glimpse of the typeset pages. She was pleased that they'd chosen Penelope Heath to do the proof-reading. Penelope could spot an inconsistency from a mile away and, to her, typos shone like beacons. It should take her only three or four days to proof the book, then Jane would make the final corrections. If everything went smoothly, *Tomorrow's Joy* would be on its way to the printers by the end of next week. Holly had not yet learned to think of the book without a pang of conscience. But the alternative – a black bag full of shredded pages – went a long way to ease her pain.

At her neat desk in the reception area, Lois was smiling brightly. "Meeting tomorrow, five o'clock," she said in answer to Holly's greeting. She loved the way everybody practically skidded to a halt when they heard that.

"Good news?" Holly asked – just as all the others had done.

"Who knows?" Lois adopted an air of mystery. The truth was that Tim had threatened to bop her on the head if she said one word about the meeting.

"You *must* know," Holly wheedled.

"Not a thing," Lois said with an infuriating smile. "I'm afraid the matter is not open for discussion."

"Can't you give me a *hint*?" Holly begged.

"Sorry, Holly, I'm afraid not." In spite of her frustration, Lois was pleased that, if nothing else, she was able to lift the mood of depression. But even she wasn't sure what was in the air. She was still trying to sort out several puzzling events which had taken place the day before. John Barrett had spent his time on the phone with Tim Brown, not Simone. Roland Green snapped her head off when she phoned to tell him that he would be expected at Pagett at four o'clock tomorrow, but that wasn't unusual. Why did he have to be there an hour earlier than anyone else? she wondered. Before she'd recovered from that, Lucinda Rockingham had

rung and positively barked at her and Tim Brown
had asked, several times, for an outside line. That
was unusual. Things were definitely buzzing at
Pagett. She could throttle Tim. How could he deny
her such a gorgeous, meaty subject for one of her
lingering gossip sessions? But Tim probably *would*
cosh her or, worse still, fire her, so she had to
contain herself.

Holly went straight to the typesetting
department. The pages looked so different now, so
professional, nothing like the large, double-spaced
type she was used to seeing on her laptop. The
text was almost lost in the centre of the wide-
bordered pages. There were no acknowledgements,
just a dedication. Holly had thought long and hard
about this. In fairness to the unknown author and
in keeping with the story, she'd dedicated the book
to *Single Parents Everywhere*. She turned quickly to
the back of the bundle, four hundred and eight
book pages, so different in total from the
manuscript.

"Doesn't it look *wonderful?*" she asked Jane
Scott.

Jane shrugged. "What's with you, Holly? It's no
different from any other book."

Holly bit her lip. If she kept on making inane
remarks like that she couldn't fail to arouse
suspicion.

"It's the first time I've had full responsibility for a
book," she explained earnestly. "I suppose I feel
sorry for Emily Howard and want to it be special."

Jane smiled at her fondly. "You're a real softie,

Holly, but I suppose in this cynical world of ours that's very refreshing."

"Let's phone the couriers and get this off to Penelope right away, I'll give it the final check when she's finished and then it's all yours," Holly said, her cheeks flushed with embarrassment.

"Will do. You've heard about the meeting, of course? Who do you suppose is going to take over Pagett? The American firm?" Jane asked.

"I haven't an idea. We don't really know if that's the reason for the meeting."

"It must be. You only have to look at Lois's stupid grin. She's bursting to discuss it all – but apparently Tim's muzzled her good and proper."

"That's a first," Holly laughed.

"I'll try her again at lunch-time, wear her down," Jane promised wickedly. The moment she heard about the meeting, Jane had come to the conclusion that her appointment must have been approved by the new owners – God bless them, whoever they were.

"I don't think she'll tell this time," Holly conjectured. "Still, we've only got another twenty-four hours to wait and then all will be revealed – or not!" Holly was so hyped-up about the book she found it difficult to be miserable.

In the art department, Marianna Berry was pinning illustrations to the big notice board. They had discarded the idea of using a photographic model and agreed that a brightly-coloured illustration would be best for the cover.

"Hi, Holly. The drawings have arrived, come and see," Marianna invited.

Holly crossed to the board, she was almost afraid to look.

"They're *fabulous!*" she said excitedly. "Even better than I dared hope."

"That's what I thought," Marianna agreed.

They were still staring at the coloured sketches when Jeremy Hide, their marketing manager, popped his head round the door.

"Come and see these," Holly said delightedly.

"I must say Gemma has surpassed herself this time." Jeremy shook his head as he examined the illustrations. "I envy people who are able to draw and paint like this. Just look at those faces, full of pathos yet not in the least depressing. They're fantastic."

They stared at the illustrations.

"I think I'll get you the magnifier," Marianna said.

She passed the magnifying glass to Holly. "Take your time."

Holly looked carefully at every line of the drawings, every nuance. "I've made my choice," she said five minutes later.

"What's the verdict?" Jeremy asked.

Holly shook her head. "Not yet. Tell me which you prefer," she said as she passed him the glass.

Jeremy studied the designs. "OK. Your turn, Marianna."

"I know which is my favourite."

All three of them had made the same choice.

They agreed that it was the jumble of children that had swayed them. Marianna removed the three drawings which they'd rejected and they crowded around the remaining illustration with smiles on their faces.

"Look at the frazzled expression on the mother's face." Marianna's artistic eye was spot on as usual. "This will make a wonderful cover, Holly. I think we've picked a real winner."

"I agree," Jeremy said. Mentally he was already planning his presentation.

"What happens next?" Holly asked. Although she'd worked in publishing for years, she still wasn't used to the process.

"We select a typeface, decide whether the title or the author's name goes at the top. I don't think that we could better the colours that Gemma has chosen, do you?"

"They're perfect," Holly agreed. "On a white background?"

"Yes. A nice glossy white . . . black type, embossed, yes?"

Again they all agreed.

"Then what?" Holly wanted to know.

"The illustration is sent to the bureau – the reproduction house," Marianna explained.

"And they print it?" Holly asked.

"No. They put it on to a large glass drum and scan it. Then it's returned to us on disk. We bring it up on the computer screen and check the results. At that stage we add the typography – the title, author's name, the blurb, newspaper or magazine quotes if there are any. When we're satisfied with that we send the disk back to the repro house. They run out films and when we've given it a final check, the films are sent to the printers."

"I'm ashamed that I'm so ignorant," Holly admitted. "I've never taken much notice of anything except the manuscripts. Simone always took care of the rest."

"As soon as proof copies of the book are ready, I'll get them to the journalists and magazines for comments," Jeremy promised. "We must set up another marketing session with Annabelle and the rest of the sales people and make a final decision as to how we present the book. But let's get tomorrow's bash out of the way first. How about first thing on Friday – if we're still in existence?"

"Fine by me," Holly said calmly, but longed to do it right away.

"Right you two, off you go. I've got a ton of work to do," Marianna said. She dismissed them from her mind as she returned to her littered desk. Holly wondered how she could ever manage to find anything in that muddle of photographs, colour swatches, author blurbs, and general papers. But she knew Marianna produced brilliant covers.

Holly's office seemed quiet by comparison. She inserted a disk into her word processor and, with a grimace of distaste, began to edit. She wasn't enjoying the book and was surprised that Simone had accepted it. Simone couldn't have read it properly before passing it on to her. She was tempted to print out the first fifty pages and dump them on Simone but with all that was going on, that mightn't be such a good idea. After all, as Tim said, by this time on Friday they could be out of business.

It was her weekend to stay with Liz and Robert, and she could hardly wait. She *must* remember to tell Terence that she'd be home late tomorrow – her turn to cook dinner. Perhaps she'd take him out instead. If the news was good she would feel like celebrating, if it was bad, she certainly wouldn't feel like cooking. Terence was so good-natured, he would fall in with whatever she suggested, whatever was easiest for her. So unlike Derek. Her thoughts flew back to the unopened letter which she'd casually tossed aside. She still had that to face.

Holly turned back to the screen with a sigh and, after a couple of minutes, was thoroughly muddled. A new character had appeared from nowhere, one that sent her whizzing back through the computer pages to find out if she'd missed something. The story no longer made sense. She pressed her save button, typed in the numbers of the pages she wanted to print and lazily watched the sheets pile up in the out-tray.

Simone's office door was open for a change. She had pushed her chair back from her desk and, lost in thought, was clacking a pen up and down between her teeth. Holly stood quietly in the doorway. Simone was probably as jittery as the rest of them. Holly had no way of knowing that Simone was compiling a list of ingredients for the dinner she was going to make. Her first time to cook a meal for Ian Trent. "Can you spare a minute?" she finally asked Simone.

"Sure," Simone said as she saw the puzzled look on Holly's face. She put down her pen and slid the chair back to her desk.

"It's this book, I'm having a problem with it. It's not . . . your usual style," Holly said as tactfully as she could.

"Show me."

As Simone read the first few pages, her frown deepened. "I *hate* this. Where did it come from? It isn't one of mine, I've never seen it before. It's more like one of those awful books Roland turns out – all those long descriptive passages that lead nowhere. Where did you get it?"

"It was on my desk, marked urgent."

"Not one of mine, Holly."

The two women looked at each other. Surely Roland wouldn't have had the nerve to sneak it in? He always used his own assistant, a free-lance editor who worked from home.

"I wonder if Roland's assistant has done a bunk?" Simone mused. "Not that I'd blame her one bit."

"I *knew* that it wasn't your sort of book. I've never heard of the author, have you?"

Simone shook her head and pursed her lips. "I'll swing for that man one day. What does he think he's playing at, wasting your time like that? He's hardly put in an appearance for weeks."

"Oh I don't care, I'm just glad to be rid of it," Holly said with relief.

"Heard anything else about tomorrow's

meeting?" Simone probed reluctantly. She disliked being kept in the dark as much as the rest of them.

"Nothing." Holly shook her head.

"Heaven knows what Tim said to Lois, I've never known her so tight-lipped."

Holly smiled, everyone had wondered the same thing.

"Would you fancy a sandwich at lunchtime?" Simone suggested.

A year ago Holly would have died for an invitation like that but today she planned to bank the advance she'd received for *Tomorrow's Joy*. The cheque lay accusingly in her bag and she needed to be rid of it.

"I'd love to but I'm afraid I can't." She didn't elaborate. Again, pangs of guilt attacked. Simone would have a fit if she knew why she'd refused.

"Some other time." Simone stretched and ran her fingers through her hair. "Leave these pages with me and drop the diskette back, I'll tackle Tim about this." This would be the perfect excuse to visit him. She hadn't seen Tim since the meeting had been announced. Also it would serve as another useful black mark against Roland.

* * *

Peter Flood stood behind the shuttered blinds of his office and ate his lunch. He never ordered anything with garlic on Wednesdays – the day Holly Grant paid her weekly visit to his bank. He'd made up his mind that he would take the plunge today and invite her out. On his security monitor he could see customers queuing at the busy counters, nevertheless he gave the blind a nervous tweak to make sure that he didn't miss her.

There she was. He threw the end of the pitta bread into his wastepaper bin and hastily wiped his chin on the soggy paper napkin. He smoothed his hair, then sauntered casually towards the counter.

"Mrs Grant!" he declared in a surprised voice. The tellers either side of the counter exchanged grins. Peter was so predictable.

"Hello, Mr Flood." She smiled warmly at the manager who had always been so helpful. "I was hoping to see you today, I'd like to bank a cheque for the friend I told you about."

"Come into my office, we can discuss it there."

More knowing winks passed between the tellers. The man behind Holly muttered sourly about the equality of the sexes.

Peter dusted the chair with a clean handkerchief and felt like a fool.

"It gets very dusty in here," he said.

"I'm sure, all those machines . . . " Holly could see he was nervous and hoped he hadn't changed his mind. It was difficult enough to take the money, but banking it in a fictitious name was another thing. Pure, unadulterated fraud, she reminded herself.

"Emily Howard's cheque has arrived. Remember? I promised to do her banking for her?"

"Certainly, I do. That's fine." Normally he wouldn't have agreed to open an account for someone he'd never met, it was against all the rules. But anyone with half an eye could see that Holly Grant was totally trustworthy. Besides, the cheques to be lodged in Emily Howard's deposit account would all be issued by the publishers for whom Holly Grant worked. How kind she was to look after Mrs Howard like that. He couldn't begin to imagine the misery of being stuck indoors for the rest of his life, how sad for the poor woman.

Holly opened her bag and passed him the cheque. He smiled at her as he pressed a button on his intercom.

"Can you deal with this, Debbie, please," he said to the slim, young woman who answered the summons. "A deposit account has been set up for Mrs Emily Howard. Make a note, please, Mrs Grant will deal with all her transactions."

Holly recognised Debbie, she'd handled lodgements for her several times in the past year.

"It won't take long," he explained as Debbie closed the door. He cleared his throat nervously. "I was wondering, Mrs Grant . . . or may I call you Holly?"

"Of course, please do," Holly agreed.

"I have seats for the theatre . . . on Saturday . . . and I . . . I thought you might care to join me." For a decisive man, with a highly responsible position, he knew he was acting like a stammering schoolboy.

"I would have liked that," Holly said with a smile, "but I'm spending the weekend with my sister and her husband in the country."

Peter Flood's face fell. There were a dozen woman who would be happy to go with him, but they were not Holly Grant.

"Perhaps another Saturday?" he suggested.

"Thank you, but I'm afraid I spend all my weekends with them." Holly appreciated all the help and sympathy that he'd given her, especially in the early days of her separation, but the further away from this man and her guilty conscience she could get, the better. She was sure that if she did accept an invitation go out with him it would only be a matter of time before she tripped herself up.

"Mid-week, maybe?" he persisted.

Holly titled her head to one side and frowned. "It's really so kind of you," she said. "Unfortunately it's always so late by the time I'm finished . . . "

She was grateful for Debbie's knock at the door. Holly put Emily Howard's deposit book in her bag and stood up to leave. "I'm sorry that we couldn't get together, but thank you for asking me." Holly hoped that her message had got through, to him.

"I'm sorry too." He smiled understandingly. Obviously she hadn't recovered enough from her marriage break-up to become involved with anyone else yet – scars like hers took time to heal. He would give her time. Try again after a few months.

Holly made her escape as gracefully as she could. As she walked along the busy street, she saw nothing, no one. To her great disappointment the bank-book in her bag was no less recriminatory than the cheque had been. And now that she came to think about it, how could it be?

Holly dumped her heavy bag on the floor and knocked on Terence's door. There was no answer. She wanted to tell him about tomorow's meeting and about the cover for her . . . *Emily's* book. There I go again, she sighed.

She refused to open Derek's letter until after she'd eaten, not that her meal was up to much; some left-over salad, an over-ripe wedge of Brie and a slightly bruised apple. She heated up a couple of frozen bread rolls and made a pot of real coffee. What would Derek make of this little banquet? She shuddered to think.

If only she had the strength of character, she'd ignore his letter, at least until after tomorrow. But grudgingly she admitted defeat and began to tear at the flap of the envelope. As the paper ripped she could hear the rattle of keys and the sound of Terence's door.

She dashed into the hallway. "I'm glad you're back. I wanted to tell you that I'd be late tomorrow," Holly said breathlessly.

"My meeting this afternoon went on a lot longer than planned so I had a bite to eat with the client. But don't stand there, come in," he invited.

"Are you sure?"

He gave one of his eyebrow-waggles. "I'm always game to entertain a lovely lady in my den of iniquity."

Holly collected her key and closed her door.

"What a day!" she said as they waited for some coffee to perk. "They've called a meeting tomorrow afternoon at five o'clock. We couldn't get any more than that out of Lois, but the general buzz is that tomorrow we'll find out who the new owners of Pagett will be."

"I'm delighted, it's been a nerve-racking wait, hasn't it?"

"I suppose. I've been so busy with the book I haven't really given it much thought."

Terence knew that was true. He'd been slightly surprised by Holly's single-mindedness, she was totally wrapped up in that book. He didn't want to dampen her spirits but, if Pagett ceased to exist, then so too would the book and her job.

"You should have *seen* the illustration for the cover, Terence, it's wonderful," she said dreamily.

She looked wonderful, her whole face alight. He wanted to sweep her into his arms, hug her.

"Is that what you have there?" He pointed to the folded paper in her hand. She had almost forgotten about the letter, crumpled and still tightly clutched in her fist.

Her enthusiasm vanished and the corners of her mouth drooped. "No. It's a letter from Derek."

"Oh?"

"It came this morning but I didn't open it, I was just about to when I heard you."

Terence refilled their cups. It wasn't up to him to give advice but, if he'd been in her position, he would have handed it straight to his solicitor.

"Would you read it?" she asked plaintively.

"Are you sure? It might be private."

"I've no secrets from you." Except one, she added to herself.

"OK. Here we go. *My dear Holly . . .* "

"Huh! *My dear Holly,* indeed. Hypocrite," she snorted.

Terence began again. *"My dear Holly, I suggest that we meet to discuss the subject of divorce. Obviously I haven't made myself clear, I will not negotiate through solicitors or any other third party. But I have a proposition to put to you and it will be well worth your while to hear it. If next Wednesday, at 8 pm, suits you, we could meet here at the flat. Sincerely, Derek. PS Do not bring The Bitch with you, or anyone else. This matter is private and between ourselves."*

Holly stared at Terence in alarm. "I can't go, I don't want to see him again," she wailed.

"You don't have to. Give the letter to Vincent Harper, he's your solicitor, let him deal with it."

"But you read what the letter said, he won't negotiate through solicitors. Perhaps *Derek* is scared – of Bunny Bly's husband – I mean," she babbled.

Vincent Harper had refused to allow her to accuse Derek of adultery.

"We need definite proof," he'd told her.

Holly had been totally opposed to having Derek followed but she'd sensed Vincent's growing impatience with her. Finally, fearing that he would refuse to represent her at all, she agreed to his plan but on condition that the surveillance lasted no longer than one week. She was terrified of running up a huge bill. But her fears were unfounded. On the second night of his vigil the detective managed to sneak several excellent photographs of Bunny Bly entering and leaving Derek's flat.

Holly thought that she'd got over her fear of Derek, yet here she was quaking at the thought of spending any time in his company.

"It's up to you to decide, Holly." Terence said.

"I know," said Holly. "I don't want to meet him but perhaps he'll agree to a divorce now. I should go and hear him out. I definitely don't want him anywhere near my flat again, once was enough."

"Why can't he just contact you through your solicitor, why does he have to see you in person? I don't like it, Holly."

"Nor do I, but you don't know how intransigent Derek can be. Even though he's guilty of having an affair with Bunny Bly he's probably not prepared to lose face."

"No, he's just content to ruin *your* face – the vicious sod," Terence said acidly. "Holly, you don't have to reply immediately. Sleep on it. Perhaps in the morning you'll have a clearer picture. But if you do decide to meet him, I'm going with you." Terence held up his hand as she started to object. "Don't worry, I'll wait outside. At least that way, if there's any trouble, I'll be near by. You can always throw something through the window to get my attention – Derek for preference."

"You're so good to me," Holly said. She stood up to go and, on an impulse, leaned over to kiss his cheek just as he turned his head. Their lips met and, in that brief moment, Holly was aware of all Terence's pent-up yearning and tenderness.

"Goodnight," she said softly and fled.

. . .

Simone sprayed perfume in the general direction of her ears, on her wrists and behind her knees. After one last glance in the mirror she dashed into the kitchen to put the finishing touches to her well-disguised meal. Although they'd howled with laughter at the time, she had never forgotten the experience of one of her college friends, a hopeless cook who wanted to impress a new and sophisticated male friend. She had bought the best of everything in, ready-prepared food from Marks and Spencer. The dinner was an unqualified success. Over coffee they discussed her studies, then she asked him what he did for a living. "I'm a food buyer for Marks and Spencer," came the reply.

Simone wafted to the door on a cloud of Hermès. She had bought the soft, clingy dress especially for tonight. Ian whistled his appreciation as he handed her two bottles of ready chilled wine.

"I'll put one in the fridge, why don't you open the other?" she suggested nervously. It was a long time since she'd entertained, even longer since any man other than Mark had crossed her doorstep. For a second she thought of Mark and his wife-to-be, with regret.

"OK to use the glasses on the table?" Ian called,

as he noticed the rows of cutlery. His heart sank, he and Brigette hadn't eaten lunch until four o'clock. He hoped that he'd be able to do justice to Simone's dinner.

"Hungry?" she asked as they clinked glasses.

"Starving."

"It won't be long." Simone offered him a plate of hors d'oeuvres. "How was your day?"

"Not bad. Yours?"

"Frustrating. But, I think something's going to happen at last."

Ian nibbled half-heartedly at a carrot stick. "You mean Pagett have found a buyer?"

"Could be. Let me get the first course then I'll tell you about it." Sunlight still filtered into the room but Simone lit the candles.

The deep-fried cheese and cranberry sauce purses were extremely good and slipped down easily. Ian listened carefully to everything she had to say. It certainly sounded as though there would be an announcement tomorrow. He hadn't mentioned Brigette's book yet but tonight was beginning to look like the ideal time; a couple of bottles of wine, candles, perhaps a brandy after the meal . . . Yes, this could be the moment.

He begged off the soup. "My waistline . . . " He patted his slim stomach.

"Do you have many books lined up for publication?" Ian asked as he tucked a piece of Cajun chicken under an oil and balsamic vinegar flavoured lettuce leaf.

"Yes, we do. But we're concentrating solely on

the next couple of months, everything after that must wait."

"So you're not taking on any new books?" he said casually.

"No, positively not. I've already had to inform several of our regular authors that their books are on hold. This morning I had a call from one of them, they wanted to withdraw their manuscript, it had been accepted by another publisher."

He picked at the lemon tart. "So what would happen if someone gave you a manuscript now?"

"I'd send it back. We've been doing that for the last few weeks. Why do you ask?"

"My sister . . . she's written a novel. A terrific read according to her. It took an age to write. Under normal circumstances, I might have asked if she could send it to you. But . . . "

"Under normal circumstances I would have said, do."

"It's not important, just a thought." Ian sat back in his chair and smiled at her. "That was a superb meal."

"Coffee?" she asked, eyeing the half-finished tart on his plate.

"I don't think so, thank you. I think the heat has robbed me of my appetite," he said.

"Brandy?"

"That would be lovely."

Simone switched on the CD player and suggested that he chose some music while she poured their brandies. They sat contentedly in the half-light and listened to a Brahms lullaby. Ian glanced surreptitiously at his watch. Should he make a move on Simone now or wait until the results of the meeting were known? To make love to Simone could hardly be classed as a hardship and he was sure that she wouldn't push him away.

He drained his glass and moved closer to her. This time she was sober.

Chapter Thirty-Four

All pretence of work had stopped and, by three o'clock, Pagett's staff were as taut as violin strings.

Lois greeted John Barrett in her usual friendly manner. "Hello, Mr B, haven't seen you for ages."

"Hello, Lois, it's been a while. Is Simone in her office?"

"She is. Everyone's here today . . . "

"Could you tell her I'd like a word?" He was very fond of Lois but, given half the chance, she would happily chatter on.

Simone frowned into the phone, the last person she wanted to see today was John Barrett. She had an extremely unforgiving nature.

"Send him in, Lois," she said reluctantly.

He looked tanned and fit, Simone thought, as he closed the door and sat himself down.

"What brings you here, John?" she asked coldly.

"I came to introduce you to your new boss."

"You *know* who it is?" Simone bent forward eagerly, aloofness forgotten.

"I do. It's *me*."

"*You?*"

"Surprised?" He asked. Her face was frozen in shock. "Simone?"

"You!" she repeated.

"Me! I'm sorry that I had to keep you in the dark, but there was nothing to be gained by telling you until everything was signed and sealed . . . "

A dull flush of anger spread across her lovely face. "Not even a hint, John?"

He shrugged. "I wasn't at all sure that I'd be successful in my bid."

"That's understandable, but I was the one who told you about Pagett. Surely you could have trusted me? Who else knows about this?"

"Only the Lords and Tim Brown."

"Tim Brown! The *snake*, he never said a word . . . just let me worry on."

"Tim had an important part to play in the negotiations." John shifted impatiently. Why was he sitting here arguing the toss with Simone? "Well, your worries are over now," he said quietly.

"So presumably you intend keeping me on?" she asked sarcastically.

"I . . . er . . . yes." He wasn't sure that he liked her attitude.

John's hesitation brought her carping to a sharp halt. Shock or no shock, this was hardly an auspicious beginning.

"Forgive me, I'm knocked out by your news. Congratulations, John, I wish you all the luck in the world."

"Thank you. I wanted you to be the first to know. We'll arrange a meeting – for next Tuesday perhaps. Then get down to the finer points but, for now, I'd like to offer you the post of editor-in-chief."

Simone followed the swirls of the wood grain on her desk. Editor-in-chief, a hell of a climbdown from heading your own publishers, she thought sourly. "What exactly does that entail?" she asked.

"You'd be responsible for all the books Pagett produce. You'd approve or veto any new staff members. In other words, be involved in the running of Pagett. If you accept the post, you'd also get a handsome raise and a bonus," John ended.

Simone swivelled her chair gently from side to side. On the face of it, it sounded like a good offer. With John as the boss, her job would be secure. The uncertainty of the last few weeks was something she never wanted to experience again. But if she was to be chief editor, where did that leave Roland Green? Roland was due in at four o'clock – that much she *had* ferreted out of Lois.

"It's an interesting proposition but, quite frankly, I can't on working with Roland Green," she said.

John's lips twitched. "You do surprise me!" he teased. "Relax, it's not going to happen. I'm seeing him later."

Simone pumped the air with her fist. *"Yes,"* she shouted triumphantly.

John knew that news would please her. "The type of books that interest Roland will no longer be part of the Pagett list," he explained hastily. "Our immediate future is in mass market fiction – paperbacks mostly – except, of course, for those few authors already published in hard cover. I don't need to spell it out for you, Simone, we have quite a climb ahead of us. But I'm confident that we'll be back in the black within a couple of years. By the way, Arthur Lord will remain with us on a consultancy basis."

"With a plan like that, we can't fail," Simone agreed, equally confident. "Holly and I . . . I presume Holly stays?"

John nodded and let her continue.

"Good, we've always worked well together. With Roland's fanciful books out of the way, we should storm our way back into solvency in no time."

"That's the general idea but with one change, Holly will replace Roland, become an editor in her own right. Kathy, of course, will remain as children's editor."

John watched the light leave Simone's eyes.

"But Holly's my assistant, I need her."

Arthur had forewarned him, so Simone's reaction came as no surprise.

"You *do* need an assistant, I agree. But not Holly. When everything has settled down, you can hire a new assistant."

"Any other new appointments I should know about?" The sarcasm was back but John ignored it.

"Tim Brown will be Pagett's managing director. He and my son, Sean, will control the budget, although Sean will be guided by Tim. Jane Scott will become production manager and Marianna Berry chief art director."

"I must have misunderstood you, I thought that

staff appointments were to be my domain," Simone persisted.

John could see the steely determination which drove her.

"And they will be, but initially, I make the decisions," John said in a firm voice. He was quite prepared to give Simone her head in some matters, but he was determined to keep her on a tight rein for the moment.

"In order to cut costs, I intend to move out of this building. There's masses of space in our South Kensington offices – they'll be rent free. You might enjoy redesigning them, that is if you're not overloaded with work. Our present tenants move out at the end of the month but I'm sure they won't object if you want to have a look around before that – get an idea of what's needed."

Simone nodded.

"There are dozens of aspects to be discussed – should you decide to stay with us, of course."

Simone looked at him quizzically. "Of course I intend to stay, I've put a lot of time and effort into Pagett. I want to see it flourish just as much as you do."

John's determination wasn't lost on Simone. What was his role in all this? Did he intend to take part in the everyday business or would he be content to let her and Tim take over?

"Do you plan to move to London?" she asked, slyly.

"Good heavens, no. I'd have no time for my writing if I did that. I'll keep a watching brief, be available if there are any problems. Naturally as chairman I'll attend board meetings but, other than that, I want no active part in the company. Incidentally, I presume that you'll continue to publish my books?"

"I think you can safely assume that we will," Simone replied with the first trace of a smile.

"I'd better scoot along to the boardroom now, although I doubt that my meeting with Roland will be as pleasant as this one," he said ruefully, though Simone hadn't made it easy, either. "See you at five, we'll have a drink to celebrate. But until then, not a word to anyone, I'd like to have my moment in the sun, see people's reaction."

Simone pulled her thumb and index finger across her mouth with a zipping motion. "Good luck with His Highness." She smirked.

"See you at five o'clock," John said.

* * *

Roland Green was twenty minutes late. Without warning the boardroom door opened with a crash and he swaggered into the room. He gave John a supercilious glance, and pulled out a chair. He sat down carefully, hitching the knees of his trousers to avoid creases.

"Why are you at this meeting?" Roland enquired insolently as he arranged the cuffs of his shirt to his satisfaction.

"Good afternoon, Roland. In answer to your question, *I called* the meeting."

256

"*You?* Why you?"

"Yes, *me*. Chairman of Pagett Publications." John disliked throwing his weight about but he wanted to put this obnoxious man in his place. The chore which he'd dreaded – informing Roland that he was about to be made redundant – was becoming easier by the minute.

"I see," Roland said laconically as he arched his eyebrows.

"Let me come straight to the point, your services will no longer required by Pagett." Never in his life had John spoken to anybody quite so bluntly.

"And why is that, may I ask?" Roland's face showed no emotion.

"My accountants carried out a thorough investigation of all Pagett's finances and the majority of your books showed a loss. In the foreseeable future, we aim to concentrate on mass market fiction . . . "

"Don't bother to go on," Roland interrupted imperiously. "If you want to immerse yourself in that pulp-fiction world, be my guest. Oh! But I forgot, you already contribute to it, don't you?"

"Very successfully," John reminded him.

"Well, I have no wish to jeopardise *my* literary reputation. Of course, I will expect a hefty redundancy payment, but I'll leave that to my lawyers."

"You will receive the normal payment, nothing more . . . "

Tim Brown's prearranged call was perfectly timed.

"Yes, Tim. . . . Trudy Friel? . . . She wants an update for her column? . . . Tell her I'll phone her later, by then I'll have more information for her. Yes, OK . . . yes I'll let her know who stays and who gets the bullet. OK, Tim, thanks."

"Does that mean that my redundancy will be splashed all over that viper's column?" Roland's complacency vanished.

"She just wants material for the paper," John said innocently.

"Sure! And Roland Green provides it." Roland's face turned an alarming shade of purple.

"Of course there is a way to avoid the publicity – resign."

"You cunning bastard," Roland spat. "That's blackmail."

"I wouldn't call it that, *face-saving* perhaps." John was having a ball.

It was wrong of him, he knew, but he was sorry that Simone wasn't here to witness Roland Green's downfall. Everything she'd said about him was true. He was arrogant, rude and pompous and, luckily for John, enormously vain about his literary reputation.

"So what you're saying is that I should walk away from Pagett with nothing to show for all those years of work?"

"I'm suggesting that, from your point of view, resignation would be a preferable option. I *am* willing however to offer you a . . . a parting gift, shall we say. Also I guarantee that the details of this meeting will never be made public, either now or in the future."

"And you expect me to believe that?" Roland sneered.

"I am a man of my word. Please don't judge *me* by *your* standards," John retorted. "I'm running late and have a couple of urgent phone calls to make. Would you like to give me your answer now or would you prefer to let me know what you decide later?"

"After you've spoken to Trudy Friel? Not bloody likely. I resign. You and your pathetic little company can go to hell."

As he reached the door, Roland turned. "No doubt that frigid little harridan, Simone Pearse, is behind this. I won't forget today. Perhaps Trudy Friel might enjoy hearing about your cosy little dinners together, those *editing* lunches . . . "

"How *dare* you?" John thundered. "If you utter as much as one word of slander, I'll have you in court so fast that your bow tie will spin. And, after I've won my case, I'll go out of my way to make sure that the real reason for your dismissal is the most talked-about event in publishing history." John rose furiously from his chair. "Now get out, before I throw you out."

The boardroom table was littered with the remains of the celebratory meeting. John twirled his champagne flute and smiled at the memory of those dazed but contented faces. He had a good feeling about Pagett's future.

Chapter Thirty-Five

"Careful with that bag," Holly warned her sister. "There's a bottle of champagne in there."

Liz's eyebrows rose. "Champers, why? What are we celebrating?"

"All will be revealed. Drive," Holly instructed mysteriously.

"No tell, no lift." Liz folded her arms, planted her feet apart and leant stubbornly against the car.

"Ah, come on, Liz, let's save it until Robert can share my news."

"OK," Liz conceded reluctantly. "But you look very smug."

They lay on a moth-eaten rug under the shade of a gnarled apple tree, the cottage garden evocative of childhood summers – the scent of roses, the delicate perfume of lavender and old-fashioned pinks. Bees hummed lazily and overhead the sky was a cloudless blue.

Holly watched Liz's every change of expression as she read a manuscript copy of *Tomorrow's Joy*.

"Holly! Stop looking at me, you're making me nervous." Liz dashed a hand across her eyes to wipe away her tears.

"Sorry." Holly turned away and instead began an in-depth examination of the tree's branches. Should the need ever arise, Holly felt confident that she could recite whole passages from the book. She had taken great care to change the names of the characters, alter locations, the sex of the children, even the nature of the ailments suffered by the various relations that her main character, Amy, had to contend with – but was that enough? Was there anything else she could have done in order to disguise the story?

Restlessly, she twisted and turned on the rug. "Fancy a cup of tea?"

A guffaw of laughter from Liz greeted her suggestion.

"What's so funny about a cup of tea?" Holly asked.

"It's not the tea, it's little Eva – imagine writing her name on the iced buns with a felt tip pen."

Holly laughed too although she preferred the author's original version, a satisfying half-hour spent colouring the test card on their antiquated television screen. She was convinced that whoever had written the story had written it from experience. How anyone could cope with five children under nine, rampant poverty, a dying mother and a father suffering from Alzheimer's, was beyond her. The poor soul was also responsible for a batty old aunt who regularly put her council house up for sale, and a cousin on the run from his unsympathetic debtors, not to mention the police. Honoria – or *Amy*, as she now was – had been deserted when child number four turned one. Her husband's sudden disappearance had prevented her from telling him that number five was on the way. With a life like that, how could anyone find the time to write a book?

"This is wonderful," Liz said gruffly as she turned another page.

"You really think so?" Holly greedily waited to hear more.

"It's a master of understatement, sad, funny, harrowing and completely true to life – and what a life."

"I'm convinced that it's all true."

"Didn't Emily Howard tell you whether it was or not?"

Holly pulled herself up with a start. "I . . . I didn't ask, she . . . we didn't discuss the truth of the story . . . she's a very private person," she stumbled. At least half-truths were better than none.

"Well, *I* feel it's factual, I suppose that's what makes it such a good read. I'm sure you've got a success on your hands, Holly, I'll be amazed if it doesn't take off like a rocket."

"Here's hoping." Holly crossed two fingers.

"I'm very proud of my big sister," Liz said as she picked up the next page from under the stone that she was using as a paperweight.

"No need to be." If only she could confide in Liz.

"Come on, Ms Modesty, of course there is."

"Leave it, Liz," Holly replied so sharply that Liz flinched.

"Hey! Lighten up. What's got into you?"

"I'm really sorry, it must be the strain of the past few weeks, not knowing whether I'll have a job . . . "

Liz smiled understandingly at her sister, waiting for such an important decision must be nerve-racking.

Their infrequent, minor disagreements lasted no longer than a summer shower and by the time Robert returned, they were sitting at a table on the makeshift patio, playing Scrabble.

"Run out of conversation?" He bent to kiss his wife's head then, seeing Holly's pout, kissed her too.

Liz pulled a face at him. "You wish!" she retorted and gave him a playful slap on his bottom. "It's such a glorious night we thought we'd eat outside, OK with you?"

"That wins my vote, I've been stuck indoors all day."

"Formal attire," Liz said with a smile. "Holly's brought champagne."

"Oh? Why?" Robert wanted to know.

"I've been asking her that all day," Liz told him.

"The quicker you get changed the sooner you'll find out," Holly said, pertly.

"Just look at that smug smile." Liz put the little plastic stands of tiles on to the Scrabble board and carried it carefully into the house. She didn't usually beat Holly but at the moment she was nearly a hundred points ahead.

Liz stood at the cooker stirring the lemon-butter sauce and watched Holly gathering the cutlery and the glasses, her movements almost jerky with suppressed excitement. Had Derek agreed to a divorce, she wondered? Obviously there were no new developments at Pagett or Holly would have phoned them.

"Hurry up, Robert, or I'll expire with curiosity," Liz called as she carried the food outside.

Robert twisted the champagne cork like an expert and poured the chilled, foaming bubbles into their glasses. "What do we drink to?" he asked Holly.

"The new editor of Pagett Publications."

"Oh Holly! That's incredible, that's wonderful," Liz burbled. "Wait a minute, you mean you knew and didn't tell us?"

"Now that's what I call good news," Robert said quickly.

"When did this all this happen?" Liz persisted.

"Yesterday afternoon . . . "

"Yesterday!" Liz shrieked.

"I wanted to celebrate with you both – in style," Holly explained guiltily. "If I hadn't been coming here today, I would've told you immediately."

"So Pagett has finally changed hands?" Robert asked.

"Yes, and the new owner – wait for it – is John Barrett."

"The author? *Murder and Co Ltd* John Barrett?" Liz's eyes were wide with surprise.

"One and the same. We were sure it would be sold to an American publishing conglomerate, their auditors practically squatted at Pagett for a couple of weeks. But everyone is delighted, John is such a nice man."

Liz forgot her peevishness. "You've often said you liked him."

"By the way, the champagne is a present from him," Holly said.

"In that case, here's to Editor Grant and John Barrett," Robert said as he held out his glass.

They clinked glasses and Liz, as always, demanded the full details.

"We *knew* there was something exciting afoot when a strange man, with the physique of a body-builder, arrived carrying two trays of champagne flutes in one hand and a crate of bubbly in the other. I must admit we were all gathered in the reception area at least twenty minutes before the meeting. The booze was followed by layers of stacker-trays loaded with tiny sandwiches and canapés. Instant party. Anyway, we all crowded into the boardroom and suddenly John Barrett appeared. Poor John, no one took a blind bit of notice of him. He was just part of the scenery like the rest of us. Tim Brown called the meeting to order and introduced Pagett's new Chairman. I'm sure our faces were a study, but John took it well. He made a short speech, then announced the new appointments. I was non compos for the rest of the time. Me, an editor!" Holly's words tripped excitedly from her tongue.

"So when do you begin *editoring*?" Liz asked, her face beaming.

"I'm having lunch with John on Monday, he'll give me all the details then. We'll be moving from our present building to Barrett Engineering's offices in South Kensington. He said that I'd have a much larger office. Mind you, anything smaller than my present cell and I'd have to spend the rest of my life bent double." Holly groaned.

When the champagne was finished Robert produced a bottle of vintage red which he'd been saving for just such an occasion.

Holly answered Liz's questions as best she could. Not for the first time Holly decided that Liz had missed her vocation – she'd have made a formidable investigative journalist.

The heady perfume of night-scented stock and the peace of the tangled garden made Holly all the more determined to help Liz and Robert restore the cottage and its garden to its full glory. They'd done wonders but they still needed a team of professionals to help clear some of the larger clumps of dead wood and briars. But for now, she planned to surprise them with a trip to Paris for their anniversary. The advance would pay for it, but guilt inhibited her from telling them about the trip face to face. Liz would make it difficult to lie, and lie she'd have to in order to justify the cost of the trip. Phone-fibbing would be easier.

"How's Terence?" Liz asked lazily.

"Fine. We had dinner together last night, which reminds me, I had a letter from Derek the other day. He wants to see me to discuss the divorce. I'm supposed to go to the flat next Wednesday. Terence says I'd be mad to go but, if I do, he insists on acting as my bodyguard."

Liz felt a surge of irrational jealousy. Holly hadn't

bothered to phone and tell them about her new appointment and now, as casually as if it were an office memo, she mentioned the letter from Derek. Her divorce, one of the most important events in her life, had already been well and truly discussed with Terence. Ever since Holly's arrival this morning Liz had sensed a barrier, a distance between them. Holly had changed. All she seemed to care about these days was that damn book.

Robert and Holly waited for Liz's usual outburst. It didn't come. For once, Liz was silent.

"Nothing to say, Liz?" Robert looked anxiously at his wife.

"Holly's a big girl now, quite capable of handling her own affairs." Liz's voice was ice-laden. "Besides, Terence is there now, he can advise her."

Although Liz's face was hidden in the darkening gloom there was no mistaking her bitterness.

"I have some work to do." Robert tactfully excused himself.

"OK, Holly, what's going on?" Liz demanded when they were alone.

"I don't know what you mean. There's *nothing* going on." Holly was grateful for the dusk.

"Come off it, you've been acting strangely all day. For instance, when did you hear from Derek – during the week, last week, last month?"

"Don't be like that, Liz, of course not. I was so excited about the book that I forgot all about Derek. It's been the most peculiar week."

"I'll bet. And when you finally get the promotion

to die for, we don't hear a word. What did *Terence* have to say about that? Not that I care."

"Terence thought it was *wonderful,* now that you ask. When I told him last night, he was delighted for me. I took him to dinner, to celebrate," Holly said deliberately.

The little patio crackled with tension. Holly hated rows. The family celebration she'd planned had turned into a major fiasco.

"I'm going to bed. Goodnight," Liz said coldly.

"Liz, we always promised each other that we'd never let the sun set on a row," Holly pleaded.

"The sun set hours ago," Liz retorted.

Robert never thought he'd witness such a silence between the sisters; he'd never known them to row before. They'd hardly exchanged more than a dozen words all morning and, when they did speak, their words were either barbed or snarled. He didn't intervene but he wanted to. Liz was hurt. Holly was equally wounded, her surprise had backfired and, somewhere in the middle of all this was poor defenceless Terence, blissfully unaware that his support and friendship was wreaking havoc.

"I've decided to leave this afternoon," Holly said when she couldn't stand the cold-shoulder treatment any longer.

"Suit yourself. Robert will take you to the station," Liz mumbled with her back to her sister.

"Fine," Holly replied.

Robert looked at his wife beseechingly.

"Do you want a cup of tea before you leave?"

Liz's coldness would have frightened any guest away.

"No thank you, Terence will make one for me when I get home."

Robert squeezed her arm reassuringly as the train pulled into the station.

"Don't worry, Holly, this'll blow over," he said. "Liz feels a bit put out that she wasn't told immediately. She cares so much about you . . . worries all the time."

The rhythmic sound of the wheels on the tracks irritated Holly. Sunglasses hid her reddened eyes. *If Liz invited her again, she'd refuse. Imagine letting her leave a day early like this.*

The one-sided argument continued as she let herself into her flat. It raged as she made a cup of coffee, stormed as she wrung out a blouse so tightly she was sure the creases would never disappear and finally abated, when she'd convinced herself that Liz was wrong and she was right. Comforted by that, she crawled into bed and cried herself to sleep.

Holly moped about the flat next day alternating between bouts of indignation and fits of pique. Why had Terence chosen this weekend to visit his family, the very time she needed him. She was fed up with this poky flat, tired of hacking her shins on the table and chairs. During those miserable years with Derek, she'd become expert in the art of daydreaming. It blocked out his bullying. But, try as she might, Holly couldn't immerse herself in that comforting world today a vision of Liz's face, angry and aloof, got in the way.

She pushed her meal away and drank her tear-diluted coffee.

The phone woke her. Stiffly she rose from the chair, her arm dead from lying on it. She hardly recognised Liz's sobbing voice and within seconds her resolve had melted, their quarrel a thing of the past.

"You *will* come back next weekend?" Liz said.

"Try and keep me away. I'm sure Terence will be delighted with your invitation. I'll ask him the minute he gets home," Holly promised.

With new heart Holly tidied the room, washed her dishes, then went into the bedroom to choose what to wear for her lunch with John Barrett. Lunching at the Dorchester with your boss wasn't exactly an everyday occurrence.

Chapter Thirty-Six

Simone frowned as she looked at her desk. The media reports of the Pagett takeover had brought an exceptionally crammed post bag. And so soon – the news had only broken on Friday. She pushed her hair away from her face and put the manuscripts to one side. Again her brow creased; an author due for publication in ten days' time complained that her publicity tour was far too concentrated, and wondered if Pagett was prepared to finance the hire of a nanny for her two pre-school youngsters? Simone made a note at the top of the page – *remind her, publicity is the way to sell books*. A hurried note from Patty Bowles, a debut writer, begged for even more time, she wasn't happy with her book. Simone glanced at her schedule, Patty was already way past her deadline. *Take more time – but note, schedule full for next two years,* she scribbled. It was going to be one of those days. She sighed as she opened the next envelope – yet another letter from a writer she'd turned down. This was the third time the disappointed author had written to her. From now on, this man was best ignored, there was nothing more she could say to him. Simone put his letter into the dead-tray to be filed, she must remind Holly not to get involved in this type of correspondence, a standard rejection slip was kindest in the end. God, she would miss Holly's help. There were several invitations in the bundle; two trade lunches, a drinks party given by a newly-opened bookshop, a prize-giving, another asking her to act as a judge for a major literary prize, and a request from a quirky independent television station to appear on the programme they were making about publishing.

"Coffee?" Lois called as she passed Simone's open door.

"No, thanks, Lois," Simone said. A coffee maker would be useful when she moved into her new office. She would add that to her list of *desirable imperatives* along with a dress allowance, a gold card, a mobile phone and a new car. All perfectly reasonable requests, she felt, for an editor-in-chief.

"The menus! They don't hang about," she said aloud as she read the next piece of mail. She had only contacted the caterers late yesterday afternoon.

John was anxious to get Pagett off to a good – but not too expensive – start and planned to throw a party. What with the media, reviewers, literary and advertising agents, a couple of other publishers with whom they had always had a good relationship, she and Holly had drawn up quite a formidable list. And then there were Pagett staff and authors.

"The most important guests of all," John pointed out.

Simone had almost blown a fuse when Holly suggested that Roland Green should be included for old times' sake. She was still furious that he'd managed to resign before John had had the opportunity to fire him.

How things had changed. Up until a couple of years ago, a drink and a crisp would have sufficed. But now, with the emphasis on the dangers of drink-driving, food played an important role.

John and Sean Barrett had been given the use of what John described as "A wonderful converted loft overlooking the river." All Pagett had to do was to supply the invitations and refreshments. At least Holly could help her sort this out.

"How about lunch today?" Simone suggested when Holly answered her phone.

"Fine. Any special reason?" Holly asked nervously.

"The menus for the party have arrived, I thought we could sift through them."

Holly relaxed. These days any unexpected call from Simone sent her into a blind panic. Maybe she was just on edge at the thought of her meeting with Derek. The sooner tonight was over and done with the better. She wasn't looking forward to it and kept reminding herself that she still had time to back out.

"What time?" Holly asked.

"Twelve-thirty, OK?"

"I'll be ready."

Holly gave her attention to the manuscript she

was reading. It was astonishing how quickly aspiring writers had heard about her appointment. Congratulatory cards, letters, faxes, invitations and a stack of unsolicited manuscripts had been waiting on her desk this morning. Exciting. Perhaps she could broach the awkward subject of Lucinda Rockingham at lunch. However, if Lois ran true to type, Simone would probably already have heard that Lucinda's congratulatory fax suggested that she'd like Holly to edit her from now on. The last thing Holly wanted to do was to begin her new job by poaching Simone's author. She'd prefer to build up her own stable of writers. Real writers, she thought ruefully, not mythical authors like Emily Howard.

By five o'clock, Holly had rejected all three manuscripts. Undoubtedly the brightest spot in her day had been when Simone had gleefully passed Lucinda on to her, with her blessing.

Chapter Thirty-Seven

Terence gave her a comforting smile. "You can *still* change your mind," he said as the taxi drew up opposite Derek's flat.

"No, we're here now, I'd better get it over with," Holly said grimly.

Derek answered the bell immediately and buzzed her in. Holly looked over her shoulder towards the silent taxi for reassurance.

Derek had gone casual. Her trepidation vanished as she bit her lip to hold back her laughter. His mouse-coloured hair was parted in the centre and glistened with gel, even his moustache had been treated to a dollop of the gelatinous gloop. The short-sleeved check shirt might have been OK if it hadn't been for the phony gold chain and the string vest so clearly visible at the open neck. But the combination of baggy linen trousers, white socks and open-toed sandals was hardest to take.

"Come in," he invited with a wide smile.

"I can't stay long," Holly said in a choked voice. To think that she'd allowed herself to be guided by this fashion-nightmare!

"Drink?" Derek pointed to a neat row of bottles and an even neater plate of crudités and dips.

"No thank you." She edged her way slowly towards the window. With a hand behind her back she gave Terence the thumbs-up sign.

Derek had to admit that Holly looked well. He wouldn't have allowed her to choose such a short, immodest skirt but he'd soon get rid of that when she moved back.

"Sit down, Holly."

"I'm fine here," she said stubbornly.

"Please, you're making me uncomfortable."

Reluctantly, Holly left her safe perch at the window and sat in the chair nearest to it. Derek had changed the furniture around but the gap left by her elegant little desk was still glaringly empty.

"You asked me here to discuss the divorce," she reminded him.

"Not so fast. I haven't agreed to any divorce."

"Then I'm wasting my time," she said firmly, rising from the chair.

"Sit down, Holly," he commanded.

She felt the old frisson of fear. "You've forgotten, I no longer take orders from you, Derek," she said more bravely than she felt, and remained standing.

"Please. Sit down," he invited in a more placatory tone.

"Just remember, Derek, you're not in a good position to argue." She went back to the chair. "Now, what was it you said in your letter? I would hear something to my advantage?" She crossed one leg over the other in what she hoped was a nonchalant gesture.

"Yes. I thought you'd be happy to know that I was *not* committing adultery with Bunny Bly," he said.

"So?"

"So, you should be *glad* that I haven't been unfaithful to you. There's no *need* for you to be jealous. Bunny and I were in Paris to check out a franchise that she intended to buy. She wanted my professional opinion, that's all."

"Then in that case why did she act so suspiciously, stutter and stumble when I asked her name?" Holly shot at him.

"And what were *you* doing in Paris with a man old enough to be your father?"

"Not that it's any of your business, I was there to edit Lucinda Rockingham's book, the older of the two men was her husband."

"So where was Lucinda?" he enquired sarcastically.

"Nursing a broken ankle. She was in agony and insisted I had dinner with her husband and two business friends – she didn't want me to wander round Paris on my own." She'd often spoken of Lucinda Rockingham in the past and Derek knew that they'd moved to Paris temporarily.

He let that pass. "Tell me, Holly, who put this evil thought into your head?"

"What evil thought?"

"The idea that Bunny . . . Mrs Bly . . . and myself were anything other than business acquaintances."

"The guilty looks on your faces and the fact that she was seen entering and leaving your flat – late at night. Acting most suspiciously, I might add."

"You had me watched?" Derek screeched.

Holly drew back into her chair.

"You had me followed?" he pronounced the words slowly and deliberately, his eyes full of their old menace.

Holly was back in the grip of panic. She jumped up from her chair, she'd feel a lot safer by the window.

"Sit down." In a flash Derek was out of his own chair, blocking her way. "Answer my question."

Short of pushing him, there was no way Holly could get to that window. The room began to close in around her. "I want to leave," she whispered.

"No chance. I want an explanation. I suppose that *bitch* friend of yours is responsible for this – as usual. What did you and that Pearse woman do, Holly, camp outside my flat all night?"

She could feel his indignant breath on her face as he bent towards her. "I'm leaving, now," she said.

"You're not going *anywhere* until you give me an answer."

"My solicitor arranged it."

"Why? What did you tell him?"

Holly remained silent, she could feel the wooden struts of the chair pressing into her back.

"What did you tell him?" he repeated.

"That you were in Paris with your boss's wife." She could hear the quiver in her voice.

"And?"

Holly's mind was working feverishly. "And, if you look out of the window, you'll see that I'm not alone."

Derek didn't budge. "Nice try, I go to the window and you run away. Remember, Holly, I'm not stupid. But I *am* entitled to know who's invading my privacy."

"It was a private detective."

"A *what?*"

Holly's attention was riveted to his oily forehead, the gel was moving toward his eyebrows and she prayed hysterically that it would drip into his eyes and blur them, then she could make her escape.

"This is pointless," she said quietly, arguing with Derek never worked. "Why don't we forget the whole thing? I'll wait the five years for a divorce, I don't care any more." She lowered her gaze to her shoe and began to rub at an imaginary scuff. She should have listened to Terence, this was the stupidest thing she'd ever done. What on earth had possessed her to think that Derek could change?

"Who gave you the idea of hiring a private detective?" He crowded her even more. Their faces were almost touching.

"I *told* you, my solicitor."

"I don't believe you."

"I don't care what you believe. But if I'm not out of here in another five minutes, my neighbour, Terence, will be at your door."

"That marshmallow? What will he do, flay me with his double chins?"

"No, he and the taxi driver – who's across the street – will come and get me, but not before they radio for the police."

To her surprise, Derek paled, then stretched the upper part of his body awkwardly towards the window. In that second Holly raised both her legs and, with all her strength, landed a well-aimed kick to his stomach. Derek reeled backwards and, before he could grasp what had happened, she leapt towards the door and wrenched the handle with both hands. It was locked. Unable to believe her bad luck, she pulled again. As Derek rolled on the floor clutching his stomach she looked around wildly, there was no sign of the key. The window. She ran back towards it but before she could reach it, Derek leaned out and grabbed her leg. She hit the floor with a thud.

"You belong *here*, Holly," he rasped.

"You're insane," she sobbed as the truth of her words hit her. Derek was mad, totally, utterly mad.

For a moment they both lay on the floor, winded. Derek suddenly doubled up as a fresh bout of pain hit him. Holly saw her chance. She rolled sideways and pulled a table lamp from its wall socket then, with a force she didn't know she possessed, hurled it at the window. She stopped breathing for a couple of seconds. And then she heard it, the sound of shattering glass. Drained, she fell back and waited. The noise of running feet brought her to her knees.

"Police, open up," she heard Terence call as he hammered at the door.

Derek, still clutching his stomach, rolled over and hauled himself up.

"Open the door or we'll smash it in," Terence shouted.

Derek staggered to the door, fished a key out of his trouser-pocket and inserted it shakily into the keyhole. The door burst open, almost knocking Derek off his feet. Behind Terence, Holly could see the reluctant face of the taxi-driver as he hovered in the doorway.

Terence rushed over to her. "Are you hurt?" he asked as he helped her up.

"No, I'm all right . . ."

"The marshmallow-policeman," Derek sneered and fell into the nearest chair.

"What have you done to her?" Terence demanded.

"You mean what's *she* done to *me?* I wish you *were* a policeman, I'd have this lunatic charged with assault. I still can."

"Shut up," Terence ordered. "What happened, Holly?"

"He tripped me, I was trying to get to the window. He didn't want me to leave, so I kicked him," she explained, fear replaced by a slight glint of satisfaction. "It was all a waste of time, he had no intention of discussing divorce. Now, please, can we get out of here?"

"Just a moment, you're quite safe now," Terence turned to Derek. "You brought Holly here to discuss your divorce, but instead you're up to your old tricks. This time you've gone too far, this time *I'm* a witness to your cruelty and so is this taxi-driver. This time *I'll* see to it that you're properly punished. Rely on that. Come on, Holly, let's go."

Luckily for them, Derek didn't bother to glance at the door. The driver, heavily bribed by Terence, was nowhere in sight.

"Wait," Derek said. "I'm fed up with your whining, Holly, your solicitors, your *pathetic* advisers. If you don't appreciate what I've done for you, that's your loss. I'll give you a year to change your mind, then, if you still want your flaming divorce, you can have it."

"I'll *never* change my mind. Not in a year, a century or even a millennium," Holly spat at him. "And what's more, I don't believe you. You're lying. You're saying that to stop us going to the police."

"Not true," Derek said as he wiped his dripping forehead.

"If you're serious, put it in writing," Terence insisted, grasping the moment.

"You keep out of it," Derek retorted.

"In writing, *now*, or we go to the police. A little chat with Bunny Bly's husband should prove fascinating, too." Terence said.

Derek slammed out of the chair, opened his brief case and took out a sheet of paper. Sullenly, he wrote as Terence dictated.

"Now sign and date it," Terence said looking over Derek's shoulder.

Without another word, Terence took the written promise from him, handed it to Holly and steered her out of the flat.

Safe in Terence's shadow, Holly stopped at the door. "You look ridiculous, Derek," she said as Terence pulled at her sleeve. "My advice to you is – see a psychiatrist, then find yourself a fashion consultant."

Terence almost dragged her down the stairs. "Don't push it, Holly, I'm not *that* brave," he whispered as they made their getaway.

"I won't forget this, don't think I will," Derek threatened as he slammed the door behind them with a resounding crash.

* * *

Good timing, Simone thought as her bell rang.

"Hello, darling, you look wonderful." Ian stooped slightly to kiss her.

"You don't look too doggish yourself," Simone replied with a smile. He was such a handsome man. Ian looked more like a male model than a rep for a firm which produced medical books.

"I thought perhaps we'd order Indian food tonight – if that's OK with you?" he said as he placed his briefcase in a corner. "It's been a frustrating day, one over-stocked bookseller after another."

"Let me get you a drink. I'm not that fussy to go out either."

"I've brought along my sister's book," he said casually.

He took the Bloody Mary from her and kissed her icy fingers. "So how did things go today?"

They often discussed their work and their problems. Simone enjoyed having someone objective to talk to. She liked Ian. More and more. He was good company, good fun and a wonderful lover. Husband material? she wondered, not for the first time.

They jumped apart when the bell rang. "I'll get it," Ian said as he smoothed his ruffled hair.

Simone could hear him talking to the delivery man as she put the knives and forks on the dining-room table. Quickly they opened the cartons.

"How do you fancy spending a weekend away?" Ian asked, as he crunched a puppodum.

"Sounds heavenly, somewhere in the country, away from this heat?"

"I know just the place. I can't manage this weekend, an early appointment on Monday in Glasgow, nor next week – a family wedding – how about the following Friday?"

"That's perfect, I'm tied up this weekend too," she said.

Her life was a stagnant backwater compared to his. Ian obviously had lots of friends but, so far, she hadn't met any of them. That rankled a little.

"I'll book tomorrow, I can hardly wait," he said smoothly.

Simone told him about John's party plan. "You will come, won't you?" she asked anxiously. With Ian by her side, she would be the envy of them all.

"Of course I will, if I can," he replied, sliding a seekh kebab from its wooden skewer. "When is it?"

"If all goes according to plan, next Wednesday."

Ian stuffed the empty cartons into the plastic bin while Simone made coffee. He took the manuscript from his briefcase and put it in the centre of the coffee table, then changed his mind and moved it nearer the edge.

Simone returned with the steaming coffee pot and two pretty china mugs.

"I gather that's the book?" she said when she saw the thick manuscript.

"Yes. But really there's no rush, I'm sure you've lots of others to read. I hope you like it," he said plaintively.

"Tell your sister not to worry, I'll get to it fairly quickly," Simone assured him as she switched on the television. They both liked to watch the ten o'clock news.

"Is there ever any good news?" she grumbled during the adverts.

"Good news makes bad press," Ian said as he pulled her towards him.

Being in his arms felt wonderful, so right.

As the credits rolled, Ian yawned. "Do you mind if I make it an early night?" he asked, stroking her hair.

Simone hid her disappointment. "Of course not."

She wound her arms tightly around his neck as Ian kissed her goodnight. He disentangled himself with a laugh, then stood up. "If we start that again, I'll never get out of here."

Simone put on her favourite summer nightie then settled into bed with Brigette's manuscript. The first few pages were rough, very rough. An uneasy feeling gripped her. As she reached the end of the first chapter, the hairs on the back of her neck were standing on end. She flipped quickly through the second chapter and the third. It was a sickening story, a justification of child abuse. The writing was so bad that Simone really began to doubt that English was Brigette's first language. By chapter four, the central character had become an abuser. Her partner, a convicted sexual molester, was left in charge of their child. Simone gasped at the revolting, graphic detail. Quite simply it was the worst book she had ever read. How was she going to break it to Ian that *nothing* would persuade her to publish this obscenity? Had he read it? . . . she hoped not. She couldn't bear if their friendship broke up over a book. There'd be no rejection slip this time, she'd have to find a tactful way of letting Ian's sister down. Why had she offered to read the damned thing, hadn't she learnt anything from that Maggie Tweed episode? Furious with herself, Simone threw the manuscript on the floor, turned out the light, and worried.

It took an hour of tossing and turning before she found a solution of sorts. She'd tell Ian that the book had to be agreed by all the directors then, after a decent interval, she'd return it to him, with regret. It was a compromise but it would have to do. Whatever her feelings for Ian, Pagett could never publish Brigette's book.

Chapter Thirty-Eight

Holly found herself wishing Sunday away. Liz, Robert and Terence were hitting it off so well it gave Holly the chance to retreat into her own private world. There was so much to think about, so much to do.

With their quarrel forgiven and forgotten – hugged away – Liz wasted no time. She sang Terence's praises every hour on the hour, or so it seemed to Holly. She guessed exactly where Liz was heading but she was quick to remind her sister that, until her divorce papers were signed and sealed, she was still a married woman. Holly's new world was spinning with giddy delight, re-marriage the last thing on her agenda.

"Thank you for a really terrific weekend, I've enjoyed every minute of it," Terence said as Holly nudged him impatiently to hurry up.

"We've *loved* having you. You're welcome any time." Liz rubbed his arm affectionately. "With or without my hyper sister!"

Robert shook Terence's hand warmly. "As Liz says, any time."

"What a super couple they are," Terence said as he and Holly settled into their seats on the train.

"They're a happy pair, aren't they?" Holly agreed.

"And what a dream of a cottage."

"I love it, I always look forward to going there."

"Even if it's only in body not in spirit!"

"How d'you mean?"

"You were up there, in space somewhere."

"No I wasn't. I couldn't get a word in with you lot, that's all."

Terence grinned at her. "Whatever you say," he agreed amiably and they lapsed into a comfortable silence.

"Do you fancy going for a walk when we get home?" Holly asked as they neared their station.

"No! Your idea of a walk and mine are very different. I've watched you, haring along at fifty miles an hour."

"OK then."

But he relented. In spite of Holly's promise, Terence had to ask her to slow down twice.

"I never thought I'd make it home," he complained as they stood together in her tiny kitchen, making sandwiches. "Kidding aside, Holly, is something wrong?"

"No. Why? It's been a big week that's all, new and exciting. There's so much to think about; the book, my work, the party next week, the mail that floods in – it's quite a facer. And those meetings next week. I don't even know what I have to do or say. It's all a bit scary. The marketing meeting's tomorrow. I want everything to be right for the book."

"I can understand that, but it isn't like starting a new job in a strange firm, you know everybody and I'm sure they'll go out of their way to help. Just follow their lead and be yourself." Terence noticed that the book still came first on her list of priorities.

"You're a pet, you always make me feel better. I'm sure you're right."

While they ate their sandwiches, Terence watched television and Holly checked her list of jobs-to-be-done. She packed her hold-all ready for the next day, then emptied it again and re-organised it.

"Holly, you're hopping around like a computer virus," Terence said. "Relax, or you'll be knackered in the morning."

She smelt the flowers before she saw them.

"For you," Lois said as she waved an expansive hand.

"What time do these florists start work – yesterday?" Holly asked as she tore open the first little envelope attached to the colourful bouquet.

"Well excuse me! – *All the luck in the world, congratulations. I'll be in touch, Patsy Halloran.*" Holly read aloud for Lois's benefit. She'd only met the agent once.

Holly giggled. "Listen to this one, *Congratulations, you're in the firing line now, Trudy Friel.*"

"And you are too. Have you seen her column this morning?" Lois handed Holly the paper.

PAGETT NO LONGER GREEN
BARRETT AWARDED A GRANT

With the departure of Roland Green to publishers unknown, Holly Grant fills his empty chair. This wannabe editor's tastes have yet to be tested, but instinct tells me that she won't follow in her predecessor's aesthetically snobbish, highly unprofitable footsteps. I'll eat my dust cover if I'm wrong.

Holly's smile was a mile wide. "My first press cutting," she said proudly. "It's not too bad, Lois, is it?"

"By Trudy's standards, it's terrific. Roland will go bananas when he reads it." Lois was pleased for her. Now that Holly was an editor, Lois hoped she wouldn't end up like Simone – barking orders, full of her own importance.

"You've got a stack of post again today. Don't bother to buy the paper, I'll give you this one later on. I'll try and find a vase to put those cut flowers into – they'll probably end up in jam-jars," she warned.

"You're a darling," Holly said gratefully and rushed along to her office.

Lois was right, there was a large pile of mail waiting for her attention, most of it unsolicited manuscripts. Pagett, like most publishers, preferred to work through agents. But that never deterred authors. Their masterpieces, sometimes slim, often chunky, arrived daily. A great flood of words. Holly had promised herself that she'd read everything that was sent to her but she was beginning to realise she couldn't do that. Her slush pile was growing after just one day.

With an eye on the time, Holly waded through the rest of the post. More congratulations, many of them from business firms, some from people she had never met and a letter from an author begging her to read her manuscript – *the one with a smily face in the top left corner of the envelope* – Holly smiled and admired the writer's nerve. She made a mental note to sift through the pile and find it. Lois arrived with an enormous arrangement of flowers. This was becoming embarrassing. "How nice, it's from Arthur Lord," she read as Lois waited beside her, anxious no doubt to update her information base.

"I'll miss him," Lois said.

"I'm sure he'll still pop in occasionally. Would you like to keep these flowers on your desk?" Holly asked. "There isn't an inch of space left anywhere."

"Any more and we'll be able to open our own flower shop. By the way I've dumped the others in the sink, you'll have to take them home with you. Maybe Simone has a spare vase. Will you ask her? She's crabby today. She'll probably bite my head off if I go near her."

This was the first time she'd heard Lois express even the slightest antipathy towards Simone.

"There's my phone." Lois dashed off to answer it.

"These are for you." Simone slapped a large posy of cellophaned roses on Holly's untidy desk.

"Not more flowers!" Holly said involuntarily.

"My, aren't we popular?" Simone remarked sourly as she did an eye-sweep of the tiny room. "And your own slush-pile, already." Rotten little deserter, she thought as she took it all in. She wished she could find something to wipe that grin off Holly's face. Her headache banged unmercifully.

"Fantastic!" Holly squealed excitedly as she read the letter attached to the roses. "They're from Norma Downs, listen to this, she wants to come to Pagett, wants me to edit her. If I'm interested, I should contact her. *If I'm interested!* I can hardly wait."

"Hang on a minute, back up. You can't go signing authors just like that," Simone warned. "Perhaps she won't be right for us. After all, we don't even know why she's leaving her present publisher, do we? Remember, anything like this *has* to be discussed with me first, I *do* have the final say."

"But you've always said that her books would be ideal for Pagett, you asked several times if there was any chance she'd sign with us," Holly objected.

"Yes, but she may make unreasonable demands, like a huge advance for instance, who knows. You have to leave things like that to me. I'll contact her later in the week and have a chat."

Holly's euphoria melted like marge on a muffin. Her first important author, her first break, and Simone had trodden her into the ground. Norma had contacted her, not Simone.

Simone's perfume lingered in the tiny office long after she'd gone. Thoughtfully, Holly rubbed a finger backwards and forwards across her lower lip. Norma always did well. She usually made it onto the bestseller list, around seventh or eighth place, and stayed there, or thereabouts, for a couple of months. Admittedly her last book hadn't risen higher than tenth which surprised Holly – it was one of her best. But still, she had an excellent record. Simone was jealous, that had to be the reason she wanted to hold her back. Well, to hell with Simone, let her bring her objections to the board table.

Holly phoned Norma and arranged to see her later that afternoon. She too was curious to know what had caused Norma's change of heart.

Jane Scott appeared in the doorway. "It's back," she announced waving a rubber-banded manuscript.

"Brilliant!" Holly beamed.

She riffled through the pages. Even if she said so herself, she'd done a good editing job. She could see that Penelope Heath had suggested very few changes. There were a few red ink marks here and there, a difference of opinion about punctuation mostly, nothing serious. She'd work on the manuscript tonight and give it back to Jane in the morning.

"Thanks, Jane. I'll let you have this back tomorrow. Let's get this to the printers as fast as we can . . . " Holly stopped, a pink flush rising to her cheeks. "I didn't mean to sound as though I was telling you what to do."

"Forget it," Jane said affably. Holly would soon get used to the responsibility of handling books. "What time's your meeting with Jeremy?"

Holly checked her watch. "Ten minutes from now."

"I'll be there," Jane promised. She always liked to follow a book to its conclusion.

Jeremy was waiting in the boardroom. Coffee steamed in front of them as Holly nervously sorted out her notes. Annabelle Strong, their sales rep, dashed in to join them. "Rufus won't be here for at least another half-hour," she told them. "He has an appointment with Reduced Volumes' buyer. He's hoping to unload some of Roland's mistakes."

Holly hardly knew Rufus, their sales manager.

Marianna Berry arrived with her own mug of coffee and a mock-up of the book cover.

"Here he is, the man with the money," Jeremy teased as Tim Brown eased himself into a chair.

"And don't you forget it!" Tim parried with a smile.

"Right, let's begin," Jeremy said. "I gather the author won't attend any of these meetings?"

"That's right." Holly could feel the colour rising above the neck of her high-collared blouse. "She's authorised me to act for her, anything I decide will be all right with her."

"Lucky you," Tim observed laconically. "If only *all* authors were like that!"

"So obviously a launch is out? Never mind, that'll give us more money for posters, dump bins and advertising," Jeremy said for Tim's benefit.

Dump bins – a vision of those tempting, partitioned, display boxes with their colorful headers filled Holly's mind. Large posters of the cover, whole windows perhaps, filled with copies of *Tomorrow's Joy*?

"*Tomorrow's Joy*, 'A' format I assume?" Jeremy checked.

Holly came back to the brainstorming session with a bump. She nodded. She and Jane had agreed that the standard size 'A' format would be right for this book with its mass market appeal.

"OK. Presenter kits? Promotional gifts? Any ideas?"

Pagett often included a small gift for the booksellers when they presented the kits.

"I've read the book, how about a packet of paper hankies?" Jane asked as she came into the room at the tail end of Jeremy's question.

"I've read it too," Marianna grinned. "It's harrowing, Prozac might be better, more trendy."

Jeremy laughed politely. "Holly? Have you any suggestions, given it any thought?"

Holly was ready with her answer, she'd thought of little else for weeks. "Because the children are such little tearaways, I wondered if the actual presentation folder could look as if it's been chewed. At the top right edge maybe?"

"I like that," Annabelle laughed.

"Wouldn't that look a bit tatty?" Jeremy was unsure.

"No. Not if it's frayed correctly," Holly pressed.

"Won't that add to the cost of the folders?" Tim asked, on cue.

"Not much, and remember, we're not having a launch," Jeremy pointed out. Pagett's glossy folders rarely changed. This could be a welcome departure.

"I can see we're going to end up with an enormous budget because of the money we've saved by *not having a launch*," Tim sighed, but the corners of his mouth turned up.

"So, chewed corners it is. That brings us back to a promotional gift."

"Tranqs are out, how about a bottle of gin? You know, mother's ruin – the poor beleaguered mother bit?" Annabelle asked, then wrinkled her nose with distaste at her own suggestion.

"Far too subtle," Jeremy said kindly.

"Far too expensive," Tim ruled.

"I thought of something," Holly suggested quietly. "Keeping to the children theme, how about one of those tiny teddy bears, the ones in the little cardboard containers? They usually have a message on them – *Happy Birthday*, or *I Love You*. We could use the name of the book instead. Most people can't resist a cuddly toy."

"I think that's a terrific idea," Marianna said enthusiastically. "It would tie in the whole presentation."

"I agree," Jane said.

One by one they came round to Holly's way of thinking.

"I'll organise prices on that. This meeting is going so fast, what'll I do with the rest of my day?" Jeremy asked. "OK. Advertising – magazines or radio?"

"Both," Holly pushed, cheekily.

"Perhaps you'd like a two-minute spot on national prime-time TV?" Tim laughed at the implausibility of it. "Especially as there . . . "

"is no launch," they all choroused.

"Great cabaret," Tim said.

"Would you consider a TV advert?" Holly asked innocently. She'd faint if he said yes.

"No, Holly! Absolutely not," Tim replied.

"Are you sure about that, Tim?" Jane baited.

"Swiftly changing the subject," Jeremy intervened, "do you have your A I and the author biog, Holly?"

Holly had been dreading this moment. The A I, Holly knew, was the publishers' way of getting as much advance information to the trade as possible. Concocting the fictitious author's biog had been a nightmare. Pagett liked authors to write a short profile about themselves for publicity purposes. She'd sat for hours trying to invent something suitable, but every word that she'd written seemed to scream accusingly – *liar*. Emily's biog would probably be the shortest in publishing history. Holly handed him the sparsely worded sheet. *Emily*

Howard lives in the South of England. She is the mother of five children. Tomorrow's Joy *is her first novel.*

"That's it?" Jeremy frowned. "That's all?"

"That's all she gave me," Holly lied.

"Sodding hell, Barry will freak." Annabelle pulled a face as she thought of the difficult job facing their publicist.

"Barry knows the circumstances, he's prepared to play up the agoraphobic angle for all its worth." Holly never thought she'd hear such cynical words coming from her own lips. But once this meeting was over, the necessary lies told, it would all be plain sailing.

"Where is Barry, anyway?" Tim frowned. "He should be here."

"He's with Lara Foster, she's doing radio today. We're meeting tomorrow morning, we'll sort things out then," Holly said as smoothly as if she handled this type of publicity every day.

"And the book itself?" Tim asked.

"Jane gave it to me this morning. I'll give it the final once-over tonight."

"There's very little to be done, it should be ready to go to the printers by tomorrow evening," Jane confirmed.

"How many are we printing?" Jeremy consulted his check list.

"Sixty thousand," Holly said and paled at the thought. What if nobody liked *Tomorrow's Joy,* if they fell thousands short of their expected subs? A whole warehouse of rejected books, her credibility as an editor destroyed before she'd even begun.

"I think that's all we can do for now," Jeremy said. "I'll sort out the advertising with the agency and finalise that in the next day or so."

They all made a bee-line for reception where Lois was ready with a list of their calls. Meetings were rarely interrupted unless something extremely urgent cropped up.

"Could I have a word?" Holly asked Tim as she caught up with him at his door.

"Sure, come in."

Holly perched on the edge of Tim's desk. "If it's OK with you, I've arranged to see an author this afternoon," she began. "Her name is Norma Downs. Have you heard of her?"

Tim wrinkled his forehead. "Yes, yes I've seen her name on the lists."

"I've edited a couple of books for her – with Simone's permission – and this morning I had a letter from her asking if Pagett . . . if I . . . would take her on as an author. She'd be ideal, perfect for our list . . . " Holly stopped and looked uncomfortable.

"So what's the problem?" Tim nudged gently.

"I . . . Simone seemed a little doubtful . . . Oh to hell with tact, I think Norma's too good to miss, but Simone's pulling rank."

"I see. Does Simone know her work?"

"Absolutely. She's always been keen to get hold of her, but now, for some unknown reason, she's hesitant, says she'll handle it. I'd like to grab Norma *now* before she changes her mind."

Tim sat in contemplative silence. He'd foreseen that difficulties could arise between these two, but not quite so soon. It was no secret that Simone bitterly resented losing Holly, but that was another day's work. John had stressed that he wouldn't tolerate any in-fighting or jealousy, anything that could result in loss of business for Pagett.

"I *hate* running to you with tales," Holly broke the silence, "but if I'm to make my mark as an editor, I need authors."

And who better than a well-established one like Norma Downs? Tim thought. He was amazed that Simone would be willing to pass up a sure-fire bestseller like Norma Downs. "Leave this with me, Holly. You go ahead, meet Norma. And, by the way, if you do want to meet an author, or an agent, you don't have to ask permission. Just let us know where you are in case we need to get in touch. Good luck with Norma, I'll look forward to hearing all about it."

Holly kept her smile to herself until she reached her office. It would be good to have someone on her side, especially when that someone was Pagett's managing director. If Simone wanted to fight dirty, she was ready for her.

Norma Downs greeted Holly with a warm smile. "Let me take those parcels from you. Been assaulting the shops, have you?"

Holly laughed. "You could say that. Pagett are having a party on Wednesday and naturally I've nothing to wear."

"Naturally!"

"Thanks again for the lovely flowers, Norma." Holly gave her a quick hug.

"Well deserved, I'm delighted for you. You'll make a good editor, Holly. Now, fancy a cup of tea? Did you have time for lunch?"

"I didn't," Holly admitted, "I'd love a cup of tea."

"Go on in, I'll pop the kettle on."

Holly loved Norma's study, her idea of a perfect workroom. Bright and sunny, every inch of the walls was taken up with floor-to-ceiling bookshelves. There were books and papers strewn everywhere. On the floor, on the tables. Holly flopped into an oversized chair and marvelled how Norma could ever find anything in the cheerful chaos. But Norma knew exactly what she was doing. She could lay her hands on a news clipping or a note in less time than it took to blink. She worked in organised disorder.

The study door opened with a bang. "I must get a stopper for this door," Norma said. She'd been saying that for as long as Holly could remember.

Holly cleared a tower of books from an occasional table to make room for the tray.

"You shouldn't have gone to such trouble," she objected when she saw a plate piled high with sandwiches.

"Don't worry, they're not all for you. I didn't notice the time either, I'm starving," Norma laughed.

As they ate, Holly chatted about her new job.

How Holly had changed, Norma thought as she listened. Gone was the scared, mousy little thing with the sad eyes, and in her place this assured, attractive, sweet-faced young woman, poised to

grab life by the scruff of its neck. Holly had told her
very little about herself but her eyes had always
spoken volumes, her nervousness a dead give-
away. Something had changed. Norma suspected
that it wasn't all to do with her job.

"That was lovely." Holly drained her cup.

"I suppose your burning question is, why do I
want to make a change, why *now,* after all this
time?" Norma's eyes twinkled as Holly coloured
prettily.

"Why do you want to change?" Holly asked.

"I suppose it's for that very reason, *after all this
time,*" Norma answered, enigmatically.

"I don't follow."

"I'm sure you don't, let me explain. I've been
with Roundtree Follett for years. All my writing life.
We're like an old married couple, we've become
used to each other, accepted each others' habits and
foibles. As you well know, my books 'appear' on
the market every eighteen months, with boring
regularity. No fireworks, no excitement, they just
happen. And that's the problem. I feel I deserve
better, some publicity perhaps – hype I think it's
called now – a marketing boost. I feel they're good
books, lost to a whole generation, put off by old-
fashioned covers which would stop me picking one
up to read the blurb. You know better than anyone,
my books are 'now' stories, dealing with today's
world."

Holly nodded, there was nothing old-world
about Norma's writing.

"Do you think I'm right?"

"I must admit, I've always thought your covers were a bit out-dated, bore no relation to their stories. There's nothing compelling about the covers, nothing that would urge *me* to pick one up either."

"Why on earth didn't you say this before?"

"It was hardly my place to knock another publisher's decisions."

"I suppose you're right. But you knew I wasn't entirely happy?"

"You had an odd grumble here and there, nothing serious," Holly said tactfully.

"I didn't want to be disloyal. When I gave my editor the final draft of *The Second Mrs Merriott* a couple of weeks ago, he pulled a face, then, without even consulting me, had the title changed to *Another Wife*. Just wait until you see *that* cover – a woman with a large-brimmed hat walking through a field of flowers!"

"But that's ridiculous. The book is pure inner-city," Holly objected.

"I *told* him that. But Alan's mind was made up, *you've always had those soft, ethereal covers* was his answer. I made an appointment to see Robert Follett last Friday. He was his usual charming, intransigent self. I aired my grievances but he didn't hear a word I said – or didn't choose to. They were working in my best interests, didn't my books always make the bestseller list? Didn't I trust them any more? They had their finger on the publishing pulse, all I had to do was write. On and on he went. Then suddenly I knew the marriage between

Roundtree Follett and myself had come to an end. I didn't even bother to tackle the subject of publicity, there wasn't any point. I thought about phoning you that day but I decided to wait a while, give it more thought before making any rash decisions. Then yesterday, my daughter casually mentioned how delighted she was to read that you'd been appointed as Pagett's new editor. Suddenly, I had my answer."

"I couldn't be more pleased. You know how much I love your books. Pagett will be delighted to have you on their list."

"One thing, Holly, if I do sign with Pagett, it will be on the understanding that I have some input with covers and that my books get the same marketing and publicity that all your other books do."

"That goes without saying. We're a good team and you'll enjoy being a part of it."

Norma believed her. "Obviously RF will still publish *The Second Mrs Merriott* or whatever stupid title they decide to give it but, after that, and subject to contract of course, I'm all yours."

Holly's smile dimmed. "There's something that *you* should know, and I hope it won't put you off, but we can't pay huge advances like some of the publishers."

"I know that already. I also know there are several other publishers who would be only too happy to add my name to their list, I've been approached from time to time. But my main reason for wanting to be with Pagett is because of you.

You're sympathetic to my writing, enthusiastic, and I've always liked what you've done for me. I want to head that bestseller list, Holly, be number one, not fifth, tenth, or eighteenth. And I think it could happen. I suppose you think I'm crazy?"

"No I don't. I think you'd be crazy if you didn't want to get to the top. With good publicity and marketing and that extra push . . . "

"I like the sound of that. Maybe I should make a complete change while I'm at it, use a new pen name?"

"Absolutely not, you've worked hard to earn your name," Holly said firmly. "All sorts of ideas are flashing through my mind, we'll have to sit down and talk them out. If you do have any doubts about my ability, Norma, don't forget I'm trying to earn my stripes too."

"You know, Holly, I haven't been this excited in years. I'd made up my mind that *Mrs M* would be my last book. To be honest, I'd lost heart."

Norma's family sagas had pleased a generation of women, there was no reason why they shouldn't continue to do so. But Norma was right, she needed to attract a new generation, the twenty-and-thirty-somethings.

"I almost forgot, I've brought you an invitation to the party on Wednesday. It's short notice I know, but you might enjoy it, a chance for you to get to meet everyone. Bring your daughter with you if she's free. I'd love to meet her."

"That sounds like fun. Thanks, Holly, I'll ask her."

Chapter Thirty-Nine

Simone was in a towering temper. It had been an unsatisfying week fraught with problems and she hadn't heard a word from Ian. In the shower she mentally checked her report for the board meeting. As she dried her hair she reviewed her list of requirements for her new office and, while she made up her face, struggled to find a subtle way of reining Holly in. She'd had a most unpleasant *interview* with Tim thanks to that little sneak. He'd practically accused her of putting her own interests before Pagett. Such rubbish, just because she'd erred on the side of caution about Norma Downs.

Savagely she pulled a cotton sweater over her head. She had to curb Holly's runaway enthusiasm. She was heartily sick of all the fuss over that book, you'd think it was the first one ever published – *Tomorrow's Joy* this, *Tomorrow's Joy* that. Maybe she'd been foolish to hand Lucinda Rockingham over so easily – Lucinda had quite a following. But no, just thinking about Lucinda's eccentricity drove her up the walls.

Simone threw her brief case into the back seat of her car and scorched into the traffic. She earned herself a long, loud blast from the driver behind her. She glanced briefly in her rearview mirror and saw that the driver was an elderly woman. She stuck two fingers in the air – a wrinkly like that would hardly be a candidate for road-rage. To her utter fury, when she arrived at Pagett's underground garage, her space had been taken.

"Hello, Simone," Lois said chirpily.

That's all she needed, one of Lois's gossipy monologues. "Uh huh," she replied and frowned. "Any messages?"

"Not for *you*, no," said Lois. Madame Simone would be best left alone today.

Simone's mood darkened even more. A long, complaining letter from David Conroy's agent had been rerouted to her desk. The man, one of Roland Green's authors, had apparently been promised the sun, moon and stacks of royalties. His total sales to date had amounted to fifteen copies. The agent wanted to discuss this ridiculous state of affairs *as soon as possible*. Not only did she have to deal with a pushy new editor but now she had to take the flak from an autocratic past one. This was not going to be a good day.

She flung two heavy brown envelopes on the floor by her desk. What with the party, the move, moans from Roland's authors, plus her editing, she had enough on her plate. She needed an assistant, and fast.

By ten o'clock Simone had regained her

composure. She must be calm, in control, before she went into the meeting.

Sean Barrett was sitting in her place at the boardroom table. He smiled at Simone and she returned it with what she considered to be an equally warm one of her own. He was a pleasant-looking man, a younger version of his father. Pity he wasn't a couple of years older, she thought fleetingly.

"Let's get started." Tim Brown opened his folder.

They began with sales, which were promising. There was no such thing in publishing as *enough* sales. Then they moved to reprints. The children's editor, Kathy, reported on her list. Simone's mind wandered. Could she dare suggest to Tim that *he* should cope with Roland's authors? They still had a duty to publish his contracted books. What a pity she'd discouraged Arthur Lord from making Holly their children's editor. In hindsight, that would have got Holly out of *her* hair.

Simone forced herself back to what Kathy was saying.

"I'd like to offer Keith O'Hare a three-book contract. *Lucky the Laptop Leprechaun,* has made a real impact," Kathy pointed out calmly. She had a serenity which Simone envied, and never seemed flustered no matter how difficult her task.

Their children's section was ticking over nicely and Kathy's list was already proving a valuable addition to Pagett. John had been anxious to keep publishing children's books – had a thing, he said, about kids and reading.

Again Simone's attention wavered. What *had* happened to Ian? He usually phoned, if only to say hello. She didn't even have his telephone number. She scowled as she thought of his sister's book and wondered how it would go down if she produced it at this meeting.

"Simone?"

"Yes?" she asked sharply. "Sorry, I was thinking about one of my authors."

"Your list next," Tim frowned. Normally Simone was alert, not grumpy and inattentive like this.

Simone waded through her list of forthcoming books. Two launches were imminent, John Barrett's book was on track, two of her authors needed a push if they were to be on time, and three others were waiting for contracts. She had a possible new addition, the manuscript would need a considerable amount of work but, if the author would agree to a rewrite . . .

"I have exactly the same problem," Holly interjected. "A first novel, terrific potential but the author needs guidance. This one deserves full marks for trying, sent a letter as well as the manuscript – identified it as the one with the *smily-face on the envelope*."

Simone's smily-face vanished. "The crafty little cow, I got the same letter, the same MS, she must have written to both of us."

"What do you do in a situation like that?" Sean asked. He'd been quiet so far, content to listen and observe.

"My instinct is to return it . . . " Simone scowled.

"You can hardly punish her for trying," Holly protested.

"I agree." Tim gave Simone a long searching look. What the hell had got into her today?

Simone flushed. Little Miss Goody-Two-Shoes was obviously itching to get her hands on the new author, well it wasn't going to happen.

"As I started to say before I was interrupted, my instinct is to return the MS, but I do think Claire Jones has talent, therefore I'm prepared to offer her the opportunity of a rewrite."

Holly's face was impassive and the others shifted uncomfortably on their chairs. Simone wasn't going to accept Holly's promotion graciously.

They went through the rest of Simone's schedule without incident.

"Right, Holly, you have some excellent news for us?" Tim said.

"Yes, Norma Downs, one of Roundtree Follett's bestselling authors, wants to sign with us."

"Any problems with that, Simone?" Tim asked pointedly.

"As long as she doesn't expect a sky-high advance, but then I'm sure you'll be prepared to bend the rules in her case, spend a fortune on marketing and publicity, or anything else she demands." Simone's voice dripped with sarcasm.

"That's not true, Simone," Holly intervened angrily. "I went to see Norma the other day, she's quite content, doesn't expect any VIP treatment. And as you said yourself – many times – she'd be a terrific addition to our lists." Go argue with that, you sarky bitch.

"That's settled then," said Tim, decisively. "Holly, perhaps you'll arrange another meeting with Norma, asap, then we'll sort out the nitty-gritty and sign her up. OK, we're almost finished now, let's do the book proposals for the rest of the books."

They'd filled in the details on the sheets; the author's name and address, the title of the books, number of copies to be printed, the marketing plans, publicity, launch date, everything that related to the smooth publishing of a book.

At last the meeting drew to a close.

"Will everyone let me have their list of requirements for the new offices? Naturally we can't guarantee anything but I'm sure that Sean will do his best," Tim smiled. It was nice to see someone else in the firing line for a change.

He and Sean stayed in the boardroom, fortified by a pot of Lois's extra-strength coffee.

"So, how did you enjoy your first meeting?" Tim asked as he dunked a ginger biscuit into his cup.

"I enjoyed it, it was interesting. Is it my imagination, or is there a problem between Simone and Holly?"

"You're very astute! Something is beginning to build. Obviously you know the background history – Holly always showed promise and Simone resented losing her assistant. More to the point, she's afraid that her assistant will overtake her."

"I noticed how she quickly she backed down when Holly was prepared to go ahead."

"Yes! That was an about-turn, wasn't it? As far as I'm concerned they can tear each other to shreds,

rip each other's hair out, just as long as Pagett
doesn't suffer. It's *déjà vu* – Roland Green all over
again, he and Simone were always at each other's
throats. But Holly has done nothing to deserve this.
Simone will just have to behave. If she doesn't,
she'll have me to answer to."

Sean silently applauded Tim's attitude. "Let's take
a look at those requirement lists," he said.

Tim passed him the slim folder and walked
about the room to stretch his legs.

"Jesus! This isn't a requirement list, it's a ransom
note. Listen to this – it's Simone's list." Sean read it
aloud. "A new car, a clothing allowance, a mobile
phone, a gold credit card and a coffee-maker –
she's off her head, the only thing on this list I can
approve is a coffee-maker and even that's
unnecessary. Someone should tell her that my father
is John Barrett, not John Paul Getty."

Tim laughed. "Maybe she's following in the
smily-author's footsteps – she's trying."

"Trying it on, you mean?" Sean snorted. "Let's
have a look at Holly's list. Bookshelves and a two-
year wall planner. We can live with that." He
marked the page with a tick and wrote *passed* in
large letters.

He leafed quickly through the rest of the sheets
there was nothing out of the ordinary, a request for
light, light, light, from the art department, an extra
word processor for the production department
which Tim agreed was necessary, and an enormous
budget request, followed by a page of exclamation
marks, from marketing.

"Would that I could," Sean said wryly.

"Don't take Jeremy too seriously," Tim advised. "He and I have an understanding, he suggests outlandish sums, I turn them down."

"Which leads us back to Simone. I'd like to put a pen through the lot but I'll really have to talk to Dad about this one."

"I don't envy you. But there's no panic, a few more days won't make a difference. If I may make a suggestion, don't let the others know that you've okayed their requests before you have an answer for Simone. I have to live with her!"

Sean laughed. "I take your point, good thinking. At this rate we'll have to handcuff her, but to keep her happy we'll make sure that the cuffs are made of silk."

Tim loved the analogy, this mild-mannered, humorous young Irishman was on the ball.

Simone barricaded herself in her office and concentrated her energies on editing.

When she got home, she had a quick snack and took her second shower of the day. Her headache had vanished and she was quite looking forward to the party at the new book shop. She'd heard from Rufus that it was quite magnificent and that they intended to trade seven days a week. It had been a while since she'd seen people from the publishing world, there was always a chance that some agent or other would approach her with a world-beating manuscript, a too-good-to-be-missed opportunity. She needed new blood. No way was Holly going to produce a better list than hers.

She left her car at home and hailed a taxi, at least this way she could enjoy a drink. She could have invited Holly to go with her but instead she chose to lay the guilt on Rufus. *Important for our sales,* she'd insisted. He'd have to break his date, sort out his own girl-friend troubles, they weren't her concern. Friday night or not, Pagett's sales manager should be seen at the opening.

The traffic was bumper to bumper so she sat back in the cab and relaxed. All in all, things hadn't been that bad. Tomorrow morning she was meeting Sean at the new offices, then later they had a lunch appointment with the interior decorators. He'd probably give her the go-ahead on her requirement list. Simone was quite pleased to fill her Saturday that way, it would keep her mind off Ian. She'd been positive there'd be a message waiting on her answer machine when she got home, but the green light glowed steadily, there were no calls.

She forced her thoughts away from Ian. Pagett had started out as a small but elite literary publishing house all those years ago, and had come a long way. Now, thanks to an influx of cash from John, the solid list they had, and the departure of that snotty Roland Green, they should begin to recover fairly rapidly. It was difficult to keep up with the big boys. Difficult to compete with their million plus advances, their powerful sales and marketing teams. But with her instinct for a good book and, much as it annoyed her to admit it, that little creep Holly's intuition, they should be able to keep afloat. If she had to choose between Roland the rat-editor and

Holly-the-hated, she supposed she'd have to settle for Holly, at least she'd trained her well.

The Bookcellar was enormous, three floors of books on every conceivable subject. The ground floor was devoted to fiction, non-fiction, true life and fictional crime. Simone was pleased to see that Pagett were well represented. The floor above specialised in cookery, gardening and children's books. To the left of the escalator and overlooking the street, there was a small restaurant where customers could take books and browse through them over a cup of tea or coffee and a snack. Gleaming coffee machines hissed and the tables were dotted with plates of dainty sandwiches and hot cheesy bites – not as impressive as the menu for their party, she noted. She hopped on the escalator which led to the third floor, an oasis of self-help books, health manuals and miscellaneous publications, more reference books than she'd ever seen in one place. A booklover's heaven.

There was quite a buzz by the time she returned to the ground floor. The Bookcellar had become a trawling ground for agents, sales representatives, the press, editors and the media. There were rumours about who owned the shop, some said WH Smith, others whispered Dillons, but no one really knew. A well-kept secret in the book world? Unheard of.

"Simone," Rufus called across an aisle stacked high with the latest Jeffrey Archer and John Grisham novels.

She waved as he made his way to her side. "It's a fantastic shop," she said.

"Isn't it? The escalators are a terrific idea," Rufus approved.

"Have you seen all three floors?"

"The buyer took me round when I was here last week."

"Maybe I should meet him or her?"

"Her for fiction, him for non. I can't see either of them at the moment," Rufus admitted, looking about him.

"Simone!"

"Trudy!" Simone replied in an upbeat voice. Every flicker of an eyelash would be noted by this eagle-eyed scout.

"So how are things working out at Pagett?" Trudy fished.

"Splendidly."

"And the new editor?"

"We're lucky to have her," Simone said with a wide smile.

"And Roland?"

"What about Roland?"

"I haven't heard which publisher he's deigned to honour with his presence."

"Nor I. Someone with money to burn, I imagine," Simone bitched.

"I'm sure I'll hear."

"I'm sure *if* he finds anything, you will."

But Trudy was no longer listening, her attention was focused on an argument going on in the next aisle. Simone was glad to be let off the hook. She made her way over to Gracie Johnston, an agent for two of her authors.

"I hope we'll see you at the party," Simone said after their greetings were over.

"Yes, thanks, sorry I didn't get a chance to reply."

"That's OK, it was short notice," Simone apologised.

"I see Jemima's on her own tonight, what happened to Mr Right?"

"She dumped him when she discovered his first name was Always."

Gracie chuckled. "So how are things going under the new boss?"

"Splendid," Simone had found the word to use and was sticking to it. "John was – still is – one of my most popular authors."

"So I hear."

Simone laughed. "I'm sure you did. What else have you heard?"

"That you're snogging Ian Trent," Gracie cocked her head on one side.

"If you mean I've been out with him a couple of times, then yes." Simone was reeling at the directness of the statement.

"Has he tried to unload that slag's book on you yet?"

"Excuse me?" Simone felt as though her heart had dislodged itself and was floating, free-style.

"You heard right. Jesus, Simone, he's slept his way round every editor and agent in Christendom to get the thing published."

"I haven't heard anything about a book." She was trembling from head to toe.

"You will. It's an unmitigated piece of garbage written by a foreign bird who has him truly hooked. He passes her off as his sister."

"As I said, I don't know anything about a book, but I'm sure you're wrong." Simone managed to laugh. She'd love to take a drink from the waiter at her arm but couldn't trust herself to hold a glass.

"Catch up, Simone. If you asked any woman here who's been given the Ian Trent treatment to step outside, the room would empty."

Simone's throat constricted, her tongue furred.

"And that includes you?" she asked bitchily.

"That includes me," Gracie admitted sheepishly. "But you don't need to take my word for it, check with Helen . . . and Trish over there, they got dragged down the same path."

Rufus reappeared at her side. Simone had never been so glad to be interrupted in her life. One more minute of this and she'd pass out.

"Hello, Rufus," Gracie said while Simone struggled to control her limbs.

"Fabulous shop, isn't it?" he asked.

Their voices faded. The bastard, he'd used her and apparently every other woman on two legs to try and get that piece of rubbish published. Well maybe *they'd* accepted that, but she wouldn't.

"Sorry to be the bearer of bad news, Simone. I'll be in touch," Gracie said as she spotted someone she wanted to talk to.

"Please, get me out of here," Simone begged Rufus before he could ask any questions.

"Are you ill?"

"A bit light-headed, that's all, mixed my drinks I think." Simone seized on the first thing that came to mind.

"I'll take you home," he offered.

"Thank you," she said gratefully.

Without any fuss he cleared a path in front of them.

"You sure you're OK? You're very pale," Rufus asked as they stopped outside her front door.

"I think there was something odd about the wine, I'll be fine when I lie down."

Simone certainly appeared to be sober. "You sure you don't want me to stay with you for a while?"

"I'll go straight to bed. Thanks for the lift, Rufus, I really owe you one," she said as she got out of the car on unsteady legs.

She reached the living-room before the tears fell in a great, hot, steady stream. How *could* he? Did he really think that he could get away with that? But if she hadn't met Gracie . . .

Simone curled up in her chair like a child and cried until her headache returned and all she could think of was revenge. She didn't even notice the flashing red light on her answer machine.

Chapter Forty

The loft was ideal for a party. Cooled by the river breezes blowing gently through the open windows, it was devoid of furniture, soundproofed by what appeared to be at least an acre of plush grey carpeting.

John Barrett smiled self-consciously as he posed for a photographer. The loft was comfortably crowded and wherever he looked he could see animated faces, hear the hum of conversation and laughter.

"It is going well, isn't it?" he asked his wife.

"Beautifully, don't worry," Eve assured him with a smile. She'd never known John so nervous. "The girls have done you proud, there's loads to drink and, to quote Lucy, the food is brill."

"Where is Lucy?" he fretted.

Eve stood on tiptoe. "Talking to Simone. And, before you ask, Sean's quite all right too, so go and enjoy yourself and stop worrying."

Arthur Lord's appearance was greeted with great pleasure by everyone. He was delighted to be back. He established himself in a corner near the window and was enjoying a good gossip with Holly, who positively glowed.

"That's wonderful news," he said as she told him about Norma Downs.

" . . . and Lucinda Rockingham has asked me to edit her." Holly beamed proudly.

"How is her Imperious Highness?"

"You can ask her yourself, she's just arrived."

Arthur fluttered a hand theatrically over his heart. "Am I able for Lucinda, I wonder?"

Holly laughed and waved to Lucinda and Dominic. They'd returned from Paris a few months earlier than planned.

"Holly, my pet, how are you? Arthur, you old fool, what've you been doing to yourself?" Lucinda demanded as she jutted her cheek forward to be kissed.

"Living like a Lord," he punned.

"I can see that you've recovered well. My leg's on the mend too, thank you for asking."

Dominic smiled beatifically.

"You look gorgeous, Holly," Lucinda proclaimed as she hobbled backwards on her stick to examine her editor in detail. "I love your outfit, it would look absolutely *ghastly* on me."

Holly smiled. How could Simone not like this woman?

Holly had to admit that the navy blue jacket, white skirt and collarless white blouse had been a real find. She'd discovered a new confidence about clothes. Until short skirts died their natural fashion death they'd be her trademark.

"My God, Holly, there are two of you!" Lucinda

shrieked as Liz and Robert joined them. This woman *had* to be Holly's sister, though not quite so pretty.

Lucinda stared at Liz. No, definitely not as pretty.

Holly hugged them both, then introduced them to Lucinda, Dominic and Arthur.

"Holly had a wonderful time in Paris," Liz said, fascinated to meet the woman Holly had described.

"Not as wonderful as she would've if I'd been mobile."

Holly linked her arm through Dominic's. "Well we had a marvellous night out, didn't we, Dominic?" she teased.

"Forget him, Holly, I've told you before, he's mine," Lucinda commanded and they all laughed, none louder than Dominic.

"You look sensational, the jacket's a wow," Liz whispered as Lucinda held the floor again.

"You're quite right, she does." Lucinda apparently had the ability to talk and listen at the same time.

"I'm actually delighted with it now, I wasn't so sure when I bought it," Holly confessed.

"Well *I'm* sure," Lucinda pronounced. "Don't look so shocked, Liz, Holly's used to me, every time I open my mouth I put my great fat opinion in it."

Liz was warming to Lucinda.

"Where's Terence?" Liz asked when Lucinda finally paused for breath.

"See that crowd of women over there, he's somewhere in the middle of it."

They made their way over to the knot of

laughing people. Holly left the Rockinghams with Arthur and Amanda, who had come to check on her husband, and went to find Norma and her daughter. But Norma was talking to a journalist.

"Congratulations, Holly."

Holly felt herself colour, she knew the face but couldn't put a name to it.

"Not you *too*?" the girl groaned. "It's me, Holly, *Lucy*. Don't say it, you didn't recognise me."

Holly hadn't seen her since the launch of John's last book. "You look so grown up, so sophisticated!"

"Well, that's better than my idiot brother's remark – that I cleaned up well for the occasion!"

"Take no notice of brothers," Holly advised airily without a jot of experience in that field.

"Seriously, I wanted to wish you well. Dad says you're terrific. He's delighted that you're one of Pagett's editors."

Holly still hadn't learned to accept compliments. Tonight her face had been like a lift – up and down, up and down the colour had travelled.

"I adore my new job," she admitted.

"I hear you've got a terrific book on the way. I've told Dad I want a copy when it comes out."

"I think we can do better than that, proof copies are due any day now, I'll send you one."

"Wicked! This long holiday has been so boring. I work in a pub three nights a week, but now that my exams are over and I've caught up on my sleep, the days are a drag. All my friends are either working full time or working abroad. There aren't that many casual jobs to be had in Dublin," Lucy grumbled.

"Is my daughter giving you a hard time?" John ruffled Lucy's hair.

"Da-ad!" Lucy objected. "I went through torture to get my mop looking like this."

"I'm sorry, darling," he said with twinkling eyes.

"Lucy was telling me that she finds the long recess boring."

"Yes," John frowned. "It's a shame the job she was promised in the States fell through."

"What do you want to do when you've finished college?" Holly asked the freckle-nosed girl.

"Write?" Lucy said, timidly for her.

"That's wonderful, we'll soon have two generations of writers."

"Yeh, but Dad thinks that when I have my degree I should spend some time in the business to see if I like it. Don't you, Dad?"

"I do," John confirmed.

"Good idea," Holly said. "Come to think of it, why not now?"

"Now? You mean now – as in *now*?"

"Well, yes."

"Why didn't *I* think of that," John said. "This would be a perfect opportunity. Spend some time at Pagett, get to know how things work. You could stay with Sean. I'm sure he wouldn't mind."

"Will I get paid?" Lucy asked with a cheeky grin.

"No, you won't," said John firmly.

"Oh, OK. Can I hang around with you, Holly?"

"Of course you can."

"Whoa there, just a minute," John said with a frown. "Lucy, Simone has always been . . . well, she's encouraged you . . . "

Holly had had enough run-ins with Simone already. "Will you excuse me? I'll see you later, Lucy." Let John sort that problem out.

"How are you doing?" Holly asked Terence.

"I'm having a ball. I love all these bitchy men and women and their intrigues, I could really take to this publishing lark." He lowered his voice. "Remind me later to tell you a bit of gossip I heard about Simone."

Terence looked extremely distinguished in his black suit and colourful wide tie. When had the contours of his cherubic face begun to appear? He had lost weight and she hadn't even noticed.

"You look super," she said. "When did you lose all that weight?"

"Now she asks!" Terence affected a hurt look.

"Sorry to interrupt, Holly, can I have a word?" Barry, their publicist, was at her elbow.

She introduced the two men. "What's up?"

"Bill Tripp from the *Review* wants to meet you to arrange an interview."

Holly's lift went down to the basement. She'd never been interviewed before and thoughts of her deception began a strange little dance in her head.

"I can't do an interview. I wouldn't know what to say, where to begin," she protested.

"You'll be fine, just be yourself," Barry soothed. "As an editor you're going to have to get used to having a more public face. Bill's a decent guy, he won't give you a hard time. If you don't like a question, side-step it, smile and change the topic." Barry had passed that advice on to authors more times than he could count.

Holly looked at Terence for support, he'd get her out of this.

"Of course you can do it, Holly, you can do anything you set your mind to. You'll charm the pants off him, I *know* you will." Terence encouraged.

That wasn't the answer she wanted to hear but Terence was a great morale booster. If Barry hadn't been standing there, she'd have thrown her arms around Terence and kissed him.

With her head held high, a smile firmly pasted in place, she went to meet her doom.

Simone stopped to say hello to Liz and Robert. She hadn't seen Liz for ages. "You must be very proud of your sister," she said.

Liz's eyes narrowed defensively. "I am. I've always known Holly had great potential and I'm glad that she has a chance to prove it now. But then who knows that better than *you*, Simone?" she asked with a sweet smile.

Simone drew back, obviously Holly had been feeding her stories. Liz made her feel as though *she'd* been the one standing in Holly's way. No such luck, more's the pity, she thought sourly.

"Let me introduce you," Liz said when Terence joined them. "Terence Warren, Simone Pearse."

"Lovely to meet you at last," Terence said politely. "I've heard a lot about you."

"Some of it good, I hope," Simone replied as she scanned the room.

"Some of it," Terence replied with an angelic smile that left the three of them wondering whether he was joking.

Simone smiled, touched Robert lightly on the arm to annoy Liz, and left.

She could see Trudy out of the corner of her eye and turned in the opposite direction to avoid her. As she crossed the floor she saw Ian posed in the doorway, his hands in his trouser pockets, looking coolly about him.

Heads turned her way, she resented the pitying looks from the women she instantly labelled witches. After a moment's discussion they returned to their coven.

"Bastard," she hissed under her breath.

As if in slow motion the thing she dreaded most began to happen, Ian and Trudy were converging, heading her way. Trudy, flicking ash on the pale-grey carpet, reached her first.

"Either we don't meet for months or we see each other twice in a week," Simone greeted her. But Trudy didn't reply, she was far more interested in Ian.

"Hello, Ian," Simone said coolly. "I'm sorry I haven't had time to return your calls, it's been a hectic week." That sounded satisfyingly impersonal.

Ian took her hand but Simone slipped his grasp. Mistake number one, she cursed herself silently, Trudy was bound to have noticed. Trudy with her twenty-twenty vision could probably split an atom without the aid of a magnifying glass.

"Have you two met?" Simone asked wearily.

"Once. I'm a great admirer of your column," Ian replied smoothly.

"And I'm a great admirer of your publicity," Trudy retorted.

If only I could disappear in a cloud of smoke, Simone wished, but the only wisp of smoke available was that of Trudy's ever-present cigarette.

"And what publicity is that?" Ian smiled.

Was the man mad? Fancy giving Trudy an opportunity like that.

"How are you enjoying the party?" said Simone, desperate to steer them along a different path.

Trudy gave her a knowing smirk and ignored the question. "Your publicity, Ian Trent."

"I don't understand."

"That trail of broken hearts you've left behind you." Trudy chose her words carefully. Only yesterday her boss had called her into his office and forcefully reminded her about libel and slander laws.

"Ah! But that was before I met *you*," Ian teased. "Life is one long search for the right person, don't you agree?"

"Depends how long your list is," Trudy said slyly.

"Short, Trudy, short." As he smiled at her, his eyes softened, those chocolate-brown eyes that had fooled everyone completely. "You don't have a drink, Trudy, let me get you one." Ian took the spent cigarette from her fingers and moved towards the bar table.

"*You're* on his A list, I gather," Trudy said, her eyes dreamily following Ian's tall figure.

Simone watched, astonished. The stupid bitch was actually falling for his guff, but then, didn't we all?

"I'm not on *any* of Ian's lists, we've known each other for ages."

"And the book?" Trudy probed. "Have you been asked to publish *the book*?"

"What book? Has Ian written a book?" Simone frowned prettily.

"Never mind," Trudy said quickly as the smiling Casanova returned with her drink.

Simone was torn between making a quick escape, or brazening it out. While she dithered, the decision was taken out of her hands by John who wanted her to meet an author.

Adam Bone was aptly named. Simone was not surprised to learn that this sinister-looking man, with his mane of jet-black hair and piercing cold eyes, was a horror-story writer. If a book of his was ever filmed, the casting director need look no further for someone to fill the lead role.

"Adam's just finished his first book, a futuristic, horror novel. Do you think you could take a look at it?" John asked enthusiastically.

"Not science fiction?" Simone asked. She wished John would be more circumspect.

"No, I don't like science fiction although the book does end in the first decade of the next century," Adam replied unsmilingly.

"Send me a copy, but I must warn you that you won't receive any preferential treatment." Simone smiled briefly but unconvincingly.

John curled his toes with embarrassment. There was no need for such rudeness. What had happened to the pleasant young woman he used to know – not that long ago?

"Simone doesn't want you to be disappointed, isn't that right, Simone?"

She was craning to see what Ian and Trudy were up to.

"Simone!" John repeated. Now she was being insufferably rude.

"Forgive me, what did you say?"

"Never mind," Adam said. "I'm sure your editor has other things on her mind. Nice to see you again, John."

As Adam lost himself in the crowd, John wheeled on her furiously. "How dare you treat anybody like that?"

"Like what?" asked Simone, taken aback at his vehemence.

"You were blatantly rude. Tell me, are you finding your job too challenging or have you just lost interest?"

Simone pushed her hair back from her face, a habit she had when she was nervous. "I'm sorry, John . . . I wasn't aware. But now that you bring it up, I do have . . . a . . . problem with books that are foisted on me by friends, or friends of friends. I'm wary of making promises that I can't fulfil. It's happened before. I don't want to get trapped into rejecting something that I shouldn't have taken in the first place."

"First of all, Adam Bone is *not* my friend and secondly I'm not foolish enough to expect you to publish *anything* that you consider unsuitable. But while you're representing Pagett, I expect you to be courteous and polite, no matter what."

"I really *am* sorry," she repeated in a miserable voice.

"OK. Subject closed. Now, I have some news for you, Lucy's going to spend a month or so at Pagett, learning the ropes."

"That's wonderful!" Simone's glum face lit up.

For a moment a glimpse of the old Simone showed through. John felt a bit ashamed that he'd tackled her so harshly.

Ian followed Simone's progress round the room. "I left my number, why didn't you answer my calls, darling?" he asked when he finally got her on her own. "Is something wrong?"

"Wrong? Of course not, what *could* be wrong?" Funny how things had worked out, now that she no longer cared a fig, he'd left a contact number on her answer machine.

"I phoned on Friday night, again on Saturday and on Monday," he reproached her.

"This week has been unbelievably pressured and it's not over yet. The rest of this week and most of next is chock-a-block too," she replied.

"We're still on track for next weekend, aren't we?"

"Of course we are," she cooed. "I'm looking forward to it, it'll be a *very* special weekend."

"For me too. What are you doing after the party, would you fancy going somewhere relaxing for a snack?"

"I'd adore that but I've already made arrangements."

"Can't you break them?" Ian wasn't used to being turned down.

Simone shook her head. "I wish I could break them," she said regretfully. *Over your head,* she added silently.

"In that case I might as well be on my way," he said in a disappointed voice. "I'll talk to you at the beginning of the week?"

"Leave it till Thursday, things should have eased up by then."

"OK, Thursday it is. By the way, is that Holly over there, in the navy-blue jacket?"

Simone didn't need to follow his gaze. Ian and Holly, now wouldn't *that* be poetic justice, she thought spitefully. "Yes, that's Holly."

"Pretty lady. See you next week, darling."

Simone turned her head skilfully as he leant forward to kiss her. For one glorious moment she thought he was going to lose his balance.

Liz and Robert refused John's invitation to a late supper and party post-mortem. Holly slipped a large envelope into Robert's pocket. "Don't open this until Monday," she warned. "It's your anniversary present." As she watched them drive away, she wished they lived nearer.

The Barretts, Simone, Tim and his wife took the first two taxis, leaving Holly and Terence to follow on to John and Eve's hotel. None of them noticed the figure slouched in a car, bow tie almost hidden by his jacket.

"Tell me what you heard about Simone," Holly demanded as she flopped back in her seat.

"That guy she's been seeing – Ian Trent – the word is that he's romanced every female editor this side of the pond in order . . . "

Holly eyes opened wide as Terence repeated the story.

What a louse. "Poor Simone," she sympathised.

"How did you get on with Bill Tripp?" Terence asked.

"Very well, I think. I'm doing the interview next week, he invited me to lunch. Did I tell you, I've been asked to take part in a writers' workshop? I'm really excited about that, maybe I'll be lucky and find some new authors there. Lucinda's a hoot, isn't she? Did you meet Norma Downs?" Holly prattled excitedly. Terence sat quietly and let her.

The impromptu supper was relaxing, the perfect wind-down to end the night.

"Lucy will be a live-wire to have around," Terence said as he paid off the taxi outside their flat. To everyone's amusement, he and Lucy had sparked off each other as if they'd been friends for years.

"She reminds me of Lucinda, they have the same sense of fun," Holly said with a tired smile. "I don't know about you, but I'm kermuzzled."

"I'm sure I am – if I knew what it meant."

"Exhausted, wiped out."

"That has my vote. Can you last one more minute without expiring?" Terence asked.

"Just about, why?"

"Come in for a second," he said as switched on the lights in his flat and disappeared into the bedroom.

Holly knew she'd fall asleep if she sat down so she paced about in the limited space.

Terence shyly handed her a small gift-wrapped parcel.

"What's this?" she asked.

"Open it," he instructed.

Holly peeled away the paper and lifted out a tiny lacquered Indian headdress. She looked at him quizzically.

"Take a look in the tissue underneath."

Holly unfolded it and exclaimed with delight as she discovered several miniature white feathers, each tinged along its border with bright, jewelled colours.

"They're beautiful."

With careful fingers, Terence took the largest of the graded feathers and inserted it into a tiny hole in the centre of the headdress. "I hope you like the idea – a sort of meter-of-achievement," he said. "For each success, award yourself a feather, for every hurdle you cross . . . "

"What a lovely thought." Holly's voice choked with emotion and tiredness. "I'll treasure it always."

Terence shuffled with embarrassment but it took him an effort to let her go when she gently kissed him goodnight.

Chapter Forty-One

Trudy's Friday column was remarkably subdued, she confined herself to a report of the party and a few caustic observations about Roland Green's absence. Reading Trudy's column at Lois's desk had become almost a ritual at Pagett.

Holly could feel the dead summer heat beginning to build and was tempted to phone Liz and ask if she could spend the weekend with them. But she mustn't allow herself to become dependent. She imagined their reaction to her anniversary gift; two air tickets to Paris and a three-night stay at the Hotel de Louvre. She could almost hear Liz's shrieks of excitement, followed no doubt by an in-depth enquiry – how could Holly afford such an extravagant present? But Holly had her answer ready, her pay rise would more than cover the trip – no need to mention the advance for *Tomorrow's Joy*.

Holly looked at the clock on her desk, she'd wasted half an hour. Yesterday had been the same, probably the anticlimax after the excitement of the previous weeks. She pulled herself together and began to tackle the post.

Her eyes widened. There was no return address on Bunny Bly's flowery notelet. She was surprised that Bunny had even signed it.

. . . I know that Derek has already explained that our trip to Paris was a business arrangement, nothing more. I assure you that he has eyes for no one but you . . .

He doesn't give up, Holly thought bitterly. Her mouth was dry and she felt the walls begin to close in around her. She couldn't wait to get into her new office with its air conditioning and, better yet, windows that opened. But this claustrophobia had nothing to do with the office. She breathed slowly until her heart stopped pounding. It infuriated her that Derek could still evoke such feelings of panic. Decisively, she put the note into an envelope and addressed it to Vincent Harper. He was her solicitor, let him decide what to do with it.

She added two manuscripts to the ever-growing stack in the corner and tore through the rest of her mail. The exhilaration of opening the post every morning had palled, all sorts of junk mail now reached her desk. Today, apart from Bunny's letter, there was nothing of any importance; a couple of trade invitations, literary magazines and a two-page synopsis for a book. Two pages! Holly glanced at the first page, then took a rejection slip from her desk and put it in an envelope with the two skimpily typed sheets. At Simone's instigation, Pagett's editors no longer signed the rejection slips. That kept it impersonal. Holly was happy with this system. She'd read a couple of abusive letters

Simone had received from disappointed writers. Hers was an awesome power, the only aspect of her job that she was beginning to dislike; months, maybe years, of an author's work committed to paper, then rejected on the turn of a page. Maybe in time she'd learn not to care so much but it had to be done. Anonymity helped.

Holly gathered up her replies and dropped them off at Lois's desk on the way to the Friday meeting. She was more at ease now, not nearly so nervous as she had been in the beginning.

She was surprised to see John in the boardroom. "Take no notice of me," he said, "I'm just here to learn."

The meeting was calm. They worked quickly through the sales and reprints, then discussed the new books. Simone confirmed that her *smily-face* author, Claire Jones, was willing to redraft her manuscript and Holly reported that she'd set up a meeting with Norma Downs.

"I think you should offer her a one-book contract to begin with," Simone cautioned.

"Let's see what she has to say first," Tim replied firmly.

"If I can stick my oar in here," John ventured. "Surely it would be better to have a *three*-book contract? It's not like it's a first novel, she's a popular writer, already has a huge following. How can we go wrong?"

Holly shot him a look of gratitude.

"Suit yourself, you're the boss," Simone said scathingly.

John's eyes narrowed.

Kathy told them about a hitch in the children's section; one of her illustrators was ill and expected to be in hospital for some time. The book wouldn't be ready for the printers in time, it would have to be added to the Spring list.

"Are you happy with that?" Simone asked.

Kathy shrugged. "I've no option. But I can fit it in at the end of March, the author prefers to wait rather than take on a new illustrator at this stage."

"So we'll schedule it for March." Tim made a note in the diary. "Keep an eye on what's happening. If the worst comes to the worst, she'll have to accept another date or drop the book altogether."

Sean picked up the requisition lists and distributed the folded sheets. John Barrett watched as a dull flush spread over Simone's exquisitely high cheekbones. Her request for a coffee-maker had been granted, nothing else. Her head snapped up. John met her gaze steadily. She crumpled the page, collected her notes and without any explanation, left the meeting. John turned his attention back to the others gathered around the table – their expressions and comments showed their satisfaction. Holly beamed contentedly.

If there was one thing he was sure about in all of this, promoting Holly was the best thing he'd done.

Simone slammed into her office, too furious to speak. Everything on her list with the exception of a miserable coffee-maker had been crossed out, scored through like a child's homework. It was insulting. She had to represent Pagett at all those functions, John should give her a dress allowance. How long did they expect her car to last? But to put a dismissive line through her requests like that . . .

"Yes?" she snapped as she heard a knock on her door.

John Barrett could feel the undercurrent. He crossed the room slowly and sat opposite her.

"You left the meeting rather suddenly," he said.

Simone picked up the crumpled sheet of paper. "I didn't expect this."

"So I gathered. Admit it, Simone, you were chancing your arm a bit, weren't you?"

"I don't think so, I don't think so at all," Simone said and began to justify the reasons for her requests.

John listened politely until she had finished. "I agree that you need clothes for the functions you attend, and that sometimes – not often – you need a car. Let me tell you how I see it. You've had a substantial increase in salary, earn far more than most editors – I know because I've checked. That should take care of your clothes. A gold card? You already have a company credit card, who are you trying to impress? We're quite willing to pay taxi fares when necessary, so your car is your own responsibility. You're also linked into a generous bonus scheme. There aren't too many people who'd turn down your job, Simone, believe me."

Simone swallowed her retort. Was John threatening her?

"I see," she said.

John was finding it difficult to come to terms with this side of Simone. He'd always prided himself on being a good judge of people. How could he have got it so wrong? Had Simone changed completely?

"I suggest for both our sakes, we settle this now," John advised. "If we're going to have a good working relationship, it's imperative that we're both happy. If you want to reconsider your position at Pagett, I'll understand. I'll release you from your contract and you can walk away – no hard feelings. Now, I can't say fairer than that, can I?"

He *was* threatening her. Slowly she realised she was in danger of losing the thing that meant most to her; not Ian and his manipulative lies, not Holly and her defection – she could be replaced – not even Mark. But her editorship at Pagett.

"I don't want to reconsider. You *know* how much Pagett means to me," she said. This time she meant it.

"Good. I'm pleased we've cleared the air. Now I'll tell you what I am prepared to do, to turn the cupboard that's attached to your office into a cloakroom. It will be quite small, very basic, but it'll be all yours."

"Thank you, John," Simone said meekly.

"There's something else. I want you to keep an eye on Lucy for me. As you know she'll be back in London on Monday. I think you'll have an idea if she shows any aptitude, if she's right for publishing."

"I'll do everything I can, I'm very fond of Lucy. Besides, she'll be good company," Simone said sincerely.

"That she will." John's eyes softened.

Chapter Forty-Two

Lucy breezed into Pagett the following Monday like a breath of fresh air. Simone was delighted with the distraction – it had been a long weekend. She'd toasted her thirtieth birthday alone and in tears with only a rushed phone call from Mark to celebrate the day.

"I'll take you to all the different departments," she offered. "That way you'll soon get to know who does what, and how."

Lucy watched, fascinated, as Marianna changed the background colour on one of her book covers. "I didn't know you could do that on a computer," she said as she pulled up a chair and sat beside her.

"We do it all the time," Marianna explained.

"There's a call for you, Simone," Lois called from the open doorway.

"You'll be fine here with Marianna," Simone said.

Lucy nodded absently, she was engrossed.

"Darling," Ian's voice purred. "I was hoping I'd catch you, I hated not seeing you this weekend, did you miss me?"

"Of course I did," she replied through clenched teeth.

"I know I said I'd phone on Thursday but I'll be away for the rest of the week so I wanted to make arrangements with you now. Do you have a pen handy? I'll give you the address of the hotel. Would you mind if I arranged to meet you there, it's almost on my route? I doubt if I'll make it much before seven o'clock as it is."

"That's OK."

"Good. Super party the other night, by the way."

"How *is* your friend Trudy?" Simone asked sarcastically.

Ian laughed. "I found her very amusing."

His next victim? she wondered. "I hope for your sake it stays that way. I must cut out now, someone is waiting for me. Let me have the address."

As Simone wrote she frowned, he was lashing out a bit. The Orangerie, an exclusive country house hotel, had opened its doors to rave reviews and it was extremely expensive. At least he intended carrying out his cynical exploitation of her in style.

"See you about seven? Oh, I almost forgot, have you had a chance to read my sister's book yet?" he asked casually.

"I've read *Brigette's* book, yes."

Why did she emphasise the name, he wondered? "What did you think of it?"

"Let's talk about that on Friday, I've got to go."

"But can you give me . . . "

Simone replaced her phone. At last an idea had

begun to hatch in her mind. She sat quietly at her desk and thought her plan through. By the time Lucy reappeared, Simone was smiling widely.

"What can I do now?" Lucy prowled around Simone's office. "What are all those big envelopes? Manuscripts?" she asked. Her father used those large bubble-envelopes all the time for his work.

"Yes. They're the ones I haven't got around to reading yet."

"All those poor authors sitting at home biting their nails. How do they know their manuscripts have even arrived?"

"They don't until we've had a chance to read them."

"And then what?"

Simone explained.

"I don't think I'd survive the wait." Lucy groaned.

"Just a thought, why don't you take a couple of them home with you tonight? Read them, tell me what you think."

"Brill! I'm not going out tonight, I'd love that. Will I write you a report?"

"Sure, I'll sort out a couple for you later. Now, it's time for lunch, do you want to eat here or go out?"

"What do you usually do?" Lucy asked.

"Depends how busy I am, sometimes I stay here and order in a sandwich, other times I go out for a snack."

"Let's eat here so I can get the feel of things."

Lucy washed their plates and mugs while Simone dried. "I haven't seen Holly yet," she remarked.

"She'll be back soon, she went to meet the interior decorators to choose a colour scheme for her new office."

"What colours did you pick?" Lucy asked.

"Creams mostly. I like neutral colours."

"I'd like mine . . . gun-metal and black, I'm into that."

"I'm glad you're not decorating my office." Simone shuddered. "Come on, let's go and see if Holly's back."

They bumped into Jane's hurrying figure in the corridor. "Whoops!" she said as a book fell from her hand. "The proof copies of Holly's book have arrived," she explained.

"Maybe we'll have a bit of peace now," Simone remarked.

"We're going to Holly's office, let me take it for you," Lucy was disturbed by Simone's bitchy tone. Simone had always been a bit of an idol of hers. She'd never been like this before.

"Thanks, Lucy."

Holly wasn't in her office. "Do you want to wait for her?" Simone asked.

"Yes, I'll start reading this. I hear it's super."

"I haven't read it."

"You should," Lucy said. Dad was right, Simone was jealous of Holly.

* * *

"Your sister phoned three times," Lois said. "You've to phone her immediately you get back. And Lucy is waiting in your office for you . . . " Lois's switchboard flashed. "Excuse me a minute. Oh, hi Liz, she's just this second come in, hold on."

Holly reached for the phone. "Hello Liz, you were looking for me?"

Lois watched a grin appear on Holly's face. "You're more than welcome, happy anniversary. Sorry? Yes of course I can afford it, don't worry, just have a fabulous time. Ring the travel agent when you've decided on a date. I'll talk to you tonight, and happy anniversary again."

Lucy jumped when Holly called her name. "I didn't hear you come in, I was really into this book."

"What are you reading?"

"*Tomorrow's Joy*. I hope you don't mind. Jane gave me this proof copy to give to you."

Holly's face lit up. She almost grabbed the book out of Lucy's hand.

She held it reverentially. The sepia tones of the proof copy weren't nearly as colourful as the finished cover would be but it was thrilling to see the book in print.

Lucy grinned at Holly's delight. "It must be terrific to follow a book from start to finish."

"Oh it is, it really is." Holly cradled the book in her arms. "Now at last we can get moving. Come with me to the production department."

Jane was waiting for her. "I knew you'd come dashing in here the minute you got back," she teased.

"Doesn't it look wonderful?" Holly asked.

"Not as wonderful as it will do when the real cover's on, but yes, it's great." Jane wondered how long it would take before Holly became blasé.

There were several piles of proof copies stacked on the floor. "May I have a couple?" Holly asked.

"Of course," Jane said and gave her three copies.

"Here you are, Lucy." Holly gave her back the book. "When will these be sent out?" she asked Jane.

"They'll be posted tomorrow. I've just dropped the labels off to Lois. Jeremy will take over after that."

"Anything I can do to help?"

"No, all you have to do is sit back and relax."

"I've had a super day." Lucy collected the manuscripts from Simone. "I'll start on these tonight and let you know what I think."

"Take your time, there's no hurry." Simone had selected two unread manuscripts and another that she couldn't quite make up her mind about. Her borderlines, she called them. Perhaps Lucy might help her decide.

When Simone arrived in her office the following morning, a manuscript lay on her desk. Without prompting from her, Lucy had chosen to read the borderline first. Simone smiled as she read the sharp, concise report. *Wonderfully descriptive, elegantly written, endlessly boring.*

"I haven't said the wrong thing, have I?" Lucy lolled on the visitor's chair. "I kept waiting for something to happen, but it didn't."

"No, you haven't said anything wrong, in fact, it's a very perceptive critique."

"You've read the manuscript?" Lucy frowned. Was she being tested?

"Yes, I felt the same way but needed another opinion. You've made my mind up for me."

Lucy's frown instantly disappeared and she looked pleased. She didn't tell Simone that she'd been awake most of the night reading *Tomorrow's Joy*. Now *that* was a wonderful book.

Holly listened avidly to Lucy's enthusiastic praise.

"I'm sure Emily will be happy that you enjoyed it," she said. "Terence sends his love and wants to know if you'll come for dinner on Thursday, it's his turn to cook."

"*Can* he cook?"

"Oh yes, he has quite a repertoire now. We take it in turns, me one week, him the next."

"Are you going to marry him?" Lucy asked.

The question caught Holly totally off guard. "No! And I couldn't even if I wanted to, I'm not divorced yet," she said.

"Sorry, I shouldn't have said that, you've turned as red as your lipstick."

"No, you shouldn't," Holly agreed but laughed anyway.

"Mum always says my tongue will hang me one of these days."

"You'd certainly need all the tact you can find if you want to stay in this business," Holly warned.

Lucy pulled a face. "Imagine ending a career before it even begins."

"It's not that bad. Just think before you speak, avoid confrontation and you'll be fine. Be careful. Publishing is an emotional business," Holly warned.

"How come you're such an expert on confrontation?" Lucy demanded.

"My ex-husband regarded any form of argument or adverse response as insubordination." Why she had brought this up, she didn't know.

"How terrible. I'm glad . . . " Lucy stopped.

"You're glad what?" Holly prompted.

"Wait, I'm thinking, before I stick my size eight Reeboks in it again. I'm glad that you don't have to put up with that any more," she finished triumphantly. She had been going to say that she was glad Holly had dumped the pig.

"Come on, I'll make you a coffee, then you can relax and be yourself again."

* * *

Simone waited until Wednesday before she phoned The Orangerie.

"Reception please," she requested.

"How may I help you?" a plummy voice asked.

"You have a booking for Mr Ian Trent, this weekend?"

"We do, but if he wishes to cancel it he'll have to forfeit his deposit," Plummy said sharply.

Simone ignored her remark. "I'm Mr Trent's

secretary and he'd like to know if it's possible to up-grade the room to a suite?"

"Hold one moment, please."

Simone fiddled impatiently with the cord of her phone.

"Yes, we have one suite available, our most prestigious suite," she stressed.

A euphemism for *our most expensive*, Simone noted with a satisfied smirk.

"Mr Trent *will* be relieved. I take it that you have room service?"

"*Of course*, Madam," the receptionist said.

"Mr Trent would like a meal served in the suite on Friday night. He and Lady . . . I mean . . . his partner, should arrive about seven o'clock." Simone paused just long enough to allow her supposed slip to take effect. "He'd prefer something cold, something that wouldn't spoil if they're a little delayed. What do you suggest?"

"Let me get a menu," the receptionist said. She wouldn't employ a secretary like that, her boss would be *furious* if he knew she'd almost divulged the name of the woman accompanying him. "Sorry for the delay," she said less than a minute later.

"What can you recommend as a starter?" Simone asked.

"Cold soup? Vichyssoise?"

"No. Too boring."

"Pâté de fois gras?"

"Umm, perhaps. Anything a little more . . . exciting?" Simone mused.

"Caviar?"

"Both. Yes, that'll do very nicely. With champagne."

"Not vodka?"

Simone could almost hear her raising her eyebrows. "Vodka, yes, but he would also like champagne."

"Do you have any preference? Krug, Cristal?'

"Which do *you* recommend?" I can use euphemisms for expensive too, you supercilious twit.

"The Krug, I think, it's excellent."

"Right. The main course – lobster mayonnaise is a favourite of . . . Mr Trent's."

"Certainly, we've had magnificent lobsters this week."

"Good. With asparagus and artichoke hearts? I'll leave the rest of the trimmings to you." Simone's stomach began to rumble.

"I'll inform Chef. He won't disappoint you."

"I'm sure he won't. Dessert – exotic fruits, some wild strawberries, that type of thing. And to complement the fruit?"

"Our pastry chef's *petites tartes*, a *brûleé* perhaps?"

"Make it a selection of desserts."

"Coffee? Liqueurs?"

"They'll order those themselves."

"Now let me check, you'd like to start with . . . Then drinks, vodka, champagne . . . "

"That's correct," Simone said as the list came to the end. She was almost tempted to go along just for the meal. "I presume Mr Trent left you his credit card number?" she asked. This would be a total waste of time if he hadn't.

"One moment . . . yes, he booked by credit card."

"Men! They'd forget their own names if we weren't there to remind them," Simone said conspiratorially.

"Indeed," the receptionist agreed.

"So I can rely on you, the meal will be ready in the suite when they arrive?"

"Of course," the receptionist's voice bristled.

"One more thing, a package will arrive sometime on Friday afternoon. Mr Trent would like it taken to the suite and placed on the bed." Her own voice had taken on a superior tone just from listening to the woman who, she decided, probably had a whiskery chin.

"Certainly. I understand."

"Thank you for all your help, I'm sure Mr Trent will have a very special weekend."

Simone replaced her receiver and began to laugh. Deep throaty chuckles. She only had one regret, that she wouldn't be there to see Ian's reaction. She could almost visualise his smug smile when he saw the champagne cooling in the bucket, the sumptuous meal. She could imagine him calling her name. How long would it take before he realised that he'd been outsmarted? But there was no time to revel in daydreams, there was still the florist to contact.

"Floral Revenge," a voice answered.

"I would like to send a package to someone, it's a fairly thick manuscript, one that's died the death. Can you suggest something suitable to accompany it?" At least she could be honest with this woman who specialised in revenge.

"How about our little white satin-lined coffin containing a black rose?" the florist suggested.

Simone began to laugh again. "Absolutely perfect," she said. She gave the florist the name and address of the hotel. "I'll send the manuscript over by courier."

"Perhaps we could tie it with black ribbon for you?" the florist said helpfully.

"Even better," Simone replied. That had sparked another idea. She would buy a black-edged card and use that instead of a refusal slip.

*   *   *

Simone closed her front door with a sigh of relief. The week had been endless, the Friday meeting worse than endless.

Now she could forget Pagett's problems and focus her mind on Ian. She expected his phone-call about seven-thirty. She'd practised a dozen different speeches, scathing, bitter accusations, only to change her mind. The hurt, how-could-you-approach might be more effective, but why should she give him the satisfaction? She emptied a tub of potato salad and some slices of cold meat on to a plate and decided to play it by ear.

By nine o'clock she'd edited the same pages five times. Too late for a call, was he going to arrive at her flat unannounced? Should she open the door to him or pretend to be out? She switched off the computer, her concentration non-existent. Eleven o'clock – it wouldn't take him this long, even in heavy traffic. By midnight a feeling of unease gripped her. Ian's lack of response was unnerving, she'd be screaming blue murder if anyone pulled a stunt like that on her.

Chapter Forty-Three

"Very editorish!" Lucy explored Simone's elegant new office. She poked her head round the door of the cloakroom. "This is handy," she said.

It was fortuitous that the little room attached to her office had been so easily adaptable, otherwise she wouldn't have had that either.

The three floors of offices were quite sumptuous compared to Pagett's Chelsea headquarters. A lift swished silently up and down, there was even a converted dumb waiter in which they could place papers to save travel between floors.

Lucy and Sean Barrett had been miraculous. They'd heaved and humped packing cases to all the right rooms, then leant a hand to store the contents. Sean inspected faulty plugs, connected computers and was generally available when problems arose, Lucy ran a make-shift canteen with ferocious dedication.

Holly quailed when she first saw the rows of buttons on her phone. "I'll never get the hang of this," she moaned. Lucy made her a user-friendly chart. Her magnificent new bookshelves boasted two proof copies of *Tomorrow's Joy,* a signed copy of each of Norma's books and one volume of every book she had edited so far, a total of fourteen. In pride of place on a corner of her curved desk sat the little Indian headdress. Holly sighed with contentment, this was utter luxury compared to the cubby-hole that Arthur Lord had awarded her – utter luxury compared to her cramped, airless flat. Her two-year planner was on the wall behind her desk and she was immensely proud of the off-white shag pile carpet. The shelves under the bay-window would be ideal for her manuscripts and the generously furnished office, with a sitting-room area, was perfect.

Their first Friday meeting, toasted with champagne in paper cups, was held round Pagett's kitchen table. John had sent his good-luck wishes along with the champagne. A fortnight later, at Lucy's farewell party, they assembled in the boardroom. Judging by the impromptu speeches, Lucy would really be missed. Even Simone was particularly loquacious.

* * *

The autumn breeze nipped at Holly's slim ankles like a frisky puppy. She welcomed the cooler weather. Orders for *Tomorrow's Joy* had surpassed all expectation and there was still a week to go before publication day. Her television debut next week as Emily Howard's spokesperson loomed large and terrifying. Neither Terence nor Liz could understand her nervousness. Liz was worried about the effect the job was having on her sister. For years Holly had shown such a placid exterior, now she snapped at the slightest provocation, jumped at the slightest noise. If her nerves were so on edge, now while her work-load was light, how would she cope when things got hectic?

The programme credits rolled. Liz held tightly to Robert's hand. The presenter, Daniel Robinson, a personable man in his late thirties with penetrating grey eyes, ran through a preview of the books to be discussed, then introduced Holly.

"She looks wonderful." Liz slackened her grip slightly, to Robert's relief.

Although she was practically numb with fear, a close up of Holly's face showed little of the strain she was feeling.

"Holly Grant is here tonight to represent Emily Howard . . . " He explained Emily's plight to the viewers then gave a short synopsis of the book which Holly knew had been compiled by his researchers.

"Tell us about Emily," Daniel invited.

Holly dug her nails into her hands and began her well-rehearsed story of the single mother coping against all the odds. She even remembered to include a couple of amusing anecdotes from the book.

Liz relaxed. Holly's enthusiasm gathered momentum as she talked. The camera caressed her lovely face.

"And what was your part in all this?" Daniel prompted, then sat back and waited for Holly's answer.

For the first time, Holly hesitated. "I edited the story," she said simply.

Suddenly her time was up. Daniel Robinson repeated the name of the book, the publisher and the price, then thanked her. On the monitor she could see a full colour copy of *Tomorrow's Joy*.

"You were *fantastic*," Terence said as she fell into his arms in the hospitality room where he and Barry had watched her on the monitor.

"Would you like a drink now?" the programme assistant asked. In spite of her make-up, Holly Grant was as pale as a page from her book.

"Yes, please," Holly replied gratefully.

Terence offered to pour it while the assistant, promising to be back in a nano-second, whisked another nervous-looking woman away to the studio.

"Was it really all right?" Holly asked as the fiery liquid began its calming effect and euphoria kicked in.

"As if you've been doing telly all your life," Terence confirmed.

"You were terrific," Barry added.

"It was all so quick," Holly said wonderingly.

"Eleven minutes," Barry said.

"It wasn't! It couldn't have been!"

"We timed you." Terence pointed to his watch.

As Holly let herself into the flat, the phone was ringing.

"Well done! You were super and you looked gorgeous," Liz said breathlessly.

"Barry was wonderful, he met me at the doors of the television station with a rose and loads of morale-boosting advice. Terence came with me and he was brilliant too. Then it was all over in a flash, Daniel Robinson made it so easy."

"Maybe in future you won't find it so nerve-wracking. This book's taken it out of you, Holly," said Liz, kindly.

"What do you mean, taken it out of me?" Holly demanded.

Liz bit her lip. "You've put so much energy into it, so much . . . care . . . " Liz allowed the silence to finish her sentence for her. No matter what she said, Holly would pounce on it.

"I'd better ring off, I'm whacked. Thanks for phoning, Liz. See you at the weekend?"

"See you then."

"That was a short call," Robert said as he saw his wife's frown.

"Wasn't it just? I told her that I hoped she'd be able to relax now and she did her quick-exit act."

"It'll pass, she'll calm down eventually."

"I think she's getting worse."

Robert secretly agreed but there was nothing to be gained by saying so. "How about a coffee? I'll make it."

Publication day arrived without a whimper. No trumpets blared, the traffic didn't stop and people rushed past the bookshop window without as much as a glance at the displays. Holly stood and watched. Where were all those sales going to come from? Tens of thousands of copies of *Tomorrow's Joy* had been printed, enough to fill a warehouse. At least Terence had offered to celebrate the occasion; he'd cook or they could go out, whichever she preferred. She'd chosen to eat at his flat imagining that the day would be hectic and exciting. What a burst-balloon occasion it had turned out to be. With a sigh she left her spying-post and began the walk home. Tomorrow she'd divide her lunch hour between WH Smith and Dillons, see how things were going.

"How was today, exciting?" Terence asked.

"OK," Holly replied shortly.

"OK? No fireworks?"

"OK, that's all. Just OK." I must stop snapping at him, Holly chastised herself. "A bit disappointing to be honest. I don't know what I expected, but . . . "

"But it was just like any other day," Terence finished for her. He'd experienced that feeling of anti-climax many a time, but it soon passed.

"Can we change the subject?"

"Dinner will be ready in a few minutes, will you have a top up?" He held up the wine bottle.

"No thanks, I'll wait."

Terence clattered around the tiny kitchen while Holly lapsed into a moody silence. He sneaked a glance at her, her pretty face sullen. To talk or not to talk, should he try and chivvy her out of her bad mood?

"I was approached today to do a lovely old house," he tried.

"Yes?" she replied in a flat voice.

"A huge conversion and extension."

"Where?" Holly tried to rouse herself from her bout of crabbiness, this wasn't fair to Terence.

"In Kensington, not too far from where you are."

"Oh."

"At least they'll have kitchens that you can turn around in," he said as he juggled for space on the counter top. "Come on, dinner's ready, let's eat."

Holly moved the couple of short steps to the table and eyed her plate unseeingly. After a few minutes even Terence's patience deserted him. "What do you think of the sauce?" he queried.

"Very nice."

"What is it, do you know?" he demanded.

Holly shook her head.

"It's a whisky sauce, took a while to make."

"It's good," she muttered.

"It's *bloody* good. Holly, for heaven's sake, try and forget the damn book for the evening. You look as though you've just lost one of your nearest and dearest. Nothing's gone wrong, the advance sales are excellent, the book is on track, finished, so what's the problem?"

"I'm sorry, I don't know why I feel the way I do, but I just do."

"If every book you're responsible for is going to pull you down like this, you'd be better off doing something else."

Terence's harsh words seared her. Terence, never judgemental, never interfering, was treating her like a child. "If you don't like the way I am, I can leave," she threatened. "I put up with Liz all weekend telling me I'd changed, that was when she took time off from raving about what a wonderful time they had in Paris – courtesy of the one who's changed."

"That's not like you, Holly. You were as thrilled about their trip as they were. Liz cares about you, worries about you – as I do."

"I don't need you two to care about me, I can cope, thank you. I've spent enough of my life being controlled by Derek and frankly I don't need you taking over where he left off."

"Fine. In no time at all you should succeed in becoming just like Simone, alienating the people who love you, a dedicated, hard-working loner. Liz is right, Holly, you *have* changed."

"That's it!" Holly flung her paper napkin on to her plate and grabbed her bag. "Thank you for the dinner and the lecture, goodnight Terence."

She could barely see the keyhole as she tried to insert her key. She banged the wooden door with her fist in a lather of frustration. Tears of self-pity stung her eyes then splashed her cheeks as she bolted the door. Nobody understood, *nobody*. When Terence came knocking on her door in a few minutes' time, she'd tell him how *he'd* changed, let him know what it felt like to be scolded like an infant by someone who didn't even know the facts.

But Terence didn't knock at her door. Through the thin walls she could hear his television, a comedy judging by the sound of his laughter. Worse still, she was hungry.

Chapter Forty-Four

Whether it was the plight of the author or Holly's sympathetic portrayal of her which captured the reading public's imagination, *Tomorrow's Joy* rocketed from obscurity to eighth place on the bestseller list. Pagett's publicity and marketing departments were besieged with requests for interviews and re-orders. Emily Howard became Holly's alter-ego, the children her surrogate nieces and nephews. She invented little snippets of information, something fresh and new for each radio programme or magazine article. In short, she told herself as she left the studios after one particularly harrowing talk show, she'd become an accomplished liar.

Holly's appearance on *This Morning* clinched it, and the book rose to second place on the lists.

"If only we could dislodge Peter Rayne," she grumbled at the Friday meeting.

"If that man wrote a shopping list it would become number one," Simone said with a shake of her head. Although she was heartily sick of *Tomorrow's Joy,* she still took pride in seeing

Pagett's name up there in lights. That number one spot was tantalisingly close.

"Being second to a world best-selling author like Rayne is no shame, Holly. The timing's unfortunate, there's nothing you can do except enjoy Emily's success. Perhaps next time . . . " Tim commiserated.

Holly had more or less implied that there *would* be another book, other books. The painfully familiar rush of blood to her cheeks forced her to move ahead rapidly.

"Norma's new book is coming along beautifully," she reported.

"Have you anything else lined up?" Simone asked.

"There are one or two manuscripts which show promise, I'm just waiting to hear Liz's opinion."

Liz was both articulate and fair-minded, an excellent judge. Holly was convinced that hiring her sister as her reader had been a stroke of genius. She trusted Liz's opinion and Liz had been delighted to supplement her income by doing something she would have enjoyed even as a hobby. Holly insisted she should be paid for it. Without too much hesitation, Liz accepted her new responsibility with grateful enthusiasm. She missed the income from her teaching.

As a result of Holly's appearances on television and interviews on radio, dozens of manuscripts had arrived. There were purple shadows under her eyes, her trim figure had become far too thin, a combination of skipped meals, taut nerves. Above all, she missed Terence, the easy warmth of his company, the comfort of his presence, his soothing words. And she had no one to blame but herself, he'd only tried to help her. When she came back to her flat each evening a cloak of misery descended. It wrapped itself around her and bound her tightly until she left again the following morning. She wished she could find the courage to knock on his door, tell him how much she missed him, how sorry she was that she'd stormed out the way she had. But when they met accidentally in the hall or passed each other on the stairs, there was a coldness in his manner which prevented her taking those couple of short steps. She listened for the reassuring sound of his television but more often than not lately there was only silence, an eerie quiet that unnerved her. Where was he? Who was he with? Probably spending time with someone who deserved his kindness.

Exactly one month and three days after publication, *Tomorrow's Joy* headed the bestseller list. Peter Rayne had been deposed. Lois was first with the news, of course, and the excitement at Pagett was intense. Sean came dashing in and gave her a big hug, then John Barrett phoned from Dublin to offer his congratulations, he wanted to discuss an Irish publicity tour and would see her next day when he arrived in London. Even Simone patted her arm and said, "Well done." There was no hint of begrudgery in her tone. One by one they appeared: Tim's grin wide with admiration, Jeremy and Barry to take her to lunch. Jane and Marianna congratulated her warmly and she gave them their due praise in return. Tim suggested that they should send flowers to Emily. Holly agreed. She'd take them round to the local children's home. That's what she'd done with the ones that had supposedly been delivered to Emily when the book was published. Her phone rang constantly. Lucinda Rockingham laughingly expected no less for her own book but her good wishes were warm and sincere. Liz was practically incoherent with delight. When the lull finally arrived, Holly locked herself in the toilet and threw up her breakfast.

"If only," she said to herself quietly as she passed Terence's door.

Dejected, she rooted in the fridge and found some cold chicken and the remains of the previous night's salad. Her heart bounded as her bell rang.

"Terence!" Her despondency vanished as she flung herself into his arms. "Oh Terence, I am so happy to see you," she sobbed.

He put his free arm around her to steady himself as much as her. In his other hand he clutched a bottle of champagne.

"I've missed you so much," she cried, laughing at the same time.

"Congratulations, Holly, I saw the book list in the paper this morning, you did it, well done. Top of the bestseller list." He detached himself from her waif-like frame and held out the champagne.

"Thank you, oh, I'm so pleased to see you." She stepped back and took the bottle. "Will you share it with me? Will you share my bit of dried chicken?" she asked, laughing.

Terence looked uncomfortable. "I'm sorry, I'm afraid I can't, I have an appointment . . . some other time?"

Her delight vanished. She had lost him and his friendship. He stood in front of her like a polite stranger, nothing more.

"Yes, some other time," she replied. "Thank you for the champagne. Don't let me delay you, enjoy your evening."

She waited until the door closed behind him, then cried like the child he had accused her of being.

Chapter Forty-Five

Simone stared moodily through the window. Autumn with its misty mornings and swirling leaves made her shiver. All her authors had chosen this week to act up. Claire Jones, her *smily-face* new hope, had failed to produce the pages she'd promised to do. Not a good beginning. John Barrett was a couple of months behind with his manuscript. Understandable, but it meant he'd have to rush his book. Late or not, she could hardly refuse to publish her boss's book, but it would throw their schedule into chaos. Jacki Weir, one of her pet writers, had demanded more than her usual share of ego-massaging. Simone had had to dig deeply into her reserves in order to hide her irritation. She'd patiently encouraged Jacki but what she really wanted to do was tell her to sit down and get on with it. Time was running out.

Simone checked her diary, then phoned through to Marianna to ask how one of her covers was coming along.

With uncustomary sharpness Marianna replied, "I'll let you know when the roughs are ready."

Simone banged down her receiver.

Her thoughts turned to Ian Trent and that fateful weekend. Even her attempt at revenge had backfired. Friday night, Saturday and all day Sunday she'd waited, but she hadn't heard a single word from him. Curiosity and fury got the better of her. On Monday she'd phoned the hotel.

"He left late yesterday afternoon, I'm afraid," Old Whiskery Chin informed her.

Simone asked the receptionist if everything had gone according to plan?

"Of course, Madame. At least on our part, carried out to the letter. The parcel was delivered just as you instructed. It was such a shame that Mr Trent's companion was delayed until Saturday and that she missed that delicious meal, but pressure of business I suppose . . . "

Simone seethed. A Pyrrhic victory. Only Ian could have turned revenge into triumph.

After that fiasco, Simone began to take stock of her scanty social life. She had a few women acquaintances – she couldn't call them friends – whom she could phone and chat to, or have a meal with. Most of them were in publishing like herself. The men she knew were agents, booksellers, or authors. She would never phone them socially. That, to Simone, just wasn't on. She needed to take a break, but where would she go? And with whom?

She welcomed the sound of her phone.

Her ex-husband Mark's voice was cheerful and light. She'd only spoken to him a couple of times since his marriage and they were short, unsatisfying phone calls. Somehow these days he was never very far from her thoughts.

"Hi Mark, how are you?"

"Good, and you?"

"Can't grumble, busy as usual."

"Simone, I wanted to . . . I wanted to tell you, Susie and I are . . . we're expecting a baby. I didn't want you to hear it from someone else."

Simone sat with open-mouthed paralysis. Why was this such a surprise? "Oh, Mark, that's terrific . . . lovely news. You must be very happy," she faltered when she finally found her voice.

"We are, it's all a bit scary, but I'm sure we'll soon come round to the idea."

"I'm sure you will get round to the idea," she repeated inanely.

There was an awkward silence.

"If there's no other news I suppose I'd better haul myself back to the Internet. How did we manage to communicate before the days of computers?"

"Tantalisingly slowly," she replied with a hollow laugh and hung up.

What had she hoped for when she heard his voice? A reunion? Hardly.

A baby? She couldn't remember Mark ever expressing a desire for children when they were married, perhaps it was all that bovine Susie's idea.

In her mind, she'd almost succeeded in convincing Mark that he'd made a dreadful mistake when Lois knocked at her door and ushered in the first applicant for the editorial assistant's job. There had been dozens of replies but she'd whittled the list down to four.

"Do sit down," Simone said to the nervous-looking young woman standing in front of her. While she pulled up a chair, Simone did a fast appraisal. "Let me tell you what the job entails," she said briskly.

Ellie Butler listened intently, kept eye contact and nodded.

" . . . It can be quite stressful at times," Simone finished.

"I'd relish a challenge," Ellie said. "My present job's dull, lonely. My boss is rarely there, just phones from the print works or wherever he is. I'm more or less left to my own devices all week. I enjoy being with people. Frankly, the solitude is getting me down."

Simone glanced at the CV in front of her. Ellie had done some editing for one of Pagett's competitors in her spare time.

"I see you're familiar with editing?"

"Yes, I love it . . . " Ellie explained what her spare-time work entailed, with obvious enthusiasm. She was happy to work all hours at something she enjoyed so much.

Simone heard the dull clang of a warning bell. Shades of Holly? Would this young woman be content to take orders, do what Simone wanted, or was it just a stepping-stone to editorship?

"You do understand that you wouldn't be able to work with another publisher if we took you on?"

"Yes, of course," Ellie agreed immediately.

"Do you have any questions?"

Ellie thought for a moment. "No, I don't think so. I know about the salary, the hours don't worry me, I've plenty of time. I'm flexible, adaptable, and I'll pick up the routine in no time. I don't want to sound as though I'm tooting my own horn but I've been told my work is excellent. I want to get on, be the best editorial assistant there is."

Been there, done that, edited the book, Simone thought, as Norma Downs and Holly hovered brightly on the horizon. Am I becoming paranoid? she wondered.

Simone chose not to respond to Ellie's ready smile. "These are chapters of a book, I'd like you to take a look at them," she said as she handed Ellie a large brown envelope. "I'd like you to edit them. You can either do them here or take them home with you, whichever you prefer."

"If it's all right with you, I'll work here." Ellie was anxious to get this job. Her instinct told her that doing the editing right away might earn her more brownie points, but instinct also warned her that Simone would be a tough nut to crack.

"What colour ink would you like me to use?" she asked.

Simone shrugged. "It doesn't matter, do you have a pen?"

"Two red and two blue!"

Why doesn't that surprise me? Simone asked herself.

"Lois will find you a quiet room to work in, make you some coffee."

Simone couldn't decide what to make of Ellie, whether the young woman was madly ambitious or just plain eager. But one thing she did know, three editors at Pagett was enough. She buzzed for Lois.

Lois had taken the move to their new premises very seriously. Gone were the fussy, frilly blouses and skirts, the multi-storied hair-dos. Now, reigning supreme at what the staff had dubbed the *news desk,* she wore elegantly knotted scarves or simple blouses under her severely-tailored business suits. Her hair was bobbed and gelled, combed back from her face in the latest catwalk-fashion. But her insatiable bloodhound's nose for news hadn't changed.

Lois frowned. "I'm sure we'll find somewhere for you," she said. "Do you expect to be a while?"

"I'm sure half an hour will suffice, somewhere quiet, Lois," Simone interjected before Ellie succumbed to Lois's inevitable fact-finding mission.

"Marketing? There's no one there at the moment."

"That'll do fine," Simone agreed.

Lois escorted the young woman up one floor. "If you need me, press zero one on the phone," she said.

Ellie thanked her smilingly.

"Would you like me to come and collect you in half an hour?" Lois probed.

"I'm not sure how long I'll be, I'm going to edit the chapters in here," she said holding up the envelope. "I'll find my way back to you."

Satisfied now that she knew what was going on,

Lois cleared some papers from the desk and removed them to a shelf.

"I'll be back in a moment with your coffee." Ellie seemed to be pleasant enough, givey, open, and Lois liked that.

The second applicant, Arabella Trenton-Smythe, was a different cup of tea. Lois took careful note of the casually worn cashmere coat, the gleaming bobbed hair. She resisted the temptation to rush to the cloakroom and wash the gook out of her own fair head. No matter, she assured herself as she checked her new role-model thoroughly, tonight will do.

When she left ten minutes later, Arabella also carried a brown envelope but barely glanced in Lois's direction.

"Let's hope that's the end of her," Lois muttered as the reception area's door closed with a bang.

Whether it was his brazen charm, or his exceptional good looks, Neil Sachs set Lois's heart aflutter. Now that's what I *call* an editorial assistant, Lois told herself as she led the way, seductively she hoped, towards Simone's office.

Simone disliked him on sight. The man's body language shrieked resist-me-if-you-can. And as the stilted interview got under way, his remarks about her appearance – *so delightful to work with such a pretty lady, such talent in one so lovely* – antagonised her even more. He had all the allure of root-canal treatment. She despatched him, minus the envelope she'd given the other two. She didn't care how good his qualifications were.

"We'll be in touch," she said with a smile as false as his own.

"This is awful," she groaned as the over-powering scent of his after-shave faded.

She'd seen three out of the four so far. None of them had appealed to her. Granted Ellie's corrections were good, she'd caught ninety-nine per cent of the errors, but Arabella Trenton-Smyth and Neil Sachs were non-starters. Arabella was only interested in how much free time she would have. Neil had set her on edge as he'd walked through her doorway. Simone shook her shoulders with a shudder, she'd rather work twenty-four hours a day than employ that peacock. Resentfully her thoughts turned to Holly. *She'd* fallen on her feet, found herself an assistant reader without even having to get out of bed. Holly had encouraged her to interview her sister and, although she didn't like Liz, Simone had to admit that she was more than capable of filling an important gap.

Simone pushed back her hair as she turned back to the beginning of the text. Sophie Davis was right, the central character *had* been wearing navy-blue trousers in chapter one and now they were black. How had she missed that? And indeed, how had Ellie let that slip by?

Sophie let her gaze wander about the immaculate office. The editor had excellent taste. She dispelled all thoughts of her own hit-by-an-earthquake living-room and focused on what Simone was saying.

"This is very good Sophie, very good." Simone didn't use the word excellent, but it was. Sophie hadn't missed a trick. Her punctuation was excellent. Simone had to admit that the discrepancy which Sophie had found was exactly the sort of observation necessary for a good assistant.

"I'd like you to write a letter for me – to the author of these chapters. Point out the errors, and the lack of time remaining before publication – keep it soft but urgent."

"Yes, sure," Sophie agreed readily.

"You can use my word processor." Simone cleared her screen and pushed back her chair. At least Sophie wouldn't need any computer training, she was familiar with this package. "I'll be back in about ten minutes."

Simone stirred her cup thoughtfully. Sophie was definitely the best of the bunch, ideal, but she'd made it clear that anything outside office hours would have to be agreed as overtime. What the hell do I want? Simone asked herself. Ellie was happy to work all hours and I turned her down because of that. Now Sophie wants to be paid for any extra work she does and I'm annoyed. If *I'd* been paid for all the extra work *I've* done I'd be waltzing into Pagett every day in a chauffeur-driven limo. But then, perhaps I wouldn't have become an editor, I would've remained a nine-to-five editorial assistant working for a bitch like me. That thought popped into her head without as much as a by-your-leave. I have turned into a bitch, an angry one at that.

Simone flung the dregs of her coffee down the

sink and gave her cup a perfunctory splash of water. I wonder how many calories a day my anger burns? When *did* I turn into such a monster?

After a session of long, slow, deep breathing, Simone made her way back to her office, her mind made up.

"Finished?" she asked Sophie.

"Yes, I've printed it out for you." Sophie handed her a neatly typed page.

Simone read the letter carefully, she couldn't have done better herself. Sophie had flattered the author, praised the writing and suggested that, in order to make his text perfect, he should consider the few, but relevant, changes suggested. In a firm but apologetic tone, she pointed out that his wonderful book was approaching its printing slot and that she was confident he would make the changes as soon as possible.

"I like this, it's clear and to the point yet sympathetic," Simone admitted. "Sophie, how much do you want this job?"

If Sophie was startled by the sudden question, she didn't show it. "A lot," she answered simply.

"I'm prepared to offer you the position now, but I have one reservation. Publishing isn't a nine-to-five occupation. Manuscripts do pile up. Our launches are usually held at night, six o'clock or thereabouts. If our publicity department is pushed, the editorial assistant has to fill in occasionally – out-of-town authors who need to be wined and dined or need to be accompanied to a television or radio studio. I'm not saying it happens often, but it can, and it's part of the job. *None* of us get paid overtime . . . " Make or break. If Sophie accepted these terms the job was hers, if not . . .

Sophie's brain was in top gear. How often was occasionally? She'd adore to attend the kind of events that Simone had mentioned but, with two dependent youngsters, could she afford sitters? But how could she afford *not* to take this job? Pagett paid very well but, more importantly, this was her opportunity to shin up the ladder of success. Sophie Davis, full-blown editor.

"I'm sorry if I gave you the wrong impression, I'm perfectly willing to put in the time . . . " Sophie wriggled.

"But?" Simone asked.

"No buts. Perhaps I should explain?"

Simone nodded. She'd been right. Sophie had tried it on and failed.

Sophie's colour heightened. "I have two daughters and I like to spend as much time with them as I can now that their father . . . I suppose I'm still a bit over-protective. I have good neighbours, I'm sure they'd look after the girls for me if I'm late. If I could take manuscripts home, I'd be perfectly happy to do as much work as you want."

Simone gathered that Sophie and her husband were separated. She was pleased Sophie hadn't confided in her. Obviously Sophie was not the social butterfly type, and neither was she hell-bent on climbing to the top. She would do very nicely.

"I have no objection to that. Now that we've

cleared the air, I can offer you the position. I suggest a three-month trial, and after that we can review the situation. If all goes well, we'll draw up a contract. When are you free to start?"

"A week next Monday? I must give a week's notice."

Simone held out her hand. "I'll see you then. Welcome to Pagett and I hope you'll be happy working with us."

Sophie smiled her thanks and went on smiling the whole way home. Whoever said it didn't pay to listen to gossip? Rumour had it that Simone Pearse was furious when her previous assistant was appointed editor. The word was that Simone would never again hire anybody who showed too much initiative. Now that she'd met Simone, she was grateful for all that mindless chatter she'd picked up in the typing pool at Johnson and Carew. Even more thankful that she'd persevered and learnt to edit by studying those endless manuscripts she'd typed for Bettina Carew. Her time had come at last.

Chapter Forty-Six

"One moment, please." Lois put Rick Gill's secretary on hold.

Lois's knowledge of book-world gossip was encyclopaedic and the rumour circulating in the trade papers lately was that Nancy Dell was unhappy with her long-time publishers, Berry, Barnes and Webb. Was that why her agent, Rick Gill, was phoning Pagett? Pay-back time. The secretary had asked to speak to *the editor*, she hadn't asked for Simone by name.

"Holly, Rick Gill's secretary is on the line," she said decisively.

"Rick Gill?"

"Yes, the agent."

"I know who he is. But me? Why me?" she asked. "You'd better put him through."

Holly cleared her throat nervously; the tough-dealing agent wasn't known as the *Rickweiler* because of his charm. Why on earth did he want to speak to her?

"Rick Gill," an imperious voice announced.

"Holly Grant. Good morning, Mr Gill, what can I do for you?"

"Better ask what *I* can do for *you*. I'd like to meet. Today suit you?"

"That depends. Why do you want to see me?" Holly asked briskly.

"To discuss a possible change for my client, Nancy Dell."

Rick Gill always referred to Nancy Dell as his client, never his wife.

Nancy Dell, *Nancy Dell!* Her books were money in the bank. But why would she want to come to Pagett? Pagett couldn't hope to compete with the enormous advances that most big publishers would be willing to pay an author like that.

Say something you fool, Holly instructed herself sharply. "I know her books well, I've read most of them."

"Who hasn't? What time would suit you?"

"Either noon or – let me check my diary – three o'clock?"

"Twelve o'clock. The Lanesborough?"

Holly paused, she'd be less nervous in familiar surroundings. "My office would be more convenient," she said.

"Very well. Goodbye." The phone clicked in her ear.

There must be some mistake. Perhaps Rick Gill was working through a list of publishers, preparing to set up an auction. But what the hell, it wouldn't cost anything to find out.

Holly dashed like a sprinter to Tim's office.

"Busy?" she asked when Tim looked up from the contract he was working on.

He smiled, rubbing the bridge of his nose. "I'm delighted with an excuse for a break. What's up?"

"You mean, *what's going down*!" Holly corrected him with a grin.

"Huh?"

"Rick Gill, he's coming to see me at noon."

"Rickweiler Gill?"

"One and the same," Holly laughed. "I'm as astonished as you are. Nancy Dell's on the move and, before you ask, that's as much as I know."

"Rick Gill, Nancy Dell? We're not in their league . . . "

"That's what I thought. Still, there's no harm in meeting the man. If nothing else, I'll have the opportunity to find out why Nancy Dell is bitching about her publisher."

Tim rubbed his hand across his chin. "Holly, you won't do anything foolish, will you? Make any rash promises?" he asked in a voice filled with alarm.

"Neh! I'll offer him a couple of mil for her next book, three maybe, but no more than that."

"Don't *make* those kind of jokes!"

"Who's kidding?" she asked innocently. "I'd better buzz off and make myself presentable."

Lois looked up expectantly as Holly approached.

"Do you think you could rustle up some coffee at twelve, Lois?" she asked.

"No problem. For Rick Gill?"

"Yes. He's coming in to talk to me about . . . "

"Nancy Dell," Lois finished for her.

"Lois!" Holly could hardly accuse her of listening

381

in on the call. "How do you know that?" she asked suspiciously.

"Oh Holly, don't you read the trade papers? That's old news now. Nancy Dell's contract is up and there are rumblings that she wants a change."

"You don't miss much, do you? I must confess, I didn't know. Anyway, when he arrives, wheel in him into my office, will you?" Holly spoke with more confidence than she felt. For a moment she considered asking Tim to sit in on the meeting but then decided to handle it alone. She could always call him in if the need arose.

Rick Gill was older than she'd expected. He moved with the grace and confidence of a younger man.

"Holly, my dear, how nice to meet you."

"Nice to meet you, Mr Gill." She tried to keep the quake out of her voice.

"Rick! Please," he invited graciously.

"Come and sit down, Rick." Holly led the way to the comfortable chairs in the informal section of her office.

Lois appeared on cue with a tray of coffee and their "best" biscuits. Holly suppressed a grin. Where would they be without Lois?

Rick Gill appraised the young editor with an expert's eye. Pretty face, fine pair of legs. He was pleased that he was dealing with this novice instead of with Simone Pearse.

"Milk, sugar?" Holly poured with a surprisingly steady hand.

"Black."

As Rick bent forward to take the cup and saucer, Holly took inventory; carefully-styled silver hair, immaculately tailored suit, high-fashion tie and gleaming black shoes. Surreptitiously she rubbed her own shoes against her chair.

After a few banalities and a general chat about publishing, Holly moistened her lips. "You came to talk about Nancy Dell?"

"Nancy is considering a change," he began. "She's been following the fortunes of Pagett and the idea of a smaller publishing house appeals to her. More intimate, less frenetic."

"That's very flattering, but I'd better tell you now, we can't compete with the larger publishers. We don't give huge advances. We put all our money into marketing and publicity."

"I'm well aware of your policy. But Nancy has reached a stage in her life where peace of mind means more to her than mere money. Earning her royalties is no problem," he assured her with well-buttered sarcasm.

"So where's the catch?" Holly asked cheekily. This was all too easy, too good to be true.

"That's a very cynical approach, Holly," he reproved as he helped himself to a refill.

"Perhaps, but let me make sure that I understand what you're saying. If Nancy Dell signed with Pagett, she'd be prepared to accept our standard contract, correct?"

Rick Gill smiled patronisingly, "I didn't quite say that. What I suggest is . . . "

Holly heard him in amazement. Nobody paid

those kind of royalties, least of all Pagett. If she went along to a meeting with those figures, they'd laugh her out of the boardroom. "You can't seriously expect me to agree to that." No wonder they called him *Rickweiler*.

"I'm perfectly serious," he said. "Think about it, whatever percentage you pay Nancy Dell is better than no percentage at all. Think of the prestige. A world class writer – Pagett, up there with the finest. You won't find too many offers like this coming your way and, although I can't pretend that I approve of her leaving her publishers, that is her wish. Naturally if we agree terms we'd have to iron out the finer points, presentation, publicity – she doesn't do much of that these days – covers, etcetra. That's my offer, you'd be crazy to pass it up. Besides, think what it would do for your own reputation – Holly Grant, Nancy Dell's editor." He held up an elegant hand as if seeing her name, up there in lights, on her office wall.

Despite his outlandish demand, what he proposed did seem to make good sense. But why Pagett? And why her? Why hadn't he asked for Simone? Her head buzzed with questions and doubts.

Rick Gill watched her. He doubted that Holly would be in a position to make this decision alone but if he could convince *her* . . .

"I'll have to discuss this with the directors," she said thoughtfully.

"By all means. But don't take too long. I won't insult you by telling you that any number of publishers would leap at the chance of adding Nancy to their list – heading their list."

Then why was he here? she fretted. "I appreciate that, but . . . but in this instance, I'm not prepared to make a snap decision. I'll be in touch in a couple of days." Holly rose to her feet and held out her hand.

Calmly, Rick Gill replaced his unfinished drink on the table and stood up. This *youngster* was dismissing him. Holly Grant wasn't nearly as foolish or impressionable as he'd first thought. He'd reduced better established editors than her to a fit of the shakes but, to his annoyance, Holly appeared to be neither intimidated by him nor in awe of him.

Holly waited a couple of minutes then cautiously opened her door. There was no sign of Rick Gill in the corridor. She burst into Tim's office.

"She doesn't *want* a huge advance," she said breathlessly.

"Who doesn't?" Tim asked.

"Nancy Dell."

"You'd better catch your breath, then start from the beginning." A smile touched his lips as he saw Holly's cheeks flushed with excitement.

"Rick Gill says that Nancy Dell isn't worried about a big advance, she wants to be published by a smaller house, *more intimate, less frenetic,* he says."

"Just like that?"

"Almost, but she does want . . . high royalties."

"How high?"

Holly drew a breath and blurted out the amount.

"You're winding me up, it's a wind-up."

"No I'm not. That was my reaction at first. But just think about it, we only have to pay her what she earns. It makes good sense . . . " Holly used Rick's argument to convince him. "And at the end of the day, think of the prestige, she'd really establish Pagett, we'd be up there with the big boys."

"At that rate she'll end up owning . . . " Tim's door opened with a crash for the second time in minutes.

"Why didn't you refer Rick Gill to *me*, Holly?" Simone blazed.

"Come in, Simone," Tim invited, but he might as well have saved his breath.

"Answer me, Holly, why didn't you consult me? *I* am head editor here, not you. What makes you think you have the right to deal with an important agent like Gill when I'm here?"

"Just a minute, hang on, that's no way to speak to Holly," Tim intervened angrily.

"And that's no way for Holly to behave, sneaking around talking to agents behind my back."

Holly's fury was held in check only by fear, the sensation she'd so often experienced when Derek flew into a rage. Any moment now she expected smoke to billow out of Simone's ears.

"I won't tolerate this kind of shabby treatment, stealing agents from under my nose," Simone fumed.

Holly was trembling all over. "You have no right to accuse me of stealing your agent. Rick Gill phoned me and I made an appointment with him."

"Little Ms Innocence, as if you didn't know who he was representing."

"I knew who his client was after he told me."

"Liar!"

"That's enough. Simone, apologise or get out of my office . . . "

"What's going on? I could hear you all the way down the corridor." Sean Barrett had slipped in unnoticed. "What's all the panic?"

"Who is editor-in-chief at Pagett?" Without missing a beat Simone wheeled round and demanded an answer from Sean.

"You are, why?"

"I'll tell you why, because Holly managed to siphon off an agent who should have been sent to me, that's why." Simone slammed back a stray wave of hair.

Sean looked at Tim, then at Holly's angry face. "I think we should all calm down and discuss this like grown-ups."

"Don't patronise me." Simone stamped.

"Nobody is patronising you, but I *would* like to hear what this is all about."

"I've told you, this . . . this . . . cunning little cow . . . "

"Stop that immediately," Sean ordered. "Tim, can you explain what's going on?"

"As far as I know, Rick Gill phoned and asked to speak to Holly. He represents Nancy Dell – a world-wide best-selling author," he added for Sean's benefit. "Simone feels that Holly should have passed him over to her . . . and that's about it."

"Is that correct, Holly?" Sean asked.

"What the hell do you expect her to say? No it's not right, *mea culpa,* I stole him from Simone?" Simone had calmed down to hurricane force.

Sean could feel his own temperature rising. "Holly?"

"That's exactly what happened. I don't see why I have to run to our *editor-in-chief* – as Simone likes to remind us frequently that she is – every time the phone rings." Holly couldn't resist her own dig.

Sean bit his lip to hide his smile. How right Holly was, Simone did like to throw her title around. But that wasn't the issue. "I can see nothing wrong with that," he pronounced.

"No, you wouldn't," Simone shot back at him. "You're as stupid as Holly."

"You're really pushing it, Simone," Sean said menacingly. "Just in case you've forgotten, I'll remind you. This kind of personal attack is unwise. Extremely foolish." There was no mistaking his implied threat.

Even in her irrational state Simone realised that Sean and Tim together would make dangerous adversaries. "How would *you* feel if someone did that to you?" she demanded as she fought to get her temper under control.

"Did *what*? Answered the phone, made an appointment with an agent?" Holly asked scathingly.

"Please, both of you, wait. Does it make any difference which one of you talks to him?"

"Of course it bloody well does. She's no match for him. He's one of the toughest agents in the business." Simone turned to Holly. "And what incredible deal *did* he offer you? How many millions does his client want as an advance?"

"None."

"None! She's leaving her publishers to come to us because she likes the sound of our name? Dream on, Holly."

"Simone!" Sean warned.

"Something like that, yes," Holly replied calmly.

Holly's composure only served to whip up Simone's fury.

"Oh Jesus, now I've heard everything," She spat.

"Not quite everything, she would expect a very high percentage in royalties. But as Rick said, as far as Pagett is concerned, no matter what percentage we pay her, she's a prestige author and we can't fail to make money." Holly wisely omitted Rick Gill's remarks about being Nancy Dell's editor.

"And just what percentage is that?" Simone asked scathingly.

Holly told her.

"Are you insane? You *promised* . . . "

"I promised nothing," Holly deliberately kept her tone even. "If you hadn't come in here screaming like a demented banshee I was going to ask Tim if we could call a meeting to discuss all this."

"Oh sure, and I'm Salman Rushdie's minder."

"I'm sure you'd be very good at it, you'd scare anyone away." The words were out before Holly could stop them. She drew back as Simone rose from her chair, she was positive that Simone was going to strike her.

"Arthur!" Simone exclaimed.

Arthur Lord, in town for a routine check-up, couldn't resist the urge to pop into Pagett before returning home. It was no wonder his entrance had gone unnoticed. He loathed confrontation and, judging by the raised voices, he'd walked in on a major one.

"Arthur, what a nice surprise," Tim said as he too left his seat and went towards his former boss.

"I thought I'd drop in and share the good news with you. My doctor has given the go-ahead, now I'm fit enough to take on the job of strong-man in the circus," he joked.

Arthur's arrival was perfectly timed. "Good for you," Tim said. "And what excellent timing, we were just about to break for now." Tim's glare dared Simone to defy him. "I think we should celebrate your good news, Arthur, do you have time for lunch?"

"Why not? One of retirement's little luxuries." Arthur gave an impish grin.

"I suggest we adjourn this . . . meeting until after lunch, two-thirty in the boardroom suit everyone?"

They knew that it was an order, not a request.

Simone said goodbye to Arthur and, with a glower that would douse a volcano, elbowed her way past Holly.

They all visibly relaxed. "Anyone join us?" Tim asked.

"I've already made arrangements," Holly said. This wasn't entirely untrue, she'd just promised herself a large brandy at the pub around the corner.

"Some other time," Sean said as he prepared to return to the sanity of his office on the ground floor. He was certain that Tim would want to discuss this with Arthur in private.

"That was some meeting," Arthur said when he and Tim were alone.

"Meeting my foot, more like World War Three," Tim frowned.

"You must tell me all about it over lunch."

Wearily, Holly collected her handbag and made her way to the cloakroom. It gave her no pleasure to look in the mirror, the reflection which stared back at her was gaunt and pale. She jabbed some lipstick on her mouth then threw the case back into her make-up purse. As she reached the door she thought she heard a noise – a cat? It couldn't be. She stood silently and listened. There it was again, a sob. Someone crying.

"Anyone there?" she asked.

The noise stopped.

"Who's there?" she asked again and walked towards the closed toilet door.

She knocked. There was no answer. She pushed the door gently but it was locked.

"You might as well come out because I'm not leaving until you do."

She could hear the sound of a bolt being drawn back when a horrible thought struck her, what if it was Simone? She held her breath as the door slowly opened.

"Lois!" Relief flooded through her but was

instantly replaced with concern. Lois's eyes were red and her peachy skin a mass of blotches.

"Why are you crying? What's wrong?" Holly put her arm around Lois and led her to the stool in front of the make-up mirror. "Sit here," she said as she gently eased her into a sitting position.

Holly leant against the edge of the dressing-table and waited while Lois wiped her eyes and struggled to compose herself.

"I'm sorry I got you into such trouble," Lois finally blurted out.

"What do you mean? Why should you have caused me any trouble?"

"The phone call . . . Rick Gill . . . his secretary asked for the editor and I put him through to you."

"Why's that your fault? Wait, I need to get out of here, are you on your lunch break?"

Lois nodded miserably.

"Right, let's go and get a stiff drink, then you can explain what you're on about."

Lois trailed towards her desk, her head down and her chin almost touching her chest. She unlocked a drawer and took out a box of tissues.

"Some day you must let me into the secret of those drawers," Holly teased with a grin.

There was precious little in the way of office accessories, sewing equipment or even medical necessities that Lois couldn't produce in an emergency. *Everything from sheets of plastic to knicker elastic,* was her proud boast.

Neither of them said a word until they'd taken a good sip of brandy.

"OK," said Holly. "We were up to the bit where the Rickweiler's secretary phoned and asked to speak to an editor and you put him on to me."

"That's not quite true, she asked to speak to *the* editor, not *an* editor. I know I shouldn't have done it, but I wanted to pay Simone back for all her nastiness. I wanted *you* to have the credit for taking on Nancy Dell." Lois's look of shame had Bambi-caught-in-the-car-headlights appeal. "Simone saw Rick Gill getting into his car. She practically grabbed me by my scarf and demanded to know what he was doing at Pagett, almost choked the information out of me. Then she freaked. I was really scared when she went tearing around trying to find you. I pretended I didn't know where you were. After a couple of minutes I sneaked along to Tim's office and could hear her screaming at you. I never thought it would lead to such trouble. Now you know the truth. When Simone finds out what I did, she'll fire me. I love working at Pagett . . . even with Simone snapping orders, I really love it." A thin stream of tears coursed down her cheeks.

Holly finished her brandy in a gulp. At least that explained how Gill had ended up in her office.

"Don't worry, you won't get fired, no one will know, I promise. Dry your eyes. Now, talking of orders, we'd better order a sandwich, I don't have much time."

"I'll get it," Lois offered. "What would you like?"

"Anything, I don't care. I'd better have a coffee

too." She could hardly roll into the meeting pie-
eyed, which she would be if she didn't get some
food inside her.

Energy seeped from Holly like a punctured air-
bed. She could have quite easily put her head down
on the table and fallen asleep. She was always tired
these days, tired and stressed. And guilty.

Lois returned to the table. "They're making you a
sandwich."

"What about you?"

Lois shook her head. "I'm not hungry."

"Listen, Lois, you're *not* going to be fired. Forget
Simone, forget that a secretary said *the* instead of
an. It'll all be sorted."

"But what about you?"

"Don't worry I can take care of myself, I'll deal
with our *editor-in-chief*."

"Editor-in-chief! Predator-in-grief would be a
better title. I'm so sorry, Holly, you're the last
person I want to upset."

"I told you, don't fret, this'll all blow over," Holly
assured her with false calm.

"Perhaps I will have a sandwich after all," Lois
capitulated. She had always liked Holly but today
Holly was a star.

Holly wolfed down the sandwich and drank half
her coffee. "I've got to dash, the meeting's at two-
thirty. I promised I'd phone Lucinda this morning
and, in the excitement, forgot all about her. Louise
is due back this afternoon, she had a meeting this
morning with an American publisher who was
madly keen on *Tomorrow's Joy*. She met him a

couple of weeks ago at the Frankfurt Book Fair. I want to know what happened, if he's interested in buying it. Take your time, if anyone asks where you are – ie the Predator – I'll tell them that I delayed you," said Holly.

She took a ten pound note from her wallet. "Can I leave you to pay the bill? Lunch is on me."

Lois began to object but Holly silenced her. "No arguments, no time. Thank you for what you tried to do, Lois, I really appreciate your good intention. If you do enjoy working at Pagett as much as you say, you must never jeopardise your job like that again. At the end of the day we all work for the same firm and to the same ends. Besides, what would I do without you?"

* * *

By the time they'd finished their main course, Arthur was fully briefed about the argument. He didn't envy Tim's lot. If there were times when he wished he was back behind his desk, today wasn't one of them. He knew Rick Gill by reputation but he could understand Simone's frustration. As senior editor, Simone was the obvious person for Gill to approach but still there was no justification for that kind of behaviour. Tim had tried to be impartial, but Arthur could sense that his sympathies were with Holly.

"Simone seems to exist on a diet of angst and anger these days," Tim complained ruefully. "She's put everyone's back up. She's demanding to the point of rudeness and never misses the slightest opportunity to put Holly or Kathy down. She's wary of me but even Sean got the sharp end of her tongue this morning, she told him he was stupid."

Arthur laughed. "She didn't! What was his reaction to that?"

"A subtle reminder that he was the boss."

"And how did she take that?"

"With more of the same – *her agent had been swiped from under her, it wasn't fair* – that kind of thing. That's when you appeared and was I glad to see you."

"How are you going to resolve this?"

Tim shook his head. "I honestly don't know. The cowardly way out would be to ask to Holly to hand Rick Gill over to Simone. If Simone wasn't so bloody intransigent I'd suggest they make it a joint venture but I'd rather have a fingernail removed without anaesthetic than suggest that."

Arthur shuddered. He knew just how Tim must feel and wished he could say something to ease his burden. No stress, his doctor had warned him.

The restaurant, filled with the quiet buzz of conversation, was comfortable and familiar. Arthur had eaten at Bennetts at least once a week for as long as he could remember. Their menus rarely changed; roast and two veg, steak and kidney pie, chicken and mushroom *vol au vents* the size of dinner plates, but it was good, honest, well-cooked food. During the meal, several people stopped on the way to their tables to say hello, to enquire how he was enjoying his retirement. It was kind of Tim to go out of his way and suggest Bennetts when there must have been a dozen places within walking distance of the new Pagett. The new Pagett. How that hurt at times.

Tim glanced anxiously at his watch, he was really pleased to see Arthur but his thoughts kept straying.

"Let's order pudding," Arthur suggested.

"Should you?" Tim asked as he scanned the menu.

"No," Arthur said with a grin.

"What would you like, gentlemen?" Alice, their waitress, asked. She didn't need a trendy tag with her name on it, everyone who ate there knew Alice.

No longer in the first bloom of her youth, Alice had fussed over her flock since she'd left school. She knew all about her gentlemen's wives, their children, their grandchildren.

"The meringue with some ice cream on the side." Arthur could almost hear Amanda's voice vetoing his choice. He avoided Tim's gaze.

Tim handed the menu back to Alice and opted for coffee.

"Something about this changeover is bothering me," Arthur said as he borrowed Tim's teaspoon to scoop up the last little pool of melted ice cream.

"Not as much as it's worrying me," Tim replied.

"I don't mean the row. I find it strange that an experienced writer like Nancy Dell would be willing to forego the advances of a big publishing house. She's been with Berry, Barnes and Webb for years and, if there's no major disagreement between them, she should be able to dictate terms to a certain extent. And it's not as though she's punching a clock or working in any frenetic environment . . . I agree that Pagett has had its fair share of success, and nobody is prouder of Pagett than I am, but compared to the powerhouses – and that includes Berry, Barnes and Webb – we're small fry. It feels as though there's a crack in the bell, Tim, it just doesn't ring true."

This morning's upheaval had happened so swiftly that Tim hadn't given a thought to Rick Gill's motives. He'd often disagreed with Arthur's natural caution, but maybe Arthur was right. And perhaps Simone also had a point. Holly might well be no match for Rick Gill.

"I hadn't even considered that there could be a hidden agenda." Tim's eyes narrowed with concentration. "Whoever takes Gill on will need to tread warily. But, if he's genuine, it's a hard offer to turn down."

"I suppose so, that's up to you to decide. If you can't find a solution, talk to John Barrett. He's a reasonable man and a smart one and, I suspect, not unaware of Simone's moods."

"He's in London this week doing some research for his next book. He'll be at Pagett tomorrow for the board meeting. I don't like running to him with tales, but if we can't come to some sort of compromise this afternoon I may have to."

* * *

Simone scraped the sides of the yoghurt carton; that, and a cup of coffee, would have to do for lunch today. She couldn't face the quizzical looks and snide whispers. The rest of the staff would all have heard about the row by now. The last of the smooth, custardy yoghurt stuck in her throat. Of all the insults that had come her way, this morning's was the worst, the gravest, the most unfair.

Her direct phone-line rang and she ignored it. Where was Lois? It was almost a quarter past two and she should be back from lunch by now. It had probably taken her longer than usual this morning to spread her venomous gossip. She'd deal with Lois later. The question that burned most brightly in her mind was, what should she do if they refused to hand over Rick Gill? Should she resign? Definitely, she should resign. But why should she let that little squit, Holly Grant, force her out? The very thought of Holly sent the blood pounding through her head.

Simone looked around the boardroom with pride. This was her handiwork. Her design. There were no hard edges in the room. The board table was round, the chairs curved and upholstered, even the frames on the wall had been chosen for their oval shape. She had selected her favourite combination of pastels for the curtains and the self-patterned, biscuit-tinted carpet was comfortable underfoot. She damn well wouldn't resign.

Holly was the last to arrive and took a chair as far away from Simone as she possibly could.

"One way or another we must resolve this matter before it gets further out of hand," Tim said.

"There's no need for any further discussion," Holly announced decisively. "If Simone wants Rick Gill that badly, he's all hers. We all work for Pagett and surely that's what is important." Holly would like to have been more gracious, but anything she could do to make Simone look petty . . .

Simone's eyes widened with suspicion. Tim's mouth opened and closed like a guppy out of water. Sean gave her such a look of gratitude that she almost giggled.

"Thank you, Holly." Tim was reverent with relief. Simone remained silent.

"I can't pretend that I'm not delighted we've settled this matter . . . " Tim said as he sat upright in his seat, his eyes alert. "But I think it's important that we discuss the details. Holly, can you tell Simone exactly what Rick Gill proposed?"

Simone's complacency vanished. "I really don't need any information from Holly, I'll contact him myself and set up an appointment." Simone pushed her chair back from the table.

"One minute, Simone." Tim put his hand on her arm. "There's something about this that bothers me, I still can't quite understand why a writer like Nancy Dell is anxious to . . . "

"Tim, I've told you, I'll handle this," Simone interrupted. "I'm not some impressionable half-wit waiting to be taken in by a smooth-talking agent."

"OK," Tim said hastily as her slur hit home. Holly's face was flushed with anger. "Meeting adjourned." For the first time in his career he understood Arthur Lord's policy – to adjourn meetings while everyone was still in one piece.

Sean and Holly left the room together.

"That was very decent of you, Holly," he said as soon as they were out of earshot. "Please don't let Simone get to you. You've already proved yourself to be a terrific editor and I suppose Simone finds that hard to take. There'll be other Nancy Dells, other Rick Gills . . . "

Lois looked eagerly towards them. Sean smiled at her and Lois returned his smile with interest. Now that his last girlfriend had gone her own way he'd been tempted to ask Lois for a date, but mixing business and pleasure worried him. Perhaps in a few weeks' time . . .

"That was quick, what happened?" Lois asked eagerly when Sean left them alone.

"I don't want to talk here, come into my office," Holly said. Lois followed her with a frown.

"Close the door," Holly instructed as she threw herself into one of the comfortable chairs and signalled to the one that Rick Gill had occupied not three hours earlier. "If you repeat anything I tell you . . . " Holly warned as she pulled a finger across her throat.

"I won't, I *won't*."

"I told Simone that she could have Rick Gill."

"You *what*? Why?" Lois demanded.

"Because I think she was . . . entitled to handle Nancy Dell. It's also a way of thanking her for letting me stay with her when I broke up with

Derek. But, aside from that, she's pissed off enough with me already and would probably make my life a living hell. I had enough of that with Derek . . . "

"Is Lois with you?" Simone barged into Holly's office uninvited.

"I'm here." Lois jumped guiltily to her feet.

"You were late back from lunch, why?"

"Lois was doing some work for me, I delayed her," Holly said.

"I need you to make some calls for me," Simone said sharply.

Lois obediently trotted towards the door with a backward look of gratitude towards Holly.

Holly smiled encouragingly. Any sign of gratitude from Simone would be a miracle. She made a face at Simone's well-tailored back. She was sick of seeing her dressed in beige.

Holly trudged up the stairs lost in thought and almost tripped over Terence who was pushing something under her door.

"Hello," she greeted cautiously.

"Hi! You're early, I was just leaving a note for you." Terence was shocked by her appearance, she looked strained and thin. He longed to put his arms around her.

"Come in," she invited but refused to allow herself to get excited by his visit. She'd made enough of a fool of herself last time.

Terence stooped to retrieve his note.

"Excuse the mess," Holly apologised as she took off her coat. "I haven't had time to tidy up."

"That's OK." He was happy to see that Derek's influence had been exorcised at last.

"Is there something special you want to talk to me about?" God, I'm beginning to sound as bad as Simone, she told herself.

Terence hesitated, he recognised the wariness in Holly's tone. She was entitled to be cautious, he'd never forgive himself for having rejected her. Quietly Terence crumpled the note in his hand and pushed it into his pocket. His news would keep.

"It can wait. Are you busy tomorrow night?" he asked tentatively.

"Not especially," Holly replied guardedly.

"I'm making one of my pasta dinners, there's plenty for two . . . I hate waste." Nervousness made him flippant.

"Me too," Holly fenced. "About seven?"

Terence nodded.

"You still haven't told me why you wanted to talk to me."

Terence frowned. Holly did have a right to know. "When our leases are up next year, they're not being renewed."

Holly's first reaction was one of knee-buckling relief. She'd convinced herself Terence had come to tell her that he'd met someone else and was getting married.

"Sorry to spring it on you like that." Terence couldn't read her expression. "The landlord was buzzing around with some builders this morning. I hung about till they'd gone then asked him what was going on. It took a while to get it out of him but the bottom line is, he intends to refurbish the building then push up the rents. I checked my lease and he's entitled to chuck us out. I assume your lease is the same as mine?"

"I was in such a tizz when I took the place I don't think I read it properly," Holly admitted. If that's all that was wrong . . .

"No matter what he spends on the flats we still won't gain any extra space. I asked him about that. I know you've always felt just as cramped as I have. He reckons it'll take about six months to carry out the work, and when they're ready we'll be offered first refusal. I don't know how you feel about this but if I'm going to spend more money it might as well be on a larger flat. I needed a push like this to get myself moving."

Even during the coolness between them, living next door to Terence had been a comfort. Holly had felt that she could rely on him no matter what emergency arose. Her panic subsided and the full implication of what he'd told her began to sink in. This was the beginning of the end. They'd go their separate ways. At first they'd have dinner occasionally, then, after a while, they'd drift apart. She didn't want to be parted from him.

"I don't want to move," she exclaimed involuntarily. "I want to live next door to you."

Terence felt a real twist of pleasure. "I want the same thing," he admitted. "I've been miserable, I should never have pretended to be busy that night I came to congratulate you, all I did was go to a film on my own."

"And I shouldn't have snapped at you the way I did and gone stamping off like a spoiled brat. You were so distant after that, I didn't have the courage to knock at your door and apologise," Holly said.

"That's all over and done with now. Even though our landlord's dropped us in it, I think we should toast him for getting us back together. We'll do that tomorrow, OK?"

"Sure!"

"It'll be something to remember when we're out on the streets living in cardboard boxes," Terence teased.

"I'll drink to that," Holly said. "Just as long as the boxes are side by side."

"They will be, I promise."

"Do you have time for a drink now that you're here?" Holly ventured, she didn't relish being turned down again.

"If we make it a quick one. I genuinely do have an appointment tonight. With a client," he added quickly. "May I use your phone?"

Holly heard him rearranging the time of the meeting as she scrabbled around in the drawer for a corkscrew.

"Tell me what you've been up to," she said as she handed him the bottle to uncork.

"Busy, I'm glad to say. We're working on a lovely old house in Berkshire, the new owners are determined to make it even more beautiful. That's taking up a fair bit of my time at the moment.

We've finished the offices in Mayfair and I've several appointments with builders next week. The client I'm meeting tonight is restoring an Elizabethan house, it's a beaut." Terence's eyes shone with pleasure. "I'd love to get involved in that. My main difficulty is actually getting to those country mansions. It's a pest having to hire cars, and expensive. So perhaps there's something to be said for moving after all. If I could find somewhere with room to garage a car, I might consider buying one. I don't fancy parking in the street and having it nicked."

"What a coincidence! I was thinking about the same thing the other day. I spent last weekend with Liz and Robert. The traffic in town was so bad that I missed my train. I'm sure I could've made it to the station much quicker on foot, but the bag I was carrying weighed a ton so I had to stay put in the taxi. Poor Liz, she had to wait at the station for ages. I spent the journey thinking how much easier it would be if I had a car."

"Can you drive?" Terence asked.

"No, but I'm sure I could soon learn."

"Of course you could."

Holly smiled at him. This was the Terence she knew and loved. The truth hit her with such force it almost creased her. She did love him.

"Where have you disappeared to now?" she heard him ask.

"Sorry, I think the ramifications have just caught up with me," she apologised.

"You were certainly on planet X when you came home." He laughed indulgently. "You could hardly miss *me*!"

Little did he know how untrue that was.

"Bad day today?" he asked.

Holly hesitated. "I made up my mind that if we ever became friends again, I'd never dump my worries on you."

"That's ridiculous, we've always shared our problems," Terence objected.

"Yes, but they always seemed to be my problems."

"So what, that's how life goes. I think you've had a bad day, right?"

"Kind of. A head-on with Simone, but it's sorted out now."

"Tell me."

"Really?"

"Really."

" . . . so I told her she can have him, honestly, it wasn't worth the hassle," Holly said.

"Nancy Dell? Rick Gill? Those names ring a bell."

"I'm sure you've seen her name on the bestseller list."

"No, it's not that, I'm sure it was in some other context. It'll come back to me, I'll remember. I'd better push off now or I'll be late," Terence said reluctantly.

Holly walked to the door with him and impulsively gave him a quick peck on the cheek.

"I'm so glad . . . " she said, then stopped, suddenly embarrassed.

"Me too," Terence confirmed as he fled, pink-cheeked, into the narrow hallway.

First thing tomorrow morning I'll rescue my feathered headdress from the drawer, she promised herself. It had been such a painful reminder of their friendship that she'd wrapped it up carefully and stored it out of sight.

Chapter Forty-Seven

Samantha Forrest's attitude was puzzling. The two editors had met several times at literary functions and Simone had always found her friendly and up-front, happy to discuss publishing problems in general and editorial ones in particular. But her call to Samantha earlier had left Simone wondering. She'd answered Simone's questions reluctantly, their brief conversation punctuated with hesitations on Samantha's part. No publisher liked to lose a good author but Berry, Barnes and Webb would hardly suffer sleepless nights if Nancy Dell defected to Pagett. It happened all the time in publishing. Evasive, yes, Samantha had been evasive. Simone shrugged, it couldn't be helped. The important thing was that Nancy was free to make the change – although a bit of extra information about the author wouldn't have gone amiss.

"Could you get Rick Gill for me, Lois?" she asked.

"Rick Gill," a sharp voice said.

"Good morning. I'm Simone Pearse, editor-in-chief of Pagett."

There was a short silence on the line. "Yes, Simone, what can I do for you?"

"I understand you called here yesterday while I was out. I apologise that you had to deal with one of our . . . junior editors."

"I found your Ms Grant very capable and efficient," he said loftily, cursing his bad luck. He'd spent most of yesterday celebrating his good luck.

"She is indeed, but I handle all our important agents and authors, I'm afraid she doesn't have the authority . . . "

"I see. Does that include Emily Howard? I thought Holly Grant was her editor."

Simone ignored his remark.

"Well, no doubt Holly filled you in on the good news?" he asked.

"We spoke briefly. I'd hardly call it good news. I'll come straight to the point, I'm afraid the royalties you proposed are out of the question." Simone held her breath.

Attack then defend was the way to deal with him.

"Then we have no common ground for talking," Rick responded harshly.

"Apparently not."

"We can of course approach any publisher, but for some reason Nancy has chosen Pagett," he said disparagingly.

"For *many* reasons," Simone bristled. "We have an excellent reputation, treat our authors well, do an excellent job with marketing and sales, and have just added several big names to our new list."

"Whatever, I'm merely following my client's wishes."

For ten minutes they played their cat and mouse game.

Simone replaced her receiver smugly. She had knocked him down two and a half per cent across the board. This news would keep until the meeting tomorrow. She wanted everyone to be there to hear it, to enjoy the satisfaction of teaching Holly Grant a public lesson. This would fix the little witch, show her how to deal with agents.

* * *

"Do you have a minute?" Lois asked.

"Sure, come in." Holly was glad to take her eyes off the screen.

"I'm not sure I should tell you this, it may stir up trouble again, but Pagett comes first, right?" she said mysteriously.

"Right. Tell me what?" Sometimes she wished that Lois wouldn't talk in riddles.

"You know that Simone spoke to Nancy Dell's editor at Berry, Barnes and Webb this morning – Samantha Forrest?"

"I didn't, but that's not surprising."

"Well, I put the call through and then had a chat with their receptionist, Gina Shields. We went to school together and haven't seen each other for yonks. We arranged to meet for lunch today. She hasn't changed a bit but thought I looked great," Lois digressed proudly.

411

"Where's all this leading?" Holly frowned impatiently.

"Naturally we talked about Nancy Dell," Lois ventured nervously.

"Naturally."

"Well, it turns out that Berry, Barnes and Webb didn't publish her last book, it never reached the shops."

"Wait a minute, what are you talking about? Her last book did well."

"No, the one before that did well. The latest one was turned down by her editor."

"You're sure about this?"

"I'm only repeating what Gina told me."

"Didn't she give any reason for its failure? I mean, for goodness sake, Nancy Dell is practically a household name."

"I know. According to Gina, the manuscript was so utterly useless, so hopelessly muddled, that it left Samantha no choice, she had to pull it. If Rick Gill hadn't come storming into Berry, Barnes like a headless chicken, Gina wouldn't have known anything about this. It was lunchtime and she was the only one around. He and Samantha had an enormous row. Gina could hear them yelling at each other, but by the time she was ready to go to lunch they'd calmed down."

"Does Simone know about this?"

"I haven't a clue what Samantha told her. They didn't talk for long, then Simone buzzed and asked me to get Rick Gill."

"This is awful," Holly said.

"You won't involve me or Gina, will you? I didn't know what to do."

"It's OK, you were right to tell me. I'm not exactly Simone's closest confidant but it's only fair to warn her, *important* to warn her. I'll talk to her now. And don't worry, I won't implicate you, or your friend Gina."

"Thanks, Holly. But you'll have to wait until tomorrow, Simone's just left for an appointment."

"Will you put me through to Simone?" Holly asked Lois the following day.

"Good luck."

"What can I do for you, Holly?" Simone asked, pleasantly enough for her.

"I need to talk to you."

"Sure, what about?"

"About . . . Nancy Dell."

"Holly, that matter is closed," Simone retorted sharply.

"'But, I wanted to . . . "

"No ifs, no buts, the subject is closed, do you understand?"

"It's important that . . . "

"C-L-O-S-E-D, Holly, taboo, finito, fermé, ended in any language you care to name. Get my drift?"

The phone at Simone's end went down with a crash.

"Ungrateful bitch!" Holly yelled down the dead line. "You don't want to hear me out? Let's wait for the meeting, you'll hear me then," she vowed.

They were all there early, no one liked to hang around on Fridays.

"Excuse me, Holly, there's a call for you," Lois said.

"Can't it wait?" Simone grumbled petulantly.

"Who is it?" Holly asked.

"Terence Warren, he says it's urgent."

"Pity she can't keep her love life outside office hours," Simone muttered just loudly enough to earn herself a censorious look from Tim. He hoped they weren't going to indulge in one of their verbal brawls this morning.

"Go ahead, Simone, you had something to tell us," he reminded her.

"It'll wait until Holly gets back." She wasn't going to embark on her moment of triumph while Holly was out of the room.

Holly took his call with a frown, Terence had never phoned her at Pagett before.

"Hello, Terence, something wrong?" she asked.

"Nothing's wrong, I've just remembered why Rick Gill's name was familiar and I thought perhaps you should know. I was asked to price an extension for him, a bedroom and bathroom on the ground floor of his house. It was for his wife Nancy who'd had a stroke. That's where I saw her name, on dozens of books in his study."

"My God! That explains why her last book failed. But if she's ill how can she still write?" Holly wondered aloud.

"Search me, a secretary, ghost writer maybe?" Terence suggested.

"I must get back to the meeting. Thanks a million, Terence."

"What's going on?" Lois demanded, her ears almost at right angles.

"I think we've solved the mystery. Nancy Dell has had a stroke."

Lois's eyes and mouth formed perfect Os.

"Sorry about that," Holly apologised as she returned to her seat. How had Rick Gill hoped to get away with such a deception? She was glad she was out of it.

"Now that Holly has deigned to join us again, I'd like to tell you that I've successfully negotiated a price with Rick Gill. A three-book contract with Nancy Dell at two and a half percent less than he was asking." Simone said.

"That sounds promising." Jeremy Hide was the first to speak.

"It does," Tim agreed reluctantly. "You've spoken to her previous publishers, I'm sure?"

"I have. I don't think they're too pleased about it, Samantha Forrest was quite snitty with me."

"Well, everything appears to be above board," Tim said dubiously. He still wasn't convinced that Nancy's reason for moving was valid.

Holly sat quietly and listened to the comments around her.

"Are you satisfied to take her on even though Berry, Barnes pulled her last book?" she asked nonchalantly.

"What on *earth* are you on about?" Simone scoffed.

"Nancy Dell," Holly replied innocently.

"Pulled her last book? The damn thing was on the list for weeks, don't you read the bestseller list?" Simone sneered.

"Only the books that are on it," Holly retorted with a smile.

"Holly, what *are* you talking about?" Sean Barrett demanded as he felt the tension between the editors begin to build.

Holly explained patiently, savouring every moment, "Berry, Barnes and Webb's editor turned down Nancy Dell's last book because it was so badly written. You see, Nancy has suffered a stroke."

Simone burst out laughing. "What a load of rubbish. That's the best bit of fiction I've heard for years. Well done, Holly."

"Shut up, Simone," Tim said rudely. "Is this true, Holly? If it is, why didn't you tell someone?"

"I tried to warn Simone this morning, didn't I, Simone?" she asked sweetly. "But I was told in no uncertain terms to butt out, mind my own business. But don't worry, I wouldn't have allowed her to make a fool of Pagett. I knew I'd have an opportunity to set the record straight at the meeting this morning."

Jane Scott blew her nose loudly to hide her sniggers. Marianna smothered her giggles by shuffling papers and even Sean Barrett developed a sudden bout of coughing. Only Simone, stony-faced with disbelief, failed to see the humour.

"Where did you get all this information?" Tim asked.

"Two different sources, but I'm quite sure it can be verified," Holly suggested then plunged the knife in deeper. "Would you like me to check it out for you, Simone?"

Holly had made herself an enemy for life.

Book Three

Spring the following year

Detective Inspector Michael Moore drummed his fists impatiently on the arms of his chair. Never had he been so utterly frustrated, so uncertain who the culprit was, faced with such dead ends.

He didn't regard himself as a particularly stubborn man – except where solving a crime was concerned – and didn't suffer from vanity. When he'd called his team together, he'd admitted his failure, spelt out his suspicions, then despatched them to re-interview each of the original suspects. But his officers had also drawn a blank. All four possibilities had iron-clad alibis.

There had to be something he'd missed, something that would give him his answer. Circumstantial evidence wasn't worth a jot and he didn't even have that.

He stared dully at the tape as it continued to roll. He couldn't be bothered to switch it off and continued to take his moody frustration out on the battered leather chair. Even with the help of computers, video cameras and DNA testing . . . He shot to attention. He watched, counted, then watched again. He re-wound the tape and double-checked.

"Got you!" he yelled with sheer delight.

His shout brought half the squad running into his office.

"I've got it," he said excitedly, pointing to the tape. "Look, it's all here – chapter and verse."

Chapter Forty-Eight

Holly patted the bonnet of her car lovingly. Passing her driving test first time was one of her greatest achievements.

On the far side of the carpark, she saw Simone wave to Sophie. The editorial assistant waited for Simone to catch up with her. They were as thick as thieves, those two. Nowadays Simone only spoke to Holly when it was absolutely necessary and Sophie was cool to her when they met.

To hell with them, Holly muttered to herself but lingered a little longer in order to avoid them.

"Hi, Lois." Holly paused at the news desk.

"Had a good weekend?"

"We went to the cottage, the weather was glorious and we walked for miles."

Lois pulled a face. "Not my scene," she shuddered.

Lois was so trim it was hard to believe that she hated all forms of exercise.

"Post in yet?" Holly asked with a smile.

"On your desk."

Holly riffled through the envelopes. Her phone rang.

"Congratulations, Holly, I thought you'd like to know that your decree nisi has been granted. I've written to you with the details, would you like me to fax you a copy?"

"Yes, thank you for letting me know," she said and gave him the fax number.

In six weeks she'd be free. Single. Unattached. Holly dropped the fax on to her desk and watched it curl up. She felt nothing. No sudden rush of joy, no elation, nothing. She'd heard from Derek twice in the past two months. His first letter had offered to take her back and, when she didn't reply, the second one was truculent and unpleasant – typically Derek – *he had no need of a fool like her*. She'd sent both letters to Vincent Harper. At least this time Derek had failed to find out where she lived. She must phone Liz immediately, she didn't want a repetition of their row. She'd tell Terence later.

No doubt Liz'll renew her crusade now, Holly giggled.

"I'm thrilled for you. Free at last – well, almost. Now you'll be able to concentrate on Terence," Liz said.

"Liz! Let's get the ink dry on my divorce papers before you rush me down the aisle again."

"Come off it, you know you adore him," Liz pushed.

"I do and so do you, but marriage . . . "

Holly nodded and waved Lois in.

"Liz, I've got to go, Lois needs me. I'll talk to you later."

"The couriers have just delivered this

manuscript, do you have anything to go out?" What marriage? Was Holly divorced now? Lois itched to know.

"Nope. Thanks, Lois."

Lois left uninformed but returned five minutes later. "Tim asked me to give you this, he's just dashing out."

Holly slit the envelope and her breath caught in her throat. Emily Howard's first royalty cheque. It fell from her nerveless fingers and landed on her desk. She should be jumping for joy but she felt numb. It was there, a cheque for more money than she could have imagined and all she could do was gulp air. Holly recognised the first signs of nausea and rushed to the cloakroom.

She dashed cold water on her face and examined her appearance in the mirror. Her hair hung limply round her thin face.

Pale and wan instead of rich and single, she thought as she patted her mouth with a tissue. I've got to get my hair cut. Like Liz's, a bit shorter maybe, then my face will look rounder.

She checked her watch; there was no time to hang around, she had a final meeting about Lucinda's launch in a few minutes and needed to put on some make-up.

Holly sank blissfully into the scented water. Although it was almost three months now since she'd moved into the flat, she still hadn't learnt to take its size and comfort for granted. She had gladly left it to Terence to find a flat. His connections in the building trade spread far and wide. He had pestered builders non-stop until, finally, his tenacity paid off. There were eight flats in the four-storied conversion in Wimbledon and they had become the first tenants – two flats side by side, just as Terence had promised. It was a treat to have two bedrooms. Like all the other rooms, they were spacious and airy. Holly had been totally won over when she saw the cleverly designed gardens – six attractively fenced, entirely private patio gardens. She and Terence agreed to share one which had delighted the builder. A flat with its own garden would fetch a higher rent.

She leant forward to remove a dead leaf from the potted fern at the foot of the bath, then stretched out again and continued to soak. She tried not to think about the cheque and its implications. Now she could afford all those extra bits and pieces she'd hesitated to buy a few months ago. She shut her eyes and tried to think what she needed but all she could see against her closed eyelids was the word *thief*. If only she could turn back, tell the truth. Holly pulled out the plug, she'd been down this road too many times before.

"How would you like a visitor for a couple of days?" Liz asked.

"You?" Holly's face lit up with pleasure.

"Robert is going on a course the weekend after next – the American company, remember?"

"That's wonderful! I'll book theatre tickets, anything special you want to see?"

"No, I'll leave that to you."

"We'll spend a day at the shops, have a meal out. Oh Liz, I'm really looking forward to this. I'll take the Friday afternoon off so we won't miss a moment."

"OK. We should arrive just after lunch. We're bringing back your desk and your china. Now, tell me about Vincent's letter."

Holly read it to her.

"At least Derek's paying costs and giving you a few grand besides," she said dryly.

"Vincent negotiated that."

"You're entitled to it. I'm sure that you're over the moon now that the end's in sight."

"Funnily enough, I'm not."

"You're *not?*" Liz shrieked. "Holly, you're not going to change your mind again, tell me you're not."

"Of course I'm not! What I mean is I don't feel anything, it's as if it's all happening to someone else, not to me," Holly explained.

"It's probably shock or relief, or something." Liz calmed down. "Robert's just come home. I'd better go and rescue his dinner from the oven. He'll be thrilled to hear your news."

After they said goodbye, Holly pulled her laptop from its case. She put it on the table near the window and switched on. Her days were always so busy at Pagett that she'd fallen woefully behind with her editing. She should have something to eat but was too tired to cook. There was a bar of chocolate in the kitchen, that would do. She ambled into the chintzy kitchen with its pine-scrubbed table and pretty cushioned chairs and found the chocolate. She never tired of this room, imagine, *four* chairs around the table.

* * *

"Did you tell Holly why I'm doing the course?" Robert asked as he sat back in his chair.

Liz hung her head and muttered something under her breath.

"I didn't hear you. You didn't, did you?"

"No, I chickened out. Besides, you haven't definitely decided yet."

"You know it's just a matter of tying up the loose ends." Robert looked at his wife's sad face. Poor Liz, the thought of the separation from Holly was affecting her badly. He reached for her hand and gave it a squeeze. "It's up to you, sweetheart, but I can't help feeling that the sooner you tell her the better. I understand your reluctance, really I do. But it's only for three years, four at the most. She can come and visit us in the States. Just think of what we'll be able to do with all that extra cash. The cottage will be restored at last, the way we planned."

"I agree with you, you don't have to sell the idea to me, but her decree nisi came through today, I didn't want to spoil her day by telling her our news."

"She must be delighted with that."

Liz shook her head. "I thought she would be too, but she's not. Says she doesn't feel anything."

"The reality hasn't sunk in. I'm sure she'll be pleased when it's all finally over."

"You're probably right, but if I was in her place I'd be yelling it from the rooftops," Liz said as she gathered up Robert's plates and his glass and walked thoughtfully to the sink. "I'll tell her next weekend when I go to stay with her."

"Not before? If you leave it until then, your weekend will be ruined."

"Oh Robert! I'm such a coward, aren't I?"

"Would you like me to tell her?"

"No, it's better coming from me. I'll phone her back before I lose my nerve."

* * *

Robert put his arms around his wife. "How did she take it?"

"Badly. She was crying so much she couldn't talk. It was awful, even worse than our row."

"I'm sorry, Liz."

Liz wiped her eyes on her sleeve, it was unfair to make Robert feel guilty like this. The job at Swift Pharmaceuticals was a wonderful opportunity for him. Not only had they offered to double his salary, but also to provide rent-free accommodation. They'd even promised to find work for her too. But, best of all, at last Robert would have the necessary funds to continue his research. Liz knew that, apart from herself, Robert's work meant everything to him.

Chapter Forty-Nine

Lucinda's launch was going with a swing and the cabin was well-sprinkled with journalists, many of whom had already received review copies of her book. Paris was the perfect background for her story; a young couple, broke and friendless, starting married life in a strange city.

Few people ever got the better of Lucinda and Holly had hidden her laughter while Lucinda bullied, cajoled, then demanded that Tim Brown should increase her launch budget. He finally gave in.

"I've got four interviews next week," Lucinda whispered to Holly as they seated themselves at the table.

"Five." Holly corrected. "Barry has someone else lined up for you, a new magazine, you'll feature in their first edition, photos – the lot."

"I'll probably crack the camera lens," Lucinda beamed delightedly. "Hear that, Dom, I'm to star in a new mag." Lucinda nudged her husband.

"Quite right, too, my darling," Dominic said proudly. She was a wonder, his wife.

The long boat swayed gently at anchor. Holly picked at her food and looked about her. There were several journalists from the broadsheet papers, and the tabloids and magazines were well represented too. Barry had done an excellent job. Lucinda had invited several friends, bright chatty people like herself who definitely added to the gaiety of the occasion.

It was hard to believe that so much had happened since she'd travelled to Paris.

Holly took a sip of water then cleared her throat. This was her first launch as an editor and, in spite of her notes, she suddenly felt nervous. It was time to introduce Lucinda and her book. She got to her feet.

Barry tapped his glass with a fork.

"Welcome," she began quietly. "I am the editor of Lucinda's wonderful book, *The Boulevard* . . . "

"I'll drink to that," Lucinda interrupted. Her jocularity was well intentioned, she could see that Holly was trembling with nerves. The laughter that followed relieved the tension considerably.

" . . . so any time Lucinda feels like basing a book in Rome, Madrid or even Paris again, I'd be perfectly willing to make the sacrifice and edit her there," Holly ended.

Barry gave her an approving wink as he led the applause and Sean told her that John would be proud of her. Tim smiled, but it was a worried smile as he watched the waiters opening more wine.

By two-thirty most people had drifted away, back to their desks and their routines.

"It all went splendidly," Lucinda said as she

thanked them. "I might well take you up on your suggestion, Holly – another town, another book. What do you say about that, Dominic?" she teased.

Dominic smiled, "I'll see what I can do, my sweet."

While she was waiting for the stylist to cut her hair, Holly flicked impatiently through the pages of the glossy magazine. She could ill-afford the time but her hair had become unmanageable. She stopped at the book page, read the critiques, then plunged on through fashion, cookery, and finally gardening. A beautifully designed garden caught her eye, a corner of which would be perfect for Liz and Robert's garden. But it would be years before that would happen, she thought sadly. From force of habit she looked for the name of the journalist. Roland Green. Don't be silly, she told herself, there must be dozens, hundreds, of Roland Greens. She scanned the article. Roland Green had retired from his position as managing editor of Pagett Publications to pursue the great love of his life – gardening. Holly turned back to the profiles at the beginning of the journal. Roland Green's photograph – with the inevitable bow tie – smiled back at her from the glossy page. The magazine's new gardening writer was delighted that his retirement *would give him the opportunity to visit all the wonderful celebrity gardens to be featured in future editions*.

Holly chuckled. How Simone would enjoy this!

"I'm so sorry to have kept you waiting, I know how busy you are," Ken, her stylist, apologised.

He picked up a spray bottle and damped her hair.

"You can make up for it," Holly said. "You can turn away while I tear out a couple of pages from this magazine."

"No problem. Most people do," he laughed. "Your hair, same way as usual?" He picked up the scissors.

"Not quite." Holly explained what she wanted.

"That'll work. How's life in the fast stream?" he asked as he disappeared into his own world of split ends.

Ken held up a mirror to show Holly the back of her head. He had managed to make it look even better than she hoped. Shorter and fuller than Liz's. She'd love Ken to cut Liz's hair. Her own village hairdresser was good but Ken definitely had the edge. Perhaps she could make an appointment for Liz before she left for the States.

As Holly waited for the lift to the ground floor, she wallowed in misery. No more weekends at the cottage, no more spur of the moment late-night chats on the phone and, although she would eventually find someone else on her own wavelength, no reader for her manuscripts. How could she bear it?

The lift doors opened. Liz would miss her too, Liz was the one going to a strange town, a new country. She would have to make huge adjustments. Find new friends. Start a new job.

The lift emptied and Holly followed the crowd to JP Harker's exit doors. The store was always so busy. A display of brightly coloured scarves didn't tempt her to stop. She had no heart for shopping today. She passed through the cosmetic hall with its fragrant aroma. She shook her head at a beautifully groomed girl who approached her with an elaborate glass bottle. New perfume didn't appeal to her either.

The notice – *give someone a token of your love* – above the reception desk, stopped her. Liz would have to cope with the expense of moving, how would she manage? A token would be the ideal going away present for her sister, a gift that she couldn't refuse. But for how much? Liz would object no matter what she gave her. She would think about it tonight, draw some money from her account, then come back and buy the token tomorrow.

"Yes, Holly?" Simone glared fiercely across her desk but didn't invite Holly to sit down.

"There are a couple of things – I need to find a new reader," Holly began nervously.

Simone's brow furrowed. Had a row with her precious sister, had she?

"Oh?"

"Liz and Robert are leaving soon for the States and I need someone to replace her."

"I know the feeling," she said spitefully.

Holly couldn't reply, she was mortified as she felt tears fill her eyes. This was the last thing she wanted but was powerless to help herself.

Simone stared at the miserable young woman facing her. This was about more than losing a reader, this was about a relationship that she knew meant the world to Holly.

"Look, I'm sorry, Holly, I know how close you and Liz are." That was the best she could manage. "Go ahead and advertise, or do you have someone in mind?"

Holly shook her head dumbly.

"You said there were a couple of things?" Simone reminded her.

"I thought you'd like to see this." Holly found her voice and handed Simone the pages that she'd torn from the magazine.

"Gardens?"

"Look again," Holly said as she sniffed away her tears.

"My God! Roland! So *that's* what happened to him. What's he doing writing a gardening column? That man wouldn't know an aster from an asterisk. *Celebrity* gardens. Typical! With all those genuinely talented gardening writers around, how come they pick him?" Simone demanded.

Holly managed a watery smile. "I thought you'd enjoy this."

"You're so right. He was a thorn in my side for long enough. Trudy Friel will love it." Simone's eyes sparkled with malice.

At least it will take the heat off me for a while, Holly thought as she headed for the door. On an impulse she stopped and turned.

"Simone, not that it makes any difference now,

but I'd like to say that for the first time I understand how you must have felt when I . . . when I was no longer your assistant. It took losing Liz to make me appreciate how difficult . . . " Holly faltered. "I know we can never be friends, but perhaps it would be easier for everyone, including ourselves, if we weren't so hostile towards each other."

Roland's downfall had put Simone in an expansive mood. Holly was right, they would never be friends, but they could be more civil to each other, it would lessen the tension, particularly at the meetings.

"I suppose you have a point, our . . . little disagreements don't help. And Sophie *is* a great assistant." She couldn't resist the dig.

Holly ignored it and stretched out her hand.

After a moment's hesitation, Simone shook the slender hand and smiled.

As the door closed, Simone reached for the phone and asked Lois for an outside line. Oh yes, Trudy would love this.

Simone smiled with satisfaction as she turned the last page. Sophie was spot-on as usual, this manuscript was excellent. On Monday she'd phone Gracie, the author's agent, and arrange a meeting. Maybe they'd have dinner, she might even tell Gracie about the stunt she'd pulled on Ian Trent, it was Gracie who'd warned her about him in the first place.

In a weak moment she had told Sophie what she'd done.

Simone enjoyed it when the building was quiet

like this, no phones ringing, no clatter. She'd decided that it would be easier for her to go straight from Pagett to the book-reading, use the time in between to do some editing. If anyone at the meeting had noticed the cessation of hostilities between her and Holly, they hadn't acknowledged it. It wasn't a bad thing this truce, anger was such a waste of emotion and, after all, she was the one in control, not Holly. They had to work together . . .

Simone was startled as a girl with a long chestnut plait slammed a book down on the desk.

"This is my mother's book," she announced.

Simone jumped to her feet. She had been so taken up with her own thoughts that she hadn't heard the girl come in.

"Who let you in?" she asked.

"*This* is my mother's book," the girl repeated.

While she recovered her composure, Simone glanced at a well-thumbed copy of *Tomorrow's Joy* lying on her desk. What was the girl talking about?

"Don't bother to deny it," said the quivering girl.

"Deny what?" Simone asked.

"That you stole this book. All the names of the characters have been changed of course, and the places, and lots of other details, but this is my mother's book." She jabbed the cover with her index finger.

Simone had heard that this kind of thing happened, people trying to make false claims.

"I'm sure there's some mistake. We know the author of this book, Emily Howard. Look, her name is there on the cover."

Simone wished there was someone else around. That Sophie hadn't left early to go to the dentist. With a quick glance at her watch, she realised it was almost five-thirty. The girl was so angry Simone began to feel a little afraid.

"Why don't you sit down? We can discuss this calmly and rationally."

"I don't want to sit down," she said. "I want to know why Emily Howard's name is on the cover! Who is Emily Howard?"

"What's your name?" Simone asked.

"Jennifer James, Jenny."

"OK, Jenny, you say this is your mother's book, can you prove it?"

"Yes, I can."

"How?"

"I can bring you the exercise books Mum used when she wrote it. I knew every word of that book, I was the one who copied it onto the proper paper. It took me weeks and weeks. My mother was the one who chose Pagett to publish it."

"Why didn't your mother come and see me herself?"

"She died last year."

"I'm sorry," Simone said. She was desperate to get rid of this wild-eyed creature.

"I want to know what you're going to do about this. If you don't admit you're to blame for stealing the book, I'll get legal help," Jenny stormed.

Jenny's threat was an empty one. The only contact she'd had with the law was when she'd been caught shop-lifting. It had been the most frightening experience of her life and all because of a few groceries and a bottle of 7-Up. The few measly pence she'd had left in her purse wouldn't even cover the cost of a small bottle. It was the only drink that her mother could keep down.

Jenny knew she'd been lucky to find such a sympathetic magistrate, even more fortunate when an officer of the court tucked a ten-pound note into her pocket and told her to go home and look after her mother. Told her never to appear in court again or she'd wind up in jail.

She couldn't get involved with the law again, couldn't risk losing custody of her younger brothers and sisters, watch them being taken into care.

"You're perfectly free to seek legal help, Jenny. But I must warn you, you're not the first person who's tried to claim a book which is not rightfully theirs."

"It *is* mine – ours – now Mum's gone. I told you, I have proof."

At last Simone found the way out. "OK, Jenny, here's what you do. Bring me the books and give me time to check them against the text. How does that sound?"

"It sounds as though you're trying to get rid of me. Look, I'm telling the truth. I've come halfway across London to speak to you, I could've gone straight to my solicitor or to the newspapers."

Simone sank on to her chair. It was true, Jenny could have sought legal advice. If this wasn't a hoax, Pagett had a serious allegation on their hands.

"I'm *not* trying to get rid of you, what I'm trying to do is find proof. You do understand that, don't you?"

"Don't patronise me, you're in no position to do that," Jenny shot back bravely. For a moment she wished that her family wasn't so dependent on her, that she was free to carry out her threat. But she'd promised her mother that she'd always care for her brothers and sisters and, as long as they needed her, she would.

Simone bit back her retort, getting into an argument would serve no purpose.

"When was the book sent to us? How long ago?" she asked.

"Three years ago," Jenny answered without hesitation.

"And you say it was handwritten? What was it called?"

"It was written by hand, we didn't have a typewriter or anything. It didn't have a title, Mum wanted whoever published it to decide that. I'm sure she explained all that in her letter."

"Didn't she think it strange that she didn't get a reply?"

"She was disappointed."

"But she didn't write to us again?"

"No. She thought you didn't like it. But obviously you did." Jenny's tone was sarcastic.

"Usually a manuscript would be returned within a couple of months," Simone explained. "I presume you included a return name and address?"

Jenny shifted her feet. "I told you, Mum packaged it up, I just posted it."

"Can you give me the exact date it was sent?"

"I can't remember. I know it was around March, that's all. But what difference does that make?"

"Did you register it?"

Jenny gave her a scornful glare. "I didn't think that was necessary, besides, we couldn't . . . "

"You couldn't what?"

"We couldn't afford the money to register a parcel like that," she said.

Simone's brain was reeling. There was something convincing about this girl.

"When can you bring me the exercise books?"

"Tomorrow?"

Simone rarely came into the office on Saturdays but this was important.

"What time?" she asked.

"After ten o'clock?"

"Make it eleven. You'll have to leave the exercise books with me, I'll need time to read them."

Jenny met her gaze unwaveringly. "This book meant a lot to my mother. She was a wonderful mother," she said slowly. "The story is about us, our life, I'm sure you guessed that."

"I haven't read the book," Simone admitted. "Now Jenny, I must ask you to leave, I have an urgent appointment and I'm late already. I'll see you tomorrow."

Simone took a deep breath. She'd been mega-scared at one stage, now she just felt drained.

Perhaps a dose of caffeine would revive her, give her a chance to think about this mess.

Simone nursed the mug of coffee between her fingers. Holly must be told, right away. It was just as well they were speaking again, at least now they could discuss this in a civil manner. She'd advise Holly not to tell Emily Howard anything about it for the moment.

It's probably just a try-on, Simone told herself as she dialled Holly's number. Yet there was something about the passionate girl that rang true. Would anyone as young and unworldly as Jenny try to pull off a scam like that, have the nerve to expect to get away with it? She didn't look more than seventeen or eighteen.

Holly's phone continued to ring.

Simone remained at her desk. She'd skip the book-reading tonight, finish her coffee and go home. She'd phone Holly from there.

As Simone drove, Jenny James haunted her. Those flashing eyes, her wild accusation. Maybe Holly *should* talk to Emily Howard, sound her out. But how could Emily have got her hands on the exercise books? It was a pity that she wasn't able to come into Pagett, or even talk on the phone. She'd have to leave Holly to do that. Obviously Emily felt comfortable with Holly. Holly had done everything for her; made all her decisions, handled her publicity, taken care of her banking, her covers, her editing, everything. Holly was the only one who'd ever spoken to her, the only one who knew she actually existed . . . Simone stamped on the brake pedal. The lights had changed to red. She sat there, her heart racing. *No one had ever spoken to Emily Howard . . . Holly had taken care of everything . . . the only one who knew she really existed.*

Don't be absurd, she told herself, Holly is a lot of things but that's crazy. I'm beginning to go round the twist. The motorist behind her blasted his horn and Simone moved on. She drove slowly, searching for a place to pull in. She must go and see Holly, right away if possible. She had to get some answers.

If only she had a mobile she wouldn't have to trail around in the rain like this looking for a public phone. She scowled at the two giggling teenagers as they finally left the phone box. She was soaked and Holly still wasn't home.

Chapter Fifty

After their first tearful few minutes, the sisters agreed not to spoil the weekend by discussing Liz's move to America. Holly told her about the plans she had for the weekend then gave Liz her gift.

"A thousand pounds! You're crazy, I can't take this. I *won't* take it," Liz said in a shocked voice.

"You'll need clothes – summer clothes and winter clothes, shoes, suitcases and goodness knows what else."

"I know I do, but I can't accept this Holly. You still have furniture to buy for the flat, things *you* need. It was a lovely thought." Liz pushed the gift token back at Holly.

Holly had expected her sister to react like this. "I can afford it, specially now that I'll be getting that money from Derek. Spending his money on the flat would just remind me of my unhappiness. Please Liz, take it. You've both given me so much. I've had somewhere to run to when I needed it, such wonderful weekends, your love and understanding. This is *my* way of saying thank you."

"Oh Holly, I can't, it's too much."

"You can and it's not. End of discussion. I thought you might like to spend the day at Harkers tomorrow."

"I feel terrible . . . "

"Subject closed," Holly said firmly.

"OK. But if I go, will you come with me?"

"Of course if you want me to. I thought maybe you'd prefer to do your own thing. I've plenty of work to occupy me here, I never seem to catch up at the office."

Liz wouldn't hear of it.

"We'll eat after the theatre, that way we can take as much time as you want. Now, back to today. Do you fancy poking around a couple of art galleries or would you rather go to a film? I've booked a table at a new Thai restaurant, but that's not until eight o'clock."

"In that case, a film I think. A comedy?"

"A film it is. We could both use a good laugh."

The film lived up to its publicity and their meal was perfect – spicy and tasty – and, by the time they reached the flat, they were in excellent spirits.

Liz dashed to answer the phone. "That'll be Robert, he said he'd leave it until after eleven to ring."

She listened for a moment. "It's for you. It's Simone."

"Simone! Are you sure?" Holly whispered.

Liz nodded.

"Sorry to phone so late, but I've been trying all evening. I had a visit . . . "

Liz picked up the pages beside the laptop and began to read them.

After several minutes she glanced across at her sister who'd hardly said a word. Holly's hands were shaking, her face ashen.

"Mostly I write to her, we rarely speak on the phone," Holly said.

Liz frowned and lowered the papers in her hand. Holly looked really upset, what had Simone said now?

"Six o'clock tomorrow? That's awkward, my sister's staying with me."

Holly was almost palsied with fear, her eyes rolling, her body swaying.

"Nine o'clock on Monday morning," Holly confirmed as the receiver fell to the floor.

Liz was on her feet in an instant. Holly was going to faint. She held her sister firmly and managed to get her onto the couch.

"Holly, Holly, what is it? What did she say to you?"

Holly continued to shake. She tried to speak, but no words came out.

"You're ill, I'll phone for a doctor," Liz said, her own mouth dry with fear.

"No . . . no," Holly rasped.

If only Terence wasn't away, Liz panicked. A drink, that might work. She dashed into the kitchen and opened one cupboard after another but couldn't find anything alcoholic. The fridge. Frantically she wrenched at the door. To her relief she found three bottles of white wine chilling on a shelf. Where was the corkscrew? She pulled out all the drawers. The kitchen began to look like a bombsite. The cork split and Liz pushed the remainder of it into the bottle with the handle of a teaspoon. She grabbed two cups from the shelf nearest to her.

"Drink this," Liz ordered as she wrapped Holly's paralysed hands round the cup. "Don't try and talk."

Liz took a big gulp of wine. At least that dreadful shaking had stopped, she'd never seen anything so frightening.

"Take your time, when you're ready you can tell me what's happened."

Holly sat as if she was in a trance. "It's all over, Liz," she mumbled.

"What's all over?"

"It's all over," Holly repeated and began to shake again.

"Drink the wine," Liz prompted. She didn't know what else to say.

"Tell me what's over? Have you lost your job? Has Simone fired you?"

"No."

"Talk to me, Holly. Maybe I can help."

What could Simone have said?

The phone rang again. If it was Simone, she'd ask her point blank.

"Hi sweetheart," Robert said.

Liz kept the conversation as brief as possible although she doubted if Holly would even be aware that Robert had rung.

"Holly's upset?" Robert guessed.

"Yes," Liz replied, her hand cupped round the phone in order to muffle the sound of her voice.

"She won't be pleased to hear the latest news – I don't know if you will either. Our plans have been changed, we're leaving in two weeks – a fortnight today. But there's good news too, the man I'm replacing has agreed to rent the cottage for two years and a pay a huge amount of rent."

"Not three years?" Liz asked stupidly, her mind in turmoil.

"Not at the moment. His tenure at the college is for two years, although there's talk that he might stay on at Oxford. Take a further degree. We can worry about that nearer the time."

"That sounds all right," Liz replied guardedly.

"I can tell you're having a difficult time there. I'll talk to you tomorrow, OK?"

"Bye, darling."

As Liz suspected, Holly was oblivious to the call. Liz touched her sister's hands, they were like ice. She went into the bedroom, pulled the duvet off Holly's bed and wrapped it around her.

"Holly, please, let me help you, you *must* tell me what's wrong. Nothing can be that bad."

"It is . . . but it's over now . . . you're going to be so . . . so ashamed of me."

"Never," Liz said staunchly. "I don't understand. Tell me what you mean."

"The book, they know about the book."

"What book?"

Holly looked at her sister and began to sob.

"*Tomorrow's Joy,* they know about it. Simone knows about it."

The sobbing was as bad as the shaking.

"Knows what?" Liz probed patiently.

"Knows I stole it."

"How do you mean, stole it? You edited it, you didn't steal it. It's Emily Howard's book, everyone knows that."

"There *is* no Emily Howard, you don't understand, I stole the book."

Liz's heart pumped so hard it constricted her breathing. No Emily Howard? Holly didn't know what she was saying. But if Emily Howard didn't write the book . . . "Holly, tell me again, why do you say you stole the book?"

Holly looked at her pityingly. "Because I did."

"I'm going to make us a cup of tea, do you have any whisky or brandy?"

Holly nodded. "Somewhere," she said unhelpfully.

"In the kitchen?"

"No, I think it's . . . in the cupboard in the bathroom."

"When I've made the tea we'll start again. I'm probably being dense, but I'm lost."

The tea made Holly hiccup but at last she'd stopped crying and shivering. Her cheeks burned brightly against her chalky white face.

"Now, begin again," Liz coaxed.

"I can't. I can't."

"Begin at the beginning," Liz insisted.

"I stole the manuscript. It was there. There was

no title, no name on it, nothing to say where it had come from. It was handwritten and must have been pushed into the storeroom and forgotten."

"You found it?"

"Yes . . . no . . . sort of. I found it in a box of manuscripts that Simone gave me. It was wonderful, Liz, too good to be thrown out, but that's what Simone said to do with it when I told her about it. I couldn't bear to."

"Oh my Lord," Liz groaned as Holly's explanation began to make sense.

"Go on, Holly."

"I read it twice and for something to do, I began to edit it. Change it. All the names, the incidents, the . . . everything. All I could think of was that this wonderful story, with no title, no author to claim it, was going to be black-bagged or shredded." Tears coursed down her cheeks.

Liz held her hand and sat silently. She had always talked about the book as if it was a living, breathing thing. So many things fitted into place now, Holly's nervousness, her defensiveness about *Tomorrow's Joy,* the row they'd had. It was too awful to grasp. Holly, her own sister, steal a book? It couldn't be true.

"Does Terence know about this?"

"No," Holly's voice was almost a shout. "Don't tell him, Liz, please don't tell him," she begged.

"I won't, I won't," Liz said quickly.

"Or Robert?"

"Not if you don't want me to," Liz promised. It was all too much to take in.

"How did Simone find out about this, is that why you have to see her on Monday?"

"Yes. A girl came to see her today, said it was her mother's book. She threatened to go to her solicitor, expose Pagett."

Liz gasped. This was getting worse by the minute. She mustn't let Holly see how afraid she was for her.

"But Simone doesn't know that you . . . took the book, does she?"

Haltingly, Holly began to tell her what Simone had said.

Liz listened with growing horror. If the girl brought Simone the exercise books, the truth would be obvious.

"What are you going to do?" Liz asked helplessly.

"Do? I don't know what to do. Admit it, give back the money, it's not mine."

"Could you do that without anyone else knowing?"

"Simone knows."

"Could you talk to her? Explain? I'm sure she won't want to see Pagett involved in a scandal."

"Talk to Simone? She hates my guts, you know she does. She'd be delighted to get rid of me."

"Won't you even try?"

"I suppose I could, but it won't do any good."

"Promise me, Holly, talk to her, you may be surprised."

Holly nodded her agreement, it was easier than arguing. She was tired and cold, her head ached and she couldn't think.

"I think you should try and get some rest," Liz said. "Get into bed, I'll bring the duvet."

Liz switched on Holly's electric blanket and tucked the duvet around her sister. "You'll see things more clearly in the morning. Perhaps it won't be as bad as you think."

Holly closed her eyes. She knew that Liz was trying to help but there was only one way out of this. She'd already made up her mind what she must do.

Liz climbed miserably into bed. Holly's disclosure had stunned her. What could she have been thinking of, how could Holly have done anything so dreadful? Liz turned over and tried to find a comfortable position, she was taut with nerves. What would happen to Holly? She'd be disgraced, never get another job in publishing. Liz shifted again, she couldn't bear to think about the worst scenario. Now that their trip had been brought forward she wouldn't be around to give Holly the support that she'd need. At least she'd have Terence. Liz hoped that Holly would tell him. And how was she going to act naturally? Robert was always so quick to sense her moods. But she'd given Holly her word and she wouldn't go back on it.

Holly woke to the awful realisation that faced her. She had lain awake most of the night and her head was beginning to jingle with pain. She couldn't go shopping with Liz today, couldn't face that crowded store.

"How are you feeling?" Liz asked sympathetically.

"Pretty dreadful, I've got a headache."

"Is there anything I can get for you, anything I can do?"

"There is something. Please Liz, would you go shopping without me?"

"No way. I'm not leaving you here on your own."

"I'll be perfectly all right, I didn't sleep very well last night. If you weren't here I could go back to bed and sleep this off."

"You can do that anyway," Liz insisted.

"*Please*, I won't want to sleep if you're here. Take my car, spend the day at Harkers then, by the time you come home, I'm sure I'll feel better. I'll wash my hair, be ready to go to the theatre."

"I don't feel like going either – maybe you'll change your mind, we could go this afternoon."

"No, Liz," Holly said wearily.

Liz sat and worried. How was this nightmare going to end? When would it be solved? They'd be leaving in two weeks' time and she still hadn't told Holly. She could just blurt it out. Or wait a few days, perhaps? She knew what Robert would advise. Robert, who didn't have a mean bone in his body, always believed that getting things out in the open hurt less in the end.

She took a deep breath. "Holly, I can't bear to add to your worries, but when Robert phoned last night he said that we have to leave sooner than expected – in two weeks to be exact."

Holly's expression didn't change. Liz wondered if she'd even heard her.

Holly struggled to keep a grip on reality. Her head hammered. Liz would have so much to do before she left, maybe she could go to the cottage the following weekend and help her, that is if she wasn't in jail.

"In that case you *must* do your shopping today," Holly insisted quietly after a few minutes. "You haven't much time left."

"I know I don't, you're right I suppose," said Liz ruefully.

It was almost a relief now that Liz had gone. It had taken Holly nearly an hour to persuade her sister that she'd be perfectly all right on her own. She was drained, unable to think, to function. The bottle of brandy was still on the table from the night before. Would that solve anything? she wondered. Her head throbbed. Aspirin would be better.

She found the tablets amongst the debris in the kitchen and swallowed two. She should get dressed, but instead, she returned to the living-room and flopped into her chair.

A clatter of footsteps on the stairs woke her.

Terence? As she listened, she imagined his reaction; disbelief, shock and finally, disgust. The footsteps receded.

I've got to get out of here before I go crazy, she told herself.

Although it was almost two o'clock, she couldn't face lunch. She showered and dressed, then made up her face. She threw on a light jacket and left the flat.

Chapter Fifty-One

Jenny James was waiting outside Pagett when
Simone arrived.

"I got here early," she said as she picked up the
two bundles which lay by her feet. Simone switched
off the alarms and stood aside while Jenny
manoeuvred herself and the exercise books into the
lift. The small space filled with the delicate
fragrance of Simone's perfume. How lovely she is,
Jenny thought enviously, so together.

Simone smiled at the girl with the frank, green
eyes, her hair today a cascade of shining chestnut
silk. For a moment Simone wished that *she* was
young again, could begin again, avoid her mistakes.
If only there was such a thing as a second chance.

Simone shrugged off the thought and led the
way to her office. She took off her jacket and threw
it on a chair while Jenny put the books on the desk
and freed her cramped fingers from the string
handles.

"They're all in the correct order," she said.

She slipped the string from one of the piles and
showed Simone that the books were numbered.

"That's fine, don't worry, I'll find my way round them."

"Do you want me to stay? I could help you, I'm free today."

"No Jenny, thank you. I need to be alone, do this my own way."

"What'll you do when you find out who's responsible? Will you put my mother's name on the cover? What happens to . . . "

Simone cut her short. "Jenny, you'll have to be patient, I can't give you any answers until I've read these. I explained all that yesterday."

"I know you did, but I want to know what happens when you find out that I'm telling the truth." Jenny's voice had risen.

"Jenny, Jenny! Calm down. The sooner you go, the sooner I can start reading these."

Jenny slouched towards the door with infuriating slowness. "When will I hear from you?"

"I don't know. Soon," Simone replied curtly, her patience at an end.

Simone puffed up her cheeks with relief as she heard the whine of the lift.

She must calm down herself, it would need a clear head to tackle this lot. At a glance, Simone guessed there must be at least forty exercise books in the bundles, nearer fifty perhaps. Under the circumstances it was foolish of Jenny to have left all the books, she shouldn't have done. If her accusation was true they were Jenny's only form of proof.

She unlocked the drawer of her desk and

brought out the battered copy of *Tomorrow's Joy*. She opened the book, then hesitated. If she did have to underline passages in the text it might be better not to use Jenny's copy.

Holly's office was ghostly quiet – attractive and neat like the editor herself. There were several copies of the book on the shelf beside that strange little headdress which Holly valued so highly. It was inconceivable that Holly could be foolish enough to steal a manuscript. She'd be the first to admit that Holly had given her plenty of grief but, of all the names she had called her, *thief* was not one them.

Simone began to read.

The opening lines of the book were different from Jenny's notebooks, completely different. Her eyes darted from the exercise book to the printed page, backwards and forwards, backwards and forwards her head moved as if she was watching a game of tennis.

It was beginning to look as though Jenny James was mistaken after all.

The last lines of the third paragraph were identical. She checked it again, word for word. Identical. She underlined the text in the book then made a note of the page and paragraph on a pad.

Her eyes scanned the pages. She no longer bothered to stop and take notes. There was no denying it, *Tomorrow's Joy* was a plagiarised version of the handwritten story. Holly's book was a more polished presentation but, without doubt, a substitute for the original.

Simone stared at the evidence. This was

incredible. Incredibly foolish, incredibly illegal. Worse than than – it was fraud.

Even with the indisputable proof in front of her, Simone found it impossible to come to terms with what she'd just read. Holly of all people! Those years of bitterness and subservience must have warped her mind. What other explanation could there be? What should she do now, should she speak to Holly first or report this immediately? She consulted her watch. It was almost twelve-thirty. A good strong cup of tea wouldn't go amiss and neither would a couple of Lois's biscuits.

By the time she'd finished her tea, Simone had decided what to do. She would compile a full list of the changes before she confronted Holly – start right away while the pages she'd read were still fresh in her mind. The rest she'd work on over the weekend.

Simone rolled her head in slow circles to relieve the tension in her neck then reached for the string and began to unpick the knots. Her fingers were sticky. She threw the string down in disgust, removed a pile of manuscripts from a box in the corner and tossed the books into it. Sophie would find another box. She went into the cloakroom room to wash her hands.

Implications of the fraud gripped her. If a scandal like this became public it could cause irreparable damage to Pagett's reputation. This must be kept quiet. She must contact John Barrett right . . .

A noise in the office startled her. The contract

cleaners must be early today, they didn't normally start work until four o'clock on Saturdays. It didn't matter, she was finished here anyway.

Simone hung the towel on the hook and went back into her office.

"What are *you* doing here? Where are you going with those books?" she demanded angrily.

In a split second she realised what was happening. She moved like lightning but, as she tried to snatch the box, it fell to the floor. Before she could bend down to pick it up, two hands grabbed her. Pushed her viciously. Her heel caught in the rug. She felt herself toppling backwards and put out her hand to save herself. There was nothing to hold on to. She heard the sickening crunch as her head hit the edge of the desk, felt the searing pain. Lights flashed behind her eyes. The room spun around her as she slumped to the floor.

Chapter Fifty-Two

"I thought I'd never get home," Liz said as she unloaded her shopping bags in a heap on the floor.

"You've done well," Holly observed.

"I did. Thank you again, Holly. I'll show you what I bought after I've had a cup of tea. How are you feeling now?"

"OK'ish. I went out for a while, at least my headache's gone."

"I'll go and put the kettle on," Liz said as she rooted amongst the bags. "This is for you, take a look, see if you like it."

The blouse was exactly what she'd have chosen for herself but it did nothing to lift her spirits.

They drank their tea in silence. Liz looked exhausted, obviously unused to the hustle and bustle of a London store.

The carpet was covered with bags, tissue paper, receipts and an assortment of gaily coloured clothes.

"What do you think of this?" Liz asked as she held a cotton mini skirt against her waist.

"Super," Holly said in a flat voice.

"Where've I put the top that goes with it?"

Holly shrugged. She wished Liz would stuff the whole lot back in their bags and put them away.

Liz did. She sensed Holly's lack of interest.

"What time do we have to be at the theatre?" Liz asked as she gathered up the bags.

What a pity we couldn't have gone to the play last night, she thought, but hid her feelings. She didn't want to disappoint Holly.

"It starts at eight," said Holly.

She would have given anything not to have to go to the theatre but she didn't want to disappoint Liz.

"I suppose Robert didn't ring did he?"

"No."

"He'll . . . that's probably him now," Liz said as the phone trilled.

"Hi, Robert," she answered without waiting for him to speak. "Oops! Sorry, John, no it's Liz, Holly's sister. I thought you were someone else. Hold on, I'll get her for you."

Holly's face was ashen. "Simone's told him about the book," she said. "Hello, John."

"I have some bad news for you . . . I'm shocked . . . I don't know how to say this . . . " John's voice faltered.

Holly braced herself. John knew.

"It's Simone . . . she's dead."

"Simone? Dead?" Holly repeated dully.

"Yes. Sean just phoned me, the police suspect . . . "

"The police? Did you say the police?" Holly asked.

Poor Holly, she was as stunned as he was. "The police think she was murdered."

"But Simone *can't* have been murdered, they've made a mistake, they must have," she objected.

"I wish they had."

"What happened, did someone break into her flat? Was she robbed?"

"I don't think so. It happened in the office this afternoon, Sean said. The cleaners found her. Apparently she must have forgotten to lock the front door and . . . someone got in. That's what the police think."

"Simone, murdered?"

"I'm afraid so. This has been a dreadful shock for you. For me too. I can't believe it. But I didn't want you to hear it from someone else – from the police or on the radio."

"I understand . . . at least I don't understand, but thank you."

"Eve and I are flying over tonight. I've told Sean to contact everyone else. I suppose the police will want to question everybody, Sean will probably have more details by the time I arrive."

Liz was at Holly's side, her face as pale as her sister's.

"I'll phone you when I get to London. Maybe we'll know more by then, will you be at home?"

"Yes, yes of course. I'll be here."

"Holly, pour yourself a drink. Your sister's with you, isn't she?"

"She's staying with me."

"Good. I'll phone you later. Take care."

"You too."

"What's happened? Simone murdered? What happened?" Liz asked.

"I . . . Simone's been murdered. She was alone in the office . . . the cleaners found her."

"My God! Are they sure? I mean is she really . . . dead?" Liz's voice faded.

"That's what I asked, but she is – was – murdered."

"Was she robbed?" Liz asked.

"I don't know, I don't think so, I can't remember what John said. I don't know."

They looked at each other helplessly.

"I'm sorry, Liz, we won't be able to go to the theatre. John is flying over and he'll be phoning later."

"Forget about the theatre." Liz lapsed into silence.

"She was in her office? Did someone just walk in and kill her?" she asked a moment or two later.

"I don't know. John thought she'd forgotten to lock the door. I suppose he meant the street door. We never lock our office doors, don't even have keys for them."

"Do they know who did it?"

"I don't know."

"How did John find out?"

"Sean told him, anyway what difference does it make who told him? There's no point in asking me all these questions, I've told you what John said," Holly snapped.

"I think we could both do with a drink," Liz said.

Holly could hear her pottering about in the kitchen but made no move to go and see what she was doing.

Simone, dead. She could imagine the headlines in the papers – *Editor murdered*. The police would want to ask questions. They'd probably all have to make statements. Suddenly, Holly began to tremble. What if they asked where she'd been at the time of the murder? She hadn't spoken to anybody, or seen anyone but Liz all day.

Holly put her hands to her head, it felt as though it was going to burst.

"I've made us an omelette, come and eat before it goes cold," Liz said as she put the plates on the table. "I bet you didn't have any . . . Holly! You're trembling. Here, have some wine or would you prefer brandy? There's plenty left in the bottle."

"Liz, what happens if the police ask me where I was today?"

"So what? Tell them."

"If they ask me where I went?"

"I don't understand. Where did you go?" Liz asked with a puzzled frown.

"To Norma Downs' house – she lives quite near here. I decided to deliver her manuscript myself instead of waiting for the couriers on Monday. She was out, so I came back home."

"Do you usually deliver her manuscripts yourself?"

"No, not now. But I owe a lot to Norma. I was worried about her book. What might happen when

I saw Simone on Monday, whether I'd be fired on the spot. Then what would happen to Norma?"

"She's the last of your worries. But the police won't suspect you, why should they?"

"They'll probably suspect everyone, want to know where everyone was. We'll have to answer questions . . . I thought after last night that things couldn't get any worse, how wrong I was. I'm really scared, Liz."

"Don't be . . . don't worry," Liz said absently.

"How can I *not* worry?" Holly wailed.

Liz didn't reply.

"Oh Liz, if only I'd gone with *you* instead."

"So, say you did. Go with me, I mean."

"How can I do that? The police aren't stupid, they could soon check."

"I suppose you're right."

"And when they find out about the book . . . "

Liz drained her glass. Holly's was barely touched.

"If you're that worried, say that *you* were at the store."

Holly frowned. "You mean that I was there instead of you?"

"Exactly. We're very alike, no one would know the difference."

"They would if they saw us together."

"Why should they? If they were asked, all the sales people would remember is that a woman who looked like us used a gift token. If that solves your problem – say it was you. But honestly, Holly, just because you weren't bosom-buddies with Simone, it's hardly a reason for murdering her, is it?"

"But what about *Tomorrow's Joy?*" Holly asked.

"As far as we know, no one knows about the book."

"John didn't, he would have said something."

"There you are then."

"I still can't believe that she's actually dead," Holly said.

"Nor can I."

Neither of them gave a thought to the omelettes, congealed on the plates.

* * *

Robert glanced anxiously at his watch. He had only ten minutes in which to phone Liz and have a shower. As he waited for the operator to put him through, he wondered how Liz would feel when he suggested that they go back to the cottage early tomorrow instead of Monday.

"Hello, sweetheart," he said cheerfully when he heard her voice. "How are things going?"

"Not good, we've just heard the most awful news – Simone Pearse is dead, murdered."

"What! That's dreadful . . . "

Liz told him the little she knew.

"Holly must be gutted, you must be. I . . . I just can't believe it. That's the sort of thing you read about or see on telly, never expect to hear about someone you know."

"We're shredded," Liz admitted.

"So what happens now? I suppose the police will want to question everyone she worked with?"

"I imagine so. John Barrett said he'd phone later when he has more information."

"I'll phone you after dinner."

"Leave it as late as you can. How did *your* day go?"

"Hectic. For my sake they've condensed two days' meetings into one. We're on a ten minute break now. One short talk before dinner, then we're finished for the night. I have a final briefing with one of the directors at eight-thirty tomorrow and hope to be with you by eleven. I was going to suggest that we left immediately but now you probably won't want to leave Holly."

"I don't know what to say. Could we decide tomorrow? After I find out . . . "

"Darling, I've got to rush. I'll see you at the flat, if you want to stay on, do. I'll head back to the cottage and start the clearing. You can follow by train when you're ready. How's that?"

"That might be the best idea," Liz said guardedly.

Robert's brain was reeling. There seemed to be no end to Holly's problems – not that this was her problem. But to be close to anything so horrific couldn't fail to have a terrible effect. Even Liz sounded shocked and upset and she hardly knew Simone. He wouldn't try and influence her tomorrow, Liz must make up her own mind.

* * *

By the time John phoned, Holly had spoken to almost everyone from Pagett. They were all stunned, anxious for more information. They needed to talk, to discuss the terrible murder, confess their sorrow, even their guilt that they'd spoken unkindly about Simone at times. Lois was in a dreadful state.

"I should never have called her the Predator, now I can't take it back, can't apologise," she sobbed.

"She never knew you called her that," Holly soothed. "Everyone feels terrible. We've all been bitchy at times, it's human nature."

Tim Brown's voice was terse, " . . . and why the hell was she there anyway? I spoke to Sophie, she couldn't think of any reason," he finished angrily.

Holly felt a wave of relief. Simone hadn't told him about the book, or Sophie either.

It was almost midnight before John Barrett got back to her.

"I promised to up-date you but there's not much more to add. I met Detective Inspector Moore – he's in charge of the case – and he'd like to see us all tomorrow morning. To take statements. I suggested that it might be easier if we were all together and he agreed. If you could be at Pagett by ten o'clock?"

"Of course. John, do they have *any* idea who killed her?" Holly asked.

"I asked him the same thing. He said it could have been anyone. He was keeping an open mind, wouldn't even conjecture. The only thing he did tell me was that it wasn't a break-in, the outer door hadn't been damaged."

"I see. Thank you for letting me know."

Liz waited anxiously for Holly to fill her in.

"John's spoken to the person in charge. We've all to go in to Pagett tomorrow morning and make statements. Either they don't know who killed her or, if they do, they're not saying."

"That's not very helpful."

Holly shrugged.

"What *am* I going to tell the police if they ask where I was?" she asked Liz.

"That you went shopping, that's what we said."

"But everyone knows you were staying with me, won't that sound a bit odd?"

"Well . . . you could say that I'd gone to visit someone. We're leaving earlier for the States and that I couldn't go without saying goodbye. Half of that's true although I still can't see why you won't tell the truth."

"I told you, I can't prove where I was." Tears sprang to Holly's eyes.

She's been through so much, Liz thought, what harm in telling a lie if it makes her feel more secure.

"Right, I'd better tell you exactly how I spent the day. It's not difficult, I got to Harkers just around twelve, parked in the car park . . . Now, repeat all that and we'll make sure you've got it right."

Holly went over her story twice.

"That's all there is to it," Liz said.

"You are wonderful, Liz," Holly said gratefully.

"Forget it. Holly, there's something else. Robert

wants to go home tomorrow – after his meeting in the morning. He said there'd be no problem if I wanted to stay on with you, he'd understand."

"I can't ask you to do that. I'll be all right. Once tomorrow's over, I'll be OK. Besides, Terence will be home on Monday."

"With all that's been going on I forgot about Terence. That makes me feel better. You won't be alone. Just one thing, Holly, I think it's better if I don't tell Robert about swapping places, he might not understand."

"I won't say a word. I won't tell Terence either. At least not now, maybe in the future . . . "

Liz jumped on her sister's words. "So there is a future for you two!"

Holly fired a cushion at her sister. Even though it wasn't that funny, they laughed hysterically.

Chapter Fifty-Three

The constable on duty outside the dead woman's office watched the staff as they passed the closed door. DI Moore had asked him to report any strange reactions.

Most of them averted their gaze as they passed, and scuttled by as fast as they could. Except for the dark-haired woman in the black trousers, she stopped, stared at the door for a while, then walked slowly on.

John introduced Holly to Detective Inspector Michael Moore and to Simone's ex-husband. It was the first time she'd ever met Mark. He was handsome, tall and slim with a shock of brown hair which gave him a slightly vulnerable air. His eyes were sad and faintly red-rimmed.

"Do you think I could use your office, Ms Grant?" Michael Moore asked.

"Yes, of course, I'll show you where it is."

Lois and Holly volunteered to make coffee.

"That's a good idea," John said appreciatively. "I have a feeling it's going to be a long day."

It was almost a quarter to one before Michael Moore sent for Holly.

She was a lovely-looking young woman – gorgeous blue eyes, good legs, he liked that mini skirt. Now if he were a few years younger . . . he sucked in his stomach and straightened his shoulders.

The detective was standing by her bookshelves, the lacquered headdress in his hand. She wanted to tell him to put it down, it was special.

"This is unusual," he said.

"A gift from a friend," Holly explained.

"Come and sit down, Ms Grant," he invited. "This is just an informal chat between ourselves. I'm sure you're as anxious to find Simone Pearse's killer as we are."

"Of course I am. Please, call me Holly."

"OK, Holly. Tell me something about your relationship with Simone Pearse."

Holly told how they'd worked together in the beginning, about Simone's kindness to her when she and Derek had split up and the subsequent coldness between them when she became an editor.

"Your husband didn't approve of her, did he?"

Holly was taken aback, how did he know that?

"He didn't approve of many people. He didn't trust people."

"He blamed her for your break-up, didn't he?"

"He thought that she'd encouraged me to leave him, yes."

"He threatened her on a couple of occasions?"

"Empty threats, Derek always shouted and roared. But that's in the past, now."

"So is Simone Pearse, unfortunately," said Michael Moore acerbically. "Your divorce is about to become absolute, isn't it?"

"Yes, in a few weeks," she replied.

"Do you think he was still harbouring a grudge against her, or yourself, come to that?"

"I don't know, I have no contact with him, haven't spoken to him for over a year. He was seeing someone else – although he denied it."

Michael Moore continued to fire a barrage of questions at her. He asked her about Simone's men friends, about her ex-husband, her working relationships, her popularity, how she got on with authors, their families, how she dealt with agents . . . Holly's head was spinning.

"Do you know of any author who might have had reason to . . . attack her?"

"No, no one. Except . . . perhaps . . . no."

"Except who, Holly?"

"This is silly. A friend of Simone's sent her a book which she turned down. The author was very disappointed. She tried to get her own back by placing cards with Simone's number on them into certain shops – the cards were adverts for Swedish Massage." Holly coloured and Michael Moore's lips twitched.

"What's the author's name?"

"Maggie Tweed."

"Do you know where she lives?" he asked as he made a note of the name.

"No. I'm sure that Simone could tell you . . . Oh! I'm sure it would be on her file."

"Anyone else? Think carefully."

"Not that I know of, but Sophie might be able to help you. She's Simone's assistant now. *Was* Simone's assistant."

"Don't worry, Holly, everyone forgets at first."

"We weren't close friends," Holly volunteered. "We had our set-to's from time to time, but it's difficult to believe that she's gone. I can't imagine Pagett without Simone."

"Tell me about Ian Trent."

"There's nothing to tell. She went out with him for a bit and then it was over," Holly said, then hesitated. "I don't like to repeat gossip, but there was a rumour circulating that he was using her in order to get a book published. He passed it off as his sister's book but actually it was his girlfriend's."

"And Roland Green? He and Simone didn't get on well, did they?"

"No. He didn't like her, didn't like any of us very much. He sneered at the books she edited, called them *Kleenex Fiction*. He and Simone fought all the time."

"Enough to kill her?"

"Oh, I don't think Roland would do that."

"Why do you say that?"

"I don't know. I just don't think he would. I don't know anyone who would."

"And that includes your husband?"

"Derek! Derek was a rotten husband, a control-freak, not a murderer."

"How do you know?"

"I can't imagine it, that's all. He's a bully, but also a coward."

"So there's no one you can think of who'd want to kill Simone?"

"No, of course not."

"All right, Holly, relax, we're just about finished now. Just before you go, purely as a matter of routine – where were you yesterday afternoon?"

Holly recited the well-rehearsed account of how she'd spent her day.

Sophie, dressed from head to toe in black, had been the coolest of them. Holly thought she looked slightly shaken when she came back from Simone's office.

"They needed me to tell them whether anything had been stolen or not," she explained.

"And was anything missing?" Tim Brown asked.

"Not as far as I could tell. Apart from . . . a bloodstain and a spilt vase, everything seemed to be as it should."

The flat was silent and empty when she finally returned home. It had been a gruelling day and the endless questions had caused tempers to flare. Making their statements had been a lengthy process.

After a steaming hot bath, Holly was still tense. Liz would be waiting for her call.

" . . . and then I had to give a written statement," Holly told her.

"You remembered everything I said?" Liz checked in a low voice.

"Yes. I got to the store about twelve, spent the day there. I even wrote down everything that you'd bought – *I'd* bought."

"Sounds right."

"That bit was no problem, but I was astonished how much the detective knew about Simone and about me. By the time I left Pagett I felt that *nothing* was private any more."

The television didn't help, her thoughts kept straying back to Simone. What would happen to her authors, all the books that were on hand? John would probably keep Sophie on for the moment. Now Holly came to think of it, she'd been comparatively friendly today, for her. Normally it was a nod or a brief hello. She'd jumped up and offered Holly her chair. Taken her cup from her when it was empty and washed it. Sophie was obviously worried about her job.

Tomorrow would take care of who did what. All she wanted to do was to forget the horrible events of the past few days, go to bed and sleep.

Chapter Fifty-Four

Flashbulbs blurred her vision and reporters crowded round her as she tried to get to the door. She could feel herself begining to panic. A hand took her arm and led her firmly towards the door.

"It's all right, Holly, just keep going," John said calmly.

Cameras whirred and flashed, reporters shouted their questions.

"Sorry, we have nothing to say," John told them as a policeman opened the door and ushered them safely inside.

Holly blinked to rid herself of the circles of light which had temporarily blinded her.

"I thought there'd probably be a few reporters hanging around but I wasn't prepared for this," John admitted as he rubbed his eyes.

"I suppose it's in the papers today?"

"You can say that again. Obviously you haven't read them, or listened to the newscasts. Poor Simone, she made the headlines with a capital H. Lead item in most of them," he said ruefully. "The papers and the telly have managed to get hold of some really lovely pictures of her. Full page in most of the tabloids. It's sickening. All it takes is a photo of a beautiful blonde found dead in her office, add the word *murder,* and that'll sell more papers than the biggest government scandal or political crisis. I have a feeling we're in for quite a day again."

Lois, pale-faced but alert, was at her desk.

"I'm so glad you're here early, Mr Barrett, the phone has been ringing non-stop. I keep saying *no comment* like they do in the films. Is that right?"

"Perfectly. Don't answer any questions, talk to any reporters, anybody that you don't know. They get up to all sorts of tricks. And Lois, don't call me Mr Barrett, John will do fine."

"Right, John," she said shyly.

Lois smiled at Holly. "You OK?" she asked.

"Like all of us, I suppose," Holly replied.

"Holly and I will be in the boardroom," John said. "Send everyone in as soon as they arrive."

"Before you go, one of Simone's authors phoned. She insisted she must know what's going to happen to her book. Just before she rang off she said she was *sorry to hear the news.*" Her voice was filled with disgust.

"Some people are all heart," John said angrily. "It will be a few days before we can even begin to sort things out. If anyone is stroppy with you, remind them that we've lost a colleague and a friend. We're human even if they're not."

"You bet I will," Lois said fiercely as tears filled her eyes.

"Don't cry, we need you to be strong. We're relying on you," John said.

Lois gave him a watery smile. "I won't let you down," she promised.

Holly squeezed Lois's hand and followed John to the boardroom.

"Is she going to manage, d'you think?" John asked as he closed the door.

"Yes, she's suffering guilt pangs. We all are, I suppose – things we said and can't take back now. Simone was very good to me when I broke up with Derek and . . . well, the rest is history."

"I know. I was tough on her too at times. It's strange, I was thinking last night of all the murders I've committed – in the literary sense – they never cost me a bother, just words on a computer screen. And now it's for real. I can't even bear to pass her office let alone go into it." John shuddered.

"I'm glad I'm not the only one," Holly said.

Sophie was the first to arrive.

"We were just saying that we couldn't bear to go into Simone's office," John said.

"Don't worry, I don't mind going in there, I'll get whatever you need."

John gave her a sharp look. "We need everything, but I don't suppose we'll be allowed to touch anything yet. Perhaps you could find out for me?"

"She's a hard case, isn't she?" John said when Sophie had left the room.

"She's probably worried about whether she has a job or not."

"That's true. Now that we're on the subject, what do you think, Holly? Should we keep her, can you work with her?"

"I don't know her very well. I know Simone found her competent and we certainly need someone. I'm about to lose my own reader – my sister Liz – she's emigrating to the States next week."

"Then by all means, keep Sophie on. You're going to need all the help you can get. I wasn't going to bring it up, but now that Simone isn't . . . has gone, the job of editor-in-chief is yours, if you want it."

"Editor-in-chief, that sounds very grand. I'd be happy to take it on if you want me to," Holly said.

"I'm sure you'll do an excellent job. You may find that you need a junior editor, you'll be the best judge of that. You'll definitely need an assistant, two perhaps."

John glanced at the boardroom clock, it was almost nine o'clock.

"The others will be here in a minute. I'm probably going ga-ga in my old age, but there's something about Sophie . . . I watched her yesterday, she's over-eager, ingratiating . . . " John stopped abruptly as Sophie came back into the room carrying a large box.

"I got this lot out of the office. The copper on duty said it was OK to take them, the forensic crowd have finished doing whatever it was that they had to do with them." Sophie dropped the overflowing box on the table. "I'm sure there was another box kicking around the office – maybe the police took it. Simone's schedule is here, but the detectives took her desk diary. All the unopened manuscripts are here too. Where do you want me to put this stuff?"

"Would you take them to my office?" Holly asked.

"Sure. Anything else I can do?" Sophie frowned.

"Two strong, hot cups of coffee would warm the cockles of our feet," John said with a charming smile.

"We're awful, we should tell her she's still got a job," Holly said.

"We will, but not until that coffee appears."

By ten o'clock, Pagett was in chaos. The boardroom became the focal point for the staff, their offices deserted. Lois and Jane coped with the switchboard, while Sean, John and Tim handled the calls from authors and agents. Holly and Sophie agreed that it would be impossible to attempt to make even a rough schedule until Simone's diary was returned to them.

Arthur Lord's arrival was a comfort – he'd ignored his wife's pleas to remain at home, not get involved. He had known Simone longer than any of them.

Tea and coffee cups littered the table top. They took it in turns to make fresh pots. Marianna went to the local supermarket and replenished their stock of coffee, milk and biscuits, adding a stack of paper cups to her basket.

Detective Inspector Moore arrived after lunch and took John to one side.

"I've had the coroner's report, it's definitely murder," he confided.

John looked at him in surprise. "Was there any doubt?" he asked.

"There was an outside chance that she might just have fallen although I was certain she *hadn't*. The coroner's report proves I was right. Whoever attacked her gave her one hell of a push. Apart from a broken neck, head injuries and a cerebral haemorrhage, there was severe bruising on her chest."

John's stomach lurched, this was Simone he was talking about; the jean-clad editor who'd walked by his side in Howth, had raved about the fresh, sea air. Who'd teased his daughter and sided with his wife, fallen asleep by his fireside. This was how he wanted to remember Simone.

"Something bothering you?" Michael Moore asked.

"No, just memories, that's all."

"They have a habit of popping up without bidding, don't they?" he sympathised. "I'd like to talk to Simone's assistant again, just a couple of questions, I won't keep her long."

"I'll take over at the switchboard. Shall I send her to Holly's office?"

"Yes, if Holly doesn't mind. Simone and her assistant got on well, did they?"

"As far as I know, extremely well. Anything else before I go?"

"Not for the moment."

"By the way, when do you think we can have Simone's diary back?"

"Probably later this week," Michael said.

"It's just that we need to know what appointments have been set up."

"I'll do my best."

Terence met her at the top of the stairs. "I heard the news on the radio, I'm stunned," he said as he folded her in his arms.

For the first time since the tragedy had occurred Holly felt protected, shielded from the world.

Chapter Fifty-Five

Roland Green looked round him with a sigh. This was the only way to live.

He settled himself at the table and rang for the maid. He approved of the dainty china and the pretty flowered cloth, approved of this breakfast room with its perfect view of the gardens and rolling acres beyond, admired the wonderful old house but, most of all, he approved of Lady Patricia and her reputed millions. How considerate of Sir James to have expired with minimum fuss and to leave his pretty young widow to carry on his life's work – the pursuit of pleasure.

"Good morning, Sir." The grey-uniformed maid placed a glass of orange-juice in front of him.

"Good morning, delightful morning," he replied pompously.

"Your eggs will be ready in just a moment," she said as she placed a stack of neatly folded newspapers by his left hand.

Who reads all these? he wondered as he searched through the pile for *The Times*.

The glass dropped from his hand with a crash. Shards of glass and orange juice flew everywhere. A full page photograph of Simone stared back at him from one of the tabloids.

"Oh shit! Simone – murdered! Can't be." He reached for his glasses – to hell with his image. He read every word, his heart thumping wildly. Serve the bitch right if she got her comeuppance but she didn't deserve to die, to be murdered. He must phone the magazine and see if they'd heard anything.

"The police were asking for you, Rolo," his colleague said.

"I've told you before, my name is *Roland.*"

"Cheers, Rolo, I'll remember that." He enjoyed winding him up, supercilious pratt.

Roland dashed up the ancestral staircase and knocked on Lady Patricia's door.

"Come in," she answered in a frail voice.

"Patricia, look at this." He pushed the paper under her nose.

"Don't shout, Roland, I'm fragile today. What's all the excitement about, read it to me."

She tutted and oohed in all the right places but, to her, Simone was just an unfortunate victim of murder.

"I've got to get back to London, the police have phoned. I expect because we worked together . . . " A discrete tap at the door stopped him.

"It's like a railway station in here today," Lady Patricia complained. "Come in."

"It's the police, they want to talk to Mr Green."

Roland grimaced. "They didn't waste much time. Tell them I'll be down in a minute."

"Don't tell me my house guest is suspected of murder?"

"Don't be ridiculous," Roland replied huffily.

"Well, don't worry, sweetie, I'll give you an alibi even if you did do it."

Sergeant Bill Merton took an instant dislike to the man. He was almost sorry that he had an unshakable alibi. Roland Green hadn't left the house and grounds for two days. Aside from Lady Patricia, her staff and her gardeners, a whole slew of photographers and a presenter from his magazine could testify to that. He would've enjoyed putting this patronising twit away for twenty or thirty years. No wonder Simone Pearse had fought with him.

* * *

How the hell had they found him so quickly? Ian Trent wondered. Even on honeymoon a man wasn't safe from the law. It was a good job he'd been on his way downstairs when the copper arrived at the hotel. Brigette would have killed *him* if she found out that he'd been sleeping with Simone. She'd go berserk, divorce him on the spot. At least there was no doubt where *he'd* been at the time of the murder – marriage registrars don't lie.

It was hard to think of Simone lying on the floor of her office with her head bashed in. Whatever else about her, Simone was beautiful, had been mad about him. If it wasn't for Brigette . . .

The waiter arrived with his coffee. He couldn't face breakfast, neither could he order a drink at this hour of the morning but he could do with one. He put the paper aside.

As he sipped the hot coffee he could picture the room at the Orangerie; the magnificent buffet, the champagne in the cooler. He could see the rose in its ridiculous cardboard coffin, Brigette's manuscript tied with black ribbon.

In an instant he'd realised what Simone had done and could have throttled her. He'd paced the room for almost an hour, shrivelled at the cost of the sumptuous meal then, suddenly, appreciated the humour of it. He'd been drunk as a skunk when he finally fell into bed, laughing hysterically and plotting revenge.

Ian poured another cup of coffee.

When he'd woken the following morning he phoned Brigette and asked her to join him at the Orangerie – he'd paid for the room and might as well get value for his money.

"You can rely on our discretion," the snooty receptionist had assured him.

By the time Brigette arrived he'd made two decisions; she must forget about the book and, as far as Simone was concerned, he'd do nothing. Absolutely nothing. That would frustrate her more than anything. He could imagine her sitting by her phone waiting for his call.

"I've been looking for you." Brigette sat down beside him. "Why aren't you having breakfast?"

Ian handed her the paper. "Remember the editor I told you about? Simone Pearse? While we were getting married on Saturday, she was being murdered."

. . .

Derek Grant stared disbelievingly at the photograph. He read the headline. Simone Pearse, dead? How often he'd wished she was. But still – murdered. There was a big difference between wishing someone ill and it actually happening.

He wiped his mouth on the linen napkin, then took a sip of tea. The police hadn't arrested anyone, they were following several leads.

The toast fell unnoticed from his mouth. What if they thought that he'd killed her? He'd threatened to get his own back on her often enough. What if Holly told the police that? And there was the day he'd kicked up such a fuss at Pagett, they wouldn't forget that in a hurry.

The doorbell startled him.

"Derek Grant?"

"Yes."

"I'm Detective Inspector Michael Moore and this is Police Constable Betty Holmes, we'd like to ask you some questions. May we come in?"

"Is this about Simone Pearse?" Derek asked.

"We'd like to ask you some questions," Michael Moore repeated.

"If it's about the murder, I didn't do it," Derek blurted out.

"No one's accusing you of anything, Mr Grant."

"Just because I didn't like her it doesn't mean that I killed her," Derek protested as he backed into the little hallway.

"Calm down or we really *will* be suspicious," Michael advised as he eased his way past Derek and strolled into the living-room. "Can you tell me where you were on Saturday, Mr Grant – between one o'clock and three?"

"I was out walking."

"Alone?"

"No, with a friend."

"What's your friend's name?"

"I . . . er, I . . . was with a lady . . . "

"And the lady is married?" Michael Moore finished for him.

"Yes."

"Can you tell me her name?"

"Do I have to? Can't you just take my word for it? I can tell you where we went, everything we did."

"Can anyone else corroborate your story?"

"No, I don't think so."

"Then in that case I'm afraid I'll have to insist that we talk to her."

"Her name is Bunny Bly . . . she's my boss's wife." Derek's face was brick red with embarrassment.

"And where can we find this lady?"

"Do you have to go to her house? Couldn't she go to the police station instead?" Derek asked.

"Maybe she would come here," Michael suggested helpfully.

"And her husband needn't know?"

"That depends, we'll see."

"I'll phone her now."

Derek's hands were sweating so much he could hardly hold the receiver.

"Bunny? It's Derek. Can you come round right away?"

"Derek, why are you ringing me?" Bunny said furiously. "I told you on Saturday, it's over. Finished."

"You don't understand, the police are here, they want to talk to you, want to know where I was on Saturday."

"Come off it, that's the most pathetic try-on I've ever heard. I don't want to see you or hear from you again." She slammed down her receiver.

Derek glanced at Michael Moore. "I think we got cut off," he said and dialled again. "Have you seen the paper? Holly's colleague, Simone Pearse, has been murdered."

"The woman you don't like?"

"Yes, her. That's why the police are here," he hissed.

"I'm sorry, Derek, the answer is still no. If I get involved Alan is sure to find out. We're going away next week, a start-over-again holiday. Say goodbye now, you know how you hate being late for work."

"Bunny, either you're here in fifteen minutes or I'll give the police your home address," Derek said menacingly.

"Oh sure! And lose your precious job? Who are you kidding?"

"I don't care about my job. I can find another job. Can you find another husband?"

Michael Moore took the phone from Derek. Grant was a nasty piece of work.

"Mrs Bly, this is Detective Inspector Moore. We're trying to facilitate you by interviewing you here, but if you prefer . . . "

"I'll be there as soon as I can," she interrupted in a shaky voice and the phone went dead in his hand.

"I understand that you've threatened to get even with Simone Pearse on several occasions."

"She was an interfering . . . she . . . encouraged my wife to leave me."

"Just how did you propose to punish her?"

"I . . . by playing tricks on her. I suppose I was angry at the time. I . . . I might as well tell you. I let the air out of her tyres one day, sent pizzas round to her flat – my wife was staying there – I ordered taxis and . . . sent her a joke letter telling her that her partner had AIDS."

"That's sick! Disgusting."

"I told you, I was angry," Derek insisted. "But I didn't kill her."

"Unless they're brilliant actors, I think they're telling the truth," Betty Holmes ventured.

"I agree with you. Their stories were similar but not *too* alike in detail. That's always suspicious. I doubt that our Bunnikins would cross the street for Derek Grant, never mind lie for him. She wants to be rid of him in the worst possible way. But there's no harm checking that café in case someone *did* remember them. Like they said, it was a quiet time and they were arguing. People notice things like that."

. . .

Jenny James passed her stop. She read every word of the article avidly. Sadness enveloped her, not just for the dead woman whom she barely knew but for herself, her brothers and sisters. Who could she talk to now? Simone Pearse hadn't said so but Jenny was sure that she'd believed her. The exercise books would have proved it. She must go back to Pagett, talk to whoever was in charge.

Jenny walked quickly, she didn't want to be late for work. She could think of nothing else except Simone Pearse, that gorgeous face and slim figure. If she could've chosen to look like anyone, it would have been Simone Pearse.

She turned the corner and kept up her pace. Was it possible that she was the last person to see the editor alive? There'd been no one else in the building while she was there. She began to feel frightened. What if they thought she'd had something to do with this? She had only gone there to claim what was hers. She mustn't be a coward, there was the rest of the family to think about. She'd wait a few days, then go back to Pagett, and demand to talk to Simone Pearse's replacement.

Chapter Fifty-Six

"Send it back with a rejection slip," Holly said.

"But I thought it was a good story," Sophie objected.

"It is, but I'm not prepared to edit anyone who resents being edited. The covering letter made it very clear that he didn't want even a comma changed. I don't like all the convoluted phrases he uses, the descriptive passages slow the story down. Could you imagine how he'd react if I put my pen through that lot?"

"*Treading on their angels,* Simone used to call it. I still think it might be worth . . . "

"Rejection slip, Sophie, we don't have time to debate it. How about this one? Your report is very enthusiastic."

"I loved it. The plot is excellent."

Holly decided to read the manuscript again. She wasn't sure of Sophie's ability yet.

"That's it. Fiona Carling will be here in a few minutes," Sophie reminded her.

"What's she like?" Holly asked.

"She's quirky. Really funny. She looks like a

whippet. Simone said she never eats. She told Simone that her idea of pigging out was to put *two* olives in her martini. Her MS was an utter mess, all over the place, but wonderful. Her characters are really zany. Just like her. Simone thought the book was super."

Holly was getting a bit sick of hearing what Simone did, what Simone thought. Sophie was working for her now and she was sorely tempted to tell her so.

"Detective Inspector Moore is here," Lois announced.

"Again?" Holly said irritably.

"I won't keep you long," Michael Moore said as he strode into her office. "Just a couple of points . . ."

Holly tried hard to hide her annoyance, Michael Moore's few questions had taken an hour. He'd asked her practically the same questions last week and the week before.

"I don't want to sound rude but I have an author waiting for me, she's been waiting almost an hour."

"Why didn't you say so?" Michael said with a disarming smile.

Lois popped her head round Holly's door. "Are you coming for a sandwich?" she asked.

"I can't, I'm way behind. Maybe you'd pick one up for me on your way back?"

"I will, but this is crazy – you never leave your office. You *should* have a break, the place won't fall down while you're gone."

"And the work will do itself, will it?" Holly snapped.

"Sorree! Just trying to help," Lois said lightly but looked hurt.

"No, *I'm sorry,* I didn't mean to snarl at you. That man is driving me spare. Every time I turn round he's here. All those questions. How many times do I have to tell him the same thing? Tell you what, we'll take an extended lunch the day after tomorrow, how does that grab you?"

"I'll hold you to that."

Holly could hear someone in the reception area calling "hello". A young girl with beautiful chestnut hair was standing uncertainly by Lois's desk.

"Hello, can I help you?" Holly asked.

"I'd like to speak to the editor," the girl replied.

"I'm the editor, Holly Grant."

"My name is Jenny James, I was here before – with Simone Pearse," she said nervously. "It's about my mother's book."

The blood drained from Holly's face and she could feel the pulse pounding in her neck.

"Which book is that?" she asked in a voice that didn't sound like hers.

"Tomorrow's Joy."

"You'd better come into my office," Holly said. "Please sit down."

Jenny sat on the edge of the chair, her hands clasped tightly together.

"Did Simone Pearse tell you about me? I was with her the morning she died, I mean I was here that morning . . . she wasn't dead or anything, I brought her the proof she asked for . . . the exercise books that my mother used before I copied it on to proper paper and sent it to Pagett who stole it," she finished breathlessly.

"Slow down. You say that you brought books here and gave them to Simone?"

"Yes, proof that the book – *Tomorrow's Joy* – had been stolen from Mum."

"Exercise books? There are no exercise books here."

"I brought them here, the day she died," she repeated stubbornly.

"Was there anyone else here?" Holly asked.

"No, just the two of us."

"I'm sorry, Jenny, I'm afraid I know nothing about them and everything in Simone's office was passed on to me. No exercise books."

The girl glared at her angrily. "I think I should tell the police about this," she said.

"I do too. I think that the police would be *most* interested to talk to you, to know that you were here with Simone. Alone with Simone. What time did you leave the building?"

Jenny's eyes flashed with alarm. "I didn't kill her if that's what you're thinking. Please, don't phone the police, the social services will take the kids away from me, take them into care."

"How many children do you have?" Holly asked. She didn't look much more than a kid herself.

"They're not *my* children, they're my brothers

and sisters. I look after them – have done since my mother died."

"I wish I could help you but if the books turn up . . . "

Holly collapsed on to her chair. She'd handled the interview badly, asked all the wrong questions, hadn't been sufficiently affronted that Pagett was being accused of theft. She *should* have called the police. Would Jenny stay away or would she find a sympathiser, someone who wouldn't be afraid to take up her cause?

It was the frightened look in Jenny's eyes that had given Holly the courage to challenge the girl. Jenny had folded like a house of cards when she'd mentioned the police.

There were so many other things she should have asked, would like to have known about Jenny and her life, her mother, those crazy relations. Were they real people? How much of the book was fiction, how much was fact?

If only there was a way she could send the royalties to Jenny, ease her own guilt. But she couldn't afford to take the chance – a large sum of money like that would be an admission of fraud. What would happen to Pagett? How would John stay in business without an editor?

Holly felt the prickle of tears behind her eyes. She'd cried so much last week when she said goodbye to Liz and Robert that she didn't think it would be possible to cry ever again. Even Liz's nightly phone calls from the States hadn't helped. She'd been permanently soggy for days.

Terence had done everything in his power to cheer her up. She appreciated his efforts and loved him for it but it was the sheer volume of work that had finally allowed her to push her misery aside.

She wasn't the only one with a long face at Pagett. When the funeral was over tomorrow, perhaps they'd all feel better.

* * *

Michael Moore stood at a discrete distance from the grave, partly concealed by a tree. He recognised quite a few of the mourners and the only one who seemed genuinely upset was her ex-husband Mark. He'd never been a suspect, had no motive. Pagett's receptionist was crying a lot but she was the emotional type anyway. The other members of staff were showing varying degrees of emotion; sadness, discomfort perhaps, but not grief. That may of course have had something to do with the media presence. They were here in force. Robbed the ceremony of its dignity. He presumed the rest of the crowd were authors, agents, booksellers and whoever else made the book-world tick. His investigation into Simone's background had been thorough. Apart from a couple of cousins, she had no other relatives. Very few friends.

He turned his back as they passed him. His journey had been a wasted one; of the five possible suspects only Holly Grant was present, her pretty face drawn and pale.

"How could Mark Pearse have married anyone so plain?" Marianna asked as they walked towards the cemetery gates.

"I'm sure she's very nice," Jane said.

"I'm not saying she's not, but what a contrast. Simone always looked so disgustingly glam. Did you notice how she stuck to him like a limpet? He was really upset, wasn't he?" Marianna asked.

"I suppose if you've been married to someone even for a few years it would be difficult not feel *something* for them. Anyway, they were still friends." Jane was glad that they'd reached the gates.

Lois tucked her arm in Holly's. It was a warm day but she felt chilly.

"Do you think we should all go and have a drink?" she suggested.

"Why not?" Holly agreed. "I'm sure none of us feels like going back to work just yet. I'll see if the men want to join us although I think that John and Sean have something on at Barretts. I didn't have a chance to speak to Eve Barrett. Arthur Lord has gone home, his wife whipped him away as soon as she decently could."

Tim Brown declined their offer. "I'd love to come with you but our auditors are due in an hour," he said ruefully.

"I'm glad it's over, aren't you?" Lois asked as

Holly caught up with her again. "It's been on my mind all the time."

"Mine too," replied Holly.

* * *

"Any joy?" the desk sergeant asked.

"Neh, a bleedin' waste of time and energy," Michael groused as he opened the squad room door.

Nobody in the squad room questioned him, they didn't need to, they only had to look at his face.

Michael slammed his office door and made straight for his desk drawer. He picked out the largest bar of chocolate he could find, broke off a large piece and crammed it into his mouth. Sod the diet.

"I'm going round in circles, Bill. I've never been so frustrated," Michael said as his sergeant gave him a letter to sign.

"There must be something we've overlooked, there *has* to be an answer."

"Wake me when you find it," Michael said.

Bill Merton was less optimistic than he sounded. They had ruled out the likelihood of a casual intruder, nothing had been stolen, Simone Pearse hadn't been sexually attacked. Ian Trent, Derek and Holly Grant and that twit, Roland Green, all had unshakable alibis. Michael had thought Maggie Tweed an unlikely suspect but, nevertheless, they'd checked her movements too. She was in hospital the day of the murder having an ingrown toenail removed.

Michael paced the small office then flung himself into his chair in disgust. He'd played the damn tapes over and over again. They were the only tangible material he had so he pressed the remote control and played the tapes again.

"What the hell's up with him?" Bill Merton asked as they heard Michael's shouts. "We'd better go and see."

They crowded into Michael Moore's office. The DI was on his feet waving the remote control in the air.

"I've got it," he shouted gleefully. "What a moron I am."

Nobody argued but he was too excited to notice that.

"Take a look. Look!"

Chapter Fifty-Seven

Holly noticed that Simone's parking space was still empty. No one wanted to use it nor would they go into her office. John had made arrangements to have the office gutted. He planned to turn it and the offices either side into one large open-planned room. Sophie made it known that she had no objection to using the office as it was. John found her attitude repugnant. He didn't like Sophie even though she hadn't put a foot wrong.

"Don't forget lunch," Lois reminded Holly.

"I won't," Holly smiled.

She went into her office and opened the windows. The warm air brought a sigh of satisfaction to her lips. In another week or so they'd able to use the barbecue. She'd bought a cook book and was studying it secretly. She would make Terence the best barbecue he'd ever had. She'd surprise him. He'd been incredibly kind and patient these last few weeks, ignoring her moods, her mercurial flashes of bad temper.

With her mind still on the barbecue, she began to sort out her post.

The two policemen entered her office without knocking.

"Now what?" she muttered to herself. These intrusions were becoming ridiculous.

"Ms Grant, Detective Inspector Michael Moore would like you to accompany us to the station," the taller of the two said.

"What for? I've told him all I know."

"We would like you to accompany us," he repeated doggedly.

"And if I don't?"

The other policeman took a step forward. "It would be easier . . . "

"Are you arresting me?" Holly asked, her heart beginning to thump.

"DI Moore would like to talk to you."

Holly picked up her bag and followed them.

"I have to go to the police station," she told Lois.

Lois frowned. They were really ignorant, those two, barging in like that.

"Do you want me to cancel your eleven o'clock?" she asked.

"I think that would be wise," the policeman cautioned.

"Sit here, Holly," Michael said as he turned a chair to face the television.

"Why do you want to see me again?" she asked.

"I want you to watch this surveillance video."

He sat beside her and pressed a button on his remote control. A slightly fuzzy vision of a car park came into view.

Holly frowned. What has this to do with me? she wondered.

"See the time, there on the left?" Michael asked. "The tape is a little blurred so watch carefully."

Holly could see the digital minutes ticking away. A car similar to hers pulled into an empty space. After a moment the driver's door opened. She recognised Liz instantly.

Holly's pulse raced painfully.

Michael watched her closely. He left his chair and exchanged the tape for a second one.

"Keep watching the time on the video," he said.

At one forty-two and twenty-three seconds, Liz returned to the car. She backed out carefully and left the garage.

Liz hadn't told her anything about leaving early.

Michael fast forwarded the tape then stopped it. The clock showed two fifty-eight and twelve seconds. The tape continued to play. The car reappeared. The driver waited to let a car back out then drove into the empty space.

Michael went to the office door and nodded to his sergeant. Bill Merton came into the room and stood quietly behind his boss.

On the screen Holly could see Liz walking towards a door. She could just make out the sign above it – *JP Harkers. Ground Floor Entrance.*

Why had Liz left the store? Why had she kept that a secret? Why was the time so important?

The tape whirred as Michael put his finger on the fast forward button.

"You see, it was the timing that threw me," he explained when her car came into view again. "I didn't bother to check the rest of the first tape, took it for granted that the statement you made was true – you arrived at noon, left about four. The second tape starts at one-thirty. I didn't watch the beginning of that, just rolled it on and checked the time you left – just after four o'clock. Something else I didn't notice, there were three spaces between the car and the wall at noon. See, now there are four."

Holly barely heard what he said. She could feel herself floating, the room spinning around her. *Liz* had murdered Simone, had killed Simone for her. Her lying and cheating had driven Liz to do something so alien to her nature that it took Holly's breath away. She must have gone to talk to Simone, persuade her not to prosecute her sister. Where were the exercise books, had Liz taken them? Had she dumped them somewhere? That would explain why she hadn't arrived home until after five.

Holly gasped for air. How many lives had she ruined all because of a book? Poor Simone, the innocent victim, just doing her job. Liz – she'd be extradited from the States, go to jail. She couldn't bear to even think about Robert. And Terence – kind, trusting Terence – he'd be shattered. All those lives affected. She'd never know a peaceful moment again.

Michael Moore rose slowly to his feet and faced her.

"Holly Grant, I am arresting you for the murder of Simone Pearse."

Holly stared at him uncomprehendingly. What was he talking about?

"You don't deny that's you on the tape, do you?"

Her mouth went dry, the room steadied. Liz did look remarkably like her.

Holly drew a deep breath and braced herself.

"No, Detective Inspector, I can't deny that it's me."

The End

Published by Poolbeg

Intrigue

by

Anne Schulman

From the fabulous marinas of the South of France to the mansions of Washington; Dublin's top hotels to Kildare's stud farms; the casinos of Las Vegas to the beauties of Paris.

Five strangers meet, each with their own guilty secret. One of them is going to pay with their life for something in their past.

Is it Gaby? High-flying, attractive Gaby.

Is it Edward? Cutting corners while building a career in the casinos of Cannes.

Is it Rachel? Beautiful Rachel from her poor background, shy determination spurs her on.

Is it Claude? From childhood he worked, struggled, scrimped and saved to build the perfect hotel.

Or is it Laura? Plain, down-trodden Laura. Manipulated by her conniving brother and her bed-ridden mother.

ISBN: 1-85371-336-8

Published by Poolbeg

Encounters

by

Anne Schulman

When Jane Anderson's marriage fails, she sets out to do for others what she couldn't do her herself. She welcomes a kaleidoscope of clients to her luxurious dating agency; high-powered but lonely people whose lives and biological clocks are ticking away.

Ray Parker, who built his computer company from scratch.

Kim Barrett, a stewardess on Concorde, whose love affair creates more turbulence than the aircraft.

Alex Travis, American, urbane, sophisticated and just slightly married.

Amanda Browne, academically bright but socially inept.

Kevin O'Hanlon, separated and disillusioned has left his native Dublin and desperately clings to his job in advertising.

Are any of these clients what they appear to be? Can their encounters radically alter their lives? Follow them as they weave their intricate webs of intrigue.

ISBN: 1-85371-458-5